LAIRIES

LAI

RIES

STEVE HOLLYMAN

Influx Press
London

Published by Influx Press
The Greenhouse
49 Green Lanes, London, N16 9BU
www.influxpress.com / @InfluxPress

First edition 2021. Printed and bound in the UK by TJ Books.

Paperback ISBN: 9781910312674
Ebook ISBN: 9781910312681

Editor: Gary Budden
Copyeditor: Dan Coxon
Cover design: Luke Bird
Interior design: Vince Haig

This book is dedicated to Dad, to the MA Massive, and to never sleeping again.

PROLOGUE

To make light of philosophy is to be a true philosopher.

— Blaise Pascal

MINUS-ONE

DUNCAN

He's lying on the floor, mouth open like he's sleeping, but with wide unresponsive eyes fixed on someshit above him. Inside my head I'm not in this club with the lairies and the skanks, caught up in this brawl with someone I've never met. Inside my head I'm alone and in silence. Fuck me, I'm thinking, all mute panic. I've fuckin killed the cunt.

Then bedlam returns. Pumping beats. Throbbing bass. Guys and girls gobbing off, some of them unaware of what's gone on. Where are Colbeck and Ade? Must've made a sharp exit like. And where are the bouncers? Have they even had time to react? Time slows down in situations like this but it's probably only ten seconds since I delivered a final jaw-shattering kick to the face of this fucker. The sequence of events hasn't yet registered in the minds of all the dolled-up ladies and stripe-shirted lads around me. Shock still clouds their judgement. Most people hate to see a fight, and I'm the same. I wince at the sound a punch makes when it connects with a fragile face. It's not like they portray it on TV. It's more of a thud than a cracking sound: a dull interface, understated in its subtlety, quieter than you'd expect but more devastating, a slab of raw meat thrown against a cold hard surface.

So how, then, have I ended up here in a club full of the kinda people I hate, standing over the comatose form of a bloody-faced geezer whose head I've just mashed?

Before I realise it, I'm in the corridor next to the bogs, then I'm forcing open the fire doors and I'm climbing onto the recycling bins and pulling myself over the wall with people shouting after me, and I'm away.

This is both the beginning and the end.

It is June 13th, 2003.

ZERO

SHAUN

There was the blackness, and it blanketed me, and then there was nothing.

◎

Nothing for days, and then the wall clock tick-tocking.

◎

And here it comes, The Surfacing.

◎

This is how it felt to be born. Unwombed and taking the first breath, back when I was nameless, back when I was nothing more than a cursor flickering at the top of a blank page. All clock hands snap back to the beginning: innocence, the first dilated pupil, then the steady corruption of experience.

Voices in the distance, broadcast from miles away and floating towards me on the breeze, recognisable as language but impossible to understand. And all I have is this inside surface of my skull where my thoughts dance like charged electrons trying to escape. And I'm coming up for air, ready to test my aching limbs, to uncurl from my foetal shell, to explore my own flesh with curious fingers. Gradually, as I emerge, I can count the different voices around me. There is something holding my legs down and my neck is aching. I flicker my lids, unable to open them. My surroundings are bright. I know this because behind my eyelids is a warm red, not a dead black: there is a light shining on my face. Or maybe they've laid me in the sun.

(

I think he's waking up
David, I think he's waking up

)

someone says. And I see white. Blurred patterns wax and wane in and out of focus as I absorb their colours. There is a pink smudge over me: it's my mam, and she's talking, mouthing words at me, her mouth opening and closing like a drowning fish.

◎

Tiled ceiling, four walls, two strip lights. Nausea of confusion.

◎

And here it comes.

◎

The Surfacing.

ZEITGEIST: MMIII

The real leader has no need to lead – he is content to point the way.

— Henry Miller

ONE

DUNCAN

I sat anxiously next to Ade on the settee – the faded blue one that we picked up from a charity shop for fifty quid – trying to suss out his thoughts as he held a wad of damp bog roll to his swollen top lip with one hand and gripped a can of beer with the other. When it seemed safe to speak, I said something like, Why do you keep getting yourself in these situations, man? but he didn't offer any explanation other than, Well, Dunc, someone has to do it.

Sorel was out with some mates. It was Friday night, early February, bout eleven o'clock. I was still getting used to the fact that Ade (only three years older than her and four more than me) could be the uncle of a twenty-year-old. I'd found out just a coupla weeks before all this that his dad was previously married, and that Ade has a much older brother who has a daughter who I was proper hoping to cop off with. It was for the best she wasn't there that night though: it always got her rattling when Ade got into a state, and it was happening more and more often. Course, Ade's behaviour was nothing new – there are loadsa people nowadays infected by the same antisocial disease who just wanna have a decent fuckin fight and release some pent-up tension – but his philosophy was different. He'd go out with Colbeck, this mate of his who he'd known since primary school or someshit, and they'd hang around up town, lurking in the corners of bars and nightclubs, just waiting for shit to kick off. When it invariably did, they'd jump in and reprimand the offenders with fists and feet, and they'd have a fuckin whale of a time doing it. They'd come back to the flat with bruised knuckles, black eyes, split lips: badges of honour representing the violence they'd willingly sought and dealt out.

Ade nudged me with a bony elbow and went, Oi, you ought to come out with me and Matt one night, Dunc. Fucking de-stress a bit, you know? When he says Matt, he means Colbeck; his name's Matthew Colbeck like.

No way, I goes. You aren't getting me involved in that shit. I fuckin hate violence.

Same as me, then, he replied, taking a sip of his beer and wincing as the alcohol stung the exposed flesh on his lip.

Is that meant to be a joke? I went. Every time you go out you come back bloody.

He shook his head and looked at the floor with his jaw clenched tight like he was proper gonna boil over or someshit. Then, after a few seconds on simmer, he spits, You just don't fucking get it, do you? You think I'm a fucking thug!

Course I don't, I retorted. I wanted to re-enforce the statement by adding more, but I couldn't think of anything else to say, not cuz I was lying or anything, but cuz the debate contained a much larger grey area than he was inclined to admit.

He screwed up the sullied bog roll, threw it on the coffee table and took a cigarette from the crumpled pack on the arm of the settee. He didn't offer me one though. He never does.

Where's Colbeck tonight, anyway? I asked, trying to avoid some sorta dialogue that I didn't want to be a part of.

He went home.

Oh?

Bird's got him on a tight leash.

He lit his cigarette and inhaled deep, sinking back into the settee as the nicotine rushed from lung to tributary.

I can't imagine anyone having Colbeck under the thumb, I said.

Don't be fooled, he went, holding up his cig between his forefinger and thumb and observing it. She's got him by the swingers, mate.

What's she like? I asked.

Fuck knows. Doesn't talk much. Has this condescending aura about her.

No, I goes, I meant what does she look like?

Oh. Bit of a horsey face, y'know. Cracking pair on her though.

That's the main thing, I said, but I didn't mean it. Ade's the type of person who doesn't know the difference between someone who's fit and someone who's beautiful, or between someone who's tidy and someone who's worth walking to the edge of the earth for. I never challenged him about any of that kinda stuff cuz I never dared. You should always agree with Ade when he chats to you, whether it's about politics and the ways of the world or just about his opinions on trivial shit. Cuz if you don't then the most insignificant comments can escalate into incredibly long and drawn-out arguments. He never backs down and he lives by the motto: *sleep when you're dead.*

His mobile buzzed in the kitchen. Get that for us, Dunc, he said.

Get it yourself.

Don't be a dick. My kidneys are killing me. I'll be pissing blood for days.

A slight exaggeration, but it's not nice seeing your mate in pain, even if it *is* his fault. So, I got up and fetched his phone for him. The screen said there was a missed call from Matt – Matt Colbeck like.

I picked up the newspaper from the table on my way back to my seat and looked at the crossword; I'd filled in about half while Ade was out. It was him that got me into them. He does the cryptic ones, which I'm no good at. He'd explained to me a few times the different ways that the clues work, the fact that there's hidden meanings, anagrams, ambiguity, wordplay, etc., but I couldn't get my head around all that shit. I did the quick ones instead, the ones that Ade refers to as *crosswords for bed-wetters*, and I rarely finished even those fuckers. Anyway, I'd planned on having a nice quiet night in with a few cans and the paper and a cheeky smoke from Ade's stash, but I should've known he'd come steaming in before midnight, gobbing off about the appalling state of the nation and telling me that my passivity is more dangerous than his aggression.

While he got back on the phone to Colbeck, I tried to fill in some more blanks. Eight down: false or incorrect, nine letters. Second letter R, last letter S. I stared at it for ages, trying to suss it out, hearing half of Ade's convo at the same time.

She's done what? he was saying. Nah mate. No way, you don't wanna put up with that shit. Serious, come over. Yeh, no worries. Just come over now. Fuck her, man, y'know. Honest, it's cool. Just come over here. The night's still young. Bring beers.

He put his phone on the coffee table.

False or incorrect, I goes.

What the fuck are you on about?

This clue here, I said, tapping the tip of the pen on the page. False or incorrect.

Any letters?

It's nine letters altogether. Second letter's R, and it ends in S.

Fuck knows.

He took a last drag from his cig and dropped the jeb end into an empty can on the table.

What's gone on with Colbeck? I asked, not looking up from the paper.

Argument with the bird, he went. He's coming over.

Shit, I thought. That meant it was gonna be a heavy one tonight. I wasn't up for that at all, not tonight, but I was in no place to make my opinions known to Ade cuz the flat was his and he was letting me stay with him rent-free until I found somewhere else, which was unlikely to be anytime soon.

I'm getting a beer, I said. You want one?

Yep.

I went into the kitchen and opened the fridge.

Hey, Dunc, Ade shouted.

Yeh?

I got your clue, false or incorrect. It's *erroneous*.

I knew he'd get it in the end like. Smart fucker.

TWO

COLBECK

The bitch.

That's all you can think at the moment: the fucking bitch. Two and a half years of your life. Better to have loved and lost? Bollocks, mate – better to have sat at home and wanked.

You told her that, but she was having none of it. She said she's made up her mind and this time it's over. Paranoia being as insidious as it is, her declaration makes you fucking suspicious. She's surely got some other bloke ready and waiting for her, most likely an updated model with bug-fixes on your most undesirable characteristics: a new gimmick unshackled by the silent horror of routine and unaffected by the steadily worsening incompatibility that blights your relationship like barnacles on the hull of a wrecked ship. The catalyst for this latest in a long series of fall outs came when you told her a couple of home truths, namely that: a) the only reason you ever moved in with her was because she pressured you into it; and that b) you were in fact far happier before she put the old emotional blackmail screws into you, back when you lived with your mates and saw her two or three evenings a week. 'Oh, for God's sake,' she replied waspishly, 'don't try and make out that you didn't want us to get our own place. You wanted this too.'

Yeh, right. The main reason you agreed to all this shit was – as is so often the case with stagnant relationships started too young and falling prey to the steady decay of adulthood – to avoid an argument. You weren't particularly chuffed about leaving your own house, thereby forgoing the late-night drinking sessions with the lads and snubbing the cheap rent that comes with house-sharing, to move in with her: a moth who's since chewed unrepairable holes in the fabric of your very being. But, of course, she doesn't see it like that. She's got it into her head that she's 'a fixer' and she reckons it's her duty to somehow save you. Fucking save you? From what?

'From those waster mates of yours, for a start,' she says. Now that's a fucking laugh. At least your mates don't all live with their fucking parents. She says that you're jealous because her friends have money. I'd have money too, you feel like telling her, if I hadn't wasted so much of my life with a materialistic bitch like you.

'You're such an idiot when you've had a drink,' she insists. 'Look at the state of you. Why do you always have to throw your weight around? For someone who's supposedly intelligent, you seem pretty stupid to me. Beating people up isn't big and it isn't clever. What is it that you're trying to—'

'Shut the fuck up,' you tell her, slurring slightly. When she bitches at you and you're in this state of mind all you want to do is put your hands around that whining throat of hers and rattle the life out of the cunt. It's not her fault you're so angry. But she's always the one that gets scalded when your boiling hot steam comes out sideways.

She says that tomorrow she's going to move out of the flat. In that case you're moving out too, and you tell her that you aren't taking any of her shit with you either. If she doesn't have a place to store it all, tough. It can stay here, and if the landlord seizes it when he finds out you've pulled a fast one then it's not your problem.

'You're so selfish,' she says, shaking her head in disbelief. 'I was hoping we could at least be friends, but you've really blown it now.'

You laugh so hard you nearly shit yourself.

'I'm selfish?' you say, your voice wobbling on a tightrope with rage on one side and hilarity on the other. 'You think I'm selfish? I'll tell you what selfish is: selfish is making me watch fucking romcoms every time we go to the cinema. Selfish is making me pay for your fucking gym membership even though I earn less than you. Selfish is taking up the fucking bathroom for forty-five minutes every fucking morning. Selfish is—'

'Just shut up!' she shouts. Flecks of her saliva pepper your face. 'Why does every conversation with you have to turn into an argument?'

◎

Fuck it anyway. She's staying in the flat tonight, so you've been relegated to the sofa. Fuck that. There's no way you're sleeping on the sofa in your own fucking gaff. You're going to Ade's. He knows how to have a good crack. Whoever it is that she's left you for, well, you feel sorry for the cunt. Of course, she insists that there is no one else. But it's obvious that there is. She'll have one hand on the next branch, for sure, before she lets go of yours. It could be that fucking geezer Danny who she works with – the one who rings her for late-night chats and who uses the word 'brunch' as a verb. Who talks like that in this country? This isn't fucking *Sex and the City* for Christ's sake. When you told her that, she said you were being pathetic, which is her response to every remark you make that she's unable to challenge with a valid counter-argument. If it isn't Danny, then it might be Toby. Or is his name Tony? Anyway, he works with her too. He gave her a lift home from a staff night out once, and he had the most fucking ridiculous car you've ever seen: a proper fucking pimpmobile. They'd make a good pair, them two. Or, if it's neither of those, then it's probably that fucking waiter she fancies down at the Lemon Tree. Fuck alone knows what that greasy bastard's name is, but no doubt she'll name-drop the cunt when she next feels like making you seethe a little. Anyway, The Replacement could be anyone with a cock and a pulse. You're sick of the torture.

She's locked herself away in the bedroom now and she's on the phone to someone – probably her fucking mother, who hates you anyway because the batty old cunt's got it into her batty old head that her daughter can *do better* – and you can hear her whingeing on about how this time it's over for real. You've tried knocking on the door, not because you want to talk things over but because you want to grab a spare pair of jeans for tomorrow, but she won't open it. You consider kicking it down and pretending it's someone's face, but you soon realise that in the morning, when the beer's worn off and you have to face facts, you'll be even more irate because it'll be you who has to pay to get the bastard thing fixed.

So instead you grab your crate of Belgian beer from the fridge, and shout a theatrical 'Goodbye, darling' to her as you slam the door behind you and head down the stairs. It's much colder outside than you expected, but you take the crate over to the wall in front of the flats and you sit and call a taxi. You crack open a beer using the opener on your key ring: a present from her. How sweet and fitting that you now use it to open the drink that toasts her departure from your world.

Your life has a habit of moving in circles.

THREE

SHAUN

The searing pain in my dick wakes me. What the fuck did I do last night? And whatever it was, who the fuck did I do it with? And where the fuck am I? Some girl's house? Can't be. I wouldn't do that to Steph, surely. Would I?

Eyes open. Everything unfamiliar. Vague throbbing in my head. I roll my eyes to the left, wary of any sudden motion. That's when I see him.

'Shaun. Shaun, it's okay.'

No, it isn't okay. Get the fuck away from me.

'Can you hear me, Shaun?'

Yes, I can hear you. Fuck you.

'Shaun?'

Someone else in the room. Her. She speaks.

'Shaun. Thank God.'

I try to talk, and something chokes me.

'Shhh, don't speak,' she says. Then to him: 'David, call someone.'

'I'll find the doctor,' he says, standing, and the room feels lighter without him in it.

I try to speak anyway. What I try to say is, 'The fucking doctor?' The words come out as froth. I imagine a fish foaming at the gills; filthy water gurgling in a drain. I taste blood.

'Everything's going to be okay, Shaun. I hope you can hear me. You're in hospital. You've had an accident.'

The first thing I think is: car crash. My head is full of holes. The vague throbbing is replaced with the hazy silhouette of a part-remembered dream. One of my legs is itching. I can't tell which one.

An unfamiliar face looms over me. White male. Mid-forties. Grey at the temples. Clean-shaven.

'Let me make you a bit more comfortable.'

Hands touch my body. I gargle.

'Can you hear me, Shaun? Squeeze my hand if you can.'

I do as he says.

'Good, very good.'

Why the fuck can't I move my head?

'Okay, Shaun. My name's Gianni Zaccari. People call me Zac. I'm a consultant neurologist. I know that you're very uncomfortable, but you must try not to move. You were brought here following a serious incident. You can probably feel some discomfort in your genitals. You've been fitted with a catheter. Squeeze my hand if it's causing you a lot of pain.'

It hurts, but it isn't unbearable, so I don't.

'I want you to squeeze my hand every time you feel me touch you with this pen,' he instructs, brandishing a biro in front of my face. There are teeth marks on the plastic. Perhaps he's trying to quit smoking. Perhaps it's a nervous habit.

'Can you feel this, Shaun?' He's too laid back. He's used to this.

This could easily be a dream, but I know that it isn't. It's common to be asleep and to imagine you're awake, but no one, when awake, ever truly believes he's dreaming.

'This?'

I feel nothing.

'This?'

Nothing.

'How about this?'

He taps his pen on my right knee. I squeeze.

'Very good.'

I try to speak. I try to say, 'What the fuck's going on?'

He stares at me, face as blank as an unruled page and full of sketch potential. 'I know,' he says. 'I know it's uncomfortable. I'll get the nurse and she'll sort it out for you.' Then, turning to the other two, 'Mr and Mrs Taggart, can I speak to you outside for a moment?'

He's not Mr Taggart. He's not my fucking father.

A door creaks and then clicks shut. I can't move. I sense that there is no one else in the room and I'm filled with the unbearable feeling that I'm helpless.

◎

I wake up, my head still thick with sleep. The clock says it's ten past four. It's bright outside, so it must be afternoon. I blink my eyes and swallow. They've removed the tube that was choking me. Dust floats by the window, illuminated by a sunbeam. Someone coughs, either in a neighbouring room or outside. I have no way of knowing for sure, but I sense that I am a few storeys up.

◎

There are four stages to my current existence, and they repeat ad infinitum: sleep, dream, confusion and fear. Presently I'm at stage three. Mam sits on a plastic chair pulled up close to the edge of my bed. She holds my hand, and I want to pull it away, but I can't.

'I love you so much,' she says.

Of course she does. I love her too. But I don't say that. I wish I didn't love her, but it's proving difficult to hate my own mother, even though I want to. My reason for wanting to hate her is for always taking his side, which is what led to me disowning the pair of them. I really do hate him. He's not my father, and he never will be. He knows it. So should she.

'What happened?' I ask. 'Where's Steph?'

'Steph's at home.' She clears her throat. 'Right now, we're not sure what happened. We know you were in a fight with someone.'

A sudden flush of sickness washes through me. A fight? I don't remember ever losing a fight, not since school at least, and they weren't real fights, just playground scuffles. What she probably means is that someone's hit me unexpectedly – just like when Tony got twatted in a kebab house over some petty disagreement with a gang of chavs. The difference is that Tony kicked the fuck out of them. He was arrested for that, fined £200 costs and given a suspended six-month jail term. CCTV got him and he was identified when the local paper printed stills. The lads who started it were seen as the victims and they weren't charged. But these thoughts are irrelevant now, and they fall out of my head when I remember where I am. Tony never had to go to hospital.

'Why am I even here?' I say, suddenly. 'I feel all right. When can I go home?'

She lets go of my hand. 'It's not that simple, Shaun. This was a very serious assault. You've been in a coma for almost three weeks.' A tear slips from the corner of her eye and runs along the side of her nose, and she takes my hand again, this time holding it in both of hers. 'Look,' she says, 'all this has made me realise how much I want you to come home. Why don't you move out of the flat and come back to the house? I know you and David don't get on, but this could be a chance to get to know each other. He's very fond of you and he's devastated by this whole thing. I've never seen him so upset, in fact. He's even offered to go and stay in a hotel so you can come home for a bit while you get better, if you don't want to be around him.'

'Leave it,' I say. 'I can't think about that right now. I'm so confused. What was all that stuff earlier with the doctor when he was asking me about my legs? I'm okay, aren't I? I mean, I'm not…'

I can't say it, but her maternal instinct obviously tells her what's coming. 'No, Shaun,' she says, stroking my forehead. 'You aren't paralysed. The doctors say there's every chance you'll make a complete recovery. What they've said is, and I don't understand it myself, but, anyway, what they've said is that you have some swelling on your brain. At first they were concerned that there might be some brain damage, that you could lose your speech or your sight or some of your motor functions, but they couldn't know the extent of it until you woke up. And that was only *if* you woke up, Shaun. I mean it when I say this is serious; it really was touch-and-go for a while. Now that you're awake, they're optimistic. But it'll take time. They want to monitor you for another week or so, just to make sure you're stable, and then they'll discharge you. You'll need physio but please don't worry about that for now. All the signs say you're going to be okay.'

Bubbles of relief flutter and fizz inside me but there are questions that will not go away. Is she lying? Are the doctors wrong? Are the doctors lying? And on top of it all is the horrific realisation that this really happened to me. You read about it in the papers all the time, but you don't expect it to ever actually affect you.

'Where was I?'

'In a club. Zanzibar.'

'Why did they do it?' I ask. Then I realise how stupid the question is and I wish I could swallow it back down. They did it because they did it. Probably just a case of wrong place, wrong time.

She draws her chair closer and takes my hand again. She exhales. Then she says, 'I need you to listen to me now, Shaun. There's something else. I need to talk to you about Steph.'

I hate it when people say things like that. I get the stomach pangs, the tightening in the back of my throat, the butterflies, the sickness. 'What?' I say. She remains silent so I press further. 'Come on,' I say. 'For God's sake, just tell me. It's best if you just say it.'

No. It isn't.

FOUR

DUNCAN

Sorel and me had resorted to playing Scrabble cuz the gin had run out, and Ade was at the bookies as usual. The horses were his vice of choice, but he also played the Irish Lottery as if he believed that the luck associated with that particular nation might somehow influence the results. We'd built up a decent stack of board games on the living room table cuz the telly was broken – Ade had kicked it in the previous week when he took massive offence at something someone said on *Trisha*. I'd never seen anyone destroy a TV before and I'd expected it to be a much more exciting affair than it proved to be when I eventually witnessed it. I'd envisaged an interstellar explosion of shrapnel and sparks, a flickering and buzzing of the cathode as it lost its life, smoke and lightning bolts of electricity and all that kinda shite, but it was nothing like that. His foot didn't even go through the screen like I wanted it to: it just made a big round shatter-mark, kinda like a bullet hole in a car windscreen in a film or someshit, and that was it. The fuckin thing hadn't worked since.

At college I was the Scrabble king like. But on this particular occasion I kept getting all the shittest letters and it looked like my defeat was pretty much imminent, until I banged down 'disavow' and got a triple word score on that bad boy and then the mood changed and I was like, Stick that in your pipe and smoke it.

That's not a word, Sorel goes, and I assured her that it fuckin is a word, and that I'd heard Ade use it at least twice.

Well what does it mean, then? she asked, teasing her ringlets round her middle finger. And it surely can't be spelled like that? She pointed to the letters arranged on the board. It just doesn't look right, she said.

I don't know *exactly* what it means, I admitted, but it's defo a word. And that's how you spell it, too.

She gave me one of her looks, head cocked to the left and one eyebrow raised.

It fuckin is! I protested. Seriously!

The debate was interrupted by the rattling of Ade's keys as he unlocked the front door. Here he is, I went, so you can ask him about it and then we'll see who's right.

Ade doesn't walk, he fuckin marches. He strode in, took off his jacket and gloves and threw them on the table, patted his pockets for a cigarette, tossed his keys onto one of the bookshelves, coughed violently for a few seconds, winced as he swallowed phlegm, then went, What a load of bollocks, as he sat down heavily on the sofa.

What's up? I goes.

Them fucking little shits who hang round outside the shop down the road is *what's up*, he went. I'm drawing out some Johnny Cash, right, just minding my own business, and a couple of them come over and ask if I want some aggro. I mean, fucking *aggro,* for fuck's sake. Who even talks like that?

He got back on his feet then, looking for a lighter among all the shit on the coffee table.

Here, I went, handing him some matches. I wanted to know what he was on about. He took the box and nodded at me. So what happened? I goes. And is 'disavow' a word?

His nose wrinkled. Yes, he goes, of course it's a fucking word. What're you asking that for?

Cuz we were playing Scrabble and she didn't believe me, I said, catching Sorel's glance.

Ade scoffed and shook his head. Anyway, he said. I had to give the little shits a grammar lesson. He sparked up his cig and pocketed the matches: my fuckin matches.

A grammar lesson? Sorel said, looking at me like she expected me to offer some sorta enlightenment or someshit. I shrugged.

A grammar lesson, Ade repeated. He sat back down on the settee.

You've lost me, I told him.

He cleared his throat and goes, eruditely: Aggro, Duncan, is short for aggravation, which means the exacerbation of a problem which is already present, and I was fine till I bumped into them little cunts. But when I told them that, they didn't seem interested, oddly. They just carried on gobbing off.

I laughed. I couldn't help myself. So, what happened? I goes.

One of them called me a queer, so I battered him. Then three of his mates started giving it some, and I fucking battered them as well. I tell you what, Dunc, we need a fucking cull in this country. I'd sign up for that. What we need is a few lads – big fuckers, y'know – to go and sort all these pricks out. These little twats are the type of cunts that grow into geezers – you know the ones I mean. Fucking lairies who gob off and start shit on a night out and put everyone on edge. Nip the fuckers in the bud, mate. Cos I'm telling you, the police won't do fuck all. And you know why? Because there's never enough evidence to convict, Dunc, that's fucking why. If they catch some cunt speeding or going through a red light, then it's much harder for the poor fuck to appeal. Speeding fines pay their wages, you see, and a little tick goes in the box that says 'crime solved' and then they can manipulate the stats to make it look like the streets are getting safer cos the conviction rates are going up. Well, fuck me, Dunc, I fucking despair of this country.

You can't really 'nip them in the bud' though, I went, pausing for a few secs to check he'd finished like. Some of them are only like thirteen years old. That's not a fair brawl.

I don't give a fuck how old they are, he snapped. If they're old enough to gyp me or any other cunt then they're old enough to take the consequences. The parents don't teach them to respect their elders, you see. Most of them were accidents anyway; their fucking dads should've rubbered up. The prevention is easier than the cure. You should remember that, Dunc, although it doesn't affect you really, does it, considering you never get laid?

Fuckin charming, I said, pretending to lose interest and turning my attention back to the Scrabble board and studying my letters.

Suddenly he stands up and points at me, calm into chaos as per usual, and goes, Don't just fucking sit there, for fuck's sake. Do something. Fucking say something at least! Doesn't this shit mean anything to you?

Well, what're you suggesting? I asked.

You know *precisely* what I'm suggesting, Dunc, he goes. Don't play fucking dumb. If I was out on the beat every night there'd be none of this slap-on-the-wrist bollocks. None of this taking them to the cells to sober up and letting them out with a caution. I'd be beating the pricks left, right and centre. I'd fucking relish it, mate. He leaned forward and stubbed his cig out in the ashtray, then immediately took out another one and lit it, pocketing my matches again afterwards. Then he goes, You busy tonight, man?

No, why?

I'm gonna go and hang out up town again and batter anyone who gets lairy. You fancy it? Colbeck's coming cos his bird's still on the blob with him.

Sorel winced. Fuck that, I said, before he had chance to say something worse. There's no way I'm going with you. I've told you this the past few times you've gone off on one. You'll either get yourself killed or arrested – or both.

He shrugged. It has to be one or the other, you tit, he said. If I'm dead, they'll have a hard fucking job arresting me.

What the fuck's up with you lately, anyway? I goes. You can't change the way other people behave.

Duncan's right, went Sorel. You could get yourself into serious trouble acting like that.

And besides, I reminded him, I thought you hated going out up town? You told me the clubs are full of skanks and geezers and shit music that sounds like it's been put together in ten minutes on a Bontempi in some cunt's bedroom. Don't you remember saying that?

He laughed. A short, high-pitched squawk. No, he said, I don't remember saying that. But if I did say it then I'm glad you reiterated it. That's pretty fucking funny. Sometimes I forget I'm a comedian.

So what's the difference now? Sorel asked.

He made a face at her and went, What's it to you? You go up town all the time.

Yes, I do, she said. But I enjoy it and you've always said you hate it.

It's cuz he loves scrapping like, I said.

Ade flashed me the evils and goes, I'm a lover, Dunc, not a fighter – I just happen to be good at both.

Now I was getting wound up. You what? I retorted. You do enjoy it. I can see it in your body language when you talk about it.

Bollocks, he said, ejecting a bead of spit with the first plosive. It landed on the table, and I wondered if I was the only one who noticed. What the fuck would you know about body language anyway? he demanded.

I can just tell, I said. Don't try and deny it.

No, he goes, that's not good enough.

It's just a hunch, all right? I said. An inclination like. Stop trying to catch me out.

Ah, an inclination, he said. How very Kantian of you.

He finished his second cig and stubbed it out, saying as he did so (and adopting some weird fuckin accent that was meant to sound posh, I guess, but which came out part Queen's English and part South African or someshit), I don't enjoy fighting *per se*, but sometimes it has to be done. And when you know that the person really deserves it, then yes, there is an element of pleasure involved.

I fuckin told you, I said. Why bother denying it if you're gonna admit it in the end anyway?

He lit another cigarette. Because you were making it sound like I deliberately court violence to satisfy some sort of violent proclivity, he spat. And you have no idea how much it upsets me when you say that, Dunc. You make me sound as bad as them.

You know what I mean, Ade, I said, trying to make peace and draw attention away from the fact that I didn't know what the fuck a proclivity was. It's just I can't understand it, I said.

You don't need to understand something to accept it, he went. So, you're just gonna have to put up with it, cos this is how it's gonna be from now on.

FIVE

COLBECK

A week after the argument you're still staying at Ade's, still ignoring that bitch's phone calls, and still wearing the same jeans you had on when you walked out on her. Most of your stuff is here now, in three large boxes that your mate got for you from his job in the warehouse, but you've got hardly any clean clothes, apart from work stuff. You had to get your dirty skiddies out of the laundry basket at home and just dump them in a bin bag and carry them on the bus. Now it turns out that Ade doesn't have a washing machine. He goes to the laundrette down the road and you obviously can't be bothered with that shite, not with having to go and graft in the call centre and everything.

As for your job: when people ring the bank to speak to a member of the client service team, they hear an automated message saying that calls may be recorded for training and monitoring purposes. The person listening to those calls is you. You have a scorecard and you have to answer certain questions. Did the agent use the customer's name? Did the agent authenticate the customer correctly? Did the agent speak in an easy-to-understand, jargon-free manner? And so on. Then the agent's overall grade is calculated depending on how they behaved during the call. If some fucker keeps getting below eighty per cent then the team leader comes downstairs and gleefully sacks the daft cunt.

Ade hands you an open beer and sits down cross-legged on the floor. That's one of his quirks. Whenever you're sitting on the sofa, he chooses the floor; but if Dunc is on the sofa, Ade sits with him. It's nothing deliberate; it's certainly subconscious. He's always done it. When you were at uni together, in halls, he'd come into your room and if you were sitting on the bed, he'd take the floor. If you were sitting at your desk then he'd sit on the bed, even if there were three other fuckers on it. Habit is a strange thing. You watch him cross-legged on the carpet, an emaciated Buddha, roaching a spliff and licking it down. You've always hated smoking. You never heard your granddad's voice. All you ever heard, right up until the old cunt kicked the proverbial when you were twelve, were the vile hacking sounds that emanated from his tracheotomy and the helium squeaks that caused him untold embarrassment when he tried to speak. He was a sixty-a-dayer, Dunhills, and he's the reason you've never so much as held a lit cigarette or a spliff.

'Where are Dunc and Sorel?' you ask.

He lights the joint. 'Fuck knows. Must've gone out.'

He inhales deep and holds the cancer inside him before expelling it in a grey-blue coil. You look around the flat. It's a nice place he's got here – typical student pad with mismatched furniture and garish curtains and carpets, but none of the damp walls and peeled wallpaper that you get in so many of these types of gaffs. Ade's a perpetual student: he's a member of what might once have been referred to as the non-student left. He isn't enrolled at any particular institution but he studies nonetheless. He studies newspapers. He studies youth culture. He studies the arts. And he's got enough money to do it, which is why he's never had a job. You would kill to be in his position. You remember the day you both walked into the estate agent's. 'This one looks all right, Matt,' he said. 'Let's have a look at it.' A few days later a girl was showing you round. From the way she spoke to you she obviously assumed you'd be moving in together, either as flatmates or as a pair of fucking chutney ferrets. The latter scenario of which would certainly have saved you a whole load of fucking trouble in the relationship department. But no – Ade was buying this, a three-bedroom flat, for himself. And more than that. He was buying it with cash. No deposit, no mortgage. £99,950 in a single payment. You were there when he did it. Inheritance is a wonderful thing, especially when the deceased relative in question had a top-salary position working as an actuary for a big insurance firm.

It's an enviable residence, all right, despite its charity-shop chic. There's a main living area, which is where you're sitting now, and from here there are three doors leading to three bedrooms (you're sleeping on the bed-settee in Ade's room), a kitchen and a decent-sized bathroom. The curtains have remained closed since you arrived here, and you wonder whether they've been opened at all during the time Ade's inhabited this gaff. The pyramid of beer cans and bottles on the coffee table continues to increase in both size and precariousness as you both sit sipping and Ade alternates between cigarette and joint, occasionally making small talk about the latest books he's read or about the lack of good films on at the cinema lately.

You're both in dire need of a little catharsis, so you're going out tonight, up town, to mix with some of the shit-kickers who congregate there. Pretty much any night you go out nowadays you can guarantee that you'll run into some cunt who's looking for a fight. This cunt won't care who the fight's with, or even what it's about; he'll just make sure that it happens, because that's his sole reason for being there. There are several ways for him to go about this instigation. He can choose to goad you into it, by squaring up to you toe-to-toe, or by throwing a punch, or by shoving you or insulting your bird. He can pick on your mates, usually the smaller ones, until you're so pissed off that you step in. Or he can just call you a prick as you walk past him and hope that you rise to his bait.

Any fucker who acts in this way deserves to get his face seriously fucked up. You can't understand how, or why, anyone could possibly form a cogent argument to the contrary. There's nothing quite as enjoyable as having some geezer start on you and then knocking his teeth out or shattering his fucking jaw. Mistakes are easier to learn from when facial reconstructive surgery is involved. In the town centre, you lurk like undetected cancer, watching the lairies as they crawl from under their stones, their violence swelling with every Stella sip, and when something kicks off, you jump them. You are quite literally pissing skid marks off the toilet bowl of life.

So you get your phone out and text Dunc to see if he wants to come along for the ride. He's unlikely to be up for it. He prefers to hang out with Sorel, and you can see why –

she's a tasty little ripper. Dunc ought to watch himself there, though. Ade's madly protective over her: she might as well be his daughter. Anyone upsets her or harms a single hair on her head and Ade'll fucking have them. He can flip easily although he's never yet flipped at you, or at Dunc. But she's the line that cannot be crossed. If you were Dunc, you'd stay well the fuck away. He may genuinely like her, his intentions may well be pure (and knowing him they almost certainly are), but you can never really tell how these things will turn out. You're fucking living proof of that fact.

'So, where do you wanna go?' you ask Ade. He's still sitting cross-legged on the floor.

'Wherever. It's Friday. It'll be teeming,' he says, and you imagine ants spilling from a crack in the mud.

But of course, you shouldn't think of yourself as a thug. In fact, you're the very antithesis of thuggery. You're dealing with the lairies and the geezers in a way that no bouncer or officer of the law would ever dare. You're fighting violence with violence. This is a cause you care deeply about, and the proof is in the empathy: you fucking pity anyone who acts up in front of you tonight. But you just know it's gonna happen. There's no question about it. It always does. There are just so many of these types around today that it's impossible to avoid them.

Dunc replies to your message, which makes a change. He hardly ever has credit on his phone nowadays, according to Ade, cos he's always fucking skint. He's at the pub with Sorel right now, trying his luck, fucking punching above his weight as usual. His plight is understandable. The poor guy needs to get his kicks from somewhere, and he's got fuck all else going for him: no job, no money, no quim, no qualifications apart from the ten GCSEs that he somehow fucking excelled in. Perhaps he's thinking that she might take pity on him or something. That's just the type of thing he'd get into his little head. Still, keeps him out of trouble and all that. At least he catches on to ideas quick. He bounces off Ade, whenever Ade's in the mood for it, which isn't always. He just needs a bit of toughening up.

'Same as usual tonight,' Ade says. 'We're not trouble-makers. We're just out for a few drinks, but if we see anyone acting up then we mash them. If nothing kicks off, then we get drunk and come home. If we deliberately start shit without just cause then we're as bad as them. That's not what this is about. This is reactionary. They go there specifically looking for something, and now, if they meet us, they're gonna find it.'

'Sounds like a plan,' you say. You've done this enough times to understand how it works, so there was no need for him to remind you. You've always hated trendies and you thoroughly enjoy smacking people who deserve it. This new sport of yours is the perfect combination of those key interests. Tonight, though, you're a bit distracted from the intricacies of the game, because what you're really thinking about is what she might be getting up to at the moment. Because, no matter how much of a bitch she was, you can't forget her. She fills you from the head downwards, a sand-timer flipped over as the silent countdown to despair starts again.

The landlord still doesn't know that you're moving out. Stupidly, you signed for twelve months, and that was only seven months ago. Neither one of you can cover the cost of the rent by yourself, nor are you prepared to pay half towards a flat you're not living in. You've already cancelled your standing order, and you presume she'll do the same as soon as she's cleared all her stuff out. Then it'll just be a case of trying to stop the bailiffs catching up with you, until they get bored and give up looking.

Your own legacy back at the flat consists of just a few boxes full of shit that you haven't bothered to collect yet. You don't know where the fuck you're going to live because you can't bunk up with Ade forever and you're fucked if you're moving back in with the prescription-pill-addicted old cow who shat you into the world twenty-three years ago. The more you think about what that fucking ex of yours has done to you, the more you hate her. You're not only pissed off about it. You fucking despise the girl. You are utterly hollowed out because of her. Your single cell split, grew into her, rejoined, evolved, and now that she's fucked off you're incomplete. 'Well, you were in love,' is what she'd say if she was here now. And yes, you were in love. But you never saw her making the same fucking sacrifices you did because *she* was in love, did you? The little—

'You want another beer?' Ade says, shattering the ice in your head.

'Yeh, go on,' you say, and he gets up and heads to the kitchen, leaving you alone on the settee.

The alcohol makes you twitch. The trendy scene isn't gonna know what's hit it. About fucking time, too. These fuckers need to be sorted out. Can't handle their beer, the fucking twats. Can't have a decent night out without getting lairy. Someone spills something on their new fucking Ben Sherman shirt and they kick off. Well big fucking deal, you cunt, you shouldn't be walking round the dance floor with a pint in your hand, should you? It reminds you of uni days – you and Ade used to drink in this little pub just around the corner from the campus. The Red Lion. It was usually full of student types downing cheap shots before they went up town. But occasionally groups of geezers would turn up and the whole atmosphere would change without warning, become hostile and uncomfortable like when a scrap starts at a wedding. You remember the time Ade got hit round the head with a wine bottle: to this day he can't hear properly through his left ear. He got started on cos someone pushed in front of him at the bar and he told the guy to wait his turn. That's all it takes. This contingent will kick off at you for looking at them, for not looking at them. For looking weak, for acting hard.

You hear the bottles clink as Ade carries them from the kitchen. He has a gift for opening them with a cigarette lighter, and he sorts yours first before getting to work on his own.

'Right,' he says. 'We'll down these two and then we'll get our shit together. Did you text Dunc?'

'Yeh,' you say. 'He's with Sorel somewhere.'

'Probably fucking boring her to death with his whingeing,' Ade suggests, and you laugh, because you can see it right now: Dunc fannying on about his usual shit and her sitting there yawning and looking at her watch and saying, 'Oh dear me, is that the time?' and basically doing anything and everything to excuse herself. Dunc keeps his cards close to his chest. He treats girls like mates; never flirts, never tests the water with cocky remarks and suggestive smiles. It suddenly dawns on you that he might be an uphill gardener after all, which would explain his apparently platonic friendship with her, but this thought vanishes once you remember how bad his dress sense is.

◎

Twenty minutes later, you're out on the street, straining your eyes to see if any of the cars approaching from the bottom of the road is the taxi you've booked. The alcohol's hit you now you're on your feet and it flows through you, molten adrenaline, gearing you up for another night of loathing and violence.

Your phone rings from inside your pocket. You take it out and look at the screen. Fuck her: don't answer her call. She's probably just found out that you've been back and boxed up your stuff without telling her first. Maybe she thinks it's a bit hasty. Maybe she was hoping you'd work things out. Fuck it: she left you first. There's no going back now.

'You gonna answer that?' Ade's giving you a weird look.

'No fucking way. It's you-know-who.' You cancel the call and put the phone in your pocket.

Ade nods his head slowly and takes out a cigarette. 'What happened with you two, anyway?' he asks, sticking the cig in his mouth.

'Not a lot. She just decided to fuck off. Not that I particularly give a fuck. I fucking hate her.'

He laughs. 'Behind every great man there's a fucking crazy ex-girlfriend,' he assures you, as he sparks up and sucks in smoke.

You don't say anything. You just wish you could hate her as much as you want to. You shuffle from foot to foot, feeling edgy. It's starting to get cold now; it descends on you in no time, this weather. Half an hour ago you could've stood out here in a fucking T-shirt. Now you're rubbing your hands on your upper arms, trying to scratch the bone-deep chill out from under your skin.

Your phone buzzes again. Three times: text message. You take it out and study the screen.

'You should get in touch with her, you know,' Ade says.

'No fucking way. Let her stew for a while.'

He drags on his cigarette, holds the smoke in for a few seconds, expels it. 'What does she say?' he asks.

'Not a lot. Just, "Ring me, I need to talk to you". That's all. Fucking cryptic as usual.'

Headlights are approaching from down the street. You can tell it's a taxi because the driver slows down as if he's scouting for the numbers on doors. Ade notices too, it seems, because he takes a few quick drags on his cigarette and tosses it onto the pavement. You extend a hand to flag down the driver, and he accelerates towards you, stopping just short of Ade. You climb inside, Ade in the front, you in the back, and slam the doors.

'High Street please, mate,' Ade says.

SIX

TAG

I'm standing in a large wood-panelled room in what seems to be a stately home or manor house. Mahogany bookshelves line the walls, there's a battered old leather chair by the window, maroon curtains drawn, stepladders propped up in the corner, the scent of damp paper, dust, time. I step forward, study the spines: hardback books, decades old, sun-faded and weathered, and I can't make out the titles of any of them, or the names of their authors. All except one. It's turned face on, cover outwards, and I recognise it from when I was a kid. I reach forward and pick it up and it's heavier than I remember it being. My dad used to read this to me but then sometimes, as I got older, he'd let me read it to myself. I open the book at a random page, near the end. I'm struggling to focus on the words, but gradually they begin to form: shapes, lines, curves, like a developing Polaroid. I flick back through the crisp leaves, end to start, back to the point of origin, the beginning, the unmoved mover, the first cause: bathe in the darkness of truth, or else the light.

◎

Tone says I should just leave her. It's obvious we're making each other unhappy. We've got this weird thing going on, Steph and me. Been together for a few months now, but it feels like a lifetime. She says I'm too possessive. I say she's too flirty. Both allegations are equally true, and I guess we're both as bad as each other. She's a touchy-feely person. That's okay to some people. But not to me. She says she won't change her ways for me, and I say, whatever. She's not necessarily doing anything wrong, but that's not the point. It's what's running through her head when she does it that counts. If she's sitting on some bloke's knee – chatting in his ear, touching his arms, giggling like she does – then it just makes me think, *what a fucking prick-tease*. That's what she is. But I love her. Or I think I love her. No, I do. I do. I love her.

Tone says it isn't healthy for a guy my age to be wracked by insecurities. He says I should either be settled down with a girl I can trust or, better still, he reckons, be out every weekend getting some no-strings-attached action. The thing with Steph and me is that we just sort of happened. I wasn't looking for a long-term relationship. It just started, as these things tend to. Some people call that type of thing fate. They believe that everyone has a predetermined destiny. Try telling that to someone whose kids have been killed in a car crash. Fate doesn't exist. It's a means of escape. It's something for the jilted to take comfort in. It's a myth.

Me and Steph getting together wasn't fate. It was something else, but there was still no particular reason for it other than we were both in the same place at the same time and we clicked. For better or for worse, something about her drew me in and we started chatting and then eventually we were together and that was that. The problem is, the longer you're with someone, the more difficult it is not to be with them. Even after a few months, it seems easier to stay with them than it does to go through the hassle of breaking up. I'm not saying that I want to leave her, because I don't think I do. But she's been acting weird lately, like she disapproves of all the stuff me and Tone get up to when we're out. For a start, she hates drugs. I've tried explaining to her that she's overreacting but whenever I say it, she starts shouting. She also wants to move into the flat with me. Fuck that. It's too soon. It's unhealthy. People need their own space from time to time, and if she can't see that then it's her who's being unreasonable. I only moved out of my mam's place a couple of months ago and now I can't shut the world away because Steph's got her foot wedged in my door. I should tell her to cool it but she's not the type of girl who listens to that kind of request without getting angry.

I need to do something though, because she's taking over my life. I can't get a minute's peace with my mates without expecting my phone to ring: Where are you, what are you doing, who are you with, and – worst of all – do you mind if I join you? I'm not saying that I don't like spending time with her. I just don't think we should be together all day every day. It isn't normal. The sooner she realises that, the better.

SEVEN

DUNCAN

I wish he'd get the TV fixed, Sorel said, as the pair of us stared at our distorted reflections on the broken screen. At least we had booze now – Ade had borrowed me some money and sent me to the offy. She was sipping a G&T through a straw and the room was so quiet I could hear the tonic fizzing. There's a word for that. A word that Ade used to say like... Fuck it, it'll come to me later.

Me too, I said. But he won't. Even if he wanted to then he'd probably spend the cash at the bookies on the way to the TV repair shop.

She laughed. Probably, she said. Where is he, anyway?

Gone to pick Colbeck up from work.

She smiled. They're like a married couple, she said. It's kind of sweet, really.

You mind me sitting in here with you? I went. Cuz I'll go somewhere else if you want some time to yourself.

Don't be stupid. I like chatting to you. At least I can have a proper conversation with you, which is more than I can do with him.

When she says *him*, she means Ade.

He only ever talks about two things: alcohol and the things that he hates, she went on. And, let's face it, a lot of stuff fits into the second category.

I lifted my eyebrows in agreement.

There was a bit of an awkward silence, then – kinda like she'd been planning her next statement for a while, but she was hoping to make it look spontaneous like – she goes, Anyway, I can't stand sitting in here any longer. It's so depressing. You fancy nipping to the pub?

Fuckin nice one, I thought. I said: I'd love to, but I've got no money like.

It's on me, she went.

What?

I said it's on me. Let me buy you a drink.

Like I said, I'd love to, but—

But what? I've got it covered, Dunc. I need a partner in crime.

Fair enough, I went. You've convinced me.

And so we got up off the sofa, grabbed our coats and headed for the door.

Talking of Ade, she goes, as we headed down the stairs, why did he drop out of uni so close to graduation? It seems kind of stupid of him not to have just stuck it out for a couple more months. Does he really hate students that much?

He says that he does, but there's obviously more to it than that, I said, stopping at the bottom of the stairwell to spark up a cig. Then I continued, He was getting really bad grades because he couldn't be bothered to do the work. I didn't know him then though, it's just what I've heard. I think it was a case of him either leaving with his dignity intact, and blaming it on the fact that he hates students, or carrying on until the end and either failing completely or getting a bad grade. You know, jump before you're pushed like.

Makes sense, she said, but you've got to wonder why he didn't just work hard from the start.

It's because he hates the whole idea of universities, I told her, the whole idea of education being institutionalised. He told me that we've yet to find a system of education that isn't also a system of indoctrination – whatever the fuck that means. Plus, he always used to go on about the other people on his course, and how pretentious they were, and how they didn't want to learn anything because they thought they knew it all, and how they just wanted to get drunk. Ade did want to learn, but he only wanted to learn what he wanted to learn, if you know what I mean.

Yes, she said. I *do* know.

I held the door open for her and followed her outside. On the street, the light stung my eyes and I had to open and close them a few times to allow them to adjust. It was always dark in the flat, you see, cuz Ade never let us open the curtains. He preferred the hazy daze of nocturnal existence: often, after an all-nighter, we'd realise it was getting light outside only when the cigarette smoke and dust particles became iridescent from the faint glow and hung from the ceiling like some sorta bizarre morning fog.

I tell you what though, I went, it pisses me off that Ade dicked about at uni. If I'd've ever been able to go, then I would've worked my bollocks off. I just couldn't afford it, even with a loan y'know. And I've got no A levels.

You could at least try to get a grant or a bursary from somewhere, she said.

I thought about this for a while as we walked, then I goes, If they do have those kinda grants available then they probably only give them to really promising students.

She looked at me for the first time during the convo. And what makes you think that you're not a promising student, Dunc?

Cuz I'm a bit... what's the word? I said.

You tell me.

A bit gullible like, I guess. A bit thick.

She sighed and looked ahead again. Then she went, Don't be so stupid. I can tell you spend so much time with Ade – it's destroying your self-confidence. There's no reason you can't go to uni if that's what you want to do.

We headed up Charlton Road and cut through one of the alleys, past piles of torn-open bin bags and tin cans strewn across the ground. What a fuckin dump, I thought. The houses on either side were partitioned by wooden fences, most of which had panels missing and rusty nails sticking out at all sorts of dangerous angles. Clothes swayed on washing lines in some of the gardens – well, they're not gardens really, just yards with weeds sticking out between cobbles. An invisible string pulled an empty Coke can down the alley with the sound of an out-of-tune piano. We hop-scotched around the dog shit that decorated the tarmac in various stages of decomposition. I wondered what it would be like to live somewhere a little less decayed. Not that there was any chance of me getting my own place with no job, no money, and no fucker else to move in with.

So where are we going? I asked, trying to take my mind off it.

There's a really nice little pub about five minutes away, she said. The George.

Yeh, I said. I know it. Never been in though. Looks a bit rough from the outside, doesn't it?

Don't judge a book by its cover, Dunc, she went, as we came out at the top of the alley and turned right. It's actually very nice inside. Never many people in there. Quite intimate.

Okay, I said, I'll take your word for it.

We crossed the road and nipped through past the chip shop. There were a few little shits sitting on the graffitied wall around the back, eating chips and gobbing off. They gave us geezer stares as we walked past but none of them said anything until we were twenty metres or so ahead, and then they started shouting shit at Sorel like, Oi, give us a blow job! and, Get your tits out!

Pathetic, isn't it? I said, trying to seem classy and trying to cover up the fact that I was actually pretty scared of these little fuckers.

Yep, she went. They've probably never seen a pair of tits in their lives, let alone had a blow job.

Now this comment fuckin turned me on. There was just something about her that made it so sexy when she said anything even vaguely lewd. It wasn't just the fact that she was fit like (cuz I'd gone so long without any action at this point that I was starting to find ninety per cent of the female population doable, you get me): she had something else, something transcendental. I wished I was one of those blokes who's amazing with women like, so that I could charm her. I knew that it wasn't ever gonna happen though, so I just kept quiet and we continued to walk.

After a minute or so's silence, she goes, This way, it's quicker, and pulled me towards another alley.

How do you know about all these shortcuts? I asked. I've lived on this estate for months and I don't know about half of them.

She grinned at me and went, I like exploring. When I first moved in, I used to wander around in the daytime because, let's face it, there's not much else to do. And it's even worse now that the TV's broken.

True, I said.

Here we are, she said, as we emerged from the other end like ten metres from the door of the pub.

Nice one, I went. I guess all that shit I've read about girls having no sense of direction is bollocks after all.

I think she liked that one. I could just tell.

EIGHT

COLBECK

You're pretty battered when the cabbie drops you in the town centre. You wander around for a bit past rabbles of stupid lairies out for a night of debauchery and violence. The streets are full of them in various states of drunkenness – people laughing and shouting shit; short skirts queuing outside clubs with blokes lumbering past, jaws hanging as low as their pavement-scraping knuckles; groups of revellers squabbling over taxis; lost sheep bleating down mobile phones trying to locate their flock. You and Ade wade inconspicuously through the sludge.

Some cunt shoves past you in the street and you hard-shoulder the fucker to show him who's boss. Ade strides up ahead, cig hanging from the corner of his mouth, weaving his way through the skanks and spastics. The rum is swilling with the beer in your stomach like a fucking sluice and you've got a film of sweat on your back that's making your shirt stick to your skin beneath your blazer. Ade's wearing a white T-shirt with the words *Bachelor of Arts* emblazoned in black marker. 'Here,' he says, stopping outside one of the clubs on the high street and cocking his head at the sign. You nod and shuffle to the back of the queue.

You wait in line. It's pathetic really, like being back at school. At lunchtime they'd line up each of the five year groups separately, in accordance with some fucking ancient rota, and then they'd check everyone's hands to make sure they were clean and let in two kids at a time. The only difference here is that they aren't checking hands. They're checking bags, wallets, pockets instead. You don't know if they're looking for drugs or weapons or both, and you don't give a fuck either way because you wouldn't be so stupid as to try and sneak that kind of shit inside here. If you're gonna drop a few bombs and get chewy then do it before you reach your destination. If this is impossible then buy your drugs inside the venue. That way, if anyone gets caught bringing them in, it's gonna be whoever intends to sell the fuckers. And as for weapons – well, you're not into that shit. It's ungentlemanly for a start, and the desire to carry them usually disappears with the onset of pubic hair. It carries a whole different connotation, to hold a blade – even if it's only for self-protection. It acts as a barrier between the violencer and the violenced; it distances the perpetrator from the recipient.

You get your phone out and send another text to Dunc, telling him you're up town and that he should fucking get over here and stop trying to get his end away with Sorel. Then you send a text to the bitch, informing her that you don't want to meet up with her to talk about anything because there's fucking nothing to talk about, and you tell her that she'd better stop fucking texting you, the stupid cow, or else you'll block her fucking number. Ade's got his phone out as well – he's ringing up to see how many minutes he's got left cos he was going on about phone credit problems in the taxi earlier. Ade's JC has to go a long way nowadays. You'll pay your way while you're staying with him, no bother, but Dunc doesn't pay any rent because he's never got any cash. Sorel wants to contribute, but Ade won't take anything from her. Whenever she goes and buys food or whatever he tries to pay her back, and if she really insists she doesn't want it then he just hides the money in her room when she's out. He's avoiding what he sees as 'unnecessary expenses' and stretching out what's left of the cash he inherited. He gets one more instalment – when it's gone, there's no more coming in, unless he gets a job, which you wouldn't wish on fucking anybody.

There are these three giggly girls in front of you in the queue, chatting to each other, clearly pissed, winding you up to fuck. You dig a fingernail into your side. They're a bunch of what you'd call fairy-tale blondes – fucking Grimm. For Christ's sake, you fucking skanks. Shut the fuck up. The hatred for it all is killing you, killing you, killing you.

Finally, you get to the doors. The bouncers say, 'Wait a sec, lads,' and you nod and smile politely. Ade's looking edgy; he takes out another cigarette and lights it with the nub of the last. You feel the anticipation fill your stomach: will you go home bored and deflated, or will you get a chance to put your life on the line for the sake of the greater good? 'Okay, guys,' says one of the bouncers, ushering you in. You pay three quid each at the kiosk – holding up your expired student card with your thumb covering the date for a quid discount – and get the fuck inside and make tracks to the bar for a round of shots before you get onto the beers. There's no order in the pack in here, people just crowd together hoping to get the attention of the limited number of bar staff. Ade manages to get served before you do. He eyes you over his shoulder and raises his hand to his mouth asking what you want to drink. You make a V sign with your fingers, Churchill style, and he knows without hesitation that you want a Smirnoff. Ade's dodgy ear means you often have to rely on semaphore; he'd never hear you over the fucking relentless pumping shite that dribbles out of the speakers in shitholes such as this. He gets the shots in and orders a couple of ciders to wash them down.

You edge out of the rabble to where there's a bit of elbow room, neck the shots and take a couple of cider-sips each.

'Look at all these cunts,' you say, pointing out a few of the worst ones. A group of lads in the seated area on the opposite side of the room have got your attention. They're setting fire to their shots and covering the tops of the glasses with their hands, then using the vacuum to stick their glasses to their palms. One of them is a right fat cunt, and he's sticking his glass to his flabby, gammon-nippled tits, much to the delight of his fucking droogs. After this risible display, they're sucking the gas out from under the glasses with straws and then necking the shots back. What the stupid twats don't realise, of course, is that when they set their drinks on fire, they're burning off the alcohol and making it less likely to fuck them up. Regardless of this, they're falling about all over the place, shouting to each other and acting like they're the hardest cunts in the world, arguing about whose round it is next and that kind of shit, pointing at the skanks and making suggestive faces. The back of your throat contracts as you feel the rage come. You've got your fucking eye on them.

Ade's seen them too. He's doing that same fixed stare that he always does, unbroken, uncompromising, unrepentant, holding his cider glass to his lips and staring at them over the rim as he enjoys slow and steady sips. He brings his glass down, takes a cigarette, lights it. He never looks away: his stare as sharp as a hypodermic needle, his pupils glittering like drops of morphine in the lumen.

'Come on now,' he says, eventually. 'Let's go over there. If I look at them much longer then I'm going to puke.'

You melt into the crowd. A few girls seem interested in Ade, nudging each other and whispering. One even goes as far as to dance up in front of him, but he ignores her and pushes past. She looks at her mates and shrugs as if to ask, 'What the fuck did I do wrong?' The old cliché that actions speak louder than words has never been more apt than it is in this fucking place where it's too noisy to hear anything anyway. You mingle with the lairies. The time-bomb ticks. Somehow you find yourselves back at the bar and, evidently, it's time for more drinks. Your round now, but Ade gets there first again – must be cos he's so tall. He stands out, fucking oozes charisma. You take your drink and brass him up for the round. Then it's over to the opposite side of the club to check it out.

The DJ says something over the PA. You don't hear a word the cunt says, and if you were a betting man you'd fucking bet none of the twats that cheer at him do either. They're too pissed to care. Mutton dressed as mutton all round you. Fucking cellulite city. No sense of self-worth whatsoever. Bile rises in you. Chest pounds and nostrils flare.

The minutes drip by, and run into hours. You lose track of whose round it is. Your eyes scan the room: some red-faced cunt grabbing the arse of a lonely girl that looks about fifteen. Some geezer with a bulldog tattoo arguing with his other half. A group of girls trying to fend off the unwanted attention of a gang of polo-necked arseholes wearing office lanyards. There are no jokes. The only thing that's funny is reality. Who was it who said that? Ade would know. It doesn't matter anyway; it's irrelevant, like all the newly-formed friendships sparked off in this place; the conversations between pissed-up strangers that seem so enticing now but tomorrow will fade to forgotten faces and misnomers and numbers typed hastily into mobiles with no name assigned. The falsity of it all makes your face ache.

Where the fuck's my drink? you wonder. Did I neck it? And where the fuck's Ade? Seem to have lost him somehow. Can't see his head poking out above the crowd any more.

What kind of twat needs to come somewhere like this to get with a bird? The sort of place where it's so loud you can't have a decent conversation, the sort of place where every skank is so pissed up she can't see properly, the sort of place where petty trivialities make enemies out of friends?

You hate them all.

It's like the end of *Othello,* where Iago's manipulation has been discovered and they fucking drag him off to torture him and he still won't reveal his motives. That's you. Your hatred doesn't need justification. It is not redeemable. It is not answerable. It just *is.*

And yet you can't stay away. You can't *not* pick this scab. It's like you're driving past a mangled car with the roof caved in and the radiator iron all bent up like tusks, and you really have somewhere better to be, but you still stop and watch them cut the bodies out. The more often you're out at night, the more you hate the reality you're faced with. The more you hate it, the more you want to kick back against it, and the more you kick back against it, the better you feel. Since addiction always obliterates sensation, it is the rush of the violence itself that brings about the subsequent withdrawal, as opposed to the withdrawal starting only when the violence is taken away.

There's Ade. Back at the bar again. You have no idea how long you've been in here. A litany of alcohol swirls in your stomach, a lethal cocktail of intoxicants. One more won't hurt.

Then you see them. Three geezers giving grief to some girl. They're giving her a good groping even though she's made it clear she's having none of it. You watch them, stepping from foot to foot as you wait for Ade to return with the drinks, which now seem irrelevant. Fucking come on, Ade. There's a bone to be picked here. Don't let it slip away. You spot him manoeuvring his way through the crowd with his hands full. You try to get his attention but fail to do so until he's a metre away, at which point you grab him by the arm and turn him towards them. He clocks them within a couple of seconds and passes you your drink, which smells like rum and Coke despite you requesting a JD. A swift nod of the head from Ade and you're after them.

The problem with places like this is that you can't have a decent fight without getting thrown out by the bouncers. So, when it comes down to it, you've got two choices. You can either give the cunts as good a kicking as possible within a few seconds and then scarper, or you can give them a bit of a teaser and get them outside to finish it off. You opt for the former, and there's no time to discuss it with Ade, so it looks like that's what's going to happen.

'All right, gents,' Ade says, when you're face to face with them. Two of them are standing up, one is sitting down with a different skank who looks slightly more interested.

'What?' one of them shouts back. He's shouting because of the volume of the music, not out of aggression. The one who's sitting down chatting is either too drunk or too engaged in conversation to notice you. Perhaps it's a bit of both.

'I said, "All right, gents,"' Ade repeats.

'Oh,' the geezer replies, a thin smile rising on his face like blood in a paper cut. 'Who's asking?'

'I am,' Ade says, and he lights a cigarette.

'What's your fucking problem, mate?' the other one interjects. The third one, the one who's sitting down, still hasn't turned around. Probably thinks you're here to socialise.

'He doesn't have a problem,' you shout back.

'Okay…' he says. Both of them look confused. You make sure you're staring them down.

'Yeah,' you continue. 'He has no problem at all. But I do.'

'What?' They look at each other then back at you. 'What fucking problem?'

'I didn't like the way you were behaving with that girl over there,' you say, and you point to her so they both know who you're talking about.

'What?' They look at each other again. You can't tell if they're denying the accusation, or if they simply haven't heard what you said because of the noise. But before you can repeat yourself, Ade gets in there.

'I'm sorry,' he says, loud enough for them to hear him and firm enough for them to know that he isn't taking the piss. 'What my friend said is that he didn't like the way you were molesting that girl over there.'

'What the fuck are you talking about?' one of them gobs. 'Just get out of my fucking face, you dick.'

You turn to check that their mate is still sitting down and behaving himself, oblivious. He is.

'We saw you,' Ade continues, 'from over there.' He points to the edge of the dance floor. 'You were grabbing at her, and she pushed you off, and then you waited until she turned round and you did it again. Then she shouted at you, and you tried to grope her tits.'

The geezer gets it now. His smile widens as he turns to his mate, nods, every bit the cheeky chappy.

'So fucking what, mate?' he says. 'I'm here for a laugh, mate, aren't I? A fucking laugh. She didn't seem bothered, did she?'

'I think she did,' Ade says.

'And me,' you agree. 'I didn't like it at all.'

'Oh fuck off, mate,' the other one says, and he gives you a little shove.

That's enough for you.

You smash your forehead onto his face so hard that you can't tell if the horrendous cracking sound is his nose or your skull. He doesn't hit back. He's too shocked, crouching down with blood gushing from his face and soaking through his scoop-necked top. He's saying something, it might be, 'Oh my fucking God,' but you can't make it out. Ade holds the other geezer back but he's struggling to get to you, and he's shouting all sorts of shit which, again, you can't hear. The prick just won't get the message and back off, and eventually Ade has to get his arm round the geezer's neck, and get his head down, so that you can deliver a few well-aimed kicks to his temples until he hits the deck.

You've got the attention of the third fucker. He shoots up off his seat like something's bitten him on the ballsack – so fast, in fact, that the table tips over, spilling drinks all over the skank that he's spent the last half an hour trying to chat up. Fucking classic! Ade gives him a shove – not hard enough to knock him over, but hard enough to let him know that if he tries anything, he'll be spitting teeth – and he immediately takes the hint and steps back, holding up his hands.

This whole episode, from the slap of your bonce on the guy's face to the present moment, lasted no more than fifteen seconds. A circle in the crowd has opened up around you already, and people scramble to get out of the way. It's time to go. Fucking fast.

You excuse your way to the opposite side of the club. You're disorientated and this place is a fucking maze, so you have to hope Ade knows where he's going. Once you're past the bar, you stroll casually towards the far corner, towards the welcoming smile of the doors. You want to pick up the pace, but you know that'll look dodgy. You keep looking back over your shoulder to see if anyone's following, but all you can see are punters dancing and chatting.

You reach the doors an age later. There are a couple of bouncers standing there, in the hallway, smoking cigarettes and talking. Ade calmly tells them, 'Mate, you need to get over by the dance floor, there's been a punch-up,' and so off they fuck without either thanking or challenging him.

Back on the street now, and it's pissing it down. You fall out of the club in euphoric ecstasy, throwing your arms around Ade's shoulders and roughing him up like a footballer congratulating his teammate for a fucking awesome goal. You feel your forehead and notice there's a nasty lump coming up and a bit of a split in the skin. Fuck knows what state the geezer's face is in. It's time to call it a night and get back to the flat – you can't be fucked with wasting any more money. You stand and wait for Ade as he shelters in the club's entrance and lights a cigarette.

'Taxi?' you ask when he's done.

'Yeh,' he nods.

You head back up the high street. There's a taxi rank at the top of the way and there's usually a long line of cabs pulled up by the side of the road around this time of night. When you get there, though, there are no taxis, just a group of lads standing under a bus shelter.

'Might as well just wait it out,' you suggest.

'Yeh, defo,' Ade says.

'I think those lads are waiting too,' you say, nodding at them.

Ade looks at them over your shoulder. 'Probably,' he says. 'We should let them get in the first one.'

'Yeh.'

You decide to go and stand with them underneath the bus shelter, even though there's not much point cos you're already about as wet as it's possible to get. You nip across the road and it's only when you're about three feet away that you notice their faces in the glow of the streetlamps. They're the geezers you saw when you first got into the club, the ones who were setting fire to their shots. And they notice you, too.

'Oi,' one of them says, aggressively. 'What the fuck were you two looking at earlier?'

'Nothing,' you say, glancing at him, caught off guard.

'Yes you fucking were,' the guy says. 'You were fucking staring me out. You got something to say?'

He's slurring his speech, obviously drunk. You can't decide whether to batter him or let it drop. He's a big fucker, this one, and his mates aren't much smaller. They're all squared up in front of you, staring at you intently with jaws clenched and chests inflated like toads in mating season.

'There's no problem,' says Ade. 'We were just watching you setting your shots on fire at the bar, that's all.'

Suddenly, and for no apparent reason, one of them grabs Ade by the face and smashes his head against the side of the metal bus shelter. There's a painful sound like a gong being hit, and for the first time ever, you see Ade hit the floor.

Not for long, though. He springs to his feet, narrowly avoiding a kick in the mouth. You're ready for action now. Funny how adrenaline kicks in just when you need it to. All four of the spastics are getting stuck into Ade, so you get hold of a couple of them and hold them back as best you can, but they're fucking strong. Ade's managed to knock down the one who first hit him, and he's stamping on him so ferociously that you're actually worried he might kill the fucker. You take one of the others out with a punch to the stomach, and then give him a few jabs in the kidneys to make sure that he stays down, but another one manages to grab your arms from behind, and the fourth delivers a few cracking punches to your face. As soon as the third punch connects, you feel your nose give way and you know it's broken. It's happened to you before and it's weak as a result. Ade's still stamping on the first guy's head in the same frantic way that someone might stamp on a campfire that's got out of control. You shout at him to come and get these two fat fucks off you. He takes the first one down with a right hook, but as soon as that cunt hits the floor, another one – the one you knocked down first – gets up again. These guys are giving it their fucking all, and for a moment you can envisage this shit going on until you're all dead, or at least unconscious.

One is still holding your arms, but you bite him on the biceps and he jerks backwards, yelping like a kicked dog. Ade's taking care of the other one, and by the time that cunt goes down, he's had enough and stays put. You notice that one of the guys who fell first is using his elbows to lift himself off the ground, and you shout at Ade to warn him. He stamps on the geezer's fingers, grabs him by the scruff of the neck and smashes his face into the concrete. You feel the thud through the soles of your shoes.

Now there's only one of these cunts left to deal with: the one whose arm you bit a chunk out of. You and Ade get to work on him: the guy's fucking wider than you are tall. Ade manages to get the fucker onto his knees by delivering some fast punches to the face and throat. Once he's at waist level, you kick fuck into him until he slumps face down and continue kicking him till he stops moving. It's still raining, but fuck the taxi. You both leg it up the road, leaving all four geezers in the bus shelter.

'How the fuck did that happen?' Ade shouts back at you.

'Fuck knows. I wasn't expecting that,' you say.

You carry on up the street: Ade is sprinting but you're too unfit for this shit.

'Get down here,' he says, and you nip off the main road into a car park and collapse next to some recycling bins.

You hold one of your nostrils shut with a finger and blow a rocket of snot and blood onto the concrete. Then you do the same with the other. You touch your nose and it feels a bit weird, but you can't work out what's wrong with it. One side of Ade's head is bleeding but most of the blood is already congealed, which is probably a good sign – no stitches necessary and no questions asked. He's got a real shiner coming up too and a garish-looking split on his top lip where the wound from the other night has reopened.

He tips his head back and rests against one of the bottle banks. You tilt yours forward to let as much blood flow out of your nose as possible. You can't be doing with this holding-your-head-back-to-stop-a-nosebleed shit, because it makes the blood run down your throat, which tastes like fucking muddy Guinness and makes you nauseous.

Ade takes out a cigarette and sticks it in his mouth. He doesn't light it yet, though; he just turns to face you, and stares for a few seconds, like he's sizing something up.

'What?' you ask.

'Your nose is facing the wrong way,' he says, finally.

'Fucking what?'

'It's facing the wrong way. Your nose.'

'What fucking way is it facing?' you ask, putting your hand up and feeling it again.

'Sideways,' Ade says, and he takes a lighter from his jacket pocket, spins the flint, and puts the flame to his cigarette.

'Fucking sideways?' You run a finger along the bridge, but you can't form a mental image.

'It must be broken,' Ade says. He takes a long drag on the cigarette, then coughs violently and gobs out the phlegm. It hits the tarmac with a splat.

'Yeh, it's broken. Feels the same way as it did last time I broke it anyway,' you say.

'I didn't know you'd broken it before,' he says.

'Yeh. Not fighting. Kneed myself in the face when I was a kid, on a bouncy castle. Fucking agony, it was.'

Ade laughs and takes another drag. 'Looks like we're walking home,' he says. 'We can't get in a taxi looking like this. The fucker'll freak out.'

You nod. 'But let's sit here a minute first,' you suggest. 'I need a rest. Running makes me sick.'

It's still early – it's ten past midnight, and for many the fun's just getting started. You listen to the distant sounds of revving cars, whooping revellers, honking horns, shouting lairies, laughing skanks, all set against the surprisingly calming muzak of late February rain on concrete. You are soaked to the bone and you don't care. Your nose and your knuckles are throbbing, and you can feel the blood pumping in your temples and crunching in your ear canals. For a brief moment back there, as kick followed punch followed stamp, you lost yourself. The world went away, and there was nothing but the furious silence between the screams.

NINE
DUNCAN

The George and Dragon is a quintessential old man's pub: dark and dusty inside, full of faces as gnarled and weathered as the wooden tables and scratched wooden floor. They do guest ales, darts, cards and dominoes and they don't serve any food apart from crisps and scratchings. Hard-looking old geezers cradle their pints and stare vacantly at the bare walls. Smoke clings to every surface and a middle-aged woman stands behind the bar, wiping down. It's the sort of place where you don't fuck about, where you drink alone, where you go when there's no one left to drink with.

We were sitting at a table in the corner that had four chairs around it but was prob only big enough for two people like. Sorel had just got another round in, but before I had a chance to take a sip, my phone buzzed in my pocket, a text message from Colbeck.

```
From: Colbeck
To: Dunc
```

```
where the fuck
are u?
```

I texted him back explaining that me and Sorel were bored in the flat, so we decided to nip out for a drink. Sorel stirred her gin and tonic with the straw and took a coupla sips. I watched the bubbles rise in the liquid. Effervescent! That's the word I was thinking of earlier. Fuckin told you it'd come back to me. There's a term for that, you know – lethologica. It means having a word on the tip of your tongue like. Fuck only knows how I know that, but I do. It prob comes from living with Ade for so long. He reads the dictionary when he's taking a shit. He's been doing it for nearly a year now, reading it from cover to cover like most people would read a novel. He reckons a good vocabulary is the best weapon there is, but I'd like to hear him say that if he wasn't as hard as fuckin nails.

Sorry, I went, looking up from my phone. I'll be as quick as I can. It's just Colbeck wondering where we've got to.

Checking up on us already, are they, she said, and I couldn't tell whether it was a joke or a remark of genuine annoyance.

I finished my text and picked up my glass. Cheers, I said.

Cheers, she went, and we clinked.

What's goin on anyway? I asked, keen to strike up another convo. I mean, how come you've come to stay with us? If you don't mind me asking like.

Not at all, she said, looking at the drink in her hand instead of at me. Basically, I split up with my boyfriend last month.

I widened my eyes to show interest, but she didn't look up.

I didn't want to go back to my parents because that'd be weird after living with him for so long, you know?

I nodded. There's no fuckin way I could go back to my parents, I thought. Fuck that. They practically pushed me out.

She went on: So, anyway, I had to find somewhere to go. I didn't have enough money to get a place of my own. All my friends either still live with their parents or they've moved in with boyfriends and stuff, or gone away to uni. So I couldn't really stay with them either. Me and Aidan have always got on well. He's been more like an older brother really. So, I decided to ring him.

Same as Colbeck, I goes.

How do you mean?

Well, he was living with his girlfriend somewhere. I dunno where cuz I never got invited over. I never even met her. Anyway, they ended up splitting up and so that's why he's here now. If they really have split up, I mean. Ade reckons this type of thing happens between them all the time.

I didn't realise, she said matter-of-factly, taking another sip of her drink. Anyway, you've heard my story. What about yours?

I don't really have a story, I said.

Everybody has a story, Duncan, she went. What's the story you tell most often?

I just looked at her.

Well how come you live with Ade, for a start? she said.

I found my cigarettes, took one out, lit it with a match which took two attempts. People ask why I use matches not lighters and it's cuz they're easier to find – you can hear which pocket they're in when you shake your jacket like. Ade reckons lighters were invented first, before matches, which is kinda weird when you think about it, and I quite like that. There was no ashtray, so I leant over and grabbed one from the vacant table next to us.

I was living with my parents, I said, exhaling. They were hassling me every day about doing something with my life. Cuz I'd dropped out of college, and I had no job, and – the way they saw it anyway – I was just sponging off them. But that's nonsense cuz I never asked them for money. I wouldn't have fuckin dared. But anyway, they made a point of telling all their friends about it, making me feel like a complete loser, and in the end I'd had enough of it. So in the middle of one of our arguments, which were happening pretty much every day by then, y'know, I just said, fuck this like, and came to stay with Ade.

She looked at me for a second or so after I'd finished chatting, stirred her drink, then took a sip. I had another coupla drags from the cigarette. I lifted myself up off the chair a bit cuz my boxers were sticking in my arse, and hoped I'd done it discreetly.

Then my fuckin phone buzzed again. I took it out, apologised to her for the interruption, and read the message.

From: Colbeck
To: Dunc

nice of u 2invite
us u dick. we r
goin out 2nite r
u cumin?

I put my phone back in my pocket. I couldn't be arsed to reply.

Sorel drained her glass and shook the ice about a bit. You want another? she asked.

I did, but instead I said, We should be getting back. You've already spent too much on me.

She winked at me and got up out of her seat, assuring me she had it covered. *Fuck me,* I was thinking. *She's too fit. I need to control myself here. Cuz if I start to fancy her too much then living with her's gonna become a complete nightmare. And she's obviously not interested anyway.* But she looked proper tidy that day, even though she was only wearing jeans and a skinny T-shirt. I was already starting to worry about whether I'd made a dick out of myself at all, and about whether my hair looked okay, and about whether I was boring her or whatever. Proper fuckin stressful it was. I was also worrying about what'd happen if I knocked a drink over, or fell off my chair, or spat when I talked or got a bogey like, or said something dickish. *Fuckin hell, Dunc,* I thought. *Need to calm down here. She's only a girl. We're only having a coupla quiet drinks as friends, fucksake.*

She returned, a pint in one hand and a glass of something else in the other: we were mixing our drinks so much by that point that it could've been pretty much fuckin anything.

Cheers, I said, and we clinked again. I was worried about an awkward silence opening up, so I went, Colbeck's been texting me. He wants to know if I'm gonna go out with him and Ade tonight. I'll tell him I might join them later, just to keep him happy. I'm not really going to go though.

Can't say I blame you, she said.

```
From: Dunc
To: Colbeck

mite meet u l8r.
still in pub
```

I sent the message and put my phone on the table next to my pint glass.

This is fun, she said. We should do it more often.

Fuck yeh! I thought.

My phone buzzed again. Fucksake.

```
From: Colbeck
To: Dunc

dont be a knt. cum
trendy bashing with
us. i am iago!
```

What the fuck's that meant to mean, I wondered. What the fuck is iago? I didn't like the sound of it anyway. I remember thinking – it sounds like loco, which means mad, only iago sounds worse, like fuckin tribal or someshit. I was well in the mood for drinking by now, but I was feeling a bit full from drinking that last beer too quick. I fancied something a bit shorter.

Shall we do some shots? Sorel asked, as if she'd climbed into my head and read my fuckin thoughts like.

Serious? I went.

Nothing wrong with a couple of chasers, she said, as she got up and headed to the bar.

I texted Colbeck back asking him what the fuck he was going on about, glancing up periodically at Sorel standing at the bar. She had the most heavenly arse I'd ever been privileged enough to witness and from this angle I could enjoy it in all its glory. I finished texting and took my cigarette from the ashtray, took a coupla drags, leaned back in my seat, glanced at her again. I'd not eaten yet and I was worried that the drinks were gonna go to my head, but fuck it: I'd started now so I might as well carry on. The worst thing you can do once you've started drinking early is stop.

Here you go, she said, placing the glasses on the table next to the empties we'd accumulated. She was drinking something different to my vodka. Something dark. I wondered what it was, and I wondered what she'd taste like after she'd drunk it. She sat down opposite me.

So tell me, I said. How long were you with your ex for? As long as it's not a touchy subject, I mean. I don't want to pry or anything.

It's fine, she said. It's good to talk about these sorts of things. I was with him for quite a while. Over two years. He was my first serious boyfriend, or at least my longest-lasting. I started going out with him when I was seventeen. God, that sounds so young, doesn't it?

I'm just dreading turning twenty, I said. It's the fact that I won't be a teenager any more that scares me the most. And the fact that twenty sounds so old, y'know?

Yeh, she said. At least twenty-one doesn't sound as old as twenty, in a weird sort of way.

When I thought about it, I realised she was right.

So what happened with your boyfriend? I asked. She looked a bit annoyed, so I apologised.

Duncan! she said, sternly. You've got to stop being so paranoid. If I didn't like hanging around with you then I wouldn't have invited you to come for a drink with me, would I? And if I didn't want to talk about something then I'd tell you.

It's just that Ade always tells me that I'm too nosey, I goes.

That's because Aidan would rather talk about what he wants to talk about as opposed to the things that you want him to talk about, you know?

Of course I knew, but I didn't say anything.

The reason I split from my ex is because he hit me, basically, she said.

My eyes dropped from her to the ashtray and refused to budge. I mean, I'd seen blokes hitting girls on TV and in the newspapers and shit like that, but I'd never actually met anyone who it'd happened to. Not until then.

What the fuck did he do that for? I asked, my eyes still fixed on the ash and fag ends.

He had problems, she said. Drink, drugs, emotional issues, the usual. Sometimes he'd get violent. He always used to punch walls and things; he'd smash stuff up, rip doors off their hinges. One time I got in the way. It was a stupid argument that escalated and I can't even remember what started it. I left him that night and I haven't seen him since. I sent my dad to get my stuff.

Has he tried to contact you? I asked.

Yep, she said, taking a quick sip of her drink but leaving the shot untouched. He rang me about twenty times a day for the first few days. I didn't answer. Apparently, he'd been ringing my parents as well. But I didn't call him back. He must've got the message anyway because he doesn't ring any more.

I can't believe Ade hasn't killed him yet, I said.

That's because Aidan doesn't know. He never even met him, and I'd rather keep it that way. He's bad news, and his friends aren't much better. I'm far better off without him. You're the first person I've told about this, and you've got to keep quiet about it, because if Aidan ever finds out then he'll end up getting himself arrested.

That made me feel kinda weird like. The idea that she'd confided in me about this shit but told no one else. She had a way of making people feel important when she chatted to them, mainly cuz she looked straight at you most of the time and didn't let her eyes wander. She'd play with her hair and her bracelets and jewellery, but she'd look you right in the eye, hypnotic and captivating. I was thinking about this guy who she was with and wondering what the fuck was going through his mind when he smacked her. Some people don't realise how fuckin lucky they are.

How did you hide the bruises? I asked. Didn't people get suspicious?

There were no bruises. Well, not very noticeable ones. When he hit me, he got me right in the face and all I got was a massive nosebleed. So I just told everyone that we split up after a big argument, which is true, just missing certain details. But that's for the best, I think.

Wouldn't it make you feel better if someone hit him back? I goes. I hoped she didn't think I was volunteering like.

I thought about that, she said. I honestly don't think it'd make any difference to me. I mean, he did what he did, and the consequence is that I never want to see him again, and hopefully I never will. If I told Aidan, then he'd try to sort it out with violence and the whole thing would be dragged up again. It's really not worth it. And, what's more, he isn't worth it. He's not worth wasting the effort on.

That's admirable, I went. Completely opposite to Ade. I can't believe you two are related. Although he always tells me that in order to win an argument you have to understand both sides equally. He reckons he got that from studying philosophy, y'know. And so, I've tried to see the things he's been saying lately from both sides. I agree with you that all this 'going after lairies' shit won't solve anything, but I can totally understand why he wants to do it.

But you could understand both sides equally and yet disagree with one, she goes. Or you could disagree with both.

True, I said. I'm not sure what I agree with any more.

She bit her bottom lip and nodded slowly.

What about Colbeck? she asked. I don't feel like I've really got to know him. What's he like?

I dunno, I went. I've not known him that long. Him and Ade studied together at uni and they've known each other pretty much forever. I think that Colbeck kind of looks up to Ade, so he might be easily led. I really don't know.

Please don't get yourself involved with this whole thing, she told me. I don't want to see you get hurt.

I should've paid more attention to that last part.

TEN
SHAUN

Alone in the metallic half-light of a deserted hospital ward, just after 3 a.m. On the university campus down the road there's a clock that chimes on the hour: a constant reminder of how slowly time moves when you can't sleep.

My mam's words, over and over and over in my head.

Shaun, on the night this happened to you, Steph was raped.

Oh fuck. I don't want to think about it, but I can't help myself.

You and her had some kind of falling out. She went off on her own and she was attacked. They found her passed out in a toilet cubicle.

Whoever did this to her, whoever did this to us, I'll get him. I'll find him.

It's the not knowing that kills you; the fact you're not feeling the same thing she's feeling. You've no tangible experience of her agony and so you don't understand what you should or could do to help her. You ask yourself whether she'll ever want to see you again. You wonder who's talking about her behind her back. You imagine the whispering of concerned friends, rising to a low murmur and then a steady hum, all of them saying that she deserves better than this. Saying that she deserves better than you.

And they're right. She does. Because in one way or another, you might just have caused this.

What the fuck did I say to her that night? What did we argue about? Mam didn't seem to know. Steph sometimes gets wound up when I'm drunk; she says I get too aggressive. But that's only when I'm provoked. That excuse doesn't cut it, though. She says that it scares her.

I hate this.

The memories must be in my head somewhere. The debris of snapshots and fragments. I just need to find and assemble them. So I go over the events as I remember them, up to the point where it all goes black.

I know that Big Tony and I were planning a big night. He came over to my flat for a few drinks and a couple of spliffs and he brought some MDMA with him. He turned up with his sports bag slung over his shoulder, on the way back from the gym – I have this memory of him saying, 'All right, dude, you've gotta check this shit out!' He said he'd had a bump before he went in and that he'd been able to bench-press fifteen kilos more than usual. Steph and her mates had arranged to meet us in Zanzibar, after they'd been to a few bars first. I was pissed off about that. The night was going to be a messy one, and I didn't want her to be there to see the sort of state I got into when I went out with Tone. I'd been trying to persuade her that she should just have a night with the girls, that there was no reason for her to come and meet up with us. Don't worry about me, I said. Don't feel guilty about it. I'll just see you tomorrow. Spend some time with your mates. I said this as if it was for her benefit, but of course it was really for mine. There are no memories after about eight that evening, and by that point me and Tone were already pretty mashed. I know that we *did* meet up with Steph, but only because that's what I've been told. And something happened and we argued: maybe me being drunk and stupid and starting on her, or maybe her starting on me because of the state I was in.

It's the not knowing that kills you.

Someone saw her. She was upset. Perhaps she was crying. Alone and vulnerable. Let down by her bloke again. And he sees her, and he approaches her, asks if she's all right, offers her a drink.

She accepts.

He leads her over to the bar. She's tipsy and she's hurt and she trusts him. He hands her a glass. She chats for a bit then excuses herself. He waits. Watches for the telltale signs of the drug taking hold. Then, when she's out, he's onto her. He has to work fast. He might get caught.

How long was he actually with her? How long does it take for those kinds of drugs to work, to stop working?

How does she feel when she wakes up? Does she know instinctively that something has happened to her? Or does it slowly dawn on her, this horror? Is it one of those things you're aware of straight away, or does it take her a few minutes to work out? Did he come inside her? And does he speak to her while he's doing it? Biting her neck and breathing heavy in her ear?

What about the gaps though, the memory-holes? Mam told me Steph's saying she can't remember much about any of it. I've taken all sorts and still remembered everything I got up to the night before. So how fucking much did he have to give her?

Whose fault is this mess? Does she hate me? What the fuck did I say to her?

It must've been quick. Tony got ejected from a club once because some girl was giving him head in the bogs and the bouncers caught them; looked over the top of the cubicle and saw him, his cock still wet from her saliva as she wiped her mouth. The bouncers look out for that kind of thing. And the toilets in clubs are always rammed. How the fuck did he get away with it?

Him. Who the fuck is he? Old and lonely? Young and fired up on amphetamines? What does he look like? He has a name. He has a family.

And what am I to Steph now? A bloke is supposed to protect his girlfriend. I didn't. Big Tony is always good to have around when something kicks off. He's a terrifying individual when he has to be. We should've been there for her, but we weren't.

I need to see her. I need her to know that I'm sorry. It seems as though I'll always be sorry. I'll always regret that night. But these are just words. She's probably spent the last few weeks being told that everything will be okay by people who should fucking well know better.

It's the not knowing that kills you.

My friends, her friends, our friends. All talking behind our backs. Did you hear what Shaun did? He got off his face on mandy and alcohol, had an argument with Steph and abandoned her, and then she got raped. Two lives ruined, hers and his, and it's basically all his fault. He's such a twat. He's in hospital at the moment. He got hit. Probably throwing his weight around as usual. Cunt deserves everything he gets. He's lucky he's never been smacked like this before. How the fuck could he do that to Steph? She could do so much better.

In this place, there's just too much time to think things over, and there's nothing to block it out.

You can lie to everyone except yourself.

It's the not knowing that kills you.

ELEVEN
DUNCAN

We finished the last coupla drinks simultaneously and slammed our glasses down on the table. Last orders had been called ages ago but there'd been a bit of a lock-in and it was nearly fuckin one in the morning now. Sorel goes, Home time, I think, and I nodded. Just let me light a cig first like, I said.

She stood first and I followed her, sparking up at the same time. I picked up our glasses and put them on the bar on the way out.

I enjoyed that, I told her, as I buttoned up my parka. Thanks for all the drinks.

No worries, she went. You can get them in next time.

We stepped out into the street. She looked proper fit, fitter than usual, I reckon, but perhaps it was the beer goggles. Anyways, I specifically remember thinking – cuz Ade and Colbeck had gone up town like – we were gonna have the flat to ourselves when we got back and so I'd better start thinking of some interesting shit to chat to her, seeing as my one-liners were pretty much exhausted. Perhaps I could put on some soft music and dim the lights or someshit. That's the way to woo a girl. Whatever Ade and Colbeck say to the contrary, the birds love a bit of fuckin romance.

The problem I had, of course, was that it pretty much went without saying that at some point Ade would burst into the room with Colbeck in tow, guns blazing, completely shattering the atmos, spitting shit about all the lairies they'd spotted up town and gobbing off about what a load of cunts they were, throwing their weight around with promises of revisiting this hatred upon them tenfold while Ade chain-smoked his way through a twenty-deck and grebbed periodically into the kitchen sink and Colbeck patted him on the back and assured him it's all good unless there's fuckin blood in it. Plus there was the fact that if Ade caught me trying it on with Sorel he'd be more than likely to rip my balls off, and on top of that I had the small obstacle of getting her interested in me in the first place like. But all in good time. I'd get her to like me, I was sure of that, cuz I had to. I just hadn't worked out how to do it yet.

She led the way and I followed her cuz I was unsure how to retrace the shortcut we'd taken earlier, and I was enjoying the view of her arse besides. As I trailed behind her, I secretly prayed that she wouldn't lead me through the alleyway again, cuz I knew there'd prob be some right dodgy fucks hanging out up there at this time of night. I didn't say anything though, cuz if I did then I'd look like a proper dick, and I wanted her to feel safe with me. To my fuckin horror, she made a right and headed straight down it.

I moved closer to her, hoping she'd think it was cuz I wanted to protect her, but in actual fact it was the opposite: I wanted her to protect me. Fuckin hell, Dunc, I thought.

You need to stop being such a fuckin wimp. Solid as seawater like.

You're quiet, she goes, when we were about halfway from the haven at the mouth of the alley. What you thinking about?

I dunno, I said. What I was actually thinking about was that thing where people go, 'Is the glass half empty or half full?' and I was trying to apply it to our current position in the alley, wondering if we were halfway from the entrance or the exit seeing as we were right in the middle of the fuckin thing, and wondering which view, if any, was more optimistic.

She looked at me, not slowing her pace at all.

What? I went, probably a bit too defensive in retrospect. Then I shrugged and said something like, I was just thinking about all kinds of stuff, y'know, nothing in particular.

Are you scared? she asked, with a coy smile that made her look even fuckin fitter than before.

No! I goes. Course I'm not scared.

It's just that you're walking really fast, she said, still smiling.

Am I?

Yep.

Okay then, I admitted. Yes, I'm scared. I hate walking up dark alleys at night.

Aw, she said, and she took my hand. Fuckin result! Despite making myself look like a scaredy-twat, I'd finally initiated at least some kinda physical interaction, so I was kinda a step or two closer to my end goal, without really trying. Nice one!

We reached the top of the alleyway and turned left. We cut through from the back of the chip shop – the same way that we walked down from earlier – and then took another left onto Charlton Street, and all the time she still held my hand until we were on Wedgwood Road by the offy, where she sorta changed her grip so that our fingers interlocked like. Fuck me, that girl was turning me on. I knew that if I said anything else, I'd more than likely make a dick out of myself, so I just kept quiet. This is fuckin great, I thought: I'm pissed enough to feel it but I'm not feeling ill or falling over. Most of the time I either overdid or underdid it on the alcohol front – at house parties I'd either be the one passed out in the back garden at midnight with my face in my own stomach acid, or else the only person still awake at 6 a.m., raiding the alcohol cupboards of some poor fucker's unsuspecting parents.

We were still holding hands when we got to the front door. At this point, she let go and looked in her bag for her keys. I took the opportunity to light another cigarette. I knew that if I played it right, if I didn't say something stupid to ruin the moment, if I just kept her smiling, then I could get her. You know when you get that feeling, when you know that you're in? Well that's the feeling I got right then, you get me?

I don't have my keys, Dunc, she said. You got yours?

Probably, I went. I felt in my pockets and found them after a coupla seconds of rummaging.

Lucky, she said. We could've been waiting out here for hours.

We took the stairs to the flat, which is on the second of three floors. But when we got there the door was open. We looked at each other, just like they do in films when someshit's obvo amiss. Then I poked my head round the door, kinda like I'd imagine a soldier looking out from behind a barricade after heavy shellfire, wary of any sudden noise or movement.

The first thing I saw was blood: a few spots on the floor, and a smudged handprint by the light switch, which was switched on. The second thing I saw was Ade, sitting on the settee with a cigarette between his lips, casually filling in some of the blanks I'd left on the day's crossword.

Where the fuck's all this blood come from? I goes, stepping into the room with Sorel, frightened that I might find a corpse or someshit in one of the bedrooms. I mean, Ade often comes back bloodied-up, as you know, but fuckin smearing it on the walls was a new one. He turned round slowly, calmly, like he'd already anticipated us entering, and that's when I noticed the cut on his head.

Aidan! Sorel shouted, clocking the dried blood stuck to his cropped hair at the same time as me. What've you done now?

Hello there, he said, cheerily. Half of the cigarette dangling from his mouth was ash. You can always tell when he's pissed. His head goes like one of them nodding dogs, like he's got Alzheimer's or someshit. I strode over to him and held an empty beer can underneath his chin until the ash dropped into it.

Your blood's all over the wall, Sorel said, pointing towards the door. For God's sake, Aidan, what've you been doing?

What? he said. He was talking a bit slow like, kinda slurring. Then he seemed to realise what the fuss was about cuz he went, Oh! That's not my blood. It's Colbeck's.

Fucksake, I went, sitting down heavily beside him on the sofa. Sorel shook her head in disgust, or amazement, or whatever. And right on cue, I heard the bog flush and then the bathroom door opened and in stepped Colbeck.

What the fuck…? I said.

How do? he went.

I nodded back at him, but Sorel was looking at him kinda weird. What's happened to your nose? she asked him. It's facing the wrong way.

Ade's face twitched a bit, like he was having a stroke or someshit, and then he proper cracked up. As soon as he caught Colbeck's glance they were both pissing themselves, slumped over the settees, jerking like someone was going at them with a cattle prod.

What the fuck's so funny? I demanded. Cuz if you could see it from my perspective, you'd understand it's no fuckin laughing matter.

This got their attention for a bit but then they were off again worse than before: Ade now had his face in his own lap like he was performing autofellatio or someshit. Sorel moved closer to me and we watched them, her standing and me sitting, both of us in silence and shock. The effects of the alcohol had worn off the instant I stepped into the flat. I was proper pissed off at them, too, cuz I'd planned on cosying up with Sorel and they'd totally fucked it up.

Please excuse me if I forget to laugh, I said, bitterly.

Fucking lighten up, Dunc, Ade giggled, sitting up now, scratching his bollocks, adjusting himself. Then he goes, Look at the state of Matt's face, man! It's absolutely fucked!

And then he was off again with his squawking.

Fucksake, you two, I said. I went over to Colbeck, who was rolling on the floor, and jabbed him in the ribs with my foot. Not hard like, just a bit of a prod to get his attention. Come on, I goes. Get up, man, you're getting blood on the carpet.

Hey, Dunc, Ade called from across the room. You seen my cig? Think it fell out my mouth when I was laughing.

You dick, I went. That could start a fire – haven't you seen those fuckin adverts? Get out the way and let me look. I stepped over Colbeck's hefty frame.

It's okay, Ade said. I can see it now. It's there. He pointed towards the nub on the floor, and the black mark it'd burnt into the rug.

I snatched it up and dropped it into the empty beer can. I managed to make eye contact with Sorel, and when I went into the kitchen, she followed.

This is getting out of hand, she went, when I shut the door behind us. Are they on something?

Like drugs? I asked

Like… anything, she said.

I dunno, I told her. It's probably just the rush from kicking the shit out of someone.

It looks to me as if someone's kicked the shit out of them, she went.

I'm sure they gave back as good as they got, I said. I was about to continue but Ade shouted at me from the living room.

Dunc! There's a bottle of Jack in the secret cupboard. Bring me a double. No ice.

I heard Colbeck say something, but I couldn't make it out.

And one for Colbeck, Ade shouted through the door. On the rocks for him, though.

It's ridiculous, Sorel said, when the silence returned. How can they justify beating someone up just because of what they look like?

It's not about what they look like, I said. It's totally non-discriminatory. Then I realised I was starting to fuckin sound like them, and I had to stop for a coupla seconds to get my train of thought back. I went on: It's people who get lairy, people who cause trouble, people who kick off, that sorta thing.

Well, she said, folding her arms. It's pathetic.

Ade shouted again from the living room: Yo, Dunc! I don't hear much activity in there. You fixing us that drink or what?

I grabbed the door handle and shoved the door open. No! I spat, glaring at him. I'm not fixing you that fuckin drink. If you're sober enough to walk then you can get off your lazy fuckin arse and make it yourself, you cunt.

And I slammed the door.

I heard Colbeck go, Ooooh, handbags at dawn, boys, and both of them laughed.

Sorry, I said, glancing at Sorel and wondering who or what she was thinking about. But you know what Ade's like, I goes. I can't talk any sense into him. He's got his own agenda and he won't take any notice of what I tell him. He knows I'm not going to get involved in it; that's all I can say.

She started to say something, but then the kitchen door opened and in staggered Colbeck.

Hello, ladies, he said, and he took a couple of glasses from the draining board and rinsed them out under the cold tap. His nose was still bleeding: he had to keep sniffing to keep the blood from dripping onto his clothes, which were already covered in it anyway. This was gonna be a hospital job for defo, I thought. He'd wake up tomorrow and he'd look in the mirror and fuckin shit himself.

I think you've had enough alcohol for tonight, said Sorel, taking him by the arm and ushering him away from the sink.

No way, he said, shaking himself free. He looked Sorel up and down, holding his gaze on her tits for a few seconds, and I know she noticed him do it because she adjusted her top and folded her arms again. Then he goes, The night is young. Join us for a tipple.

He opened and closed a few cupboards, obvo trying to find the elusive Mr Daniel's. When he succeeded, he held the bottle aloft and inspected it against the kitchen light. Marvellous, he said, still sniffing back the blood.

I imagined it trickling back into his throat. He poured out a couple of glasses, triple measures in each, then opened the freezer and removed a tray of ice. I watched as he allowed one, two, three cubes to drop into one of the drinks.

Come on, Matt, Sorel goes. Why don't you just go to bed?

Gonna play Sega, he went.

What? I said. You can't play Sega, the telly's fucked.

Oh yeh, he went. Haha.

And he picked up both glasses and headed back into the living room, leaving the freezer door open and the tray of ice melting on the counter.

TWELVE

COLBECK

You've heard that when a soldier kills someone for the first time his immediate reaction is to want to kill someone else. You don't know whether this little piece of worthless trivia is true or not, and you don't care either, but one thing's for sure: every time your fist shatters a jaw, every time your boot connects with fragile genitals or vulnerable temples, every time your fingers jab at eyeballs, your only desire is to do it again and again and again.

But it wasn't always this way. What about the first time? What accidental collision of atoms set this new universe into motion? As it happens, the first time wasn't at school; it wasn't one of those coming-of-age events where you kick the fuck out of the bully who's been tormenting you for years. The first time you threw a punch at someone was much more recent than that: it happened when you were at uni with Ade, when a pissed-up student-football-team cunt decided to start something that he wasn't man enough to finish. He obviously expected his teammates to have his back, but they didn't. And the reason they didn't have his back is because he was the biggest of all of them and you still put him on the ground. After you did it you stood over him all adrenaline-drunk and wondered whether you should kick his face in. But you quickly decided, no, he's had enough, there's no need. That might have been the end of it all, and you might have taken a very different path in life, were it not for something that happened later on that evening.

It goes something like this: after you smack that cunt it all kicks off a little bit – no more punches are thrown but you end up getting separated from Ade in the pushing and shoving that follows. You find your way out of the bar through one of the patio doors; it's summer and there's a paved area outside where people can go and get some air or do some covert fingering or whatever. By the time you finally get hold of Ade, over text message on your 3210, it turns out that he's already left, and he's halfway back to the student digs you share because he assumed you'd left as well. Outside, the patio is deserted. You do a quick minesweep of all the half-finished drinks abandoned on the picnic tables just to get yourself as fucked up as possible before making your exit. Then you're heading up towards the far end of the patio – the opposite end from the doors to the bar you just vacated – and you're nipping up the steps onto the street, rounding corners and skipping kerbs on complete autopilot as you make your way home.

There's a commotion up ahead and you walk towards it with your head down and your collar up. You keep your balance by following the white lines in the centre of the road. As you get closer, you can hear two or three voices – girls, pissed up, veering between hysterical sobbing and frantic panic. Nearer now, you can see there's some sort of stone monument or war memorial with a couple of benches beneath it. There's a barefooted girl lying on one bench with her head lolling over the edge and a thin stream of puke connecting her chin to the pavement. Her mates are crouched beside her, rocking her head backwards and forwards and slapping her face and offering her water that she's way too fucking out of it to drink. One of the girls stands up and begins pacing clockwise and anticlockwise round a three-quarter circle, phone to her ear, gobbing off into it. You pass by them, glancing fleetingly in their direction and shaking your head in equally measured doses of disgust and amusement.

'Hey!' one of them shouts. 'You! Come here! We need help.'

You slow your pace. Out of habit you turn and look around you to check it's actually you she's addressing, but it's pretty pointless cos you know already that's the case. You suddenly start to feel a lot less drunk and your first instinct is to cross the road and pick up speed and just get yourself the fuck away from them. For fuck's sake, you're thinking, can the superhero not get a few fucking hours off work?

'Please!' she shouts. 'She's in trouble.'

It's at this point that some dichotomy stirs, catches, and tugs inside you with one part saying *leave it now...* and the other telling you to go to their rescue. It's as if your mind is urging your legs to keep moving, to keep walking in the opposite direction, to move on, move on like those Biblical cunts did before the Samaritan came by – but your legs refuse to comply because they know there's an unquestionable moral obligation to help. You're stood absolutely still in the middle of the road now, with your back to them. You turn around.

'Please!' she says again. 'Can you help us?'

Your legs, without permission, propel you towards the bench where the three girls are assembled. One of them is in a bad way, flopped over like her bones have been softened in vinegar, her groans punctuated only by convulsions and spasms and a horrid gurgling sound frothing out of her gob like elderly lungs succumbing to pneumonia. As you approach, despite the apparent gravity of the situation, all you can call to mind is the pet guinea pig you had when you were younger – and you can't even remember the cunt's name right now, fucking Flopsy or Mopsy or something like that – who did exactly the same thing shortly before it was boxed up and taken away to be put down.

'Christ. What the fuck's wrong with her?' you say.

'She's had her drink spiked,' one of the friends sobs. 'By some guy.'

'What guy?' you ask.

'I don't know.' The terrified eyes widen and fix on yours. 'We don't fucking know! Just someone she met in there.'

'In where?'

'There,' she says, pointing vaguely back down the road, towards the various gutter-clubs that line the pavements in this part of town.

You notice that you've taken your jacket off and you're laying it over Flopsy on the bench.

'Has someone bothered to call for help yet?' you're asking. 'And are you sure about this? How do you know she's not just pissed?' You flatten the arms of the jacket to increase the surface area, to cover her up as best you can.

'She doesn't even drink,' comes the reply. 'She's meant to be driving us home.' She pauses to light a cigarette then goes on: 'I fucking told her not to take a drink from that lad she was with. I knew he was dodgy.'

'Is an ambulance coming?' you ask.

Before anyone can answer, the girl on the bench jerks suddenly and pukes all over your jacket. She's moaning – a low, almost inaudible humming sound escaping her lips every time she exhales.

'Here. Use my phone,' you say, pointing your mobile at her mates. 'Ring an ambulance.' These are words, formed by your mouth, that you have no control over. They are not coming from you.

'We already have. We rang ten minutes ago.'

'It'll be here soon, then,' you say. 'Don't worry.'

'Will you stay with us?'

'I can't,' you say. 'I need to go.'

'Please. Please stay with us until someone comes.'

Her eyes are wet with tears. You can see for the first time how young and frightened she is. You want to turn and get the fuck out of here, right now. But you can't.

'How old are you?' you ask. 'I'm serious. How old are you? And how old is she?'

'Sixteen,' the girl responds, pointing to herself and the second girl. 'And she's seventeen.' She nods towards Flopsy.

'For fuck's sake,' you say. 'You shouldn't even be out here.'

Jesus Christ. You sound like a fucking granddad.

'Please!' the other girl says.

You realise that you're going to stay with them until help comes. For whatever reason, that decision has already been made. They're young and they're stupid and they're naïve, and perhaps you'd hate them on a different day, but you can't walk away and leave them here. You feel a strange protective urge that you can't recall ever having felt before. Besides, if she really has been spiked, then you might run into whoever's done it, and then the girls can confirm his identity and you can – well, who knows? There's a new twitching feeling inside you that just won't subside since you smacked that guy earlier, and you know you could easily turn someone's face inside out again if they crossed you. But before you can confirm any of this to them, someone behind you says, 'Excuse me, sir?'

A scruffy, straggly-bearded cunt, with a crooked roll-up hanging unlit from the corner of his mouth, and the hungry jawline and greasy nocturnal pallor of a smackhead, steps out from behind the war memorial.

'What?' you demand.

'What it is,' he begins, 'is that I'm just asking people if they can spare a little bit of change so that I can get into a hostel or something like that, so that I—'

'So you can buy fucking drugs, or booze, you mean.'

The girl on the bench pukes up again, more this time, wetter and heavier, and her mates try and comfort her between their own whimpers.

'No, no,' the guy goes on. 'I just need—'

'Look!' you say. 'Fucking look at her! This is going on, right in front of you, and you fucking dare come over here and ask us for money?' You turn around and face him square on and get right up against him, your chest touching his. You're bigger than he is. 'Fuck off,' you spit.

'Maybe I can help?' he suggests.

'Fuck off before I tear your fucking face off.'

The guy breaks eye contact for a second and glances over your shoulder. He sees the girl, cocks his head, and makes a clicking sound with his tongue.

'Put something under her head,' he says. 'Here.' He offers you a plastic carrier bag with a rolled up sleeping bag inside it.

'No thank you,' you say. 'Go away.'

'You need to support her head,' he says, unrolling the sleeping bag, 'and you need to lift her legs onto the bench and bend them under her. Make sure she lies on her side. Keep her warm. Give her water but make sure she only sips it.'

'We've done all that,' one of the girls says. 'Why the fuck won't she stop being sick? Will she be okay?'

'You just have to keep her warm and keep her on her side and get the paramedics out,' the guy says.

'Doesn't that go without saying?' you reply. The spite is rising up inside you and you're finding it almost unbearably hard to keep it at bay.

He lays the sleeping bag over the girl. It's filthy and it fucking stinks. 'I know first aid,' he goes on. He lights his cigarette with a cheap lighter. 'I learned it in the army.'

You turn to him. 'Really?' you ask.

'Really,' he says. He turns his head to the side and blows smoke. 'Happens a lot,' he shrugs.

The girl's breathing has slowed a little and she's stopped panting and jerking. Her mates have quietened their sobbing and you suddenly feel very cold without your jacket despite the summer air. A couple of minutes later, two First Responders arrive and ask the two conscious girls a few questions. Ignoring you and the other guy, they sit the patient up and put a blanket round her, and you take the opportunity to get your coat back and roll it up to stop the puke getting on your clothes.

You ask the girls if they're going to be okay. Can they get home? Do they have any money?

'My dad's coming to get us,' one of them says. 'He's five minutes away. I think we're going to follow Chloe to the hospital.'

'Okay,' you tell them.

Meanwhile, the guy is collecting his sleeping bag and packing it back up inside the carrier and tightening the straps on his rucksack. He checks he's got everything, and you realise he's about to simply fuck off, without saying anything.

'Oi,' you say, as he takes the first steps away from you.

'Yeah?' he looks up at you.

'Fucking take this, okay?' You hand him a fiver and some change.

Slowly, he takes the money from you and puts it in his pocket.

'I don't like handing money out,' you say. 'I'd rather have taken you to get some food or something. I suppose I'm inclined to believe you'll spend it on getting fucked up. But, have it. It's yours.'

The guys nods. 'Thanks,' he says. 'What's your name?'

'Matt.'

'I'm Nathan.' He extends his hand and you shake it.

Then the two of you walk off in separate directions without saying another word to each other.

When you're just out of clear sight of the bench where the girls sit with the paramedics, you stand and keep watch for fifteen minutes until a dark-coloured estate car pulls up on double yellows with its hazard lights lit up. An older guy gets out and engages in brief conversation with the girls and the ambulance crew. You can't hear what anyone is saying but there's a lot of nodding and some pointing, and you see the guy is wearing tracksuit bottoms and a long T-shirt like he's just got out of bed. The girl on the bench, still wrapped in blankets, is helped to her feet and chaperoned into the back of the ambulance. The other two girls get into the back of the car. The doors slam, the engine revs, the hazards are switched off, and they all drive away. You watch the blue and red lights disappear around the corner, trace the reflections in the glass of the shop windows until they're gone completely.

◎

Up until then, you'd largely internalised your diatribe against the horrific state of affairs that greeted you as standard on any given night out. You'd always treated it as something that had to be put up with, like rising beer prices and your increasing student debt. Maybe the football guy in the bar pushed you over the edge. Or maybe it was just a combination of him catching you pissed, bad-tempered, and with Ade at your side. Because you and Ade will always look out for each other. You can't imagine Ade ever getting involved in a fight that you wouldn't jump into in a second. And it works both ways – a reciprocation neater and more beautiful than anything within mathematical law. Any time you need help to put someone down, you don't even need to ask. It's an unwritten ethic that exists between you; a common courtesy like saying please and thank you or offering your bus seat to an old lady. And there comes the second part of it – the desire to protect what deserves to be protected. Was there a time when you would have let the guy in the bar get away with it, not wishing to cause a scene or put yourself at risk? For sure. Was there a time when you would have just walked past those three girls on that bench, not wanting to get involved? Yes, probably. Was there a time when you would have smirked at them and said, 'Serves them fucking right'? Good chance of it, yeah.

But something changed that night. Something inside you. You've never felt the same way since. It's like the first time you have sex. Whether it happens when you're pissed and not expecting it, or whether it happens after weeks of planning and getting the mood right and all that bollocks, something changes. You feel different the next day. You might try to hide it, but you act different. You walk with more of a swagger. You talk to your friends differently. You'll never be the same person again.

You are a different person now. There's no going back. The man you used to be doesn't exist any more. He is extinct, existing only in photographs and fading memories. Every end has a beginning, and the thought of this both scares you and spurs you on.

THIRTEEN

TAG

It was just another day.

June 13th, 2003: Friday night. We're off out as usual. It's 7 p.m. and I'm in the flat ironing my shirt. I don't have an ironing board, so I'm using the poker table I bought second-hand at a car boot when I hosted a flat-warming poker tournament. Then the phone rings. I snatch it from its cradle.

Hey, I say. I already know it's Tony cos he's the only one who knows my landline number.

I'm on my way, he says. Won't be long.

I hear thc flint spin on the lighter as he sparks up a cigarette. There's noise in the background; it sounds like he's walking along a busy street. You managed to get hold of anything? I ask.

Yeah, he says. He inhales smoke. I hear the crescendo of music from a car stereo as it drives past him, then fades into the distance.

How much did you get?

Wait and see.

He says that he has a call waiting on the other line. Says he'll see me in a bit, and then he hangs up. I carry on ironing the shirt. I'm shit at ironing, especially shirts. I can never get them to lie flat enough. I've been doing this one for ten minutes and it looks just as bad as it did when I started. The creases are still there, just in different places. That's one thing I miss about living at home – free laundry service. Just dump it all in a filthy pile and it miraculously disappears, then reappears a few days later washed and dried and folded up. But the self-sufficiency is a small price to pay to get away from David, the bloke who's pretending to be my father. What happened is that my mam and him had an affair which went on for about a year. At the time I had no suspicions and as far as I know my dad didn't either. Then suddenly it was all out in the open. She came clean about it on a Sunday evening when I was in the pub playing pool. I got back home and the shit had hit the fan. Dad said he was moving out for a few days. But a few days passed and he didn't come back. Then a week, then a month. Then the divorce claims were filed. And he's still a wreck because of it, living in a one-bedroom flat on the other side of town. He's drinking and he's on disability. Job gone, family gone, life gone. And if it comes to apportioning blame then at least half of it has to go to David. That's why I hate him so much. She's not much better. When mam asked him to move into our house – no, not just our house, but our fucking *home* – I really went off on one. I threatened to kill the bastard. I said I'd get in there when he was asleep and take a hammer to his skull. But he moved in anyway, obviously unfazed by my threats, which I had no real intention of ever carrying out anyway. I wanted to try and be mature about the whole thing and I knew it'd only stir up the shit if I stayed, so I had to move out. There are always extra hours going at work, and it's shift stuff that pays well, especially when I do nights, so putting aside a bit of extra cash for rent and bills wasn't a problem. That was two months ago, and I haven't spoken to either of them since. She calls my mobile every few days, but I ignore the phone until it stops ringing. She's sacrificed her family for a younger man with an executive job and a car with a fucking two-litre engine. Pathetic. Talk about a midlife crisis.

I, on the other hand, am having my own quarter-life crisis. I don't know whether it's abandonment issues that are preventing me getting close to people or what, but I feel like I'm trapped whenever I'm reliant on someone else, or whenever someone else is reliant on me. Like Steph, for instance. It's early days and this is meant to be the honeymoon period, but when I remember that she's meeting us tonight it doesn't give me butterfly-flutters of excitement in my gut. To be honest, it just puts a bit of a downer on the whole thing. I don't think it's too much to ask: sometimes I just want to have a night out with the lads, but whenever I say that, she kicks off. Am I being selfish? It's good to have some time to yourself, away from each other, to pursue your own interests – isn't it?

The problem is that my own interests tend to lie in activities she actively discourages – like letting yourself go a bit at the weekend when I'm not on earlies at work. It makes me edgy when she's around, especially when I'm on pills. I've told her that I've stopped dropping them, but of course I haven't. I'll be having a few later on and then I'll have to deal with her. It's a strange relationship. We've been together about five months, which is longer than I've spent with anyone else apart from Michelle, and that was when I was sixteen. But Steph always wants to be around me, and she doesn't understand that it's unhealthy. She's already made advances about moving in here, but I've told her that the flat is only a temporary thing and that it'd be a waste of time for her to bring all her stuff around only to have to shift it all out again in a couple of months. That's keeping her at bay, for now.

There's also the problem of uni. I got good grades in college. I was going to move away, but I decided to have a year out. That turned into two years out. I'm twenty now, and I'm really determined to move away to uni next year. It's one of those things where I just know that I'll regret it if I don't do it. I've lived round here my whole life and I want to see somewhere new. Didn't even go abroad till I was seventeen. Whenever I talk to Steph about it, though, she says I should just stay here and go to the uni down the road. She says that it's as good as anywhere else. I tell her no, it isn't as good as anywhere else, because it's an old polytechnic and with my grades I should be going to one of the red-bricks. But every time I say that, she kicks off. She says that I'm obviously not as serious about us as she is. My side of things: I *am* serious about us, but she needs to learn to be a bit less fucking clingy. She's acting like we're married. Tone knows all about this because I've moaned to him a few times about it, usually while drunk. Now he calls Steph my wife. He'll say, How are you, man? And how's the wife? I laugh it off because it irritates me and you know what mates are like: show them that something's getting to you – like a joke about shagging your mam, for example – and they'll only say it more.

Fuck the shirt. It'll have to stay creased. I stand up and shake it a bit, then I put it on a hanger and hook it over the curtain rail in the living room. Tone reckons that ironing's pointless. Says he's never ironed anything in his life.

Speak of the devil. The door opens and in he strides with his sports bag slung over his shoulder. He always walks in without knocking. He knows that he doesn't have to.

All right, dude? he asks. He draws the word out: duuuuuuuude. We clasp hands and bump shoulders.

He goes over to the fridge and takes out a beer. Then he lifts two four-packs from his bag and puts them inside. Want one? he says.

Yeah.

He hands me a can and cracks his open. He sucks up a greedy slurp and takes out a cigarette.

So? I ask.

In the bag. Have a look.

I lean over and take the bag from him.

Front pocket, he says.

I feel around and find a baggy. It's got about five grams in it.

Fuck me, I say. We can't take all this. What the fuck is it? Coke?

Nah, he says. I'm going off coke. It's too subtle. This is pure MDMA, like what they put in Es. You've gotta check this shit out.

I've only ever had it in pills, I say. What do you do? Snort it?

No! he recoils. It's fucking rank. I get sick off the taste of the shit, I can't even gum it. So we bomb it.

How come you bought so much?

Nick's just come back from Europe, and he brought this stuff back with him, but he's got far too much and he's shitting himself about getting caught. He's practically giving it away now, and he's still making a profit. That's why he got so much. He said it was fucking dirt cheap.

How did he bring it over without getting caught?

Fuck knows. Big dealers like him, they have their ways. He's shoved baggies up his arse before now.

I look at the powder. It doesn't seem quite so appealing any more. I open the beer and take a swig.

I'm thinking, some of this, a few bars, and then Zanzibar, Tone says.

Sounds good. Anyone else out?

Usual.

Should be a good night.

Defo, he says. Especially when we get some of that stuff into us.

I can't get too fucked up, I say. The Steph thing.

Fuck that, he says. She needs to chill out. She's got you under the thumb, mate. I aren't having a go or anything, but it's none of her business.

She doesn't see it like that though. She's like my parents; she doesn't know the difference between use and abuse. She thinks that you're an addict if you have one line.

I like her and everything, Tone says. She's a good laugh. But you shouldn't let her get in the way of you having a good night.

She's coming later, you know. With some mates.

Any fit ones?

Amy's all right.

You'll have to introduce us.

No probs.

Anyway, he says, I'm gonna smoke this fag and then bomb a bit of that stuff. You having some?

Yeah, I say, but only a small one to start with. I can't get too fucked up and I don't know how it's gonna affect me.

He shakes his head in disapproval but says, No worries.

◎

We sit chatting shit and sipping beers while Tony smokes. I get up and grab us another drink each. When I get back, Tony takes out some Rizla and starts preparing the bombs. What you do is pour some powder onto the paper then scrunch it up into a ball and swallow it. Tony reckons it's no different from taking a pill. Safer, if anything. The paper dissolves in your stomach and the powder gets into your blood.

When he's done, he points to a bit that's left on the mat. Gum that, if you want, he says. Seriously, it makes me fucking sick.

I lean forward and dab a little bit with my finger. He's right. As soon as my tongue touches the contaminated area inside my top lip I feel like retching. It's an overpowering chemical taste, and it reminds me of the varnish my parents used to put on my nails when I was younger to stop me from biting them. I take a few swigs of beer to rinse my mouth out.

Don't say I didn't warn you, Tone says. Anyway, this one's yours. He hands me the tiny ball of screwed up Rizla, swallowing his own with a gulp of booze.

I place it on my tongue, linger for a moment, swallow, wince.

And wait.

FOURTEEN
DUNCAN

There's someshit I need to straighten up here before I start getting ahead of myself. Cuz you're probably wondering how someone like me – eighteen years old at the time, unemployed, a total waster in the opinion of my parents – met Ade: a malcontent dropout uni student with a huge inheritance and nothing to spend it on other than his own self-destruction. It was a weird chain of events that led us to become mates, the sorta chain of events that you might call destiny if you believe in that kinda shite. Let me tell you bout it.

I was in the library browsing for monographs to help with one of my art projects at college during the second year of my A levels. This was the university library, across the road from the college campus, because the two institutions were affiliated with one another. We were meant to have gone to a library induction at the start of the course, but I'd missed it cuz I was stoned and I'd never had cause to go since. In fact, I'd never been to a library before, apart from when I was really young and we had to go there once a week with school. So now that I was here, I was having proper difficulty using the computer database that shows you which books are in stock and whereabouts on the shelves they're located. I went over to the customer service desk to ask for help, but there was no one there, apart from one other guy who appeared to be waiting for assistance himself.

You look lost, he said.

Pretty much like, I goes.

Well, he said through gritted teeth, I've been standing here for five minutes waiting for someone to come along, and you're the first person I've seen. Fucking customer service my arse.

I laughed.

What's up anyway? he went. Maybe I can help.

Oh, I said. I'm trying to find these books.

I handed him the piece of paper that I'd used to jot down a few titles and their references from the computer. He took it from me and looked at it for a long time without saying anything, long enough for him to have read the list three or four times. Then he said something that I'll never forget. He said: Fuck that shit.

Sorry? I asked.

Fucking art, man, he said, taking a deep breath and handing back the piece of paper. Then he continued, Don't see the point of it, myself. Reality doesn't exist in pictures. Words are the closest we can get to it. I mean, some pictures are cool to look at, but when people talk about the transformative power of art and all that, I just don't buy it.

I didn't know what to say, so I just goes, I think art can be just as expressive as words.

No way, he said, turning his whole body to face me for the first time. Why do you think that?

Art can describe some things which words can't, I said.

Bollocks.

It's true.

Such as?

Like colours. You could spend your whole life trying to write a description of a colour. But if you showed the description to someone who'd never seen the colour, then it wouldn't help them at all. They'd have to see the colour on paper. And everyone sees colours differently, so they say, so it's a personal thing.

He looked me up and down, which was pretty fuckin intimidating cuz he was at least half a foot taller than me and he held himself in a way that made it seem much more than that. What's your name? he asked.

I told him.

You a student?

Yeh. At college though, not uni.

He grimaced slightly, like I'd just offered him a type of food that he didn't like. Then he went, So what you studying?

When I told him that I was taking English Lit, he seemed surprised. So, you're taking English *and* art? he asked. Man, that's a weird combination.

Why?

I just never thought they sat well together. For reasons I explained a few sentences ago.

Oh.

I've finished uni, he said. (I found out later, of course, that by 'finished' he meant 'dropped out' as opposed to 'graduated'.) I didn't go to this one, though. But I have a library card that lets me come in here and read. I'm just not allowed to take the books out. Not that anyone would notice if I did – he raised his voice at this point so everyone could hear – seeing as there are no fucking staff!

I felt proper uneasy by this point. I made an excuse about my car being parked on double yellows, even though I can't fuckin drive, and hoped that he wouldn't ask for a lift or someshit.

No worries, he said.

I turned to fuck off and he shouted after me, I'll catch you around, I guess. I'm Ade, by the way.

◎

Next time I saw him was in a pub about three weeks later. I was with a group of mates and I recognised him straight away, cuz he's so weird looking like. As soon as I clocked him, I looked away and prayed he hadn't seen me. But he did see me, and he came straight over with his pint.

We chatted for a long time that night. He was in the bar on his own, he said. He'd come down to play on the gamblers. As he was leaving he told me he was usually here at this time of night, so if I ever fancied a drink, I should nip down and meet him and he'd buy me one. He liked chatting and debating about shit, he said.

I have no idea why, cuz I had plenty of other mates to hang out with, but I took him up on his offer. I walked down to the pub the next night and he was there, just as he'd said, and within a few weeks we were having all-night drinking sessions at his flat down the road, watching films from his extensive collection. We watched all sorts: *Withnail and I, Fear and Loathing in Las Vegas, The Fugitive, Twelve Angry Men, The Filth and the Fury*. He still used a video player –

loadsa people I hung round with had jumped on the DVD bandwagon a coupla years before, but Ade had no intention of going digital. It's called a film for a fucking reason, Dunc, he informed me. Anyway, around 9 a.m. he'd go to bed and I'd fuck off back to my parents' place, knowing they'd be at work and I could skive off college and get some kip without being disturbed like.

A few months later, after I dropped out of college and ended up in a bit of a state with nowhere to stay, I called him. I moved in later that day. It was just us two for ten months or so, and then Sorel moved in, and then Colbeck a coupla weeks later.

Fuckin Sorel. She was still on the top of my fit list, you get me. It's just that – with Colbeck and Ade's casual violence and my lack of JC and my paranoia and all the worrying about the future or lack of it – there was a bit too much going on for me to take shit to its full potential. But Athens wasn't built in a day. Or is it Rome? I get a bit confused, see, cuz there's that other saying, y'know, It's all Greek to me like. And then there's fuckin When in Rome, do as the Romans do. Ade used to say that sometimes. I'd ask him, Why the fuck do you have to go to nightclubs for a scrap? If you like fighting, then start doing karate or someshit. But he'd just say, We do it in nightclubs because when in Rome you do as the Romans do. And then I'd be like, What the fuck?

Ade told me that, in philosophy, first of all you need a premise which is the statement which you set out to prove or disprove at the start of an argument. Ade's premise, in this case, was that anyone who gets drunk and gropes a girl, or gobs off, or starts a fight with someone, deserves their comeuppance. That's fair enough, but it doesn't mean he has to be the deliverer of that comeuppance. And Colbeck, I'd come to realise, was just as bad. Those two always took shit too far because they thought it was funny. And they also thought that the only justification they needed for their actions was the hatred that burned inside them. I figured that sooner or later the hatred would fizzle out. Either that or they'd burn everyone around them to keep themselves alight.

FIFTEEN

SHAUN

When the consultant turns up, I'm half asleep. Mam's gone to pick up Jodie from school, says she'll be back later on this evening. I find it easier to sleep during the day than at night. Maybe I've become afraid of the dark.

The first thing I see when I open my eyes is the red clipboard he's holding to his chest. It triggers a memory I haven't thought of in years – sitting in a science lesson at school, being told about how red is a warning sign. Dangerous insects, blood, stop signs, brake lights. All red. The fact that I remember this gives me hope. It means that my memories of the night when I was brought here could perhaps one day be triggered in a similar sort of way. They are in my head somewhere. I can sense them like shadows. Words on the tip of my tongue. One day I will tease them free and spit them out like grape seeds.

'How're you feeling?' he asks. It's Gianni Zaccari, Zac. The name doesn't suit him. Neither of them do. They hang on him like ill-fitting garments. He looks too old to be called Zac, and he's not handsome enough for Gianni.

'I'm not too bad,' I say. 'Bored and confused.'

He unclips his pager. 'Your leg and arm?'

'No better.' I turn my head and look at my left arm. It dangles pendulous and heavy over the edge of the bed like a broken wing, and it doesn't feel like a part of me at all.

'Just a bit of a chat, really,' he says. 'I've come to tell you a bit more about what's going on – treatment and prognosis-wise. Ask me anything you want to know.'

I'm not sure if I'm ready for this. I wonder if he knows more than he's letting on. I wonder if he knows about Steph. I wonder if he knows who did this to me. These are the things I want to know. But I don't ask him. It doesn't seem like a normal thing to do.

He glances at his pager and then clips it back onto his belt. 'So,' he says. 'First things first: you're suffering from a closed head injury.'

'Closed?' I ask.

'Yes. That simply means that the injury occurred inside the brain and didn't result in any breaking of the skin or the skull.'

'Right.'

'When we talk about brain injuries of this type, we categorise them as ABI or TBI – that's *acquired* brain injury and *traumatic*. ABI is where something happens to the brain such as a stroke or aneurysm. TBI is where there's some external factor acting upon the brain, such as a car crash or an assault. Yours is the latter. But the effects of the injury in either case can be very similar.'

My eyes are still locked on the red clipboard. 'How serious is it?' I ask.

'Well,' he goes on, 'the part of your brain that's damaged is called the parietal lobe, which is located here.' He leans forward and touches my head above my right ear. 'This is why you're suffering from paralysis in your left leg. The right parietal lobe controls the left side of the body.'

I swallow.

'The problem,' he continues, 'is that when someone is punched in the head, as you were, the brain has to follow the movement of the skull. Because the brain is soft and jelly-like, this movement can cause stretching in the nerve fibres which run through the centre of the brain. This can have a profound effect on motor functions, but it is often temporary.'

As he says this, he cups his hands together, demonstrating the movement of my head and the resulting impact on my brain.

'So what are you saying? Will I get better?'

'Your condition will certainly improve, but everybody is different. Some people recover fully from this type of injury. Others get back some, but not all, of their movements. For some people, there are no obvious physical effects but there are other symptoms such as changes in personality, memory loss, headaches. We're optimistic, but we can't be absolutely sure what sort of recovery you will make until we begin physiotherapy with you. We need to keep you in a bit longer; keep an eye on you. But it won't be all bad,' he says, leaning closer. 'Some of the nurses make me wish I was twenty years younger.'

Fuck this. He probably means well, but his joke seems sick and inappropriate and just not fucking funny. To me it translates as, 'You're a cripple now, but don't worry, because there are a few girls about the place that you can gawp at. It's not as if you'll be able to do anything other than look any more.'

He starts talking again before I have time to react. Maybe he never stopped talking. Maybe my imagination cut him out. I can't process information and listen at the same time. 'The other thing that you need to think about,' he says, 'is what you're going to do when you're discharged. Do you live alone?'

'I have a flat. I haven't been there long.'

'How's your relationship with Mum and Dad?' he asks. 'They're local, aren't they? You'll need a lot of help at first. Maybe a longer-term care plan as we move forward. Can you make arrangements to stay with them, or for them to stay with you?'

No fucking way. 'I can't move back in with my parents,' I say.

'I know, I know,' he says, the fake empathy and man-to-man mateyness making me detest rather than trust him. 'It feels like a step backwards: like you've finally flown the nest and now you have to go back. But that sort of support will give you the best chance of making a full recovery. You're a strong lad. You'll get there.'

No. I'm not doing it. I'm not having anything to do with David. I fucking hate him. I can't go back to live with them. I can't. I fucking won't.

◎

After he leaves, I snatch sleep in blocks of ten or fifteen minutes.

It isn't real sleep, though. It's like a void between consciousness and dreaming. It's like being in a coma. People always assume that a coma is some kind of sleep state, but it isn't, because when you're in a coma, you're actually neither asleep nor awake. The whole sleep-wake cycle is switched off; the brain synapses aren't firing like they're supposed to. You don't even dream when you're in a coma. You're like a TV, not paused, not off or on, but on standby. I never knew that before I came here, and even now I can't recall who told me. Could have been Zac, or I might have overheard it. While I'm in this void, I keep getting these visions – I can't call them dreams because I'm lucid and I'm fully self-aware. I see myself in hospital, then I see myself at home having discovered that the whole ordeal was in my imagination, having learned I was never attacked at all, and Steph is fine and I'm fine and it's all good; then I see myself talking to Steph and she looks different, see myself crying on the bus the day after my dad left.

When I'm awake I'm thinking about Steph and I'm thinking about my leg and my arm and about the prospect of being in this state forever. I'd rather be dead. It sounds melodramatic, but I couldn't come to terms with that sort of stress: never able to do anything for myself, always a burden. I imagine my flat, my possessions gathering dust. The clock that Steph's parents gave me still ticking on the wall. Empty beer cans strewn across the floor, ashtray full to the brim with Tony's fag ends, a stack of dishes in the sink. Just as I left it when I walked out of there for the last time, that night.

Inevitably, my eyes give way to tears.

I don't try to fight them.

Steph.

I never treated her as well as I should have. She knew that just as well as I did.

But she didn't leave.

Someone else inside her. Fuck. Fuck.

He's out there somewhere.

When Tony turns up, I'm going to get some info. I know that I'm not going to like what I hear. He's going to tell me who I was fighting with, and what it was about. The police are going to come and talk to me as well.

I never made the most of my days. I was either at work, or sitting around at home, getting stoned, going out to bars, pubs, clubs, drinking until I fell over, arguing with mates about shit that didn't matter, constantly being told I was going off the rails. Would I ever have really got my shit together? This is the life-changing moment that everyone always speaks of – the thing that kicks your feet from under you and makes you appreciate what you always had but never really cherished. I know this: if I get better, then I won't slip into my habits again. I'll sort my life out. I'll move away if I have to, if Steph will come with me. We'll do the whole 'new start' thing. But I might not get better, and Steph might not want to come with me.

I wonder if Steph will want to see me at all. I wonder if she'll want to have anything to do with me. She hasn't visited yet and I don't blame her. I can't use my phone in here and I feel completely cut off. And what the fuck are her parents thinking? They never approved of me; they never approved of any of her exes, either. They always thought she was selling herself short. One of those girls who always goes for the bad lads. She has a decent job – one with opportunities – and she's been to college. Her parents thought she was throwing her life away with me, but they were too polite to say it to my face. Or perhaps they were scared of me. I mean, I have this demeanour. People think I'm intimidating. I don't fight as much as some people, but I can if I have to. Tone doesn't often let it get that far, though. Tone's good at calming shit down.

It dawns on me, suddenly and horribly, that whoever hit me might be in a state himself. What the fuck if I glassed someone? It hadn't occurred to me that the police might be coming to see me for any reason other than to get my side of the story, which, of course, doesn't exist any more.

There's too much to think about. Too many worries. Too many what-ifs.

Time drips by as I wait for Tone to turn up. If he does turn up. He's shit at keeping appointments. But he knows more than I do, and I need his answers.

SIXTEEN
COLBECK

Fucking hell, your face is sore. It's a damage-control thing. You've gotta block the pain out though, because it's Friday and you and Ade are off out as usual. Speaking of which, an update: last Monday, which is student night round here, you saw this geezer giving out to a fucking taxi driver. Right in the middle of the street he was, calling him a dirty Paki bastard and a fucking terrorist. The cabbie just drove off in the end, and fuck knows what the argument was about, but you and Ade followed his abuser down the street afterwards, and waited till you got the chance, and then you jumped him, keen to teach him some manners. It wasn't much of a fight cos you took him by surprise. You had to be quick. Although no one was watching, this took place in a busy part of town with loads of takeaways and pubs and cashpoints and shit. So you got him into this alleyway between a butcher's and a baker's, believe it or not; a few punches from Ade and he's on the floor, and then it's stamp stamp stamp from you and lights out.

You roll him over and find his wallet in his back pocket, open it up, fucking sixty quid in there in crisp folded purples.

You take the notes out, replace his wallet, then screw up the cash and shove it in this cunt's bloodied gob so that when he wakes up – or when someone finds him, whichever occurs first – it's going to be obvious that this was no mugging. This was something else. He'll wake up and he'll think, 'Surely those fellow white boys haven't attacked me cos they've seen me giving out to the taxi driver?' Yes yes yes. Fucking A. That's the sheer beauty of unprejudiced retribution.

Later the same evening, there was the episode in the toilets of this bar called The Ember Room. You smacked this bloke cos you'd heard him boasting to his mates about the fact that he was intending on driving home pissed. They all thought this was fucking hilarious, and, as luck would have it, you found yourself alone with him in the toilets around half an hour later.

So you said to him, fucking pedagogically like, 'I'm afraid that I take exception to what you said earlier about drink-driving. If it were only your own life that you were endangering then it'd be fine by me, but unfortunately your actions could maim or even kill other road users and pedestrians.'

The cunt thinks this is hilarious and asks if you're high. Then he tries to hug you. You take him down with couple of punches to the jaw, leave him on the floor, blinking up at you, his head dangerously close to the urinal trough into which you both pissed in unison less than a minute ago. He lies there, eyes glazed, confused and bloody, and you return to Ade, not forgetting to wash your hands.

There have been other similar altercations – too many to remember the details. Tonight, there will be more of the same: both of you are enjoying this shit more than you ever imagined. It feels so right, so justified; it feels like you're doing justice for the innocent, for the victims of the yob phenomenon. They shall cower in silence no more. This is perfection. It's utopia. It's a justified and endless vendetta against an entire generation of filth.

Your phone buzzes, and you sit up on the bed. You look at the display. It's her. You still haven't spoken to her since it all kicked off. You pick up the phone and look at the screen for a bit longer, trying to decide whether or not to answer the call. Then you press the green button.

'What?' you say.

'It's me,' says the voice on the other end. Distant, faint, broken.

'I fucking know who it is,' you say. 'What do you want?'

'I've been ringing you for ages,' she says. 'I've left you messages.'

'I know you have,' you tell her.

'Why didn't you reply?'

'Because I couldn't give two fucks about whatever it is you have to say. In fact, I couldn't even give *one* fuck.'

She starts to cry. Pathetic cow. 'I've made a mistake,' she says, 'I shouldn't have called. I just…'

'You *just* what?' you demand. 'Come on, you *just* what? Fucking what, exactly?'

'I've made a mistake,' she says. 'I shouldn't have split up with you.'

'Well, it's too fucking late now,' you say.

'You sound different,' she stammers. 'Why are you so angry? I thought that by now you might be ready to talk.'

'There's nothing to talk about,' you say. And you hang up.

Within a few seconds, it's ringing again. And, of course, it's her.

For fuck's sake.

You press the green button.

'What now?'

'Please don't hang up,' she shouts, even before you've finished your two-word sentence. 'Just listen to what I've got to say.'

'Fine,' you tell her. 'For Christ's sake just get it over with.'

'You were right,' she whimpers, sobbing uncontrollably. 'You were right.'

'About what?'

'When you got suspicious,' she stammers. 'I was sleeping with someone else.'

Now, if you had anticipated this phone call ten minutes ago, and if you had considered what your response to her revelation would be, then you're certain you'd have thought you wouldn't give a shit. After all, she's the bitch who's completely fucked everything up for you. But now that you hear it, now that your suspicions are confirmed, now that you know that she really has left you for some other fucker, your rage is off the fucking scale: nought to sixty in two seconds flat. You feel your hands shaking. You feel your stomach turn over and your chest tighten. You feel a sharp pain in the top of your cranium. Your Adam's apple rises to choke you.

'You… fucking… what…?' you say.

'You were right,' she wails, sniffing and panting. You imagine her jerking spasmodically. 'You were right…'

You're so angry that you can't shout. You can't say or do anything. You're frozen cold.

'Matt?' she says. Then, slightly louder, 'Are you still there, Matt?'

You let the phone slip out of your hand. It slides onto the bed then rolls onto the floor with a dull thud. You stand up, slowly; you can still hear her voice emanating faintly from the phone on the carpet: 'Matt? Hello?' Sob sob. 'Hello?'

Then it's here, as if you've burst out from under water.

The nearest object to your hand is Ade's alarm clock. You pick it up, hurl it at the radiator. It connects, clangs, hits the floor. You grab the doors of the wardrobe. Ade's wardrobe. Pull the whole thing over. 'Can you hear this, bitch?' you scream. 'Can you fucking hear this?'

Next you attack the bookshelves. Then your CD rack, remembering as you do so that around thirty per cent of its contents are jointly owned by her. 'Can you fucking hear this, bitch?'

Your voice is already hoarse.

'You fucking slut! You fucking slut!'

You turn the bed-settee over. It remains permanently open nowadays. It hits the bedside cabinet which also topples, the drawer falling out and Ade's stash spilling onto the carpet.

'You cunt! I fucking hate you!'

And you pound the walls with your fists until the paint is smeared with blood, and you imagine it's the face of the guy who's fucking her or the face of one of the lairies up town and you stamp on your phone, which is still on the floor, and as you do it you wonder if she's hung up yet.

You stop. Take a deep breath. The alarm clock on the floor is still ticking. You step over the wardrobe, which is lying diagonally across the floor, and you stare at the clock for a few seconds.

You raise your foot above it, then bring it down. Once, twice, three times.

Silence.

You stand, alone and trembling, for about half a minute. Then there's a staccato tap on the door.

'Who is it?'

'Me,' says Ade.

'Oh,' you say. 'I've damaged your room a bit. I'll pay you back.'

'Can I come in?'

'Not really.'

'Okay…'

You hear him take a drag of a cigarette. Then he says, 'Okay,' again, and then silence returns.

You wait a while, then you say, 'You're still there, aren't you?'

'Yeh,' he says.

'I guess you'd better come in, then.'

The door opens a crack. The first thing you see on the other side is the red cherry of the cigarette. Then the door opens a bit wider; it can't open to its full extent because there's so much shit on the floor after your little episode. Ade pokes his head through the gap and looks first at the mayhem you've unleashed, then at you.

'Fucking hell,' he says, cigarette still in his mouth.

You nod in agreement.

'What's up?' he asks.

'It's okay,' you tell him. 'I'll tidy up all this shit and I'll replace anything of yours that's broken.'

'That's not important,' he says. 'What's gone on?'

'Do you really need to ask?'

'Oh. I thought you'd dealt with that shit already?'

'So did I.'

He takes a long drag of his cigarette. Then he says, 'Right. I'm going to skin up. Fucking stressful shit, this is.'

He manoeuvres his head back round the door and shuts it after him.

You collapse on the floor, your head in your hands. Your whole body shakes. She's out of your fucking life now; you've been telling people how much you fucking hate her; you could list a hundred reasons why you're better off without her; she was bad for you, selfish and uncompromising, and yet you can't imagine feeling worse than you do at this moment. Fucking bitch.

'Hey, Matt,' Ade shouts from the next room. 'You want a smoke?'

'I don't smoke,' you shout back. 'You know I don't smoke.'

'Yeh,' he says, then after a pause, 'it might calm you down a bit.'

'I don't think so,' you say. 'Fucking killed my granddad, that shit did.'

'Oh,' he says. 'I didn't know he was a toker.'

'Very fucking funny.'

'Sorry,' he says. 'You want a drink then, or what? We're going out later, remember?'

'No.'

'What? You never refuse a drink.'

'I don't mean that,' you shout back to him. 'I mean, no, I'm not coming out. I can't deal with that tonight.'

You hear footsteps and then the door opens, and his head nips round again. He looks you right in the eye with that horrible stare of his.

'Fuck that,' he says. 'No better way to release the tension than by beating seven shades out of some lairy cunt. Who knows, you might even run into her.'

God help her if I do, you think, and God help me too. Because right now you're capable of anything.

For the first time, but not the last, you are invincible.

SEVENTEEN

TAG

The MDMA is making me fidget. I snorted a bit of it, contrary to Tone's advice. Now I know why he's so against doing that. I shuffle about in my seat, unable to focus on the TV or the conversation or the third pair of bombs that he's sorting out on the mirror he's removed from the bathroom wall.

Fucking get these two down us, he says, gesturing to the neat piles of powder nestling side by side on the shiny surface, and then I'll call us a taxi and we'll get up there.

He flattens out a tenner and places it on top of the powder, then runs his debit card over it a few times to get the crystals out. What's up with you anyway? he asks. You're red as fuck.

Am I?

Jesus, Tag, you look fucked.

I think that shit's cut with something, I say.

Tony looks pissed off. This is the purest around, he says. There's nothing better. All the rock stars and actors in Hollywood, yeah? They're doing coke – not MDMA, like, but coke – and even that shit's only half the quality of this,

I'm telling you. Nothing better than this around here at the moment. Nothing at all. Nick'll be there later. Ask him.

Did he ever get back with Sorel?

Not officially. But he banged her last week, apparently.

Fair play. She's fit.

Fucking right she's fit, he says. He screws up the Rizlas and offers me the mirror. As soon as I see my reflection in it, I shake my head.

Go on, he says, almost pleading. Just one more before we go.

Last one, I say, taking the mirror from him.

I reach forward and pick up one of the bombs. I put it in my mouth and swallow it.

That's the spirit, he says. Get it down ya.

I pass the mirror back, sit back and collapse into the settee, and at first I feel marginally better than I did a few minutes ago. I lean forward and gum a bit off the mirror once Tone's finished. That was a fucking mistake. A moment passes before it's onto me: the pounding heart and shakes and cold sweat prickling my back.

Fuck, I hear myself say. Bad idea. Definitely should have had more willpower and not bowed to peer pressure and all that shit they tell you in school when they're lecturing you about the perils of recreational drug use.

Aggggh! shouts Tony, throwing back his head. I'm up for a fucking good night now, man. Proper fired up!

The chemical taste has gone from my gums, but it's in my throat now, metallic and bitter. I need to wash it away with something, and I've finished my third beer, and the half-bottle of cheap vodka. There's a glass of stale water on the table, so I pick it up and take grateful gulps.

You all right there? says Tone.

No, I say. I'm fucking dying. My face is on fire.

He laughs.

Gonna be a good night, he says, nodding his head intently. I'm gonna ring that taxi.

He goes into the kitchen with his mobile because there's no signal in my living room. I sit and ponder the bombs dissolving in the acid of my stomach while he makes the call.

Tenby Street, mate… yeah… how long, mate?… What?

I get up and walk round the room a couple of times, trying to get my circulation back on track and trying to make myself feel a little less fucked-up in general. Steph thinks I'm off all drugs, which I have been for a couple of weeks, but Tony's pick-up earlier today coupled with my general lack of willpower provided the perfect excuse. She won't be happy if she finds out, and I can't be doing with an argument tonight. I've got to get this shit out of my system and sober up a bit.

Couldn't understand a word they were fucking saying, Tone says, as he tosses his mobile on the settee. And they couldn't understand me either. I was like, Tenby Street, mate, and he was like, Stanley Street? and I was like, No, mate, fucking Tenby Street, fucking T-E-N-B-Y like. You'd expect them to be able to speak English, you know? I aren't being racist or anything, like, you know I aren't like that. But you'd expect them to be able to speak fucking English.

I wipe sweat from my forehead.

What's up with you now? he asks.

I'm a bit fucked.

Good! That's the fucking idea. I'm gonna roll a fat one.

I can't handle that at the moment, I say.

Course you can. It's what you need, believe me. MDMA is an upper, yeah? He taps me on the shoulder like he's trying to punctuate his lecture. An upper, mate, yeah? he continues. So what you need is a downer, to balance it out, yeah? He takes his skins and baccy out of his shirt pocket and gets to work. Sit down, he demands. You're making me nervous.

Sorry, I'm just on edge. It's your fault for giving me that last bomb.

Tag, he says, as he starts to crumble some green into the papers he's stuck together. Can I ask you something?

Yeah, why? I might not answer it though.

You seem dead edgy around Steph lately. Are you worried she might be seeing someone else, or something?

Despite the effect of the drugs, I'm quite taken aback. She wouldn't do that, I say.

He shakes his head. I aren't suggesting she would, he says, a little too defensively. It's just the way you're acting lately – it's kind of weird. I've not seen you like this before. You seem really wound up whenever you're with her.

It's nothing, I say. We just sort of pick at each other sometimes. But the good outweighs the bad.

He licks the skin and sticks it down.

Tone doesn't know it, but he's exposed a raw nerve. That's not what I want when I'm fucked. What he's just said has only brought to the surface what's been playing on my mind for weeks. I can't think about things like this when I've got a head full of alcohol and drugs. I just replay the question over and over to myself, until my whole brain mechanism seems to slow down and I don't even understand what I'm asking myself any more.

A thought can't be made to just go away. It can hardly even be ignored. It's like having a favourite colour. My favourite colour is blue, and I can't stop myself from preferring it to other colours. I don't have as much control over my mind as I want to. And I can't stop thinking about her with someone else. Why the fuck did Tone have to bring that up? It's fucking settled then. I can't keep burying it. I'll have to have a chat with Steph about it, explain to her why I'm worried and why I think she should understand my concerns. Not tonight though. That's a fucking disaster recipe if ever there was one.

My thought process is interrupted by the crackle and fizz as Tone fires up the spliff.

But, yeah. We need to talk.

EIGHTEEN

COLBECK

It's been fifteen minutes since your little room-smashing episode and you're getting ready to hit the town with Ade. He's right, as usual: the best way for you to release the tension is to find some twat who's in need of a good kicking and then duly administer it to him. There was another story in the paper today about the lack of security in clubs. They're thinking about introducing shatter-glass bottles to some of them, for fuck's sake, to stop them being used as weapons. Last week, some opinion piece about the blight of feral youths terrorising suburban streets. And yesterday, on the news, a forty-year-old father of three, beaten unconscious in front of his wife and kids because he asked a group of lads to stop swearing on the bus. The offenders: five white male youths, fifteen to seventeen. You wish you'd been there. You'd have said to the bloke and his family, 'You go and find a seat somewhere else. I'll handle this.' And then you'd have summoned the rage (all you have to do is think of *her*) and you'd have got to fucking work on all five of the lairy cunts. Would you have won? Probably not. But you can guarantee that at least one of them would have lost a fucking eye. And that fact alone makes your own suffering worth it. You could be bloodied, broken and swollen beyond recognition, and it would still be your victory.

'We're never going to change anything, you know,' Ade says, when you've finished telling him all this.

'What do you mean?' you ask.

He's wearing a tie tonight. He straightens it in the mirror and says, 'We might make ourselves feel better about the situation, but we're never going to change it for anyone else.'

'It might teach people a lesson,' you say.

'I doubt it,' Ade says, lighting a cigarette. 'But I tell you what, it's fucking good fun. I despise my generation so much. The best way to understand how something works is to break it open, after all.' He sits down on the sofa, crosses his legs, and taps ash into an empty beer can.

'One of the things that fucks me off the most is the fact that no one's interested in important things any more,' you suggest. 'No one cares about education, or about books, or about culture, and that shit's fundamental. A basic knowledge of those things should be something to be proud of. It's cooler nowadays for geezers to act as thick as fucking pig shit than it is to act intelligent.' You're aware, at this point, that even talking about these people makes your stomach flip cartwheels, and there are just so many of them to choose from, ready and waiting for a good fight, desperate for it, out on the prowl.

'Anyway,' Ade says, 'the irony is that people can't separate us from them. I mean, look at Dunc and Sorel. They can't understand the difference between vigilantism and recreational violence. Me and you, we wouldn't fucking harm anyone who was just out having a good night and minding his own business with his mates. We'll only bother those who make a nuisance of themselves: people who act up, start on someone else, hassle girls who've made it clear they aren't interested. That's why it feels so fucking good.'

'Yeah, well,' you say. 'Girls love a bit of rough. I'm starting to think they're just as fucking bad.'

'Careful where you're going with that,' Ade says.

'Not all of them,' you say, your ribcage tightening its grip on your heart with every thought of her fucking betrayal. 'The skanks I'm talking about represent the minority, same as the lairies do. Unfortunately, there are times when the many have to suffer as a result of the few.'

Ade picks up the bottle opener from the table and spins it in his hand, over and over. 'It reminds me of being at school,' he says.

'What do you mean?' you ask.

'What you just mentioned,' he says, looking at the bottle opener, not at you. 'I don't know about you, but when I was there, sometimes the whole class would be punished just because a couple of people were fucking around. At the time I hated it, but now I understand why it happened. It happened because the teachers wanted the innocent ones to put pressure on the guilty ones, to say to them, "It's not fair that all of us are being punished for the shit that you two or three people are doing." But of course, it never worked like that, because the majority were always too scared to confront the troublemakers. The situation here is the same. A small percentage of people cause the trouble, but everyone suffers for it. There's tension in the bars. Tension on the streets. Bus drivers, shopkeepers, paramedics, taxi drivers get assaulted. The idea that's put forward by the media is the one that says *all* young lads are thugs and *all* young girls are slags. But people know – they must fucking know – that it isn't the case at all. But no fucker has the balls to do anything about it.'

'Except us,' you say. The jangling of the bottle opener in his hand is starting to get on your nerves.

'Yeh,' he says. 'Except us. We're the only idiots who'll take a stand.'

'I wonder what the papers would make of all this,' you say. 'Like, what would the headline be? Something sensationalising the violence, I guess – making out that we're the bad ones.'

'Exactly. What do you get for randomly glassing someone nowadays? Eighteen weeks in prison, maybe? But what do you get for defending yourself or someone else? Two years, three years? It's always the same in court: *Mr-such-and-such, fucking mitigating, says the defendant feels genuinely sorry for what he's done. The offence was out of character and he has expressed true remorse. He is sickened by his actions that night.* Well, fuck that, because I'm fucking sickened too. I'm sickened that he was out on licence when he did it. I'm sickened that he's done it before, that he'll do it again, and that he'd be doing it right now if he hadn't been caught this time. He'll be back on the streets in a few months, and fuck it, because if I run into the fucker, I'm not going to wait for him to strike first. Don't let there be a next time. Now you've got him, now you've got him *this fucking time*, you might as well make an example. Gouge his fucking eyes out. Make him suffer like his victims suffered and continue to suffer. Cut his tongue off. Infect him with the latest disease in the name of medical research. Tear his nails out. Beat him, torture him. And when you're done with him, release him back into society a broken man who thinks, "I will never, ever do that again." Then people like us wouldn't have to do the dirty work and risk losing our own fucking rights in the process.' He sighs, shakes his head. 'But it won't happen. As a society we've gone too far now.'

He places the bottle opener back on the coffee table and stares at the floor, still shaking his head. If you didn't know him as well as you do, you might think he was going to cry. 'Fuck this,' he says. 'I'm getting a beer.' He gets up off the couch.

'Make that two,' you say.

He disappears into the kitchen and comes back with two frosted bottles and a freshly lit cig hanging from his mouth. He must be getting through fifty smokes a day at the moment.

He opens your beer first. To your fucking dismay he keeps hold of the bottle opener and starts jangling it again.

'What was going on back there?' he asks, taking a sip. 'How come you smashed up my room?'

'She rang me to tell me she cheated on me,' you say. 'Fucking bitch.' Shit. You shouldn't have said that last part. Fuck. It draws attention to the fact that your nerves are still raw. You don't want to show your emotions. You don't want anyone – even Ade – to know the extent of your turmoil. You'll get her for this, the little slut. The little cunt. She was born of the earth's detritus. You'll fucking get her for this. You take a gulp of beer from the bottle.

'Was she telling you that shit to rub salt in the fucking wounds or what?' Ade asks, looking up from the bottle opener that he's still fucking spinning in his hand.

'To be honest,' you explain, 'I think she was going to ask me to get back with her. But I didn't let her get that far. I fucking told her what I thought of her. She'll probably stay with that cunt now.'

'And so you destroyed my flat in the process,' Ade grins.

'Yeh,' you say, 'and now I feel like a dick. I'm sorry.' Ade raises his eyebrows and you add, 'I shouldn't have reacted like that.'

'It's all right,' he assures you. 'I probably would've reacted the same way.'

It's time to call a taxi. Ade gets onto it and you sit on the settee glugging beer from the bottle. Duncan and Sorel, you're thinking again. What the fuck is really going on there? If it *is* just friendship, then its ostensible purity makes you fucking jealous. You couldn't do it, you know that, because you'd end up wanting to take it further. Maybe they're fuck-buddies, and you couldn't do that either. You'd become attached. You've always been the same. One fuck is all it takes. You need to work on that, need to tone down your emotions. It's 2003 and a fuck is a fuck, nothing more, nothing less. It doesn't mean you have to make tea and toast for each other afterwards. You think of the girls in the queue outside the club the other week, and you think of your ex. You had her on some kind of pedestal once, but she's no better than anyone else. You were friends back then, before all this started.

Your head is twisted inside. You know this is going to end very badly. You can feel it. Someone is going to get killed, or worse. But you can't stop. You work in the call centre five days a week and get your weekends off. Those forty-eight hours of recreation, along with an occasional Monday evening student night adventure, allow you to expel all the stress accumulated between 8 a.m. on Monday and 5.30 p.m. on Friday. All the tension born of the stories you've read in the papers, of the customers whose petty arguments you've listened in on over the phone, of the crumbling of your relationships, of your hatred for everything and everyone and everywhere. You're reclaiming the clubs for the people who deserve better. You're relegating the skanks and lairies to the gutter where they so rightly belong. Let them fight among themselves, wipe each other out. Destroy everything, everyone. You hate it all. You feel as though you're all this country has left. You realise now that you've felt this way for much longer than you were previously inclined to admit. All she did was provide a catalyst that quickened the burning fuse. While you were with her, you and Ade were already going out, meting out punishment on behalf of the violenced, but never to this extent. This nihilistic hatred is nothing but a cancer, the mutation of which was initially caused by the toxins all around you, and then perpetuated by your own self-multiplying cells – your own desires, fears, false hopes and ruined expectations. It eats away at you, gnawing at your perceptions and your morals, chewing up your ambitions, making the good flesh bad.

And now, despite the fact it wants you dead, you live for it.

If it's taken away from you, you might as well not exist.

You smile inside as you realise that you're more than prepared to die for it.

THE NATURE OF THE MOTH

Buy the ticket, take the ride.

— Hunter S. Thompson

NINETEEN

SHAUN

I'm reading *The Sun* when Tone arrives. As ever, his Lacoste bag is slung over his shoulder and he's chewing furiously, like he's dropped a few.

'All right, mate,' he says, as he dumps the bag on the floor. 'How you feeling?' He looks around at the other beds on the ward. There are five of them, all unoccupied. 'Where the fuck is everyone?' he asks. 'I thought hospitals were meant to be overcrowded?'

'Not this one, obviously,' I say, folding the paper and putting it on the table by the bed.

'I tell you what, mate, you were fucking lucky. I thought you were a goner.'

'I know about Steph,' I say. I hadn't planned to tell him that, but the words just fall from my mouth.

He's obviously caught off guard. 'Who told you?'

'My mam.'

'She wants to see you, mate, y'know,' he says. 'She's got people looking after her, don't worry. Friends and family like. Give it a bit more time. You two had a bit of a row.'

'I know that as well. How do you know she wants to see me?'

'Jade told me.'

Jade's his younger sister, and she's a mate of Steph's. 'Did Jade say anything else?' I ask him.

He manoeuvres a chair over to the bed and sits down. 'Like what?'

'Like… anything,' I say.

'You mean about what happened to her.'

'Yeah.'

'Police are dealing with it.'

'And?'

'They're trying to get the guy. But there were some issues. Something about DNA – they couldn't get anything because Steph didn't report it until a while afterwards. There's no CCTV in that club. Hardly any of them have it, it turns out, but you don't realise that until you need it. There's a camera on the street but it wasn't working. Shame it wasn't the same for me when I got done for that scrap a while back, ey?'

I'm starting to feel agitated now. 'Well, why didn't she report it straight away?'

He coughs and messes with his eyebrow-ring. 'Maybe she thought no one would believe her. I've seen stuff about that sort of thing like, in the paper. People don't report it because they're worried they won't be taken seriously. You see, you got into a fight with someone, because you thought he'd been with Steph.' He obviously notices my body stiffen because he quickly goes on: 'No. I know what you're thinking. It wasn't the guy. You were just drunk. Getting stupid ideas into your head, you know. You started on this bloke and his mates came over and dragged you off, and that's when everything kicked off. And I mean it, mate – it fucking *kicked off*. I've never seen nothing like it.'

'Do you know who they were?'

'No idea. They scarpered afterwards. We'd already called an ambulance for Steph, after we found her in the bogs, but it took fucking ages to arrive and in between us calling it and them arriving she must have just come round and walked out of there. Everyone was so preoccupied with what you were doing that there was no one to stop her. It wasn't until the next day that she even found out you were in hospital. I obviously got hold of her to check on her, but by that point it was Saturday afternoon, and she didn't even know she'd been attacked. Like, she literally knew nothing about it. She couldn't remember getting home, couldn't remember anything from about midnight onwards. She thought it was just the drink. She hadn't heard from you, but she thought that was because you were pissed off at her because, well, you had a row like I said.'

'Was I being a dick?' I ask, starting to feel sick again.

'You were just drunk, and fucking wired.'

'Aggressive?'

'Yeah, obviously. But it was a big night.'

'What did I fall out with Steph over?'

'Fuck knows, mate. I weren't there. It was when we went to the club. She was already in there with some mates. Amy and Bex and Jess, I think they were called. You were texting Steph, arranging to meet up with her. You went to meet her by the bogs and came back fuming. You were saying to me that it was over, that you hate her, blah blah blah.'

'Fuck.'

'I don't know what she'd done though. I think you were just acting up, cos you were battered.'

'Is this all my fault?'

'Shut up, man. Course it isn't your fault.'

'I don't believe you.'

He stops chewing. 'People fall out with their birds all the time. Then the next day they get back together. And people have fights all the time, and then they go home. You were just unlucky.'

'But if I hadn't fallen out with her, she would've been with me all night, and then she wouldn't have got—' My Adam's apple snags on the word; it's quite literally stuck in my throat. I have to say it quietly, like the fucking dirty word that it is. 'She wouldn't have got raped.' I shake my head. 'And if I didn't start on those blokes, I wouldn't have got hit.'

He thinks for a long time, pulling at a thread on the edge of the bed sheet. I watch him do it, watch him wrap the loose end round his finger and try to tease it free, but it's not quite long enough for him to get purchase on it. Eventually he loses interest. He says, 'I'm not talking about that shit anyway. It's fucking stupid. The important things now are helping Steph and getting you back on your feet. When are they letting you out?'

I take his hint and change up the conversation. It's not getting us anywhere. 'I don't know. Maybe a week or so.'

'What happens then?'

'Nothing. I go back to the flat, get on with life.'

'No offence, man, but how the fuck are you gonna to go back to the flat? It's up three flights of stairs and there's no lift. How're you gonna cope with that?'

'I'll find a way.'

'Wouldn't it be easier to move back in with your rents?'

'No, it wouldn't.'

'Why?' he demands. 'It's because of Dave, isn't it? Fucking hell, mate, he can't be that bad.'

'He fucking is that bad!' I shout.

Tone wasn't expecting that. 'Sorry,' he says timidly, losing his usual foghorn. 'I'm just thinking of you, mate. Thinking about what's for the best.'

'What's for the best is that I get the fuck out of here and get better,' I say. 'I don't care where else I go, but I'm not going back to theirs.'

Tone's chewing again now, even more frantically than before.

'What?' I ask. He's acting really fucking weird and I can just tell he's holding something back.

'Nothing.'

'Do you have any idea how many times I've heard that since I've been in here?' I say. 'And how many times I've had people looking at me like they know shit that I don't?'

He sighs. 'It's just that I was chatting to your mam, you know, when she told me you were awake and that I could come in to see you. And she said that you probably wouldn't be able to look after yourself for a long time, that they weren't sure what the diagnosis was—'

'You mean the *prognosis*?'

'Yeah, probably. Anyway, she said you were moving back in with them and that they'd already started changing stuff in the house.'

'Changing what?'

'Adapting stuff. Getting you a different bed, a seat in the bath, that kind of shit. It's one of those beds where you have a remote control on the side that raises different bits of it and stuff like that. Like old people have.'

'You serious?'

'Yeah, man,' he says. 'I thought you knew about that. I mean, I thought it was kinda weird, with you and Dave not getting on and stuff, but I thought you might've agreed to it, because, you know.'

'No, I don't know.'

'Well, because, sort of… don't take this the wrong way, mate, okay?'

'Just say it.'

'You're like, disabled, aren't you? Not forever like, but temporarily. Temporarily disabled like.'

'I'm not fucking disabled. I'm going through a recovery – there's a difference. It just means I'm out of action for a while. I spoke to the doctor the other day. There's every chance I'll get better. My mam and David don't know what the fuck they're talking about. They weren't there. I spoke to the doctor on my own.'

'Even so, man, it's gonna take time.'

'I'll be fine in the flat. I don't need to be fussed over the whole time. I'm not a kid. Christ, I've only just moved out and already they're trying to get me back.'

'Mate, you know you could stay at mine if there was room, yeah?'

'I know that,' I say. 'And I'm grateful, but it doesn't solve the problem, does it?'

'Not really.'

The mood in the room suddenly grows colder, a cloud passing in front of the sun. I shiver.

'I need a fag,' says Tone. He says it like he doesn't really want one, but like he has to get out of this fucking place for a few minutes.

'Okay. You coming back in after?'

'Yeah.' He gets up off the chair and grabs his sports bag, holding it up and feeling around inside for his cigarettes. 'Where do I go?' he asks.

'Just go out the front. But not in the Memorial Garden.'

'How come?'

'Because it's for a five-year-old girl who died of leukaemia. It doesn't seem right to sit there and smoke.'

He looks a bit puzzled, but says, 'Fair enough. See y'in a min. You need me to bring you anything?'

'I'm all right.'

◎

As soon as I'm alone it's upon me again. The atoms colliding in my mind and all the charged electrons rattling round my skull. What the fuck am I going to do? The mask of bravery and bravado is starting to crack. They're going to discharge me soon, because there's no point me being here using up resources that could be put to better use helping someone else.

I can't go back to them. I can't. I'd rather die.

Who the fuck did this to me?

TWENTY

DUNCAN

Well? goes Ade.

Well what?

What you think? He nodded towards the camper van: our blurred reflections stood side by side on the brightly coloured metal.

I think it's orange, I said.

Who cares if it's orange, you tit? he went, frowning. Fucking classic vehicle, this fucker. And it's tax exempt.

Cool.

Fucking right it's cool. Check out inside. He opened the sliding door on the left-hand side and we had a butcher's. Don't just fucking stand there gawping at it, he went. Get in and have a proper look. I'll put the roof up.

We both got in and I shut the door, while Ade messed around with the elevating roof which looked like it hadn't been elevated for at least a decade.

How many people can sleep in this thing? I asked, dubiously.

Four, he said, twisting his head to the side and grimacing in concentration as he fumbled with various catches and levers.

Fuckin four? I said. That can't be right. It's cramped as fuck with just us two like.

He still hadn't managed to get the roof up, and I could tell that soon his very short fuse was gonna hit the explosive. He goes, There's two bunks up there – if I can ever get the *cunting thing* open – and these seats fold out and make a double. He patted the brown fabric of the interior. Give us a fucking hand with this, will you, Dunc? he said.

I got up and started shoving at the roof while he bent the lever backwards and forwards. I could feel it starting to give way. Eventually, despite an angry squeal of protestation from the rusty hinges, we managed to open it up to its full extent, and we were able to stand fully upright, with space still above our heads.

There ya go, Dunc, he went, with a huff of satisfaction. Have a look.

He was right – there were two beds in the roof. It looked rickety as fuck though, and I told him there's no way I was climbing up there.

It's fine, man, he said, and he pulled himself up by taking his weight on his elbows and sat with his legs dangling in front of my face.

Don't just stand there, he snapped. Come and feel for yourself. It's secure, man, no worries at all.

I slowly made my way up there beside him and sat with my hands on my thighs, ears peeled for any sounds of imminent breakage like.

See? went Ade. Sound, innit?

Yeh man, I nodded. How long can you keep it for?

Until my parents need it back, he shrugged. If I scratch it or anything, though, they'll fucking kill me, believe. They've lent me all the accessories too. Gas bottle, sleeping bags, all that bollocks. It's even got a shitter.

Really?

He lowered himself back down and lifted up some of the seat covers to show me inside. That thing there, he goes, is like a canvas cubicle that you pitch outside the van. And you can buy some sort of portable chemical bog to go in it. Fucking luxurious, mate.

I was gonna interrupt him and tell him that it wasn't really a 'shitter', as he put it, it was just a fuckin tent. But I thought better of it.

Loadsa storage too, he said. We've got everything we need here for a proper road trip.

Indeed, I said, trying to sound up for it, whereas in fact I was thinking about how fuckin cold it must get in here at night. And about whether or not it was actually fuckin roadworthy. I put this to Ade.

Smooth as fuck, mate, he said, punctuating the affirmation with a nod of his head. Just had an MOT. My parents had it done up, y'know. New exhaust, new steering rack. It's had an oil change and new brake pads, and two new tyres. This van's been going for nearly thirty years, and it'll be going for another thirty, I'm telling you.

I'll take your word for it, I said.

Fuck that anyway, went Ade. You like it or what?

Well, it's got character, I'll give it that, I confessed, as I slid down and scouted for hidden compartments.

So, what you reckon about a road trip? he asked.

Are you actually serious?

Proper serious, man, of course. Me, you and Matt. Just get away for a week. Load up with booze and go wherever we want.

I'm up for it, I told him. Anything to get some fuckin activity in my life like.

Sorted, he said. I knew you'd say yes. It's not as if you've got anything better to do, is it, you sad bastard.

◎

Let me bring you up to speed, cuz quite a bit had been going on since Colbeck first moved in with us.

We decided to go away on a bit of a road trip cuz Ade thought Colbeck was getting a touch of cabin fever. He – Colbeck like – was acting weirder than ever. He'd been sacked from the call centre because of some argument he'd got into. I don't know the full details of it, but it was something to do with Colbeck sticking up for one of the younger girls who worked there, because he felt that this manager was bullying her. So it started off kinda justified, I guess, but he took it too far and made some remark that he was going to *boot the manager up her baby-maker*, which is kinda the worst sort of threat you can make in the workplace, cuz it counts as both violence and sexism, or perhaps even sexist violence. So, he got fired, and he'd started signing on with me. He didn't seem bothered about it: in fact, he said he reckoned it was about time he got some money off the state – he said he'd paid taxes all his working life and he was sick of all the dole scroungers sitting on their arses spending his money. No offence, Dunc, he was quick to add. He said that it was only a temporary thing – that he needed some time off to get his head straight. But I knew differently. Once you're on the dole, it's difficult to find the motivation to get a job. I mean, when my life had some structure, like when I was at college and shit, I was defo more content than I was when I slept until three in the afternoon and spent the days getting drunk and stoned. Everything changes when you've got nothing to get up for: your sleeping patterns, your place in the social hierarchy and, most importantly, your state of mind. You become sluggish and lazy. You lack energy. You drift through life, not touching the sides. I know, cuz I lived like that for over a year.

With all three of us now unemployed, we spent a lot more time together, sitting in the flat with the curtains closed, watching TV and getting films out from the rental place down the road. We lived on toast and microwave meals, smoked contraband cigarettes bought in two hundred decks from a bloke in the pub, and drank no-frills gin and vodka with flat tonic from a plastic bottle. Colbeck seemed to be suffering a lot cuz of what happened with his ex-bird. After he trashed Ade's room, he seemed kind of embarrassed, and he stopped talking about her. Up until then he'd at least had the time to call her a bitch or a slag during casual convos about their time together. But not any more.

I thought the road trip was a bad idea. Colbeck and Ade were still going out a lot, getting bloodied like, but I'd resigned myself to the fact that I'd never change them and that I had to just let them get on with it. At least I got to chat to Sorel when they weren't around. We kinda bonded over their violence, in the sense that we both disagreed with it. But I knew it'd be different if we went away – I'd either have to go with them or stay in the van in the freezing cold on my own. It was hard to decide which was worse.

It was Sorel that persuaded me to go, actually. She explained that if them two went away without me there'd be carnage. She wanted me to go cuz she thought that, if I was there, my presence might help to calm them down a little or someshit. Now, this shit didn't convince me then, and it still doesn't now, but you know what shit was like with me and Sorel, how I fuckin doted upon practically everything she said, and so I couldn't say no. I know people say that all the time, when in actual fact they really *can* say no – but this was different. It was as if that little two-letter word momentarily left my vocabulary, and I wasn't fuckin clever enough to come up with a synonym. So anyway, within a few days Ade had convinced his parents to lend him the van, and we were deciding what'd be the best day to set off. Ade even forked out for a new TV from the local Smack Converters, taking the opportunity to have a dig at me at the same time. He said that Sorel was gonna need something to keep her entertained while we were away in the absence of my constant wittering.

And, cuz you're probably wondering, I hadn't got with Sorel yet. I was still working on it. But, y'know, Rome, Athens, whatever – neither of them was built in a day, you get me.

TWENTY-ONE

TAG

Immediately after getting out of the taxi we are accosted by a six-foot-tall kangaroo handing out flyers for a new Aussie-themed bar. Most new bars around here only stay trading for a few months then go bust and get boarded up, before they reopen with a new name and new branding. The two-for-one on selected drinks offer is enough to entice us so we head there, me feeling slightly more human now, but with nerves jangling because of the mixture of spliff and mandy.

The place is already full when we get there. There are Aboriginal-style paintings on the wall and all sorts of clichéd Australian memorabilia – nostalgic prints from *Neighbours*, posters of Castlemaine XXXX labels and Crocodile Dundee, and boomerangs hanging above the bar. The bar staff are all wearing those hats – you know, the ones with the corks hanging from the brim to keep the flies out of your face – and the whole atmosphere is plastic but cheery.

Tone decides to take advantage of the cheap drinks

straight away. There are no tables or booths available, so it looks like we're mingling. He squeezes his way to the bar to get us a couple of pints each.

My phone goes off and it's like the little bubble around me suddenly pops and I'm back to reality. Fucking Steph. Can't leave me alone when I'm out. She either doesn't trust me or she's more into me than I am her. I read the message, it just says *love u babe where r u?* and I instantly feel guilty. I reply, telling her I love her back and that I can't wait to see her, which is not the truth. I mean, mates and girlfriends are entirely different things. Tonight, I just want a night out with Tone and the boys and I know that seeing her is going to put me on edge. Because I can't get as fucked up as I want to when she's around, because she always looks at me disapprovingly and takes me to one side and says things like, 'You've had enough, Tag, you're embarrassing yourself,' which is such complete bullshit. Whenever she says that, I'm not embarrassing *myself* at all. I'm embarrassing *her*. If I want to get fucked up and fall over or get boisterous then I will. It doesn't bother me, and it doesn't bother my mates either.

That's why I was so worried about dropping bombs back at the flat with Tone. If this was just a normal night out, then I wouldn't worry about getting too fucked up. When Steph's not around there's no such thing as being too fucked up. But she disapproves of such behaviour. She doesn't do drugs, and she thinks that anybody who does is automatically an addict. She doesn't understand the line between dependency and recreational use. So, in her mind, no matter how infrequently I do it, it's always something to cast a shadow over our conversations, something to make her send me to sleep on the couch at her parents', something to embarrass and upset her.

Tone returns with the drinks. He has to make two trips – it turns out he's ordered five. He hands me my couple and we move to the middle of the room where there's a pillar with a ridge that we can rest our drinks on. We've got two beers each, but he's got something else in a shot glass that looks fucking deadly.

What you got there? I ask. I have to lean right over to him; the noise of the music and conversation around us makes it impossible to communicate at a normal volume.

B52, he shouts back.

He takes his lighter from his shirt pocket and sets the liquid on fire, then sucks the whole lot up through a straw. He shakes his head, face red and eyes squeezed tight shut and watering.

Fuck... me... he mouths, slamming the glass down and taking a sip from his pint.

What was in that? I shout.

What?

I said what was in that drink?

Oh. Absinthe, Baileys and vodka. Fucking lethal, mate. Fucking lethal.

I take a look around. Some real beauts in here tonight, all smooth legs and low-cut tops and painted eyes. Reminds me of what it's like to be single but I force myself to think of Steph instead. Still, the drugs are playing fucking havoc with my brain and I imagine her with someone else in some seedy bar somewhere, right now, somewhere in this same town, mocking me. Why do I do this to myself? I feel a black mood coming on now, like the drug comedown is already underway, and I know that I have the option of drinking my way over it and hopefully getting merrier, but from my past experiences there's the real danger that I'll only make it worse.

I take my chances and pick up my drink.

TWENTY-TWO

COLBECK

What a fucking joke your life has become. You are officially unemployed and of no fixed abode. You need to get that bitch out your head for good. She's such a mindfuck. You planned to pay a visit to her and her new boyfriend, the one who she was sleeping with while she was still with you, to piss through the letterbox and spit on her floor and then give that fucker a good beating and fucking petrol bomb the gaff or something. But there's no point doing that, seeing as you'd only be doing it to upset her and, from what you gather from the tirade of fucking text messages that the stupid bitch still keeps sending you, she's fully moved out of your ex-flat and she's back with her parents. You went back and picked up the final few boxes of your stuff ages ago, and now you're storing them at Ade's parents' place cos there's no fucking room for them anywhere else. The other bloke, whoever the cunt is, might still be on the scene, but maybe not. All you can do is to act completely indifferent and not give her the pleasure of knowing that you're still torturing yourself over her months later. Hopefully, one day you might run into the pair of them when you're out and about.

In an attempt to get your mind off all this bullshit, Ade suggested a road trip. You agreed, cos you're sick of the sight of this town. You've been to all the bars, had loads of fights, and you want a change of scenery. You don't get the same enjoyment from it any more; it's like a relationship turned sour. You want new thrills. New skanks and new lairies. New places and new faces to smash. The acerbic disgust and hatred burns an acid-hot hole in your gut with the screaming precision of a thousand cigarette burns. What's happened so far in this sad tale is merely a prelude to the carnage you intend to inflict on the non-generation in the weeks to come. There's a saying that suggests it takes many more muscles to frown than it does to lash out and mash some cunt's face in, but that's not to suggest that violence represents the easy way out. You're exhausted. To hate in this way requires non-trivial effort. First, it needs a host, warmth, nurture. It must be shelled-in and fed and looked after, and given regular exercise and breaks from boredom. It's a peculiar kind of hatred that needs to be kept happy. It needs to play nice. Then, once it has been exercised sufficiently and built up its strength and exhibited confidence, it must be captured and put back in its cage and kicked and beaten until it lies cowering and wet-eyed in the corner. It must be taunted and mocked and prodded at until it has lost all sentience, until it has chewed out its fur and torn its claws and broken its teeth gnawing the metal bars that lock it in. Then, and only then, you can leave its door off the catch and wait for someone to walk past and look at it the wrong way. Geezer, skank, what's the difference? You hate them equally. You've watched the sluts tottering in their high heels, arse cheeks hanging flabbily beneath pussy-pelmet skirts; seen them puking and pissing and screaming in the streets, heads lolling, doner meat and chips spilling onto the pavement; watched them fight with their boyfriends, get fingered and fucked and rough-housed against phone boxes, spit at door staff and taxi drivers and takeaway workers.

'Matt?'

Fucking worthless cunts.

'Matt?'

Ade stands in front of you.

'Yeh?'

'I've spoken to Dunc. He's up for it. When do you think we should go?'

'I don't care,' you say. 'It's not like I've got any plans. Just sort it out between yourselves and let me know.'

Ade sits down on the couch opposite you. He takes out a cigarette and leans forward to pick up a lighter from the coffee table.

'I reckon we should go tomorrow,' he says. 'The weather forecast's good for the next week. If we're gonna be sleeping in the van, then I'd rather it be warm.'

'That's fine,' you tell him. 'Anything I need to bring?'

'Just yourself,' he says, lighting his cigarette, 'and beers. And anything else you want. Don't forget your toothbrush.' He grins.

Dunc comes in and sits next to you. 'You got a fag?' he says to Ade. 'I'm running low, y'know.'

'You're a fucking fag,' Ade says. 'No, I haven't got one. If you're running low, buy more.'

'Come on, fucksake,' says Dunc.

'Buy your own.'

'I would buy my own,' Dunc says, 'but I've got no fucking money, in case you hadn't noticed.'

'That's no good,' you tell him. 'We're going on a road trip. You're gonna have to get money from somewhere.'

He thinks for a moment. 'I've got that covered,' he says.

Ade laughs. 'What the fuck are you talking about?'

'Give me a fag and I'll tell you,' he says, and you look at Ade, and Ade shakes his head and says to Dunc, 'Fucking hell, I don't think I'm gonna be able to stand being stuck in the van with you for any longer than a few minutes. Just have a fag, for God's sake.'

He tosses the pack over to Dunc.

'Nice one,' Dunc says. He takes a box of matches out of his pocket.

'So,' Ade says, 'how are you intending to get money? Please enlighten me.'

'He's probably gonna smoke a bit of cock,' you say. 'He'd enjoy that.'

Dunc smiles and lights his cigarette. 'I'm going to scam people,' he says.

'Ha!' Ade says, starting to laugh. 'And how exactly are you gonna do that? You're about as subtle as a ten-foot knob in a room full of fannies!'

'The same way I scammed you out of this fag, Ade.'

Ade isn't amused. 'You're a cheeky little cunt you are, Dunc,' he spits. 'Remind me to work out how much you owe me so far for back rent and booze and food and shit, and I'll bill you for it, yeh?'

'Fuck this,' says Dunc. 'When are we leaving?'

'Tomorrow,' you and Ade say, in unison.

'Thanks for all the notice like,' Dunc says.

'As if you need notice for anything!' Ade argues. 'It's not like you actually have anything else to do. You've said that yourself.'

'You know what I mean,' Dunc says. 'I just didn't expect it to be that soon, that's all.'

'Well,' you tell him, 'you'd better get packing.'

Ade finishes his cigarette and takes out another one.

'You smoke too much,' Dunc says.

'And you talk too much,' Ade replies. 'But if you can live with my bad habits, then I can live with yours.'

TWENTY-THREE

DUNCAN

I woke up earlier than usual, around ten-thirty like, and sat up in bed and smoked a cig, which got me thinking about when the fire brigade used to come and give talks at school. They always used to point out the dangers of smoking in bed cuz, apparently, it's too easy to fall asleep with a fag in your hand, and then, before you know it, the cherry's fallen off the end and onto the sheets and then you're all up in flames like fuckin Icarus or someshit. The flat was always too cold in the morning though, even in summer, and so I'd much rather take the risk and sit in my warm bed and smoke than get up. And if I did set the place on fire then at least it'd fuckin warm us all up a bit.

Colbeck and Ade weren't up yet. If they were then I'd hear them, as always. Colbeck's morning routine involved making beans on toast (with an egg on weekends – he only allowed himself two a week cuz he was worried about cholesterol or someshit) and playing music on the kitchen stereo. I often got woken up either by his singing or by the smoke alarm going off when he got distracted and forgot to pop the toaster up. The timer on it was fucked, see. That was my fault. I turned it on its side once and used it to grill some bacon, and the fat dripped down inside and fucked something integral to its operation. Colbeck had told me that it was okay to do that: he said that when him and Ade were at uni together, they lived in this proper shithole with no cooker and no hob so they 'cooked' everything using a microwave and toaster. He said you can cook anything, pretty much, using those two methods, but they don't publicise it on the packaging of the food itself cuz if they did then the companies that manufacture ovens would sue them for loss of revenue.

Ade's morning routine was an altogether different, breakfast-of-champions sorta affair, involving black coffee, half a deck of fags and violent coughing fits. At the moment, though, I couldn't hear any of the sounds I'd become so accustomed to, and so I knew that it was safe to sit in bed a while and wait for one of them to surface. I stubbed out my fag and reached over the edge of the bed to pick up a three-day-old newspaper. I'd been attempting the double-speed crossword in this one for a coupla evenings with no luck. I decided to look at the cryptic clues instead, to see if they might shed any light like.

One across: *High-flier ruined by exposure in tabloid.* Six letters. Well, I'm fucked if I know what that's all about, I thought. I scanned through some of the other clues but they all seemed equally daunting. Shit like *Boat in waters going west (5)* and *Damp fog hides nothing (5)*. I mean, fuck that. I tossed the paper back onto the floor, lit another cigarette, and picked up the copy of Plato's *Republic* that Ade told me to read. This was the first time I'd opened it since he convinced me that it would improve my mind. It all starts here, he'd told me. Fuck the pre-Socratics. Even you'll be able to work through it. It's completely readable. After that you can do his *Theaetetus* and then *Metaphysics* by Aristotle. With my help you'll be rattling through fucking Wittgenstein and Heidegger like a boss before the year's out. Get your breath back over Christmas and then we can start on Eastern philosophy in the new year.

I'd been reading about shadows and caves for about fifteen minutes when, from the hallway, I heard a vile hacking sound, sorta like a broken lawnmower, followed by the squeak of a door handle. I heard the pull cord in the bathroom click as someone pulled it, more hacking and spluttering, and the retch-and-splat sound of phlegm being coughed into the bog. Then came the noise of the flint spinning on a cigarette lighter, then more coughing. Ade was up.

Yo, Dunc, he shouted a few seconds later. You awake or what?

Yeh, I goes. Just reading a bit.

We're leaving in an hour, he went, cos I want to drive to the coast down south and find somewhere where we can park and stay over.

Okay, I shouted back.

I folded over the corner of the page and placed the book on the floor. Then, grudgingly, I got out of bed and shivered as I pulled on my combats and my red New York hoodie. Ade had told me to pack some stuff last night, but since we were only going for a week I was only gonna take the essentials like. I figured I'd need two pairs of trousers, cuz I could easily get away with wearing the same pair three times, apart from the fact that the other two would take the piss and call me a grebo or someshit. I reckoned four T-shirts should do the trick, and I was wearing one of them, so I grabbed three from the heap of clothes on the floor. (There's no point in hanging anything up, Ade told me once. Just put the fucker on and smooth it out a bit. The creases fall out after an hour or so. I never put anything in my wardrobe, and I wish I'd never bought it. It took me all day to build the fucking thing and I've never used it. What a fucking waste of time.) Then I found some boxers and socks, and I decided on a pair a day. I grabbed my parka, and another hoodie, and I stuffed it all into the holdall I'd hurriedly filled when I fucked off from my parents' place for the last time. Ade's book went on top, to show him that I at least had the good intention of reading the fuckin thing, and the crossword page from the paper, and a few pens. I needed booze and fags, but I'd get them en route, you get me, cuz I was proper low on cash and I needed to work out a way to convince one of the other guys to lend me some like.

I went into the living room and smoked another cig. Only five left in the pack now. Soon enough, Colbeck was in the kitchen with the stereo blaring, and the smell of burnt toast was filling the air.

I thought you only had an egg on weekends? I goes, after seeing him get to work with the frying pan and spatula.

Special occasion today, Dunc, he went. And besides, this is the last chance I'll get to use a proper cooker for a week.

Fuckin good point, I said. Borrow me some food, yeh? I'll pay you back.

Will you fuck! he said. I know what you're like with money.

I went to protest, but he said, Seeing as I'm in a good mood, I'll do you some beans on toast.

Nice one, I said. What about an egg?

Are you taking the piss?

Sorel's door opened. Hey, she said.

Fuck me, she looked fit. She was wearing a big baggy T-shirt, probably one of Ade's or her ex's or someshit, which came down to like six inches above her knee; and her hair was a bit of a mess, kinda tousled; and she'd got nothing on her feet, which as you might know, I've got a bit of a thing for. I always found her at her fittest when she wasn't trying to be fit.

Hi, I went.

Can I have a word with you in here a sec? she asked, and I fuckin melted. Colbeck gave me a look that was part *what the fuck?* and part *you jammy cunt* like.

I sauntered into her room, trying to act cool, trying to look her straight in the eye cuz I'd already noticed she wasn't wearing a bra. This was the first time I'd been in there since she moved in. Prior to that, Ade had used the space to store his books and stuff, so I'd occasionally wandered in and out when I was borrowing things from him. Some of the books were still in there but they were stacked in neat towers against the wall opposite the bed, next to a pile of clean laundry. My heart fuckin skipped a beat when I saw two black thongs and a single pair of red French knickers at the top of the pile. I took in the rest of the sights while I had the chance (fuck knows when I'd get to be in here again): a half-empty glass of water on the cabinet beside the bed, a white teddy bear holding a heart with 'Be Mine' written across the front, a pack of face wipes, some photos of people I didn't recognise.

I've got you something, she said. I wanted to give it to you last night, but you were in bed when I got back from work.

Sorry, I went. I needed an early night. Smoked a bit too much weed, I think.

She frowned. Anyway, she goes. Here it is. She picked up something from beside the bed and handed it to me. It was a small black notebook.

What's this? I asked.

It's a notebook, Dunc.

I laughed. Lowest form of wit, I went, and she smiled.

People who have interesting stuff to say should keep a journal, she goes. Have you ever written one?

No.

I've kept one since I was about eight, she said, unsticking a strand of hair from her top lip.

I'll give it a go, I went.

Really?

Yeh, defo. Why not?

At the time I didn't know how important that notebook would prove to be. Cuz if she hadn't given it to me then I never would have sketched the things that happened, and if I hadn't sketched the things that happened I would have forgotten the details, and if I'd forgotten the details then I wouldn't be able to write this. Is that fate? And if it is, would it have been better for me to have forgotten?

Colbeck shouted from the kitchen, saying my food was ready. I told him I'd be there in a sec. Just as I went to leave, Sorel grabbed the sleeve of my hoodie.

Dunc? she said. Please try to keep an eye on those two.

I will.

Promise?

Yeh.

Say it then.

Say what?

Say you promise.

I laughed. Then I promised her.

Colbeck shouted me again: Are you coming or what, gaylord? I went back to the kitchen and he handed me a plate of beans on toast and I took it and sat down. There was no brown sauce left, so I had to make do with red, which doesn't go as well with beans but, y'know, beggars can't be choosers, like Ade says.

Colbeck sat opposite and stabbed at the yolk of his egg with his knife. I always try to make the yolk last as long as possible. I don't get people who burst it and dip stuff in it or someshit. I remembered this fuckin riddle of Ade's that he got me with once: which is grammatically correct – the yolk of an egg *is* white, or the yolk of an egg *are* white? Fuckin think about it.

Colbeck leaned over close.

Oi, he said, in a hushed voice. What was going on in there?

Nothing, I said. She was just giving me something.

He raised his eyebrows.

Fucksake, I said. She was giving me a notebook. She wants me to keep a diary.

What the fuck for? he asked, gobbing pieces of his precious egg down his chin.

Cuz she says it's important, I went.

He squirted a blob of sauce on the edge of his plate. Well, if she says it then it must be true, he said.

What's that supposed to mean?

Nothing, he said. I was just making an observation.

What observation?

Just the observation that lately you seem to be doing a lot of what she tells you to do. Seems a bit weird to me. What's the point in writing a diary, anyway? You're not exactly fucking Pepys, are you?

He grinned at his own joke, a joke I didn't even fuckin get, exposing the skin of a baked bean stuck on one tooth.

You want to fuck her, don't you? he said.

No! I goes. Fucksake, Colbeck, keep your fuckin voice down.

You do! he said, pointing his fork at me accusingly and allowing a huge grimace to spread across his face. I can tell! You want to fuck her!

Fuckin keep your voice down, I said again, cuz even though there was music playing in the kitchen, her bedroom door was still ajar.

Methinks he protesteth too much, he said irritatingly, shoving another forkful of mush in his mouth.

Fuck this, I goes, and I picked up my plate and took it into the living room.

Come back, Dunc, he said. Come on, I'm only messing.

I ignored him. I sat down on the sofa and turned on the TV with the remote. I stared for a while at some chat show bollocks with guests on a stage being publicly humiliated by some smarmy fucker with a microphone. Then Sorel came in and sat beside me.

What time are you leaving? she went.

Ade said in an hour. That was twenty minutes ago.

We both stared at the TV. She might've been watching it; I was just looking at it while I finished my food. At this particular moment, I was kinda regretting the fact that Ade bought a new one, because it gave Sorel an excuse not to chat to me, and chatting to her was one of the highlights of my life at the time. I took the notebook from my pocket and turned it over in my hand, not noticing at first that she was watching me.

It's called a Moleskine, she said.

Why?

She laughed. Because that's what it's called, she said.

Oh, I went, feeling a bit stupid like. Then I asked her, Is that important?

I think so, she told me. Van Gogh, Picasso, Ernest Hemingway, they all used these notebooks to write their ideas and stuff in.

You serious? I asked.

Yeh, she went, I'm completely serious. And Sartre used them.

Who?

Jean-Paul Sartre, she said.

Oh. Who's he?

He was a French philosopher. Ask Ade.

I will, I said.

She took the notebook from my hand and flipped it open. Look at this, Dunc, she goes. There's a pocket in the back here. So you can tear interesting things out of magazines and save them, stuff like that.

I really appreciate this, you know, I said, taking it back from her.

Well it's the least I could do, she said. If you weren't here, then I'd have moved out by now.

She put her hand on the top of my thigh. Oh fuck. Fuck fuck fuck. I didn't say anything, cuz anything that I did say would ruin the moment, cuz I'm so good at that. We just sat there for about half a minute, her with her hand on my leg and me frozen rigid. Then Ade appeared.

You ready, nobby? he asked. We're off in ten.

You said we weren't going for an hour?

Yeh, I know. But that was then. And this is now. And now I'm saying that we're off in ten.

Fair enough, I went. I'd better grab my stuff.

I picked up the notebook and got up off the sofa and I carried my plate into the kitchen and put it in the sink. Then I nipped into my bedroom to collect my bag. I went back into the kitchen to wash my dishes before Ade had a chance to bollock me for it but Colbeck was already seeing to them, which was pretty fuckin unusual.

Ade told Sorel to ring him if there was any bother, saying he'd be straight back here if she needed him. They hugged each other, her telling him that she'd be fine and him telling her that he was only trying to look out for her. Then I said bye, and thanked her again for the notebook; and although I wanted to hug her like Ade did, I'm not one to initiate these sorts of things and she made no move either, so it was just an awkward see-you-next-week instead. Colbeck had packed a fuckin enormous holdall and he struggled to get it on his shoulder as I followed Ade through the front door and into the hallway. Ade just had a coupla supermarket carrier bags and a twenty-four-pack of beer.

I'll say bye here, said Sorel. I don't want to go outside with bare feet.

Okay, I goes.

Ade said something like, Get a move on, Dunc. We're only going for a fucking week. It's not like you're heading off to the Somme. He set off down the stairs with Colbeck following.

I turned to go after them, but Sorel was like, You going to give me a hug then?

I tried to act casual, put my arms round her shoulders, gave her a squeeze. She's shorter than me and slimmer and hugging her made me feel bigger than I actually am somehow, and I liked it.

She kissed my cheek, still over her shoulder.

See you next week then, she went, and I let go of her first so as not to seem too fuckin eager.

Bye, I said. I'll text you.

Then I headed down the stairs without turning round, and I hoped she was watching me.

On the street, Ade was smoking a cigarette and holding an open can of beer. What the fuck are you doing? I asked. You've got to drive in a min.

Just having one for the road, he said.

Colbeck heaved his holdall through the side door and yanked it up onto one of the seats. Shotgun front, he went.

There was no point arguing with him, so I climbed into the back and made myself comfortable between Colbeck's bag and Ade's crate, which now contained twenty-three beers. I felt in my pockets for my cigarettes, took one out, lit it.

Am I okay to smoke in here? I shouted to Ade. He was still standing on the street.

Yeh, he said. Make sure you put the fag ends somewhere though. And don't burn the fucking seats, because if you do then it's me who's gonna have to take the shit for it when my folks find out.

No probs, I went, and I sat back.

After a while I noticed something. Ade, I said. There's no seat belts.

I know, he goes. There's some in the front though.

Well, that's no good to me, is it? Considering I'm sitting in the fuckin back?

Colbeck laughed. He was holding a beer now as well. Fuck knows where that came from.

It isn't a legal requirement to have seat belts in the back of a camper van, Ade assured me.

I'm sure it isn't, I went, but I've seen your driving.

It'll be all right, Dunc, Colbeck said. This thing probably only goes fifty miles an hour. And if we crash then the windscreen will stop you.

That's not funny, I said. If we did crash, and I died, you'd have to live with that comment on your conscience for the rest of your life.

Ade laughed, perhaps at Colbeck's comment, perhaps at my reply, perhaps at something entirely different. Are we all ready now? he asked. Cos I'm good to go.

He crushed the can and threw it into one of the bins outside the flat. Looking at all the paper and polystyrene trays and plastic forks and general shit all around us, for once I wished other fuckers would follow his example.

Yeh, I'm ready, Colbeck goes. I slammed the sliding door shut, throwing the nub of my cigarette down a grid at the roadside first.

Fucking road trip, said Ade, with a grin. And he turned the key in the ignition, and the van choked and spluttered a bit, and then he revved a few times and we were off.

TWENTY-FOUR

SHAUN

I've been anticipating this moment since I first found out what happened to me.

I'm watching the clock on the wall when the first copper walks in. I spend at least an hour a day watching that fucking clock. I count the seconds into minutes into hours into days. It's my therapy. With each movement of the second hand, I move further away from the accident – although I know, of course, that this was no 'accident' in the literal sense – and closer to full recovery. It's hypnotic, watching a clock. Sometimes I don't realise I'm doing it. A watched pot may never boil, but a watched clock still ticks.

He's wearing a hat and a stab vest, which seems unnecessary in a deserted hospital ward. He looks tall, but it's difficult to tell exactly how tall someone is when you're lying on a bed looking up at them. He strides over to me, nods, removes his hat and smiles in a chummy sort of way. I'm not really into the police. They put me on edge even when I haven't done anything wrong – which, in my defence, I usually haven't. Most of the time I'm a model citizen. In case you're wondering, I'm not one of these people who refer to them as pigs to sound hard. I get it: they have a job to do, and it's not an easy one. But they don't make it any easier for themselves. Whenever I see them, which is usually when I'm up town, they're always either bollocking people for being too drunk, too loud, too disorderly, or they're posing for photographs with the revellers and letting pissheads try their helmets on. It's like being at fucking school. The worst teachers are the ones who try to be your friend. That's a mistake, because they're not your friends. They're not your peers. They get it into their heads that they understand the youth of today, because they think that they can remember what life was like when they were young. That might be true, but it doesn't mean they know shit about life today. Only ten years ago, I remember the world was a different place. Some would argue that it was safer, but I don't claim to know anything about that. From what I can see, it was just as bad – there were still terrorists, still murderers, still rapists. All I know is that it was different. So any fucker from a different generation who claims that they understand what growing up feels like in 2003 – well, sorry, but they don't know what they're on about. The key is to embrace the differences. The last thing someone wants to hear when they're going through something bad is someone else saying, 'I know exactly how you feel,' followed by an example of something irrelevant that happened twenty years ago.

It's a sad fact, really, but the police are fighting a losing battle. No one respects them any more. People like me are wary of them because they see us as scum, and they're far too quick to tar us all with the same brush and assume that we're up to no good when we're really not that bad at all and we're just trying to have a good time without hurting anyone. On the other side of the coin, the fucking high-flyer with his two-point-four children and his company car and his three-bedroom semi hates them because he thinks that they always take the side of the criminals.

Anyway, this copper comes over and introduces himself as John Kelsey. He's about forty years old, with a shadow on his face like he's one of those blokes who has to shave every five minutes. He's joined a few seconds later by a skinny, twitchy little ferret that he introduces as Constable Adam Pass. I'm not paying much attention to what else he says, because I'm reminded of a joke from years ago – something to do with police officers and cunt stubble – in the same way as the doc's red clipboard reminded me of science lessons at school.

Pass looks much younger than Kelsey. The way he grins at me suggests that we've just been introduced by a mutual friend.

Steph always says that I judge people too quickly, but I take as long as I need. Sometimes it takes weeks before I think I've sussed someone. Usually it only takes seconds, but my opinion very rarely changes once it's formed. I get off to a bad start with Kelsey because he refers to me as 'young man' and I really don't like it. It's not just that though. It's the way he looks at me. *Oh yes,* he's thinking. *I've seen your type before. A thug. A binge-drinker. A yob. Not so hard now that you're lying in hospital are you, sonny?*

'Were you expecting us?' Pass asks, obviously eager to get the ball rolling and impress his partner.

'Yes,' I say.

Kelsey asks Pass to get some chairs. There's a stack against the opposite wall, and Pass scurries over to fetch a couple, tail wagging as he brings them back.

'Let's start with what you remember,' suggests Kelsey when they're both sitting down.

'Where do you want me to start?'

'The day you were attacked.'

'I remember up until about eight in the evening. I'd arranged to go out with some mates, and one of them – Tony – he came over to my flat for a few beers first. The last thing I remember is getting into a taxi with him.'

'Tony's full name is…?'

'Sorry. It's Anthony Redding.' Pass makes a note.

'And where were you getting the taxi to?'

'To the town centre. High street, where all the bars are.'

I want to tell them that all this bollocks is irrelevant, and that all they should be interested in is catching the people who did this. It doesn't matter what the fuck I was doing up until it happened. All that matters is that it *did* happen. Steph got raped, and I got the shit kicked out of me. The only thing that stops me from saying this to them is the fact that I want to be as helpful as possible for Steph's sake. They'll no doubt be speaking to her again once they've heard my side, and I don't want them to report back to her that I was an uncooperative prick.

'Who else was there?' asks Pass.

'No one. Just me and Tony.'

'No, I mean who did you meet up with?'

'I don't remember. I know that I met up with my girlfriend, Steph, but that's only because Tony told me when he came to visit. There are a couple of other guys we usually meet up with – I can give you their details if you like? – Jake Anderson and Darren O'Brien. Also, Tony's mate Gaz. But I don't know his surname. A couple of others.'

Pass keeps scribbling. Probably best not to mention Nick the dealer.

'What I need to get to the bottom of,' Kelsey says once his partner has finished writing, 'is what went on once you were all together inside the club. Did anything unusual happen between you and Steph that night?'

'Such as?'

'An argument.'

I don't understand why he's asking questions that he quite obviously knows the answer to already. I tell the truth, because there's no point in withholding it: 'Apparently we had an argument, yeah.'

'Apparently?'

'Yeah, apparently. I don't remember, but Tony told me.'

Now they're looking at me like they're the hardest fuckers in the world, like they're a proper pair of tough cops from some fucking seventies TV show and they're going to take me into an interrogation room somewhere, pull the blinds down, and fuck me up. The atmosphere in the room has become thick and tense and I can't work out what they're getting at. Their line of questioning is making me edgy. I wish there was someone here with me. Aren't I supposed to have a solicitor present or something? I consider putting that question to them, but I don't because it'll make it look like I've got something to hide. The problem is, I don't know whether I've got something to hide or not because I can't fucking recall anything that's happened.

'And why don't you remember?' Kelsey asks. Pass is just sitting there, staring blankly, like he's there for decoration, or there to make the other one look more important.

'Isn't it obvious?' I say. 'I'm in hospital because I have a brain injury.'

'So you remember nothing about the attack?'

'That's right.'

'Quite convenient, isn't it?'

'What are you on about?' I ask.

'I'm just saying that it's quite convenient that you remember everything up until things started to happen which could incriminate you and your friends.'

'Do you think I'm lying?' I stammer. 'For fuck's sake! Why the fuck would I lie about this?'

'You were using drugs that night, weren't you?' he says, ignoring my question.

'I can't remember.'

'We can take a sample if you like. Certain substances stay in the system for weeks. It's illegal for you to refuse to give us a sample, by the way.' He grins sardonically. 'Why don't you start telling the truth?' he suggests. 'Help us to help you.'

'I smoked a joint at the flat, before I came out,' I admit. Then I add, 'In the privacy of my own home.'

'You see,' says Kelsey, 'that's very strange. Because thirty seconds ago you said that you couldn't remember whether or not you were using drugs. And yet now you say that you were using drugs at the flat.'

Pass licks his lips.

'You can't blame us for wondering,' Kelsey continues, 'if you might suddenly remember what happened later on that evening.'

'Let's stop messing around,' I say. 'What are you trying to accuse me of? Why would I lie about this? My girlfriend was raped, as you obviously know already. I'm stuck in hospital, and no one knows how long it's going to take for me to recover. Come on – why the fuck would I lie about it? I'm telling you everything I know. I want these people caught. They've ruined my fucking life. They've ruined both our lives. Mine and Steph's.'

The silence that follows seems to last forever, but it's really only five seconds. I know because I keep glancing at the clock.

'Okay then, Shaun,' Kelsey says. 'Let's start from the beginning. You and your friend, Tony, are in your flat. You are drinking beers before you go to meet some friends in the town centre. You're smoking cannabis.'

'Yeah.'

'There was something else you were taking, wasn't there? Something a little… a little stronger.'

He means the MDMA. Okay, so they've got me bang to rights then. But surely it's not that serious a crime? Not when it's taken in the context of everything else that went on afterwards?

'You know what we're talking about, Shaun, don't you?' Pass says, grinning like a paedo with sweets.

'I don't remember,' I lie.

'Well perhaps we can wait a minute or so then,' Kelsey says, looking at his watch. 'It took you less time than that to remember last time.'

'Oh, come off it,' I say. 'What are you talking about?'

Please don't call my fucking bluff, I'm thinking.

He waits, still looking at his watch, playing on the drama like this is a fucking Oscar performance.

'Okay then, Shaun,' he says eventually. 'Since you refuse to cooperate, I'll say it myself: ketamine.'

'What?'

'Ketamine,' he repeats.

It takes a while for it to dawn on me what ketamine actually is. I don't tend to know drugs by their proper names, only by Tony and Nick's slang.

'I don't think so, no,' I say. 'I wouldn't have thought so.' I consider it again, physically straining to remember. 'No, I really don't think so.'

'Well, let me tell you, Shaun,' says Kelsey, 'that a quantity of this substance was found in your jacket on the night that you were brought here.'

'That doesn't make sense,' I say. 'Why didn't anyone tell me?'

'Because no one, apart from us and the member of staff who found it, knows.'

'I really don't think so,' I say again. 'I don't know why I would have been taking that.'

'Well,' Kelsey says, 'it's a popular recreational drug. God knows why, though. It's vile stuff. We see the damage it causes all the time, don't we, Pass? Turns a man into an empty shell, doesn't it? Isn't that right?'

Pass nods animatedly. 'Awful stuff. Vile.'

Kelsey continues. 'There's more though, Shaun. This is the exact same substance that was used to drug Stephanie Harrison. What's more, as far as we can tell, it came from the same supply as the drug that was found on your person – which, by the way, was one of the purest strains we've ever seen. We have the glass she drank from. We're certain that further tests will confirm it.'

There's something about his manner that suggests he's lying. They don't really have the glass. They probably don't even know for sure that she was in a K-hole when it happened. But still, it makes sense. They think I did it. Fuck. What if I did?

'Let me tell you what I think happened,' offers Kelsey. 'I think that you and your friends were out, taking drugs, and your girlfriend disapproved of this. You had a big falling out. And you, in your inebriated state, proceeded to slip something into her drink to get her out of the way for a while.'

'Fuck you,' I spit. 'I wouldn't do that. Ask anyone.'

'I assure you, we already have. I think that someone in your group of friends saw what you did, and they decided to, shall we say, *use the situation to their advantage*.'

'None of my mates would do that either!' I shout. 'This is completely ludicrous!'

Kelsey gets up and paces over to the window.

'Shaun,' he says, turning to face me. 'I think it's time you started telling the truth.'

TWENTY-FIVE

COLBECK

Fuck yeh. You're on the road, just like Jack Kerouac and Hunter S. Thompson. Dunc's in the back with his fucking notebook and pen in hand, writing shit down. Christ only knows what he's got into his head this time. Perhaps he sees himself as some sort of gonzo journalist, or maybe he's writing little love notes to post to his beloved Sorel back home. He's really in there but he still doesn't realise it cos he's so utterly shit with the birds. You should probably take him to one side and explain that he needs to give her a good seeing to before she gets bored of him and shacks up with someone else. You can tell that she's up for it. It's the things she says, the way she says them, the way she plays with her hair and flutters her eyelashes and purses her lips with a fixed stare into the middle distance when she's talking to him. That jammy little fucker. You don't know how he's managed to blag his way into that one but it's definitely in the bag, whether he realises it or not.

'Yo, Dunc,' Ade says, eyeing him in the rear-view. 'What you writing?'

'Just thoughts, things in my brain, y'know,' Dunc says, coyly.

'Things in your brain, eh?' Ade considers. 'Page must still be blank then.'

You laugh. Ade doesn't, but his top lip twitches ever so slightly.

'Shut the fuck up,' Dunc snaps. 'It's important to write shit down so that you can look at it later in your life and see how things have changed.'

'What a load of bollocks!' Ade says. 'That's what your memory's for, you tit. Anything you don't remember isn't worth knowing, in my book. Who's been telling you all this shit?'

'Sorel,' you say.

Dunc kicks the back of your seat. 'Don't be a dick, Colbeck,' he says.

'Sorel?' says Ade. 'What you doing with Sorel?'

'Nothing,' says Dunc.

'You seem to be spending a lot of time together,' Ade remarks.

'So what?' says Dunc. 'Is that illegal?'

You jump as a lorry driver sounds his horn. Ade's overtaken without checking his blind spot again.

'Maybe you should keep your eyes on the road, yeh?' says Dunc. 'Instead of taking the piss.'

'Maybe you should stop flirting with my niece,' says Ade.

'If I want to flirt with her, I will,' Dunc says. 'You can't stop me. You don't own her, fucksake.'

Ade undoes his seat belt and turns round in his seat. 'Just you watch me stop you, mate.'

'It's not going to come to that anyway,' says Dunc, ducking out of the boxing ring as quickly as he stepped into it. 'We're just friends. In case you haven't noticed, you two've been spending quite a lot of time out of the flat lately on this stupid vigilante mission of yours.'

'Oi,' you say. 'Less of that, if you don't mind. It's a very worthwhile cause, not to mention satisfying.'

'Of course it is,' says Dunc. He's getting a caustic little tongue on him lately, that little fucker. You've got to applaud him though, giving as good as he gets and all that. It's all banter at the end of the day. 'Anyway,' he continues, 'neither of us has anyone else to talk to apart from each other, so it's obvo we're gonna get close.'

Fucking obvo! Why the fuck does he talk like that, for God's sake? It doesn't even sound good. You need to inform him of that at some point. Not right now though. You'll save it for another time.

Ade fastens his seat belt again. 'That's fine,' he says. 'You can be friends. Just make sure you consider her out of bounds.'

'Why?' Dunc asks.

'Because she is.'

'She isn't.'

'Yes she is.'

'She isn't.'

'Guys,' you interrupt. This whole thing is getting right on your fucking tits. But you don't say so. You just say, 'There's no need to argue,' then you turn to Ade and tell him, 'There's nothing going on with them two, I was just taking the piss.'

'I know nothing's going on,' says Ade. 'She's got more fucking sense. I was just reminding Dunc of that.'

'Got any music?' you ask. You want to change the subject. Ade's an erratic driver at the best of times and you don't want him in control of a vehicle when he's in a shit mood.

'Yeh!' says Ade, banging his palms on the steering wheel. 'Dunc, pass the CD bag over.'

'Which one's the CD bag?'

'I'd imagine it's the bag that's got the CDs in it, you cock,' he says.

Dunc rummages a bit.

'This one?' he asks.

'Is it a bag?' says Ade.

'Yeh.'

'And does it have CDs in it?'

He looks inside. 'Yep.'

'Then it's the CD bag. Pass it to Matt.'

You take it from him and sift through. It's either going to be *London Calling* or a Tom Waits compilation. You opt for the former.

'Light us a cig, Dunc,' Ade says. 'There's some in the carrier bag next to your feet.'

You take the CD out of the plastic sheath and slide it into the player. Sit back, open a beer, and shut your eyes.

TWENTY-SIX

DUNCAN

To: Sorel
From: Duncan

hey. jus thought I'd
txt to say hi. still
driving - ade says
he knows a place
dwn south he went
wen he was younger
hope ur ok xx

To: Duncan
From: Sorel

Thanx 4 the msg!
Jus at home bored
thank god 4 new tv!
Hope ure using the
present!
xox

To: Sorel
From: Duncan

already wrote 3 pgs!
those 2 r takin piss
obvo. Only bin away
3 hrs and already
getting on my tits
xx

To: Duncan
From: Sorel

glad ure putting it2
gud use! wot they bin
saying then? txt
back xox

To: Sorel
From: Duncan

u dnt wana kno
m8 xx

To: Duncan
From: Sorel

Oh I do ;-)
Tell tell tell!
xox

To: Sorel
From: Duncan

shit bout me n u.
askin why we
hang round 2gether
n shit xx

To: Duncan
From: Sorel

wot u sed to them?
xox

To: Sorel
From: Duncan

just that we get on
well and that they
leave us on our
own n so we've
got close x

To: Duncan
From: Sorel

wots wrong with
that? xox

To: Sorel
From: Duncan

they reckon sum
thing is goin on x

To: Duncan
From: Sorel

so wot if it was?
xox

What the fuck does that mean? I thought. Is she asking me out here or what? Cuz if I take this the wrong way then I'm gonna look a proper dick and I obvo don't want that. Why do girls have to be so fuckin cryptic all the time? Why can't they just spell shit out in black and white and say exactly what they mean? It'd make my life a whole lot fuckin easier if they did.

I typed a reply, my thumb working hyper-style on my phone's keypad. But when I tried to send it, I'd run outta fuckin credit. Shit. I didn't want her to think I was ignoring her. This was the fuckin crux of the whole convo, you get me.

Colbeck, I went, anticipating his negative response like. Lend us your phone a sec.

I don't have a phone, remember? I broke it.

Bollocks, I spat. You ordered another one ages ago. I saw the box arrive and I've seen it in the flat. Don't give me that shit. That's like the worst fuckin lie I've ever heard.

Why do you need to borrow it? he goes.

So I can send a text.

Who to?

A friend.

What friend? You haven't got any fucking friends!

Ade laughed.

Don't be a dick, I said. Come on, it's an emergency. Please let me borrow it.

What's the emergency?

It's nothing that concerns you, I went. Just let me send one text, please.

If it doesn't concern me then it can't be that much of an emergency in my opinion, he went.

Fucksake, I said. This is ridiculous. I don't know why the fuck I even bother sometimes.

Keep your hair on, dicky, he went, turning round and giving me an irritating little smirk. He handed me his phone.

Nice one, I said.

```
To: Sorel
From: Matt C

hey it's dunc. run
out of cred. Will get
sum asap then chat
2 u more. Txt me bak
on my fone x
```

I sent the message and gave the phone back to him, making sure that I deleted all evidence from the Sent folder first.

We nearly there yet, or what? I asked Ade. I thought you said it wasn't far?

Almost there, he said. Bout half an hour.

So we going out tonight then? went Colbeck.

If you like, said Ade.

I immediately got one of my panic-twinges. You'd better not get yourselves into any shit, I said. That's not what I came out here for.

Fucking hell, Dunc, went Ade. Just chill out.

I don't want to get arrested, I said, that's all.

You won't get arrested if you don't do anything, Colbeck interjected.

Yeh, but what if you two get locked up? I asked. Then I'll be stuck miles from home with no way of getting back.

No one's gonna get arrested, went Ade. We'll just go out and have a few drinks and a laugh, nothing serious.

And why should I trust you? I asked. Everywhere you two go you get yourselves into some kind of shit.

Well you can sit in the van if you like, Ade suggested, while we go out.

How exciting, I said.

My phone buzzed. I picked it up and glanced at the screen.

To: Duncan
From: Sorel

ok hun that's fine.
speak 2 u soon xox

I stared at the message for a few secs after I finished reading it. I must've been in some kinda shock or someshit, but it was beginning to sink in: I might actually be able to get with her. I wished I hadn't come on this fuckin road trip.

Should've stayed at home with her and made the most of having the flat to ourselves like. But, I reminded myself, she suggested that I should come to keep an eye on these two, and so, although I had to be away from her for a week give or take, it didn't matter cuz at the end of the day it was gonna get me into her good books like. The prob was, though, that if them two got into some sorta shit she might look upon me unfavourably cuz she asked me to watch out for them. And so, against all my instincts, I was beginning to feel that if those two ended up going out somewhere I was gonna have to fuckin go with them. And that scared the shit out of me.

What you looking at on your phone? goes Colbeck, snapping me out of it like.

Just a text message.

Who from?

None of your fuckin business!

Fucking hell, Dunc, Ade goes. What's up with you? Time of the month or what?

Shut the fuck up, Ade, I went.

Fuck this, said Colbeck. I'm putting some more tunes on.

Okay, I goes, but please put on something better than the last forty minutes of shit.

That was the fucking Clash! Ade went.

Who? I goes.

Colbeck shook his head and said, Don't tell me you've never heard of The Clash.

Nope.

You're about as cultured as my left bollock you are, Dunc, Ade goes.

It's not my fault that I've never heard of them! I said.

Whose fault is it then? he asked. I didn't reply, so he

started doing that fuckin annoying thing he always does where he repeats the question again and again like, going, Whose fault is it then, eh? Whose fault is it?

I dunno, I said. It's just not my fault.

Right, Colbeck goes. Enough frivolity please, gentlemen. Duncan, allow me to educate you.

Go on, I said.

He said summat like, The Clash were one of most important bands to come out of the punk scene. You've heard of the Sex Pistols, yeh?

Probably not, Ade interrupted.

Oi, I told him. Then I turned back to Colbeck. Yep, I've heard of the Sex Pistols, I said.

Well, The Clash were better musicians, certainly, but they also had a more diverse musical style. They experimented with different genres, pushed the boundaries, man, you know?

Well, I still don't like what I heard.

Poor misguided fool, goes Ade.

By the end of this trip you're gonna be a musical connoisseur, Dunc, Colbeck said. You'll be a Bachelor of Arts, all but.

I wouldn't count on it, went Ade.

Anyway, fuck that, goes Colbeck. He rummaged around in the appropriately named CD bag that Ade was gypping me about earlier. You're gonna fucking love this one, he assured me, taking out a disc.

Who is it? I asked, dubiously.

Fleetwood Mac.

Aren't they that really cheesy band from the fuckin seventies? I went.

No they fucking aren't, you cheeky little twat, Ade snapped.

Colbeck slipped the CD into the stereo and turned it up. I loosened the elastic on my notebook and started writing again.

TWENTY-SEVEN

TAG

Fuck. Shouldn't have had that bomb in the toilets before we left the bar, but Tone insisted. Head still spinning and nerves still jangling. Feels like my feet are sinking into holes as I step along the pavement. Tone's up ahead and I see him smiling at me over his shoulder through my tunnel vision. It's dark now. It's still warm though, and everyone's out in their summer clothes. I imagine my nose bleeding, but every time I put my hand to my face to wipe it, it comes away clean.

I momentarily forget where I am. I'm in between a bar and a club: it could be anywhere, and for a few seconds I don't know where I'm going or why I'm going there. I feel my phone vibrate in my pocket and I take it out, but no message. Just my imagination. A phantom text. Someone hunches at the edge of the road, vomiting into a grid while his mates laugh and one of them pats him on the back telling him to get it all out. Tony turns left and climbs three concrete steps and I realise that we're here, wherever here may be, and I know it's time to compose myself and act sober because they'll turn me away if I don't.

Oh fuck. Steph. She'll know straight away that I'm fucked. I hope she's not in here yet. She texted me earlier and said something, but I can't remember what. I could always go and sit in the toilets for half an hour with a glass of water and ice and make myself look presentable before I find her. Now someone appears right in front of me. My eyes are level with his neck. White shirt, black tie: funeral attire. Security. Can I see some ID, please? I reach into my back pocket, take out my provisional licence. He studies it. Have a good night, lads. He hands it back and we're in.

First things first: bar. Water seems like a sensible option. I'm slightly reassured because I obviously don't look as bad as I feel; the security let me in all right. At first I think I've lost Tone, but then I realise he's behind me. So much noise. Impossible to think straight. My eardrums resonate with each thump of the bass drum. I find the bar. My phone vibrates. I take it out. Didn't imagine it this time: it's Steph, asking where I am and if I'm on my way yet. I don't reply. I'm not ready to face her. We'll just end up arguing, I can sense it. There's a shit mood still lurking in the back of my head behind the drugs and alcohol. I'm angry and I don't know why and the thought of seeing her makes me even more angry because I know what she's like when she's had a few drinks and I know what I'm like when I've had a few drinks and it's not a good combination. It's vibrating again. I take it out. Incoming call: Steph. Just leave me alone for once. Why do I always have to answer to you? I cancel the call. I'm going to have to text her soon though, or she'll think that I'm ignoring her, which I sort of am.

They don't do tap water at the bar so I have to pay two quid for a bottle. They take the lid off and tell me that I can't keep it. I ask why not. Because, with the lid on and full of water, the bottle could be a heavy and dangerous missile if someone threw it. I take the bottle, minus cap, and head to the toilets. Realise I've walked off without consulting Tone. Doesn't matter though. I'll catch up with him soon enough.

On the way I see Nick. Haven't seen that fucker for a couple of weeks. He waves me over.

Tag! he says. How's it going, bro?

Could be better.

You fucked?

A bit.

Do us a favour, he says. Put this in your pocket.

What the fuck is it?

Drugs, man. Fucking ket, innit. I gotta sell some to this guy outside, yeah? The fucking bouncers searched me when I came in, and they very nearly fucking found it. Don't wanna risk carrying it all on me again.

I'm not sure about that, I say. I'm wankered, I might lose it.

Oh yeah! he says, like he's cottoned on. How was the stuff I sorted for Tone?

Fucking good shit, judging by the state of me.

He laughs.

Just keep hold of this shit for me, and I'll get it back in a minute. I gotta go outside and meet this geezer.

He's really not the sort of person you should argue with. He hands me the palmful of baggies and I stick them in my jacket pocket.

He slaps me hard on the shoulder – his way of saying thank you – and heads towards the doors.

In the toilets I put the bottle on the sink and stand with

my back against the tiled wall until I feel semi-sober. When I can think straight, I text Steph saying that I'll meet her by the men's toilets on the ground floor. Less than a minute later she replies saying okay. I splash water on my face. My eyes are red and I feel twitchy. She's going to know straight away what I've been up to.

When I walk through the corridor back to the club, I can see her through the circular window in the door, waiting in the small hallway that leads back inside, looking around, suspicious of her surroundings. I push through the door and try to smile.

Oh my God, she says.

What?

You're on something, aren't you? For God's sake, I asked you not to.

I'm not on anything. I'm just drinking water.

And I wonder why that is.

Because I'm thirsty?

Stop trying to be clever, Tag, she says.

Fuck this shit. I don't need it. It's starting already. I want her out of my fucking face. She doesn't shut up though. It would be a lot better for her if she knew when to shut the fuck up.

It's pathetic, she lectures. I only asked one thing of you: don't take anything before you come out, so that we can have a good time together. But you can't even do that for me. Thank you very much, Tag. That means a lot, you know? It's nice to know where your priorities lie.

Don't talk to me about fucking priorities, I hear myself say.

What's that supposed to mean?

You know exactly what it means.

No, I don't.

You. You're always leaving me standing around while you flirt with other lads. You think I don't notice it, but I do. It happens every time we're out. And you get pissed off at me just for taking a bit of fucking MD?

Oh, so you're admitting it now, are you? she says. I don't know why I even bother wasting my time.

Stop changing the subject. I'm having my say now. You're always trying it on with other people in front of me, seeing how far you can push me. It's no fucking wonder that I have to get high to deal with it.

Oh shut up, Tag. She's shouting now. The argument stops for a few seconds as someone passes us on his way out of the toilets. He avoids eye contact.

Don't tell me to shut up, I shout back, once we're alone again. You know it's true. You know you're always eyeing up other blokes.

How the fuck did we get onto this again? It's always the same, isn't it? Every time we argue, you have to bring this up. You'll never let it go, will you? You always have to accuse me of something to make yourself feel better.

Just shut up, I tell her. Get out of my fucking face.

My pleasure, she says.

And no doubt I'll bump into you later, I say, acting like the little slag that you are.

Fuck. I didn't want to say that. It just came out.

Tears well in her eyes as she turns back to face me. What did I do wrong? she asks. Why are you so bitter to me all the time? I can't take it any more, Tag.

Stop with your little routine, I say. Just get out of my face.

And she walks off. Fuck her.

TWENTY-EIGHT
DUNCAN

Anyway, fuck that.

I was standing in the queue which trailed fuckin miles back from the club doors. Well, not miles, but fuck it, y'know what I mean. *Don't wanna be here, don't wanna be here,* I thought. I'd left my parka in the van, with it being summer and everything, so all I had was my hoodie. Now it was fuckin raining, and the chill was starting to sink its teeth in. Ade was up front, chatting to a group of girls. He looked a proper dick in his sunglasses in this weather and at this time of night, but I knew he'd prob use it to his advantage somehow. Tell the girls he's in a band or someshit; anyshit to appear important. Colbeck was yet to join us. He went to get some JC out bout ten minutes before like. Should be back by now, I thought. But he would've phoned if there was any bother.

Earlier, we'd parked the van up and sat around for a bit, not really knowing what to do with ourselves. Then Colbeck and Ade had spent a while setting up their phones, and my phone as well, so that we could all speed-dial one another just by holding down a single button. So, if I wanna get hold of Colbeck, I just hold down '2', and if I want Ade I hold down '3', and they set their own phones up in a similar way so they could get hold of each other and me. What they're forgetting is that Ade and me are always running out of credit, and even if I did have some, them two never answer when I call anyway. Plus, if someone accidentally sits on their phone and calls the other person, then the other person might think something is up when it isn't and then they'd be proper rattling. But false alarms aside, I still couldn't really understand why they were doing all this shit. I mean, most normal people don't have their mates on speed-dial 'just in case they get jumped', which is the reason Colbeck and Ade put forward for having set the whole system up when I asked them about it. For people who supposedly hate getting involved in trouble, and who claim they try to avoid it, trouble seems to find them a hell of a lot. I mean, look at me. I'm not hard and I don't look it either, so I'm easy pickings for any fucker who fancies a scrap. But no one's ever started on me. Well, once, but more about that later. Most people just go about their day, and if they see something kicking off they walk around it and keep their head down, and ninety-nine times out of a hundred they get on just fine. There are some proper dickheads out there like, for sure, but the majority of them aren't fuckin concerned with the likes of you and me. They're more concerned with other dickheads who might get in their way and pose a problem. And yet Colbeck and Ade have the gall to take the piss out of me and give me shit for being a pacifist – or, as Colbeck had put it earlier that day, being *benign*. At least by hanging out with them I got to learn some new words, but never enough to keep up with them.

I'm looking forward to going out with you later, Dunc, he'd gone, even though you always just stand in the corner looking benign.

Ade acknowledged him by shifting his eyes from road to rear-view and emitted a squawk.

I asked Colbeck what *benign* meant. Naturally, the prick wouldn't tell me, and Ade was too busy laughing and trying to steer the van straight. This shite went on for, like, five minutes, which is much longer than you'd think. I bided my time and, after the leaves had settled over the mockery, I went, Guys, tell me what it means, fucksake. This shit's proper annoying me. And Ade just erupted, and I mean fuckin erupted; the laughter spewed out of him and spilled down his chin like lava, y'know. And Colbeck was like, Look it up, you fucking catamite!

Luckily, we stopped at a service station mid-afternoon. Colbeck needed his fuckin carbs and Ade just wanted to roll a cigarette. His straights had run out, so I'd been rolling them for him for the first part of the journey, but he got pissed off at me, said I wasted tobacco and rolled them too fat. So me and Colbeck left Ade in the van and found the shop, and I sauntered over to the bookstand between the magazines and CDs and tried to find a fecking dictionary. I found the word and had a butcher's. Fuckin harmless. Benign. Harmless.

Back in the queue, Colbeck appeared, striding up towards me, hands in pockets, hunched over from the rain.

Let us in then, you dick, he said as he squeezed between me and the girl in front. Tell you what, I'm soaked right down to my fucking nads here.

Oi, you prick, I said. You can't just push in. Go to the fuckin back! and the girl in front of me turned round and flashed a grin at us both, and Colbeck got talking to her, and she let him in front of her in the queue, and then he let her go in front of him, so that he was in front of me. Fuckin unbelievable. I tried to conjure an insult to throw at him at the next opportunity but nothing original enough to faze him came to mind. He carried on chatting to the girl and her mates, but I wasn't interested. I was too busy thinking about Sorel. Colbeck prides himself on his ability to charm anyone in any situation though, reckons he can chat his way in and out of anything. He'd been going on all night bout how he needed to get his end away soon, to help him get over his fuckin ex and all that, and so I presumed he'd be on the pull. Not that it was any of my business like. He'd tell me all about it the next day anyway: I'd get all the sights and sounds and fuckin smells of the experience whether I wanted them or not – which, for the record like, I fuckin didn't.

The girls Ade was chatting to up ahead got let inside, so he swaggered back over, same dark glasses still covering his eyes. I let him in front of me without argument. Colbeck was there after all. Two against one like, two against one.

◎

The shit that I was scribbling in my notebook in the van earlier that day was a kinda brief history of my family like. I don't know what made me want to write it, but it seemed worthwhile at the time. My relationship with my family is very different from Colbeck's and Ade's relationships with theirs. Colbeck used to whinge about his mum a lot, but, like Ade, he lived with his rents until he moved to uni, and then afterwards Ade got the flat and Colbeck house-shared for a while before he moved in with his ex. But me, although I officially lived with my parents until I dropped out of college, I've kinda been moving round from place to place since I was fifteen. Always staying with friends for weeks at a time and that. I stayed at my parents' house every few weeks, usually when the folks of whichever mate I was staying with felt it was time for me to get out from under their feet for a bit, but my own house always felt like a place between places that were also places between places, if you get me. It never really felt like going home. Each time I left for a few weeks, something would change that would make my bedroom feel a little bit less like mine when I came back. First it was shit like posters being taken off the walls and CDs getting moved into a box in the attic. Then new duvet covers, new curtains, followed by a full-on fuckin refurb. It wasn't that long before my room was no longer referred to as 'Dunc's room' at all – it was referred to as the 'guest room', and whenever I happened to occupy it, that's all I was – a guest. I was just someone who was sleeping there for a short while and then going elsewhere. That's the problem though – I was always going elsewhere. Until I moved in with Ade, I was never in the same place for long enough to bother using it properly. I never unpacked my stuff or really filled the space that I was in.

At the time, I blamed the fact that I dropped out of college on all this shit. I wish I'd stuck it out now, cuz Sorel's got me interested in going to uni. But now, looking back, the real reason that I dropped out when I was eighteen is simply cuz I couldn't be fuckin arsed with education. Proper fuckin waste of time, I thought. I took English Lit, Political History and Art. Art was cool as fuck cuz I got to do pretty much whatever I wanted as long as I produced something towards a final project. So I filled books with sketches of different things in different styles, using ink, pencil, charcoal, whatever, just to experiment and develop my technique. I also made collages using words and images based around different themes, and I enjoyed the freedom of it. English was okay at first cuz we got to discuss shit, but I didn't want to write essays, I wanted to write thoughts. When I told this to my tutor, he told me that writing thoughts doesn't pass exams, and I thought, what a dick like, and I said, Well, in that case, maybe I should pull out of the course.

But I didn't pull out cuz there were some proper fit girls taking English, and it was a good opportunity to chat them up, obvo. Well, not chat them up as such, just argue the toss with them, which some of them seemed to like. Some of them, I stress, because others hated me with a passion. Eventually, though, I failed the exam cuz the set text fuckin bored me, and I had to repeat the whole year and pass in order to carry on with it, and a few months into take two I thought, fuck this shit, I've got better things to do. And as for Political History, they lost me in the second week with the fuckin Luddites.

After I'd quit college I alternated between sitting about the house and lying in bed. My parents got proper pushy about that, telling me to get a job and everything, and telling their friends that I was work-shy, and basically doing all they could to get me out from under their feet. When I rang Ade after that final argument, he told me to get my arse over there right away, which is what I did, and I've been there since. I've never paid rent, just given him a bit of money for bills and shared beer and stuff with him, whenever I've had it. So although Ade takes the piss out of me, and although he fuckin winds me up to the point where I want to kill him, and although I don't agree with his views on society and the world, and although I don't have his knowledge of philosophy and literature, and although he was acting like he didn't want me to get it on with Sorel, the fact of the matter is he's done more for me than any other fucker ever has, and I'll always be indebted to him for it.

When I first started living at the flat it was just me and him and we became really good friends. Not just mates like, but friends. He tried to get me chatting about shit, but I didn't have the patience – or intelligence – for it. That's why he was always lending me books and telling me that he was going to enlighten me. Talk about the fuckin educated thug.

With all respect to my parents – although they probably don't deserve my respect – they're a bit fuckin odd. For example, they sleep in separate single beds in the same room, and my dad has his own TV and DVD player and shit in the converted garage. So instead of sitting with his wife in the evenings and watching *Emmerdale* or *The Bill* or someshit they sit in separate rooms, indulging in separate pleasures, living separate lives. And that shit's fuckin weird. I mean, who fuckin does that? Get a fuckin divorce, fucksake, cuz it clearly isn't working. Or maybe I'm wrong. Maybe it *is* working – maybe this is the absolute epitome of a good marriage: they never argue, never get under each other's feet, never have to miss their favourite TV shows for the sake of the other. Ships that pass in the night and all that. They don't have to compromise, ever. All my other mates' parents, the ones who aren't divorced, they fuckin fall out all the time over the stupidest things. My mate Jay told me that his parents once had a proper tiff – a massive blazer of a row like – cuz they couldn't agree on whether to have roast taters or fuckin mashed one evening, and they didn't have enough taters to cook both.

◎

Mashed. That's what I am now, you get me. Sitting here months after, spliff in hand, looking at the stuff I scribbled and thinking about how wrong it all went and about how I should've got out of it when I had the chance. Because what's done is done now, and it won't ever change.

TWENTY-NINE

SHAUN

Fuck them, they know nothing about me.

They're just testing the water, that's all. I know it and they know it. They're trying to make me confess to something that I didn't do. Trying to catch me out. Trying to convince me that I did it. Get the case over and done with. Get a scapegoat. Fill in their paperwork and file it and sweep the truth away.

But what if I *did* do it?

No.

I didn't. I know that. You can know things without remembering them. It's called instinct. I know the sort of person that I am, and I know the sort of person that I used to be. I've done some stupid things, I've made some bad decisions, but I didn't do this. There are some things that I would never do.

I broke the 'no use of mobile phones' rule and got Tone to find out the info for me – the legal repercussions for drink spiking. He thinks I'm curious about what will happen to the offenders when they're caught. He has no idea I'm asking in case the police pin it on me. He texts me back in his typical, almost indecipherable manner: *hey m8 i askd sum1 I kno did law @uni. Up2 10yrs in nick 4 spiking evn if no attack happnd evn longer stretch if did.*

I run through what they've told me. The ketamine in my pocket. Can I account for that? Yes. Big Tony and me must've been on it that night, perhaps to help us come down from the MDMA. Or: the stuff Tony thought was MD was actually ket. They look pretty much identical. If they really did find Steph's glass, then the fact that the residue matched the stuff in our stash is explainable too: we must've used the same dealer. So, if I approach Nick then maybe he'll be able to tell me who else he sold to out of the same batch. The lack of witnesses is understandable, too – people feel intimidated, people were pissed-up and don't remember, people are covering for their mates... maybe people just weren't paying attention. There's no CCTV footage so there's no real account of what went on.

Then I realise, and it hits me hard: I'm thinking about this as if I'm plotting a cover-up. As if it really was me that did it. Is that what she thinks? Is that what my friends think? Is it even what I think? It's as if my mind is telling me two different things: firstly, it's saying that I didn't do it, because – if I had done – I'd know about it. Regardless of the fault lines in my memory, I'd just know. On the other hand, over and over it keeps saying, what if I did do it? How would I ever really know for sure?

Is that why she hasn't been to see me? Have they told her I'm a suspect? When Tony said that her family and her mates were helping her through it, did he also know about all this?

Perhaps I'm not a suspect. Maybe they were just trying to shit me up a bit. They haven't formally questioned me or documented any of it officially. If I was a suspect, for real, then surely they'd have to take a statement from me?

◎

'Have you spoken to the filth?' I ask her – my mam – when she comes to visit in the early evening. 'And have you spoken to Steph?'

'They're not called the filth,' she says, 'they're called police officers. And yes, I have spoken to them.'

I try to dismiss her condescension with a flick of my hand. 'And Steph?' I ask.

'No.'

She looks at her hand and picks a tiny fleck of nail varnish off one of her fingernails. She looks at it for a while then lets it drop to the floor. Then she looks back at me.

'What?' I say.

She stares at me for a long time, then, choosing her words carefully, she asks, 'What were you and Steph arguing about?'

I'm taken by surprise. 'Where did that come from?' I ask.

'I was just wondering…' Her voice trails off.

'I don't remember,' I say.

'They were asking me about it.'

'Who're "they"?' I say, irritated. 'The filth?'

She looks at me coldly and nods. I put my good hand to my face and wipe the sweat from the creases of my nose and underneath my eyes.

'What else did they say?'

'They were just asking how you and Steph were getting along in the weeks before the… well…' she says.

'Before the what?' I say. 'Before the accident? I've told you, this wasn't an accident. This was someone's idea of fun.'

She's silent for a while, and I stare at her.

'They think I spiked her drink,' I say suddenly. I don't mean to say it, but it just comes out, like a surge of vomit after a swig of sambuca.

'Yes,' she says, blankly.

'What? You mean they said that to you?'

'They didn't say it. They implied it.'

'That's just as bad. They're putting the screws into you. Making you doubt me. Making me doubt myself.'

She wipes a strand of hair from her face. Then I see it. In her eyes.

'You think I did it too, don't you?' I say. My voice is almost a whisper.

'No!' she says firmly. 'Of course I don't.'

'You do.'

'Shaun, why are you saying this? Of course I don't think that.'

'Would you hate me if I did?'

'Why does it matter? I know that you didn't.'

'That's not what I asked,' I say. 'What I asked was, if I did it, would you hate me?'

'No,' she says, too quickly. 'No matter what you did, I'd never hate you.'

She takes my hand. I pull it away, but she grabs it again. My eyes are welling up, and she probably notices, but I turn my head to try and stop her from seeing.

'What if they arrest me?' I say. 'There's no way of proving that I didn't do it.'

'And there's no way of proving that you did. That's the good thing about democracy, Shaun. Innocent until proven guilty.'

'But it doesn't work like that, does it?' I say. 'As soon as someone's had some bad shit said about them, then it doesn't matter whether or not it's ever proved. People always assume the worst. If I get arrested for this, then it won't matter whether there's any proof or not. People will still think I did it. Even if I was able to prove I *didn't* do it, people only remember the bad stuff. Mud sticks.'

She lets go of my hand. Bad body language? Maybe. I have to stop watching those fucking overanalytical daytime shows. 'You're getting ahead of yourself,' she insists. 'You aren't going to be arrested for something that you didn't do.'

◎

The next day, Kelsey and Pass return, and tell me that once I'm out of hospital, they want me to make an appointment at the station. They have enough evidence to charge me with administering a noxious substance under the Offences Against the Person Act.

THIRTY
COLBECK

By the time you push your way to the bar and attract the attention of the bar girl through the tangle of waving hands your head is madly spinning. The sensation reminds you of sitting on the roundabout in the park when you were younger, urging your older brothers to push you faster and faster until the trees became blurred fingerprints on the sky. At this point you'd squeeze your eyes shut and look downwards, concentrating on the blackness and motion. You'd feel the spinning from every direction, the whirlpool in your stomach, and, if you managed to resist the temptation to open your eyes, you'd feel as though you were spinning upside down, all reference points thrown off-kilter.

You realise that you're standing at the bar with a bird in front of you leaning forward showing cleavage and asking what she can get for you. You gaze on. The Guinness and ports you downed back at the van seem like such a bad idea now – why the fuck didn't you pace yourself? The bar girl is staring straight through you and she repeats herself robotically, saying, *Hello, excuse me what can I get you?* and all that shite. You say, A tap water and two Fosters please, and she complies. Keep the change, you hear yourself tell her. One for you when you clock off. Note to self: this is how you manage to spend so much money when you go out. But you know that you'll still be turning your pockets inside out tomorrow, looking for the spare tenner which you'll be sure you haven't spent. You gulp down the water and slam the glass onto the bar, then you pick up the two beers and heave your way through the mass of disgusting sweating geezer bodies until you see Dunc with his skinny arms in the air beckoning you over.

This place is rammed. Someone's spilt something on the floor, and the sole of your shoe sticks to the stain as you step on it. You push your way towards Dunc through the smell of mixed aftershaves and smoke, but suddenly some girl shimmies over in front of you, collagen-pouting with spit-slicked lips, trying to weave her flailing arms around your waist. This daft skank's dancing is more like a seizure and you step back, arms raised, drink in each hand, and take a glance at her. Her hair is pretty cool and quirky but unfortunately it's her single redeeming feature. Perhaps she doesn't get out much and so she's spent her week's budget getting a new barnet done. The ten-second evaluation flashes in your head: bad dress sense, post-preg beer gut, floppy tits like a pair of soggy Staffordshire oatcakes. Definite no-no, you decide, as you squeeze past her, shaking her off like a louse. A real Kronenbourg, you'd say. Fucking 1664 – she has the sort of side-on-heavy figure where she fucking looks sixteen from behind but when you see her face, she fucking looks sixty-four. Either way, she follows you a few steps, grinding herself against you like a pig scratching its arse on a fence post, but you show no interest whatsoever and eventually she gets the message and fucks back off under the rock she crawled out from.

'Where's Ade?' you shout in Dunc's ear, trying to overcome the generic dance beat pumping on the club's PA.

'Bog,' he shouts back.

'Take this,' you say, thrusting one of the pints at him.

'Nice one,' he replies, taking the beer from you but not sipping it yet.

You keep your eye out for Ade to make sure he's not getting himself into trouble. Within thirty seconds, Pancake Tits is back again, this time showing an interest in Dunc. He seems to be having a conversation with her; they're both shouting into each other's ears, but you can't tell what they're saying from their lip movements alone. Dunc really seems interested. Fuck knows what he's playing at. And there's no way he's bringing her back to the van, you'll throw them both out if you have to. This girl is fucking rough. Ade still isn't back from the bogs, perhaps he cracked off with someone on the way to or from. Or maybe there's a queue, or maybe he's taking a shit. It doesn't matter anyway, all that matters is that you're standing here like a spare cock in a porno while Dunc gets cosy with his new friend. Luckily, after a minute or so, he obviously clocks on that she's got a face a fucking dog wouldn't lick and that she's only after one thing. He's got himself involved now though, shown an interest, actually started chatting her up. Big fucking mistake. This is why they tell you never to feed the fucking pigeons.

Eventually you notice Ade emerge from the bogs and head for the fruit machines, so you go over to him and chat for a while. He's taken off his sunglasses and put them in his breast pocket, because it's too dark in here for him to see with them on.

You turn around periodically to check on Dunc, but after the fourth or fifth time you can't see him. The girl has disappeared too. And you think, Fucking hell, Dunc. Out of everyone you could've picked to get with in here, you picked that skank.

You walk – or probably stagger – away from Ade. You're fucking tired of this already. You want to go elsewhere. There are people all round who are irritating the fuck out of you, and you want to fucking batter a few of them but you can't because if you do then Ade'll get shitty with you later. The violence has to adhere to his fucking rules; you can't just go out and batter someone because they're annoying you. Either they have to start on you, or you have to wait until they start on someone else and then you can step in. You're not really supposed to do anything that might encourage them to start on you either, because that could be seen as goading them, which is also against Ade's code of ethics. But that's a grey area.

◎

Well, fuck them two then. Dunc resurfaces a few minutes later and announces that he's knackered and wants to sleep. Turns out he was in the shitters all along, hiding from that fucking bint that was after him. He asks Ade for the keys to the van, which is parked up at a twenty-four-hour supermarket around the corner. Then – and you can fucking hardly fucking believe this – Ade says that he's fucked from all the driving and that he wants to go back as well, to smoke a couple of joints and play some poker and that. It isn't even midnight, so you're fucked if you're going back with that pair of pussies. Fucking outrageous, it is. So you make up this lie about trying to cop off with some girl, just cos you want to linger around here to fuck a couple of these cunts up a bit. Ade says fair enough, says he'll leave the keys to the van underneath the wheel arch if he decides to sleep before you get back.

But as for you – you're blazing now and up for something. A scrap? A fuck? Another drink? There's this twat staring you out from across the room. Maybe he thinks he's safe cos he's got so many mates with him. Fucking pack mentality. But you'll teach the cunt a lesson, if you can get him on his own. See how hard he is when his droogs don't have his back. The problem is that people get lulled into a false sense of security because they think there's safety in numbers and that there's some unwritten rule where everyone's somehow looking out for everyone else. But there isn't safety in numbers at all. Not for them, anyway. There's safety in numbers for you, because it's easy to melt into a crowd if you're on your own. You are a legion of one, an undetected shadow on a youthful lung.

You mingle with the crowd on the dance floor, weaving through them so as not to be conspicuous in your solitude, but keeping near to the edge of the throng in case you have to get away quickly. You never know when something's going to kick off in one of these shitholes. When it does, it can be chaos. Gradually, you edge towards the cunt who's been staring you down. He's in a really crowded part of the club and it's hard to get to him. For every step forward you have to take two to the side, then one forward, then two to the other side, and so on, zigzagging towards him like a fucking crocodile. All of a sudden, you've got the thing dancing on you again: tyres of milk-white flab spilling out where her midriff should be. You can see the twinkle of a belly ring poking out between the rolls. She ought to fucking cover herself up a bit more, really. Dunc and Ade are probably tucked up in bed by now, and all you've got is this strange tugging sensation inside your head that seems to be weighing up the pros and cons of a potential liaison with this girl. And all you can really think is, Why not? Like, why the fuck not? Just like accepting an offer of food when you aren't hungry. Just like taking a shit when you don't really need one. Just like mashing up some cunt for no reason other than he's looked at you in a way you find funny. Like, *why not? Why the fuck not*? You let her grind on you for a bit, all the while running these thoughts round and round your mind until something in your head clicks – almost audibly, you think – and you lean forward and put your lips gently to her neck and whisper in her ear: 'Should we go somewhere?'

You take her into the bogs to give her a good fucking, without bagging up, obviously, because she's not that type of girl. There's no need to fuck her, and you have no desire whatsoever to do so, but you do it anyway for no reason other than the fact that what she lacks in beauty and grace she more than makes up for in availability. This, it turns out, makes you enjoy it much more than you expected you would. In fact, you're having such a good time with this filthy little skank that within thirty seconds you're pretty much done. You're tempted to dump your load right fucking up there, but you don't. You pull it out instead and spray it all over her top and all over her rolls of flab and all over her belly ring. Then, wordlessly, the pair of you head back to the bar – she doesn't even try to scrub the silver stain from her black clothes after she's pulled her top back down, which is the one thing about the whole affair that appals you more than her laxity. You tell her you're gonna get a drink. Ask what she wants. It feels right and proper to buy her a drink in order to complete the transaction. She wants an alcopop. She names the type and the flavour she wants but you can't make it out over the music.

But while you're waiting at the bar, sickness backwashes through you and you know you're gonna puke. It comes on so suddenly that you're amazed you make it to the bogs in time. Once in there, all the cubicles are taken, so you vomit into both sinks while watching yourself in the mirror. Snail trails of snot stretch elastically from your nostrils and you can't help but laugh between retches. There are two guys inside one of the cubicles, snorting coke or sucking each other off or whatever. They can hear you, and you can hear them giggling and whispering to each other: 'Oh no, mate! That's fucking rank!'

You turn on the taps and use your index fingers to try and poke some of the larger chunks down the plughole. Two more lads walk in and see the carnage you've caused and say, 'Eurgh! You dirty cunt!' and you consider mashing them up but before you even have time to turn round, you realise you're done with it for tonight. The fucking and the puking has really taken it out of you and you feel utterly purged, as if someone's rammed a tube up you and flushed you out. You spit in the sink then turn the taps off and push past your audience, back into the club.

THIRTY-ONE

TAG

Fuck her. The fucking stupid little slag. Shift upstairs like a storm. Where's Tone? No sight of him. Eyes red and blurred. Bar. Drink. Fit-as-fuck barmaid. Sambuca shot. Down hatch. Get me another. Under my breath: *Bitch*. Can't think straight. Can't act or walk or talk straight. Fuck this. You all right there, mate? Group of lads my age. Sound, man. Just fucked. Laughs and shoulder-slaps. Turn around. Music flows from the speakers like mud. Too loud to comprehend. Beating in my chest. Synchronised with my heart. If the beat stops, my heart stops too.

Tag?

Arms around my neck. Tone.

Yeah?

You okay, man?

Yeah.

Seen Steph?

Yeah.

You're fucked, man! Get in!

She's fucking someone else.

What?

Steph. She's fucking someone else.

I know that I'm slurring. When I try to talk more slowly it only becomes more incomprehensible. When I try to think before I speak, I forget what I'm supposed to say as I'm saying it.

Did she say that?

Yeah.

She didn't. Tag, you're fucked.

Fuck her, I shout. I'm gonna find someone else tonight. She ruins everything. She fucking ruins everything.

But why am I shouting? I think. I can't stop. It's like I'm watching myself on TV. This isn't me. But it is me. I know it's me.

Tag, leave it, okay?

Got any more of that stuff?

No, mate. We finished the last of it off.

People stare at me.

Liar! I say. They edge out of the way.

Let's get you sorted out, says Tone. Come on, man.

He puts his arm around my shoulder, a shepherd's crook, and he moves me to the edge of the bar.

Tag, he says in my ear. Tag, you're gonna get us kicked out. Don't fuck this up, okay? You know what you're like. You'll regret it tomorrow. You know that. You always regret it the next day. If you're pissed off with Steph, then stay away from her. Her mates are with her. Let her get on with her night and you get on with yours. Let's go upstairs, yeah?

No.

What the fuck's wrong with you?

Nothing's wrong with me.

Get some water, mate, okay?

Get me a fucking beer.

I'm not getting you a beer. Get a bottle of water, then I'll get you a beer.

◎

I sip at the water. Tastes metallic. Tone's gone somewhere. I look around, eyes half open, floor melting into the ceiling, and I can't see him.

I prop myself up on a cigarette machine.

Fuck this. I'm going to find her.

I limp towards the stairs. Knock into two blokes. The water I'm still holding splashes me. I try to apologise. They mutter something back.

At the staircase, I grip the rail. Step down one step, letting the rail take my weight. Then I place my two feet together before I take another step down. It could take minutes, but I remember nothing. I'm at the bottom. Lights flash around me. Toilet sign. Push through double doors. I'm inside. Stagger to sink. Support myself with my arms. One other bloke in here, standing at the urinals, cock in hand. Get into the cubicle. Seat down, sit down, head in hands.

Fuck.

Fuck.

Fuck.

THIRTY-TWO

COLBECK

You remember the girl from earlier: the memory is foggy but there's something about leaving her waiting for a drink, and for all you know she could still be standing in the same spot like a dog told to stay, and you realise that you need to get out of this place before she sees you. You're covered in spit and snot and puke and spunk and you're in no mood to socialise. You're not feeling quite as edgy having both blown your load and thrown your guts up, but the whole room is fuzzy and you have to steady yourself every few seconds as you stagger from bar to stool to pillar and back to bar again. Where the fuck has she gone? To bump into her and her mates at this stage would not make for a pleasant end to the evening's festivities. You take a look to your left – some cunt is trying it on with a bird and she's laughing with her mates and he's laughing with his mates and they're all getting along fucking famously. To your right, a group of student types are necking shots and grimacing as it hits them in the guts. Behind you someone is screaming. Not angry screaming, but *oh fucking hell I haven't seen you in ages!*

screaming. The bar staff try desperately to keep the rabble happy but it's chaos and there's no way of knowing who got in line first. Someone bumps you, says, 'Sorry mate.' You pat him on the back, slur out a drunken and drawled 'No worries.' Good display of manners, see, and you're not the sort to pick on some poor cunt that doesn't deserve it.

Sickness washes through you again. Fuck this. It's that double vodka on the rocks no mixer that you had about twenty minutes ago. Fuck fuck fuck. It's only at this point that it dawns on you that you've been drinking steadily all day since you left the flat this morning. You laugh to yourself and hang your head and dribble a bit, thinking, Fuck, definitely had too much tonight, methinks. Should prob fuck off back to the

van

Fuck!

You trip over

something and nearly

land head over shite with all these cunts making faces around you. Where the fuck's that girl from earlier got to? Oh well, fuck her. It isn't your problem. It never was your problem; the problem was always hers and hers it remains. If you see her, blank her and keep moving.

Walking to the doors of the club is like walking through a dark rotating tunnel with people stretching upwards on both sides. You stride through like Moses, and when you arrive the bouncers hold the door open and one says, 'See you again, bud,' and you want to say, 'Not fucking likely, pal!' but you don't because you can't. Everything is fucked up and out of focus. Out on the street it's stopped raining and it's warmer than you'd expected: must be your beer coat. You try to walk in a straight line but ten steps later you're on the other side of the road. So you try to steady yourself, walk along the kerb, focus ahead, one step at a time like that explorer who was lost in the Antarctic and couldn't walk straight cos there were no landmarks for him to focus on, just white everywhere, all-encompassing white; and so he had to take off his fucking wellington and throw it ahead, walk up to it, pick it up and throw it again, and so on; or so you were told once but you can't remember where or when or by whom.

This isn't working though. There's a trickling sensation of saliva in the back of your throat and it feels like drip drip drip like you're going to throw up again very fucking soon. You stop, lean against a lamp post. Are you even walking in the right direction? You get your phone out, drop it, crouch to pick the fucker up. The casing on the back is coming off a bit but fuck it. You press Menu and try to find the text option, but you can't see the screen cos of your triple vision, and, and even if you could see properly, your brain seems to have fallen out with your fingers, and so they won't press the buttons that you want them to press no matter how many times you tell them to.

You stop. Look around you. Take in your surroundings. Down one of the side streets you can hear some bloke arguing with his bird. You toy with the idea of intervening, and try and work out which direction the shouting is coming from. He's pleading with her now: 'All I asked was for you to stay sober. Next thing I know, Danielle's on the phone saying you've gone fucking AWOL. Now I've had to wake my dad up to come and watch the kids so I can come and find you. Not again, Holly. For fuck's sake. Not again.'

You half-stagger to the opposite side of the road. You can see them now, standing in a doorway. She's screaming and wailing at him and he's propping her up and trying to reason with her, saying he's sorry he shouted at her, saying will she just come with him, please, will she just come home so they can get back to the kids. 'I don't work all week for this, Holly,' he's saying. 'I don't work my fucking arse off all week for this shit.' And she sobs and he sobs too and now she's saying, 'I'm sorry, I'm sorry, I'm sorry,' and she's trying to put her arms around him and flitting between aggression and hysteria. You watch her. Even in this light you recognise the ill-fitting crop top and the beer gut; a single street light opposite the doorway she's occupying illuminates the piercing in her navel, providing proof indeed that all that glitters is most certainly not fucking gold. You feel so sick that you can barely take a breath without gagging. You turn around and start walking again before either of them sees you. And what is this you feel? Pity? Regret? Remorse? No. It is bigger and heavier than all these emotions added together. What you feel is shame. And the shame you feel makes you hate yourself, and that hatred makes you want to hurt someone, and right now you can't think of anyone who deserves it more than you.

You pick up the pace, shake yourself, steel yourself, grit your teeth and grin to yourself as if grinning will somehow make you feel better. There are three lads walking towards you from the top of the street. You watch them approaching, nod as they pass you. 'All right, youth?' says one, without stopping. You try to say 'All right?' back to them, but it comes out as fucking nonsense. You are in your own zone. You feel as though you could stride through water without getting wet. You are completely independent of your surroundings. They keep walking.

Fuck knows what time it is now. Your phone is in your pocket and your hands are too cold to take it out and look at the screen. You continue up the road towards where the van is. Or, more accurately, towards where you fucking hope to Christ the van is, because you're fucked if you can remember where Ade parked it. But this can't be right – you're heading out of town and into what looks like some kind of industrial estate. By the time you've realised this, you're standing in the middle of a car park with large warehouses looming at you from three sides, and some bins and skips with stuff spewing out of them, and a high wooden fence with barbed wire on the top.

Fuck.

You shuffle back the way you came, make it about a hundred metres, and stop for a sit down by the fence. You've shed your beer coat just as quickly as you donned it. You collapse cross-legged, hang your head, and rub your arms under your jacket, trying to fight off the cold.

And this is where you wake up, your phone buzzing in your pocket, at 5.17 a.m.

THIRTY-THREE

SHAUN

This is it then. I really am a suspect. But that's not all.

Tomorrow I'm going to be assessed, ready to be discharged. They want me to see a shrink, to make sure I'm not completely mentally fucked up after everything that's happened. If I pass that test, then they'll let me out. I'll be leaving this bed for good. I'll become an outpatient. I have to return in two weeks' time for a consultation with the neurologist. Until then, I'll be visited five times a week by a physio, and together we'll attempt to get as much use out of my damaged limbs as possible. I've lost my fight. I'll be moving back to my mam's for the foreseeable future because there's nowhere else for me to go.

It's only a matter of time before I'm charged for this. I know that. Tone came in again yesterday and we chatted it through at last. He looked nervous and he couldn't offer much advice other than, 'It'll be okay, man.' But it won't be okay unless I do something about it. What if they do charge me, and I'm found guilty? What will they do to me? What do they do with criminals who are unfit for prison? I'm only just beginning to come to terms with the fact that I may never fully recover from this. They still say I *could* make a full recovery, but that's exactly the same as saying I *could* be like this forever. I hadn't thought of it like that before. It was always a *fuck you* mentality: I'm going to get better and I'm going to get whoever did this. But now my defiance has faded and I'm starting to wonder if I'll ever know what went on that night, in that club, between me and Steph and between me and whoever else it was. Perhaps, if I'm found guilty, then I'll start to believe that I really did it. Or maybe not. What the fuck's it going to be like when I'm locked up in jail without ever knowing for certain whether or not I committed the crime I've been found guilty of?

There's been shit in the papers too. I mean, things like this happen on a daily basis in big cities, but it's pretty big news for something this serious to happen in this town. They didn't go so far as to mention my name in relation to any malicious involvement – they did, of course, say that I've been 'left brain damaged by violent thugs' and that the situation in Britain 'is now so grave that our violent crime rate is soon expected to surpass that of the rest of Europe'. But word travels fast around here and soon every fucker I've ever met is going to know about this: 'Fuck, have you heard the twist? He got beaten-up and Steph got raped, but it turns out he was behind it all along. What the fuck was he thinking? He should rot in jail for what he's done…'

Then something happens.

It's very early in the morning, a few minutes after seven. Visiting hours don't start until ten but, through a cloud of sleep, I hear my mam's voice. Within seconds she's by my bed, shaking me.

'Shaun?'

I'm half dreaming…

'Shaun?'

I open my eyes and I see her. I feel sick. What the fuck's she going to say now? What's happened that's so important? They must be coming to fucking arrest me. Oh fuck. Oh please no. Please give me more time to think about this. Another day and I'll remember. Please. Oh fuck.

'Shaun,' she says again. 'Sit up. This is very important. Are you awake?'

My eyes sting with morning grit and I roll over and try to do as she says.

'What the fuck?' I say.

'Are you fully awake?'

'Yes. Well, sort of. What's going on?'

'They know who spiked Steph's drink,' she says, 'so you're in the clear.'

The weights lift off me and I breathe lungfuls of air.

'What? Who? I'll kill him. I'll fucking kill him for what he's put us through…'

'Shhh,' she says, touching my forehead. 'You're not going to kill anyone.'

'Well, Big Tony will. Who is it? Who did it?'

'No,' she says. 'No one's going to kill him. He's already dead.'

There's no shock when I hear this. I feel numb. There's a pang of hatred in my stomach; an anger that someone else has got to him before he could be made to suffer as much as he deserves. And that's it. Anticlimactic emptiness filled only momentarily by the ebbing and flowing of the sickness that comes in waves.

'Who killed him?' I ask, shaking.

'He did. He killed himself.'

'Why?'

'Because of the guilt, I presume.'

I squeeze my eyes shut, trying to take this in.

'So how do they know he did it?' I ask.

'He wrote a letter. A suicide note.'

'Confessing to it?'

'Yes.'

'Who the fuck was it?' I say. 'Who the fuck did this? Is it someone I know? Is it someone that Steph knows?'

'I'm not sure. The police rang me late last night, but they wouldn't give me a name. They'll speak to Steph, of course, but they're not making it public yet.'

'I hate him so much,' I say. 'He's taken away everything I had.'

'It'll get better, Shaun. I promise. You've still got me. I'll always be here for you.'

I want to say, 'Well, you weren't there for me when Dad moved out, were you? You wouldn't even be talking to me now if I hadn't been fucking crippled,' but instead, I say, 'And is it all true? I mean, have the police dropped the case against me?'

'I hope so, Shaun,' she says. 'You've been through more in the last few weeks than most people have to go through in a lifetime. They're going to need to talk to you again, that's for certain. Perhaps in here, perhaps when you're at home. I wanted you to get the shock out of your system so you're ready to speak to them.'

'How did you get in?'

'I rang the ward and told them that it was an emergency, and asked if it would be okay.'

◎

She stays with me for a few hours. I feel tired but I can't sleep. This is it. Soon enough, I'll know for sure what happened. I'll know who did this and why and how. The thought of not knowing for the rest of my life was debilitating. If you know that you've done something wrong, then you can take the necessary steps to apologise for it and try and heal. But if you don't know for certain – if you think that you might've done something wrong but you can't remember to what extent you were involved – then it's worse than knowing for sure. Your mind starts to play tricks on you: running events through your head constantly in an attempt to figure it all out, only ending in confusion. Soon, you begin to convince yourself that you haven't done things that you once knew you had, and vice versa. The truth becomes inseparable from the fiction. Doubts are crueller than the worst of truths, they say. Welcome to my world. But soon, soon, I will know. The pieces of the puzzle are coming together, at last.

THIRTY-FOUR
DUNCAN

You got any skins or what? went Ade. I shook my head, cuz I knew it was best not to let on that I still had some silvers stashed in my bag. Nothing personal like, just I was so tired that I couldn't be bothered to climb over the seat and fumble for them. He'll get over it, I thought. And he'd defo do the same thing to me. Ade was like, Save us your jeb end then, and I nodded in acquiescence.

The next few days were gonna be proper hard, and I fuckin knew it. Money was a real problem for me cuz I'd already spent most of the week's dole on fags and alcohol. I had enough booze to last me a few days, and just enough cash left for a couple of days' worth of cigs, and that was pretty much it. I had too much fuckin pride to ask for any more JC from Ade. Colbeck said he was in the same boat as me now that he was signing on, but he wasn't. That fucker had savings. He joked that we might as well just mug some pretty-boy or someshit; nick his wallet for cash and plastic and then flog his iPod. At least I think he was joking when he said that, but you never knew with him. The night before, he'd got absolutely wankered and fallen asleep in a car park somewhere, and Ade had to go out at five in the fuckin morning and find him. He was acting really weird when he got back. You know that saying, where someone goes, *you look like you've seen a ghost*? Well, that's how Colbeck looked. He looked fuckin haunted: hollow-eyed, kinda manic, the appearance of someone who'd been confronted by something that had been there all along but that they'd not noticed before and would never be able to forget again.

Before we came away, we should've each figured out our minimum daily expenses: alcohol for the three of us obvo and fags for me and Ade, plus food and petrol and all them necessities. Then we should've all made sure that we could afford it. But that's too safe and too boring. Ade's money was tight too – so much so that he'd resorted to smoking roll-ups with cheap tobacco, and he'd even taken to baccy-rationing ex-con style, which meant that he had to smoke them with no filter to make up for the lack of baccy and hence the reduced dosage of nicotine. Ade had his inheritance like but apparently it was in trust and he wasn't allowed to get at the final chunk of it for another six months, which meant that in a few weeks I'd have to start paying some rent, which in turn meant that I needed to find some money from somewhere or else I'd be forced to find a job. I was starting to realise just how bad a situation I'd got myself into in the last year. I was having fun, to an extent, but it wouldn't last forever. I had to sort myself out eventually. The weight of this realisation weighed down heavier on my shoulders every day.

As I sat there in the van, I was smoking a counterfeit Marlboro – the last in the pack. When I was almost at the nub, just before the ink displaying the brand name, I passed the cig to Ade and he had a couple of drags then tossed it out the window, saying, Thanks, Little Red, your generosity is fucking overwhelming like.

What a sarcastic prick. In case you're wondering, him and Colbeck had started calling me 'Little Red' after Little Red Riding Hood, cuz of my red New York hoodie, which I wore a lot. It wasn't particularly funny or inventive, but they egged each other on and it stuck for a few days; then as soon as I decided not to wear it one day they seemed to forget about the whole thing. I didn't have to save him any of my cig, and I pointed this out, but he didn't reply so I just looked out the window and tried to think about something other than the aching vacancy in the pit of my stomach. I hadn't eaten since the previous morning, when Colbeck cooked me those beans on toast before we left the flat. This road trip was defo a bad idea, I thought. When you think of a road trip, or at least when I do, you think about all those American films where they fuck off somewhere and spend a few days cracking off with ladies and getting pissed and stoned in the sunshine. Our road trip thus far had been nothing like that. It'd been raining almost constantly, and everywhere we went was dull and grey and boring. We were down by the coast, but it was utterly banal and depressing cuz of the weather. Ade said he'd checked the forecast, but it was obvo wrong. The beaches were empty apart from litter and sewage, none of the tourist places were open, and I had to put up with Colbeck and Ade and their shit moods.

I needed a piss, so I suggested to Ade that he pull up somewhere, but the fucker just ignored me as per. Or maybe he just didn't hear me over the Fleetwood Mac CD that was still blaring on the stereo. The tinny speakers were distorting to fuck and the whole van was rattling in time to the rhythm, not that much of it was distinguishable through the muddy sound. Fuck knows how Colbeck managed to sleep through that shit; my ears felt as though they were being gone at with a pneumatic drill. No point trying to chat over the racket like, so I just sat there, staring out the window at the trees rushing past while Ade panicked silently about where his next cigarette was coming from.

Once we got off the main road, Ade unwound his window a bit and turned the volume to mute. He didn't do it out of consideration for Colbeck though, he did it so he could gyp me without having to shout, y'know.

Got a question for ya, he said, a smug grin uncreasing his face. If a tree falls in a forest and no one's around, does it make a noise?

Of course it does, I said. He knew already that I wasn't in the mood for this. I was still rattling big time from Colbeck's disappearance last night. I wanted to add something else to my sentence, but nothing came to mind, and within a few seconds I'd lost the opportunity to slip in the witty remark I'd envisaged. I picked at the tax disc holder on the windscreen while I waited for Ade's response. But he didn't say anything, so we just sat for a while in silence. When I say 'silence', I don't actually mean *silence* of course; there were all kindsa sounds going on. There was the rain tapping on the windscreen, the mechanical squeak of the wipers, and Colbeck wheezing in the back, and a whole cacophony of other noises, but Ade and I still sat in silence because neither of us said fuck all to each other. I mean, if silence exists, then I've never heard it. But anyways, I digress. All that matters is that Colbeck was stretched out in the back, hungover to fuck, while Ade drove and I sat shotgun with my feet on the dash, pen to Moleskine.

At least five minutes of unsilence slipped by before Ade told me I was wrong.

About what? I went.

About the tree falling with nobody round and still making a noise.

I sighed in exasperation. I didn't know what to say, obvo. You see, sometimes Ade will tell me something seemingly unbelievable and then go to great lengths to convince me it's true; and after successfully convincing me of its validity, he'll call me a gullible twat and say someshit like, Fuck me, Dunc, if someone said the moon was made of green cheese then you'd ask for fucking pickle with it. Other times, he'll say something which really is true, but which sounds unbelievable, and I won't believe him, and then he'll spew a diatribe of profanities and eventually he'll go and find one of his books and he'll say, Read that out loud, Dunc. Go on, read it, and his point will be proved, and I'll drop another rung on his ladder of intellect. You can't win with him either way. But I always rise to the bait and the outcome is always the same: I'm left looking like a twat.

Ade, I said, calm as poss like. If a tree falls in a forest and no one's around it still makes a noise. The snapping of the trunk makes a noise even if nothing else does. You're fuckin wrong if you say that it doesn't.

A brash response, maybe, but I was getting a bit sick of this piss-taking. Every waking hour since we left the flat them pair'd been at it: because I'm the youngest, because I never went to uni, because I'd only slept with five girls; they'd even taken the piss out of me because I've never seen the original *Star Wars* trilogy, fucksake. I've seen all the *Indiana Jones* films though. I pointed this out to them, and they shut up for a coupla seconds, then they asked me if I'd seen *Ghostbusters*. I said no, which is the truth, and they refused to chat to me for the next hour like, just to tits me off. Colbeck had a packet of pear drops or someshit, and every time I asked for one the fucker blanked me. Cuz this is what Colbeck and Ade are like. They were sent to this earth to await my arrival and then mock me at every opportunity, fair play or not. And as usual, Ade wasn't going to let this one drop.

If no one's round, then how does it make a sound? he demanded.

For God's sake, I muttered in exasperation. It hits the ground and it makes a noise. There. Now prove me wrong like I know you want to.

Barclay's tree, ejaculated Colbeck. I hadn't noticed him wake up. Then he noticed me scribbling and added, That's spelt B-E-R-K-E-L-E-Y if you wanna write it properly, knoblet.

I amended my scribbles accordingly.

George Berkeley, Ade intoned.

I turned to Colbeck. The fuck you on about? I went.

Well, have you ever actually thought about what sound is? was Ade's reply.

I'm not asking you, I snapped, I'm asking him, and I pointed to Colbeck in the back.

Colbeck repeated Ade's question.

Fine, I replied. Sound is vibrations. And the vibrations go in your earhole, and they hit your eardrum. And then there are these three bones called the ossicles, yeh, and they look like a hammer, stirrup and anvil. And they're the smallest bones in the—

So, Ade interrupted, if sound is vibrations travelling through the ear and hitting the eardrum or whatever, then how can a falling tree make a sound if there's no one's ear nearby for the sound to travel into?

I didn't say anything. Instead, I treated him with the contempt he deserved.

So in the future, think what you're saying before you say it, he goes.

I ignored him.

Ade pulled into a service area because he wanted some Rizla, and Colbeck wanted a Ginsters, and by now my urge to piss was overwhelming. There were showers too but I couldn't be arsed to have one. Colbeck opened the sliding door and jumped out excitedly before Ade had even got the handbrake on, and headed for the cashpoint to take advantage of what little remained of his overdraft. He didn't know that I knew about his ISA. I found a statement like, and had a butcher's. The document was six months old but it said he'd invested 5K.

Colbeck! I shouted as I headed into the building in search of the bogs and the shop. Borrow me a score, all right? I gotta get phone cred and once I've picked up some baccy I'll be maxed out again.

He didn't reply. He proceeded on without even turning to acknowledge me, raising his middle finger up backwards over his head.

◎

After I'd finished one of the most cathartic pisses of my life, and been to the shop, I went straight back to the van. I'd bought a pack of straights, some skins and some rolling tobacco. For the rest of the week I'd have to rely on them two for financial support, which made me feel like a twat, but that's just how it went. I expected they'd be sitting waiting for me, muttering about how long I was taking and about how I was slowing the whole operation down, or some bollocks, but when I arrived Colbeck was still away so me and Ade sat tight. Neither of us said anything. While we sat there, Ade tilted his head against the headrest and shut his eyes. I thought about Berkeley's tree.

And I'm thinking, if someone left a camcorder running in the jungle, and then fucked off miles away, and then came back to retrieve it a few hours later, then if a tree had fallen during that period of time the camcorder would have picked up the sound regardless of whether any ears were around or not. But what the fuck does that mean? Does the microphone in the camera count as an ear because it's essentially doing the same job or what? That George Berkeley's got a lot to answer for. But were camcorders even invented when he wrote that shit? I came to the conclusion that I'd best bring this up next time those two had a gyp. Cuz you've seen what it was like. If I didn't get one over on them soon then I was sure I'd go fuckin la-la.

◎

Colbeck returned, Ginsters in hand, slightly out of breath from the twenty-metre walk.

Get it? I asked.

Get what?

Twenty quid for my phone.

Did I fuck! Pay for your own phone, you dick. We all know that you spend all your credit on those *horny old granny* chatlines of yours anyway.

I went to say something, then stopped and shook my head in fuckin disbelief. Fuckin incredible. The lengths he'll go to just to get one over on me. After a moment or two I went, That's completely unnecessary. There's fuckin no need for that whatsoever. You can just about afford it. I can't. So lend me the money, yeh? I'd do it for you and you know it, Colbeck.

That's a fucking laugh! he gobbed. When've you ever lent me money in your life?

Never, I told him, But I would if I ever fuckin had any. Come on Colbeck, fucksake, man. You gotta lend it me like. Fuckin need to stay in touch with people back home y'know.

◎

Eventually, after some persistent begging from my side, Colbeck agreed to go back to the cashpoint. We compromised, see. He agreed to lend me a tenner for credit, not a score mind you, on the basis that I promised to let him and Ade have the proper beds in the van every night.

I'm not a pushover. But, as I've already explained, it's two against one. They got the two decent beds all the time anyway, cuz Colbeck was always bitching about his bad back and Ade was the designated driver, so he got it through default like. All I was doing was turning a shit situation to my advantage, and who can argue with that? I convinced him to get me some money to use for phone cred and, as a result, I could keep in touch with Sorel back home and make sure she didn't lose interest in me during the few days that I was away. Fuckin score like.

Ade, I said. Who's George Berkeley?

Ade didn't open his eyes or lean forward. He's a philosopher, he said.

What's he got to do with the tree thing?

He used it as a model in one of his philosophical enquiries.

Fair enough, I said. But what was he trying to prove? What point was he trying to make? I don't get it.

Now he opened his eyes and turned his head to look at me.

Well, he said, Berkeley had this phrase, which is *to be is to be perceived*. Only he said it as *esse est percipi* cuz these philosophers have to use Latin for some fucking reason. Anyway, it means that physical objects, like trees and stuff, have no existence away from the mind that perceives them. So the *sound* the tree makes when it's falling is only a sound if there's someone there to hear it.

I went, If that's the case, then if nobody's around to see the tree fall then the tree doesn't even exist, let alone make a sound.

At that point his face cracked into this crazed grin that made him look like fuckin Zippy or someshit. Then he went, Exactly, you fucking got it, Dunc, nice one. Now shut up and roll me a fucking cigarette. And roll it thin!

And he leaned back and shut his eyes again.

You see, at times it is possible to have an intelligent conversation with him. It's the same with Colbeck. He studied English Lit at uni, got a first, and is a fount of knowledge, a proper interesting bloke. But put the two of them together and that's it. No more intelligent conversation, unless it's for the sole purpose of winding me up.

◎

Why at the time did this convo bear so much relevance to me? Why did I write it down in my notebook so intently? I don't know. *Esse est percipi.* To be is to be perceived. This was in early June, 2003. Less than two weeks before the event that would change my life forever. To be is to be perceived. Maybe if no one saw what I did in that club then I never did it. Maybe I don't even exist.

I wish I could somehow climb back into that notebook and write a note to self. *Don't do it.*

No such luck in the real world. To be is to be perceived.

THIRTY-FIVE

TAG

An hour passes and I don't see her again. I try to sober up. Sip water in the corner of the club. I was out of order. I need to tell her that I'm sorry.

Last time I saw Tone he was with some of the other guys. I forgot that we'd planned to meet up with them. They're on the dance floor, trying it on with the birds. Most of the usuals are here: Kev, Nick, Gaz, Ando, Brian (his name's not Brian, but his surname is O'Brien, and surnames stick as nicknames sometimes), Dave, Hammo... We usually end up meeting here whether we've planned it or not. It's just what happens. I'll be out in a bar somewhere and I'll get a text from someone saying, *U out 2nite?* or something, and then I'll reply saying, *yeah, U?* and then a night on the tiles gets arranged totally off the cuff. The best nights are the ones that occur randomly – if you start trying to plan shit, trying to get people to meet in a certain place at a certain time with the intention of going to some specified place, then that's when shit starts to go wrong and the stress starts: someone can't make it; someone's fallen out with so-and-so; someone wants you to wait for him while he's at the takeaway; someone's got lucky with a bird and gone home to shag her, and so on. I've learned to go with the flow. Go out for a few drinks with Tone, no plans, and a good night will ensue.

Usually, at least. Not tonight – probably cos we planned it too much. I keep forgetting that I've fallen out with her already. That's not good. I'm not as cunted now as I was when I saw her, and I'm starting to see the error of my ways. She provoked me though: I'm not saying she's the fucking innocent party in all of this. The important thing is to find her and apologise before she rallies her fucking mates against me.

I finish my bottle of water – the third or fourth I've necked – and make my way over to the balcony. I can see most of the club from up here. I'm staggering slightly, and I feel bloated, like I could piss for five minutes non-stop, but at least I'm aware of these feelings, and that has to be a good sign. I am conscious, at least. There's a group of guys on the balcony and they say something to me that I don't hear properly, something about there being some fit-as-fuck girls in this place tonight. I laugh and they laugh too, ask my name, who do I know, that kind of shit.

It's during this conversation that I see Steph. That's probably why I can't remember the majority of what the conversation was about. She's standing at the bar, at the edge of the dance floor, chatting to some bloke, leaning close to him, speaking into his ear, all fucking touchy-feely like she always is, sipping her drink, gesturing towards his, sipping it, wincing, laughing, flirting, teasing. He's scrawny, a bit scruffy, wearing a red New York hoodie. He's some fucker that I've never seen before, not her usual type

– her usual type being tall, well-dressed, athletic, the kind of guy who looks after himself, like me – and suddenly I'm up for a fight. Don't ask me why, but it always comes suddenly. If you have time to think before you throw a punch at someone, then chances are that you won't throw it. That's something I've learned. But they're down on the ground floor, and I'm up here, so that isn't going to happen. I watch them, study the animation on their faces, watch him glance down at her tits when she leans close to him and she's unable to notice his leering.

Heeeeeeeeeeey!

A slap on my back.

Tone.

Fuck, dude, he says. Where you been?

Here. Where've you been?

I found Steph. I spoke to her. Don't worry – she's fine. Just keep away from her for the rest of the night, and by tomorrow it'll all have blown over.

I've just seen her talking to a bloke at the bar.

She wasn't talking to any blokes when I saw her. She was just with her mates.

She's fucking talking to someone! Look! I point towards the bar area but I can't see her any more – or the guy in the hoodie.

Tag, says Tone.

What?

Fucking stop it, all right? You want me to go talk to her again? Is that gonna make you feel better?

Don't speak to her. Don't say anything.

I won't say anything. Not about you. But if I find her and she's talking to a bloke – which she fucking *wasn't,* by the way – I'll just get her away from him, if that's what you want?

He doesn't wait for me to answer. He slaps me on the shoulder again and edges through the crowd to the top of the stairwell, and I see him wait patiently, then squeeze his way down the stairs, his shaved head disappearing from my view.

From the balcony I scan the dance floor, and I watch Tone weaving through, trying to find her. But he's walking in the wrong direction. Steph emerges at the opposite side, still with the guy in the New York hoodie. Tone looks up at me and shrugs. I wave my arms at him, gesticulating wildly towards the other side of the room, but he doesn't get there in time. Not in time to stop that cunt from taking Steph's hand, and leading her somewhere out of my sight.

THIRTY-SIX

COLBECK

It's the fourth day of your excursion – the middle day, since you're away for a week – and that means something momentous needs to happen. You went out for a few beers last night at this quaint little pub down by the harbour. There was no fucker in there apart from you three musketeers and the guy behind the bar and, seeing as you were the only customers, you were treated like fucking royalty. You arrived there around eight, you were half-cut by nine-thirty, and by eleven you were absolutely fucking trollied. You were feeling fairly subdued though, cos you were using the night as a wind-down period in preparation for today. Dunc's been scribbling in his notebook almost fucking non-stop for the past three days; fuck knows what it is that he's writing. He's even been saving shit like expired parking tickets and receipts to stick inside as some kind of keepsake, like one day all this shit he's writing's actually going to amount to something.

There's also the thing with Sorel. He's had his phone practically glued to his fucking hand since he got credit, and you're positive that it's her he's texting, because the poor fucker doesn't have anyone else keep in touch with. No other developments though: he's keeping his cards firmly at his chest.

London Calling is on the stereo, playing for the third time today. Dunc's in the front, supposedly navigating, but in actual fact just scribbling, and Ade's at the wheel, whereas you get the luxury of stretching out over the back seat with a blanket over you and all that, old war veteran style. You're heading across the south coast today, so hopefully there'll be some fucking knobheads from the Club 18–30 circuit out and about, seeing as it's the first week of June. The weather's been shit so far though, so all the insects have been hiding under their rocks. The plan is that tomorrow you'll start heading north again so that, by the time you get home, you'll have completed the circle. There's no scenery, and even if there was you wouldn't look at it. That shit bores you senseless. If you want to know more about a place, then you read the fucking guidebook. You can't be fucked visiting anywhere because these shitholes are all the same anyway. It might as well be called This Street, That Town. So, you tilt your head back and shut your eyes and think to the future, to tonight, because you're gonna make it count.

Somewhere on the south coast. Somewhere between sleep and dream, between the darkness and the escape from it, the thoughts pinballing inside your cranial void, ricocheting from one side to the other as your head lolls back and forth, rocked by the van's movement, occasionally coming into contact with the cold glass of the window to your right, waking with a start and dropping back into the haze again. Yeah. You're social misfits for sure, but you're the chosen rejects. That's the way

Ade and you have always referred to one another, at least ever since you can remember. Your memory isn't what it used to be. Too many batterings to the head, or maybe it's chemical. Dunc's different. He's cut from a different sort of material to you and Ade. He's a lost sheep, he can't remember which fold he came from, and even if he could remember, there's a good chance he wouldn't want to go back there. Yeah, that's it. He needs guidance. He needs to feel accepted. He's eager to learn stuff: he wants to travel around, to see new places, meet new faces, and experience new things. Soon he'll realise that it's all pretty boring, all pretty shit. The more you learn, the duller you become. The more you learn, the more you realise that there's not really very much worth getting excited about, because it's all cyclical and it mostly comes to nothing. You end up in the same place as you started, but you're just a little bit more worn down. Why? Because you've never been through as much as you have at the present moment. Yesterday, you'd been through a little bit less than you have today, and tomorrow, you'll have gone through even more. It's a gradual wearing down, a gradual erosion. The normal wear and tear of existence, the natural and expected degradation that no insurance policy will cover. It's just how it is, mate. Just how it is. So, as life's ocean has washed over you, again and again, smoothing you out and rounding off your jagged corners, it's come to pass that instead of feeling better about the onward march of existence you've in fact felt worse. You have complete contempt for everyone. Even the few people you love, the few people you care for, you feel yourself despising them at the same time simply because they're just as worthless as you are. This contempt needs no justification, no motive. It has evolved from an animal that requires tender love and care into one that needs nothing whatsoever to fuel or to nurture it. It is entirely self-sufficient. It is unselective and unforgiving. It is cathartic and it is beautiful. It is killing you.

You hate it all. The trendies, the geezers, the lairies. The pancake-titted short-skirted skanks. The beats, the bands, the bars, the generics, the fashion. The sea of euphoric waving hands across an encumbered dance floor. The DJs, the celebs, the sport. The outlook, the attitude, the whims, the drugs, the dole. You despise all things 'pop culture', all things vain, all things 'metrosexual'. You provide a kick in the face for the cult of the white trainer, a dose of iconoclasm for the worshipper of the designer-label-and-boot-cut-jean ensemble. You hate the fact that no one ever changes anything any more. Yes. That's it. All you do now is hate. Just looking at them releases vitriol into your veins. It makes you want to smash your fist into the face of every one of them. What's stopping you? It's a violent culture and violence breeds violence and violence comes full circle too and all you're doing is throwing the violence back out at them. Someone wants to look at you, to act hard, then let him stare. But if he starts anything then you're going to finish it in a thunderstorm of aggression. It's going too far, you know. It's gone too far already. It went too far long ago. The violence is insatiable. And Duncan doesn't understand what he's getting himself into.

So.

It's evening now, and you're alone again, and you're on the prowl.

You're standing at the bar trying to make eye contact with the barman when some townie guy pushes past you to get to this horrible gobby bird who's standing beside you. There's a group of fucking meatheads behind you too, getting lairy, and to make it even worse there's some slut at your back who won't leave you alone. Guess she thinks she looks good in that dress with her fat little chicken legs poking out underneath. The mirror always lies when you want it to, and this can't be blamed on light-reversal alone.

The townie cunt pushes past you again, this time heading in the opposite direction from his horrible girlfriend. These cunts have no manners. He doesn't even seem to acknowledge the fact that he's shoved into you twice, let alone try to apologise for it.

'Fucking don't say excuse me then, you prick,' you tell him.

'Oh?' he asks, turning in slo-mo and squaring up to you like a harassed football fan, shoving his face in yours. He's trying to intimidate you but it's just not washing. You've seen too much of this shit before and the mercury of your tolerance is sub-zero. He expects you to back off and offer to buy him a drink or something, but that's not your style. There's no patience in you.

So.

You stare him out for a bit then you break eye contact. You want him to think that you're scared or intimidated, because if he thinks you're scared or intimidated then he'll let his guard down and then you can fucking do him. But you need to approach this with caution because he wants to impress the gobby pigtailed cumbucket who's still lurking by the bar – he might stick one on you when you're not expecting it. Apparently no one around you has noticed yet that something's kicking off, cos people usually step back out of the way when they see this type of thing going on – apart from pissheaded friends of the guys involved in the brawl, that is, who'll usually try to intervene and break things up before the situation gets too out of hand. None of this is happening at present.

'Fucking what?' he challenges. The voice is a thickly accented grunt and the face reeks of pissy aftershave, sickly and overpowering. He's got one of those fucking stupid mod haircuts as well, and his flabby red neck jiggles sweatily on his collar like a sticky-day scrotum. His face is still in yours and you can smell the alcohol and fags on him over the stench of his cologne. Fucking repulsive.

'Oh, you've gone deaf now have you, you prick,' the geezer says when you offer no reply, and he shoves you hard into the bar, knocking over a couple of stools in the process. A few other trendy spastics have come over for a gander now that a scene's developing.

Enough of this shit, you think, and enough of this fucking 'fists only' rule that Ade's added to his fucking regulation checklist. You pick up an empty beer bottle from the bar and hit him round the side of the head with it. It doesn't break at first, so you do it again and again and again and still it doesn't break, so you twat the bottle against the corner of the bar until the glass cracks and you're left with the bottleneck, and then you stab him ferociously in the face with the jagged edge, grabbing him by the gold chain round his throat and inverting his nose with your forehead in a single motion once the flesh around his mouth is mincemeat. You throw punches at him as he goes down, and you hack at him more with the bottle, and you stamp on him and kick him in a frenzy, beating back the bouncers and other meatheads who are pulling you off him, and you stamp and you stamp and you stamp and you kick him and kick him and kick him until his blood covers your trainers and his shirt and the floor.

As the bouncers drag you away, you notice that you're bleeding from the side of your head. You don't know how it happened, but you assume someone hit you during the chaos. You're manhandled over to the fire exit where the two security guys not only eject you, but follow you into the yard outside and slam you hard against the wall, and their spit peppers your face as they shout at you to keep still and search you for weapons. You're still holding the jagged bottle-neck, laced with spiderwebs of geezer skin, and they confiscate it from you just as some of the spastic's mates burst out of the club and start mouthing off big style. Two of them are wielding bottles and they're shouting after you, warning you that they're gonna rip your fucking head off.

You, as ever, are completely calm, and as usual you're enjoying the whole sorry affair, because you know that you just have to stand up to these people and put them in their place. Next time that cunt from the bar pushes past someone he'll remember to use his manners, if he can still speak. He lost a few teeth in the scuffle; it'll be expensive to put that right. Not to worry though. It's all in the name of societal rehabilitation.

'Fucking bring it on, then,' you say, but at this point the smaller of the two bouncers is restraining them anyway. You're a reasonable person, after all, and as such the bouncers are just doing their job, which is to protect decent people like you from pricks like them. Radios are chirping with instructions from other door staff at the opposite end of the building who are too busy with problems of their own to come and lend a hand in this incident: there clearly aren't enough security personnel employed here to control the number of very pissed-off people who are scrambling over each other in an attempt to get to you.

'You're fucking dead,' one of them shouts, and you can't help but laugh, because you haven't heard anyone say that since you were about twelve. 'We'll remember you, you fucking cunt!' promises another. Both of the bouncers are trying to reason with them now, begging them to wait inside the building, telling them that they'll deal with the situation, assuring the geezers that they'll get their say in a minute. You've got a fairly decent view back into the club from here, and you can see a crowd of rubberneckers has gathered around the bar where the action took place. The cunt will probably need a few stitches in his face, and maybe a few grafts, but whatever. He'll get over it.

The bouncers get everyone back in the club. They've left you a couple of metres behind in the yard and, although no one is restraining you, you don't bother trying to escape because there's no exit for you to escape through. They force all the lairies back from the fire door, slam it shut, press their weight against it, barricade it from outside to stop them spilling out again. One of them holds it while the other piles up a few plastic beer crates in front, jamming the handle to keep it secure.

'That's actually illegal, you know,' you point out. 'If there's a fire then all the exits need to be clear. Don't they teach you that shit at Bouncer School?'

'Shut your mouth,' one of them says. 'You're in a fucking lot of trouble, okay? And unless you start co-operating immediately, you're going to be in a fucking lot more.'

You say nothing. You know when to say nothing.

'The police are on their way,' says the other. 'This is your chance to have your say about what's just gone on inside there.' He indicates towards the club with his thumb, which is almost as thick as your wrist. 'You want to tell us what's occurred?'

You remain silent.

'Well,' says the smaller of the two, 'there's clearly been some sort of problem in there. That blood all over you hasn't come from nowhere.'

'Someone got in my face,' you say, 'and so I got him out of it.'

'He got in your face?'

'Yeh. Squared up to me. Insulted me. Used threatening behaviour. So I dealt with him.'

He shakes his head. He's not buying this one bit. You could break the little cunt's neck with one hand if you wanted to, the scrawny fuck. But you don't.

'What would you class as threatening behaviour?' the big one asks.

'He shoved his face in mine and asked me what my problem was. Then I didn't answer him, cos I'm not the type to cause trouble, and he asked me if I was deaf and squared up to me and called me a prick.'

'And why would he do that?'

'Because he shoved me out of the way twice without even having the decency to say "excuse me", and so I decided to teach him some manners, which he objected to.'

'"Teach him some manners"?' asks the other one, frowning. You can tell that they're enjoying this shit.

'Yeh,' you say. 'I explained to him that it's impolite for someone of his stature to shove past someone of mine without offering so much as a whiff of an apology.'

Now they're both frowning. You need to tone down the

flamboyant rhetoric because otherwise they'll know for sure that you're taking the piss. You continue, 'And that's when he got in my face, and he shoved me, so I hit him because I was worried that he'd hit me first.'

'So, it was a pre-emptive strike, was it?' asks the larger bouncer, a hint of condescension in his voice.

'You could say that,' you tell him.

His radio beeps and he says something into it. Something about having contained the suspect at the rear of the premises. What a fucking dick. This isn't fucking *NYPD Blue*, for Christ's sake. The daft cunt obviously sees himself as a bit of a maverick, a bit of a hard man, a bit of a geezer. A bit of a fucking tosser, more like.

'What's your name?' asks the smaller one.

'Wigbert,' you say, after a moment's deliberation.

They both look at you, heads cocked, *yeh, right.*

'Well, Wigbert,' the smaller one continues. 'The police will be here shortly to deal with you. I suggest you co-operate with them.'

You weigh up the situation. You will not be getting arrested tonight. You remember reading about a soldier from an SAS patrol who strapped grenades to his belt so that if he got captured, he could blow himself up and take his captors with him. Unfortunately, you don't have this option. You look around you. There must be something you can use. Your eyes move to the top of the fence: you could scale that. But you'll need to either distract the two cunts while you do it or take them down first. If they give chase, then they'll surely catch you. At the same time though, something is telling you not to harm them. They're only doing their job, after all. Their job is to reprimand people when shit kicks off and so, in that sense, they aren't all that different to you. They don't have to be such cunts about it, but it still amounts to the same thing. The simplest thing to do would be to jump on the larger one and gouge his eyes, then kick the other one half to death. An extreme measure, but a pragmatic one, given the circumstances. Not long till the cunts in blue arrive. And then what? You'll do time. The geezer's nose was hanging off when you finished going at him with the bottle-neck.

There's only one thing to do. You clench your teeth and move towards them.

THIRTY-SEVEN
SHAUN

Dr Samantha Farnworth BSc MA PsyD sits in front of me, wide-eyed and alert, caressing her pen gently between the forefinger and thumb of her left hand. Both of us perch at right angles to her desk. This might seem like a minor detail but it's symbolic in itself, a clever design, like everything else in this room in which nothing is left to chance. It means that she can swivel in her seat whenever she needs a hard surface to press on for her notetaking exercise, but at the same time there is nothing inanimate in the space between us. She is in a grey office chair with arms and I am in a wheelchair. Of course, the set-up has been deliberately laid out in order to affect the subconscious of the subject who happens to be sitting in the position I currently occupy. It is a message which states, as bold as the fists and feet that did this to me: 'Hold nothing back. Be completely open about your feelings, for it is only if you do this that we will be able to give you the most effective treatment.'

Fucking shrinks.

Everything in this place must have been chosen for some subliminal purpose: the venetian blinds, open just enough to allow thin slats of light through, illuminating the dust; the walls, plain, unpapered, neutral; the plant in the corner; and, hanging above it, the picture of a pile of heads, a pile of arms, and a pile of legs with the caption 'DON'T TELL US TO PULL OURSELVES TOGETHER' printed beneath in stark black capitals.

The whole point of this meeting is to check my psychological profile. Basically, I have to convince them that I'm not mentally fucked-up from the attack, and that it's safe to discharge me. It's like being up for parole. Samantha Farnworth BSc MA PsyD is a pleasant character, but at no point does she say that I can call her 'Sam', and this puts me on the back foot from the beginning of the session. She's around mid-thirties: small, thin, with the posture of a meerkat on sentry. She regards me through small glasses with almost-invisible frames, and she has a very slight – but, nonetheless, detectable – tremor in her hands.

'So, you've been having some problems,' she says, with a nod of the head. 'Problems with mental trauma as a result of your injury. Tell me, how long ago did this injury occur?'

'Four weeks.'

'I see, four weeks,' she repeats. She has an odd way of pronouncing her Ws so that they come from further back in her mouth than they should do, making them sound like Rs. So instead of four *weeks*, it's four *reeks*. 'And how have your personal relationships changed in this time?' she asks. 'Your relationship with your mother and father, for example.'

'I haven't seen my dad for a while,' I say. She looks me directly in the eye, her stare so unflinching that I can't bear to return it. I continue: 'My mam has time off work. Compassionate leave or something like that. Like when someone dies. But you see—'

I consider the sentence before I say it.

'We're not a very close family,' I say. 'I wasn't too well behaved when I was younger, and I wasn't living at home at the time of the assault. I found it impossible to live there with everything that was going on. So it's sort of uncomfortable now that I have to rely on her so much. It's difficult to know what to say to them, sometimes.'

'I hear that you don't get on very well with your stepfather.'

'He's not my stepfather. They're not married. And yes, our relationship is…' I pause, searching in my mind for a synonym of *fucked-up*. 'Our relationship is strained,' I say.

'That may be a starting point for us today. To help you deal with the anger issues. From what I've heard from your mother, her partner is very fond of you.'

For a second I feel that I'm going to shout something, but the rage subsides enough for me to speak coherently. 'If he was fond of me,' I say through clenched teeth, 'then he wouldn't have wormed his way into my family and split us apart. I'll hate him as long as I live, and I don't want to talk about him.'

'That's fine,' she says, smiling. She alters her line of questioning: 'Have you been drinking a lot of alcohol?'

I'm surprised by the question and it knocks me off guard a bit. 'Not really,' I say. 'Not at all since I got attacked, obviously. I've been in hospital.'

'But you were drinking a lot before.'

She doesn't pose this as a question, with an inflection on the last word; instead, she directs it as a statement, as if she is telling me that I used to drink a lot even though this is the first time we've met.

'I wouldn't say I was drinking a lot,' I tell her.

'How much in an average week?'

'Well, I'd go out twice, maybe three times a week, and whenever I was out, I'd have a few drinks.'

'Do you know how much alcohol is the safe weekly limit?' she asks.

'Yes,' I say. 'It's about—'

'Fourteen units for women and twenty-one for men,' she says, before I have a chance to answer.

'I was actually aware of that,' I say.

Samantha Farnworth BSc MA PsyD does not seem to care, and instead seems intent on delivering a stern lecture. 'But that amount must be spread evenly throughout the week. It's no good if you say to yourself, "I haven't drunk all week so I'm going to go out now and have all my twenty-one units in one go,"' she says.

'I realise that,' I explain, 'but it's what everybody does. Everybody my age goes out and gets drunk. It's just what people do.'

'And what are you drinking?' she asks. 'Beer? Spirits?'

I want to say, 'Anything I can get my hands on!' but I don't think she'd appreciate the joke. Instead I say, 'Well, I like both, but I mainly drink lager.'

'You know how many units there are in one pint of lager?' she asks.

'Two and a half?'

'Yes,' she says. 'Slightly more than two and a half, actually, depending on what type of lager it is. Some lagers are stronger than others. So, more than two pints a day is over your recommended amount. And it's recommended that at least three days a week are kept completely alcohol-free. How many pints do you drink when you go out normally?'

'Probably ten or twelve on a good night,' I say.

She recoils slightly. I want to tell her that everybody does this, that it isn't just me, that I actually drink more than that because we usually have a shitload of shots to kick the night off and that by the time I start on the beers I've often got half a gram of charlie up my nose as well. But I don't say this. I just say, 'Not any more though. Not since I was injured.'

She shakes her head. 'It's no wonder to me that you are depressed if you have been drinking this much alcohol and then you have suddenly just stopped,' she says, still caressing her pen. I realise that, although she's been holding the pen for the whole time I've been in here, she hasn't actually written anything. Besides, who ever said anything about being depressed? I never said I was depressed, and I don't even *feel* depressed. What I feel is fucking angry. Who's been briefing her behind my back? Is this my mam's work again?

'What about drugs?' she asks. 'Have you used drugs?'

I don't see why this is necessary. It takes me back to the day when fucking Kelsey and Pass were with me in the hospital. Yes, I've taken drugs in the past, but who cares? That's got nothing to do with how I'm feeling now or why I'm feeling it. I've been crippled, for fuck's sake, and my girlfriend has been raped, and we argued on the night that it happened because I was being a fucking idiot, and this whole mess is my fucking fault. The fact that I used to take a few pills here and there or the odd line when it was offered has absolutely nothing to do with it. I want to say this, but I don't. Instead, I answer her question, politely and cooperatively.

'I used to use drugs recreationally,' I say, 'but again, not since I was assaulted.'

'Which drugs?' she asks.

'Cannabis, mostly. But I used stuff like speed and coke sometimes, too. Nothing too serious. Recreational.'

'Heroin?' she asks. 'Crack?'

'No!' I say. I realise my response might have been a little defensive, so I add, 'No, I've never tried them. Not my scene.'

'Don't be fooled into thinking so-called "recreational" drugs are safer,' she says. 'That's a trap that a lot of people fall into. They think Class Bs are necessarily safer than Class As. They don't realise the true dangers.'

Now she begins writing something. She spends around half a minute doing this, not looking up and not saying anything. I notice that her tongue pokes out of her mouth when she's concentrating.

'I'm going to write a letter to your GP,' she says, when she's finished taking notes, 'telling him about our chat today. I'm also going to put you on a course of antidepressants so that—'

'No,' I say. 'I don't need antidepressants. I'm not a weakling.'

She looks at me again with the same predatory stare.

'Nobody thinks you are a weakling (*reakling*),' she says. 'I believe that a chemical imbalance in your brain as a result of withdrawal from alcohol and drug use has the potential to cause you to have mood swings (*srings*), thereby having a detrimental effect as you adjust to the recovery process. Coupled with the stress and trauma of your accident, this could be a major setback if it isn't properly managed. When you were referred to me, the doctors at the hospital wrote and told me about all you had been through. Help is available. If someone has a headache, they take painkillers. If someone has a cough, they take medicine. And if someone is depressed, then there's nothing wrong with taking a short course of antidepressants.'

'I don't want them,' I say. 'If you give them to me then I won't take them, because I don't believe in that sort of thing.'

She sighs, puts down her pen. 'What about counselling then?' she says.

I realise that I have to toe the line. I have to keep her on my side so that she signs me off and I can get the fuck out of hospital. 'Depends what you mean by counselling,' I say.

'Coming into a room like this, once a week, talking to someone about how you're feeling, things that are angering you, things that are worrying you.'

I consider it. 'I don't mind that,' I say.

'Well,' she says. She looks at me like she wants me to say something, and I'm about to ask her, 'Well what?' but she decides to continue without my cue.

'We seem to have reached an arrangement,' she declares. 'I'm still going to write you a prescription, though, in case you change your mind, because I think that it would be extremely beneficial for you to take some medication to help you through this difficult time.'

She types something onto her computer, then messes with the printer, muttering things to herself. Eventually the thing prints, and she signs it and hands it to me.

'Thanks for your time,' I say. 'What happens next? With counselling, I mean.'

'A letter will be sent,' she says. 'You will probably be able to start in a couple of weeks (*reeks*).'

She picks up her phone and dials reception. She's still talking to the person on the other end of the line when the door opens and one of the porters enters and begins manoeuvring me, still in the wheelchair, out of the room. Samantha Farnworth BSc MA PsyD regards me with a blank expression as I recede from her view, muttering a flat 'Goodbye, Shaun' just as the porter spins me a hundred and eighty degrees and pushes me into the corridor, pausing to close the door after him.

'Man,' he says, 'for someone with such a nice car she doesn't like to smile much.'

'Maybe she's fed up of listening to other people's problems.'

'For her money, I'd listen to pretty much anything.' He pauses to open another set of double doors. 'What's going on with you anyway, man?'

'Do they pay you enough for me to tell you?'

When I turn and look back at him, he's grinning. 'Hell no,' he says. 'I'm just asking as a friend.'

'Well,' I tell him, 'let's just say I need answers to some very difficult questions.'

'About what?'

'About me.'

'Well,' he says, as he pushes me into the waiting room, where my mam sits waiting, 'I hope you find them. You're certainly the best person to ask.'

◎

Once I'm back on the ward, I get thinking about that short exchange with the nameless guy whose only duty of care towards me was to transfer me from one area of the clinic to another. The truth is that his advice was a hundred times more useful and therapeutic than the full hour with Samantha Farnworth BSc MA PsyD. I mean, why the fuck is the supposedly cash-starved NHS forking out an undisclosed (but no doubt extortionate) fee for me to sit in a room with someone trawling through information that's locked away in my head but which I don't have the key to? It doesn't make sense. It can't possibly work. But with that in mind, I think I know something that will.

THIRTY-EIGHT

DUNCAN

Where the fuck's Colbeck got to now? I asked Ade. It was bout fuckin 4 a.m. and we were sat in the van, eating claggy chips and cheese that we'd got from a takeaway in town. Colbeck disappeared halfway through the night, and we came back expecting him to already be here, but he wasn't. So we decided to sit up and wait for him. We had a few beers in the cooler like. I was drinking one, but Ade wasn't. He reckoned there's no point drinking alcohol when you're eating, because the food soaks it up or someshit, and therefore you don't get the full effects. Fuck knows whether that's true or not.

Probably getting his end away somewhere, he goes, and I considered this for a bit, and decided there was a high probability that he was correct, given Colbeck's confession a coupla days previous that if he didn't get his balls licked in the next few days like he was gonna go fuckin insane. It didn't stop the nerves twitching in my brain though: the little voices saying that he'd got himself into some sorta trouble, that he was lying half-dead in a gutter somewhere, or worse.

We'd parked up in a hotel car park. There was a sign stating that overnight parking was prohibited except for hotel guests, but we were in a secluded area, so we were clinging to the hope that we'd get away with it and not be woken up early in the morning by some fucker ushering us elsewhere. We'd taken a taxi from the town centre back to the van; it was only a ten-minute journey in the car, but too far to walk when you're bladdered and freezing like we were. We paid for it out of the money Ade won on the gamblers – he was in proper good form that night, which made a change from the usual state of affairs. Anyway, I was kinda rattling, but Ade had no phone credit and Colbeck wasn't answering my calls or texts.

Ade finished his food, screwed up the greaseproof paper and shoved it in the polystyrene tray, wiped the salt off the table, picked at his beard a bit.

You've got a bit of sauce on your face, I told him, pointing, and he got it off with the napkin.

He took out a pouch of tobacco and some skins, saying he was gonna roll a joint to put us to sleep cuz he couldn't be arsed with waiting up for Colbeck any longer. It surprised me that he wasn't concerned, cuz it was proper unusual for them two to get split up for so long, and now it had happened twice. Last time it happened – two days before like – was when Colbeck passed out on the floor in that industrial estate, and despite what Ade says to the contrary, anything could have happened to the fucker.

The last time I'd seen Colbeck was after midnight, when he was complaining about how shit the beer was at the bar where we were both standing. He said that the lager was watered down, and that if he didn't get some decent booze soon like he'd be shitting his arsehole inside out within a few hours. I asked him if he wanted to go somewhere else, and he said that he did, so I asked him to find Ade and then wait for me while I had a piss, and he said okay, but when I came back he was gone. Guess I must've taken too long or someshit. I was wondering what the fuck he'd got up to; I bet he'd ended up having a proper good night while I stood next to Ade at the gambler for most of the time, occasionally taking notes to the bar for him to get coinage.

Suddenly Ade went, What the fuck are you thinking about? I've never known you to shut up for so fucking long.

Just wondering bout Colbeck, I said. Wondering where he disappeared to and what he got up to like.

He's probably gone home with someone, said Ade. Or he's still drinking somewhere. Or he's balls-deep in some girl in the club's shitters.

Why hasn't he texted us though?

How the fuck should I know? he said. I know just as much as you do. He's probably too pissed to think about it, or he's got no credit, or his battery's gone, or he's lost his phone, or he's having too much of a good time. He'll turn up; he always does.

Maybe Colbeck did this type of thing more than I was aware. Ade knew him best, so I shut up. I watched him as he placed tobacco into the skin and spread it so there were no gaps. He always said that when you're skinning up you need to put a layer of tobacco at the bottom, then the weed in the middle, then another line of tobacco on the top. That's cuz the weed doesn't burn as easily as the baccy, he reckons, so if you don't have tobacco on either side of it then the joint'll toast and you'll have to keep relighting it. It's science, he told me. I watched as he crumbled weed into the skin, nodding to himself in deep concentration. He added more tobacco, picked it up like a delicate insect, rolled, flipped, licked it down. He took a roach and teased it inside.

Lighter, he said, meaning please Dunc could you pass me one. I patted my pockets. No lighter but I had matches like. He opened the sliding door a few inches so the smoke could escape. Then he sat back and fired it up and smoked in silence, passing it to me at intervals of three or four drags. Neither of us spoke. I thought about Colbeck, and I wondered if Ade was thinking about him as well.

Fancy game of poker? he goes after a bit.

Go on then, I said. Just a quick game before we sleep like.

Ade opened one of the compartments and pulled out his poker set.

I'm worried about Colbeck, I said, for the third or fourth time. He keeps going off on his own and it's weird. Something isn't right.

Ade looked at me and took a long drag of the spliff.

Matt's come out of a long relationship, he said, smoke drifting through his mouth and nostrils as he talked. When you come out of a long relationship, what happens is that you want to go out and fuck as many people as possible.

Why?

To get your self-esteem back, for a start, he said. He handed me the joint and started shuffling the cards, then went on: He obviously wants to do all the shit that he hasn't been able to do for the last couple of years. Such as enjoying himself and staying out and doing whatever the fuck he wants without having to answer to anyone. That's perfectly normal. His ex cheated on him, you know. So, he's gonna want to get back on the game as soon as poss to reaffirm his self-belief. That's why I needed to get him out of the flat and get him away from home. He was fucking losing his mind, mate.

I can't believe how bothered he is, I said. If this girl he was with is really that bad, then surely he'd be glad to be shot of her. Why's it getting to him so much?

Fucking hell, Dunc, he goes. Put it like this – how would *you* feel? If you were him, I mean. Let's say you're with this girl, and even though you have some fucking blazing rows and say all sorts of shit to each other you really do actually fucking love her. God only knows why you do, but whatever – it's how it is. But it runs its course and you split up with her, and you're actually pretty hurt by it, but the only way you've learnt to cope with serious emotional stuff is to pretend to your mates that you aren't bothered. Then, after all that, you find out she was cheating on you while you were together, and you can't contain the pain any more and you just fucking explode. Suddenly all your emotions and weaknesses and vulnerabilities – your fucking *humanness*, basically – is exposed. She's made a right fucking mug of you and you can't understand why she did it. You never cheated on her. So why did she do it to you? Is it because there's something wrong with you? Are you not man enough for her? Is your cock too small, or what? Who else is doing something behind your back? Who else is betraying your trust without you knowing it? Can you ever really trust anyone at all? Tell me, how would you feel if that was you, Dunc? Your mates know what she did to you, and they know how much it's hurt you, and now they know you're just putting on a front and you're truly gutted. You'd feel a right fucking daft cunt, wouldn't you?

I suppose I would, I nodded. I passed the spliff back to Ade. He stuck it between his lips and dealt two cards each. Then he handed me a pile of chips – some purple, some orange: fifties and hundreds, in theory at least. No JC was involved.

Besides, he continued, if there was any problem tonight then he would've rung us. Speed-dial, remember?

You said yourself – he might not have any credit.

Dunc, stop it now. He said he wanted to stay out so that's what he's doing. It's probably doing him a lot of good, y'know. Taking his mind off shit. Now play your blind.

What?

Play your blind, he repeated, indicating towards my chips.

Soz, I went, and I slid a chip into the centre of the table next to his. He handed me the joint and I smoked it and studied my cards: Jack of hearts and seven of diamonds.

Why did she cheat on him? I asked.

Huh? Ade looked up from his hand.

I was just wondering, why did his bird cheat on him?

Oh, he went. Cos she was a fucking skank basically.

Serious? I asked, passing him the spliff. You can finish that, I said.

Nah, he laughed. She wasn't really a skank. She was all right, y'know. She was a good laugh. I don't know what went on.

Fit? I asked.

Not bad, he said. I've told you that before. Then he pointed at my cards and went, Check or raise?

Raise you a purple, I said, and I added one to the pot in the centre of the table.

Call, Ade said, and he dealt the flop. I made a pair of sevens.

Raise you a purple, I went.

You bluffing? he asked.

As if I'm gonna tell you! I said. Just call or fold.

Ade called.

You reckon there's any chance Colbeck'll get back with her? I asked.

No way. He's proper pissed off with her. He's fucking livid. This has affected him in ways even I can't understand. And I'm no pushover, either: some people reckon you can forgive someone for cheating and get back with them and pretend like it never happened. Maybe it's true, but I think it's a sign of weakness, man. You get back with them because you're afraid of living life without them or some bollocks like that. Whereas I say, fuck them. Once a cheat, always a cheat. Fuck them off. Kick them into touch. The same goes for men who cheat as well. Fuck them off.

He dealt the turn and I checked.

Raise you four purple, went Ade.

What the fuck?

You heard, he said. Four purple. He slammed them down on the table.

You're bluffing, I went.

Put your money where your mouth is, he goes, and he extinguished the spliff and tossed the roach out of the van, then pulled the door shut.

I added four purples to the pot.

He dealt the river. Another seven! Fuck me, I thought, I'm in here. I raised the fucker all-in.

You're a shit bluffer, Dunc, went Ade. I can always tell when you're bluffing. Even when you get good cards, you're too cautious. It's in your nature. You never fucking raise all-in. You're bluffing.

Well then, I said. Take your own advice like. Put your money where your mouth is and call.

All right then, he said. I will.

He called, and I won. Fucking nice one. He was waiting on one card for a flush, he said, but he didn't get it.

Will you call Colbeck off my phone? I asked. Just to see what's going on. Or text him at least.

You fucking ring him! he said. I've told you, I think he's okay.

So I tried to call him, but this time his phone was switched off.

No luck? Ade asked.

No, I said. I hope he's all right.

Of course he's all right. He can look after himself. He's hard enough.

You're only as hard as your softest spot, I said. You told me that.

Dunc, he's gonna be okay. If he wasn't okay, then we'd have heard. The other night, for example. He got too pissed and fell asleep somewhere on his way back. You were rattling about it then as well, and again I was telling you that there's no need.

Fair enough, I went.

Honestly, Dunc, he goes. Don't worry about him, okay? He'll probably turn up here later on, still pissed up.

And I swear, exactly as he said that, there was a knock at the door, and Colbeck was saying, Let me in! Let me in, you cunts!

THIRTY-NINE

TAG

Frenzy. Where the fuck is she? She's with that guy somewhere. Who the fuck is he anyway? I've never heard her talk about any male friends. Is that because she knows I'll kick off? Or because she's hiding something? Fuck it. She's hiding something. He's fucking her somewhere. Tone's at my side telling me to stop being a dick. Saying that they've just gone somewhere to chat or to sit down or get a drink. Fuck that. He's fucking her. I know it. I know he's fucking her. I can tell from how she was talking to him. I need to leave that bitch. What's the point in staying with someone when she treats you like this? Fuck her. I don't need this stress. Not with the other shit that's going on in my life: my mam, my dad, that fucking cunt Dave and his snide remarks. Cunts with more faces than Big Ben. She should know better. Fuck her. Fuck this. I don't need this.

Fucking calm down.

Tone's got his hands on me again, holding me back, even though he knows how much I hate being restrained. It just gets the tension up and makes me want to kick and bite until

I'm let go. It makes me want to struggle with such force that the tendons tear and the muscles break free from bone. All this while screaming my throat raw: Get the fuck off me!

Tag, fuck this. I'll go and look for her again, all right. I'll go and find her.

He's chatting to some of the other guys now. I see he's got Ando's and Brian's interest. He's saying, Fucking keep an eye on him, will you? He's had some phet. He probably doesn't realise his own strength.

Fuck him. Backing out of a fight. He never backs out of a fight. He's got to be in on this as well. He must know what Steph's up to. That's why he's so keen to go down there. To tell her to cool it down a bit. To tell her that she's been compromised and that I'm fucking fuming.

What's this? Fucking Nick appears at my side, stepping out of the darkness like he's fucking teleported in from another world and slipping his hand into my jacket pocket. Just getting my stuff back, he says. Hope you don't mind.

I'd forgotten all about that. By the time I acknowledge him he's melted away; he's over there talking to Ando.

Tone's all over me again now, fussing like a fucking mother hen. You wanna sit down, man? You want anything?

A cigarette.

I don't smoke, but sometimes I get so wankered that I think I do. Tone knows this. He passes me a fag and lights it for me. I cough as the blue dust tickles the delicate membrane at the back of my throat.

I'll be back in a min, Tone says. Then he tells Nick and Ando something that I don't hear, and it makes me paranoid. I don't ask them what it was because I don't want them to know I'm suspicious in case they're in on the plan as well.

By the time I realise I've thought this, Tone's out of sight.

Nick and Ando chat among themselves. Then Ando sits down beside me, on the edge of one of the podiums on the balcony.

Come on, Big Guy, he says.

Ando's always called me Big Guy, not because I'm big but because I used to be so lanky.

I'm going to fucking kill him, I say.

Who? What the fuck's going on?

He rolls his eyes at Nick, who nods in agreement, and I feel like knocking the pair of them out.

Fucking Steph! I shout. It's always fucking Steph, isn't it? She's fucking cheating on me…

She isn't cheating on you, Ando says. I saw her earlier. She's with a group of mates. She's fine.

She's not down there any more! I say. She's gone off with someone. And don't you fucking tell me that she hasn't, because I just saw her walk off with him. And they were fucking holding hands!

Tag, just fucking calm down, all right? People're staring…

I don't give a fuck! I scream. I get to my feet, point at the first fucker whose eyes meet mine. You fucking want some? I shout. You fucking looking at something?

Ando and Nick grab me by the arms, one limb each, and pull me back down again, uttering apologies to the big cunt I've just started on. Then Tone reappears.

There's no sign of her, he says.

The words shoot out of me like I've puked them up: What the fuck do you mean there's *no sign of her*?

Fucking no shit, says Nick, looking at his phone. Sorel's in here tonight. My ex, remember? She wants to meet me.

I don't give a fuck! I tell him. All I care about is leathering the cunt who's getting with Steph. She's my fucking girl, all right? I don't like other guys with her, yeah? You fucking understand?

Come on, Tag. It'll be okay.

I look at Tone's face. He's saying this shit to me, but his eyes tell a different story. He doesn't believe a word he's saying. Neither do I.

FORTY

COLBECK

Did it really happen like that? Yes, it happened like that. It happened nothing like that. What even happened?

You stagger down deserted streets with your throat red raw from wheezing. How far did you run? Half a mile? A mile? Surely not. At the peak of your physical fitness – probably back in your schooldays – you wouldn't have been able to run that far. You've always been unfit and overweight. The side of your head is swollen. That's from when the bouncers dragged you outside and you twatted your bonce on something. Probably. Maybe you got hit again. You touch the lump above your right ear. That'll take a while to settle down. Someone once told you there's a load of nerves there. Is your jaw broken? You open and close your mouth a few times. It hurts, but it isn't stiff and it doesn't click. You check your hands: looks like you've been at a fisting orgy with five menstruating anaemics. Your shirt is torn too, like the flesh on your knuckles. That was the barbed wire plus the two bouncers pulling your legs as you scaled the fence. Is that what happened? Yes, that's exactly what happened. It happened like that. It happened just like that. It happened nothing like that.

A face staring up at you as you kick it in. A face that plants delicate kisses upon a young son or daughter. A face a wife once fell in love with. The first face regarded by a child as it opened its eyes to the world and took its first breath. A face that has a family. A face with loving parents. A face with something to live for. A face with something worth dying for. A face with laughter lines and weathered skin like cling film on a frame of bones. A face with memories, secrets, aspirations. A face with everything you ever wanted. A pleading face. A face whose rheumy eyes betray the very humanity lost on you. A deflated face. A defeated face. A face. Face it, it was just a face. Is.

Yes. Is. Is a face. A face with everything you ever wanted. A face to destroy. A face to shatter. A face to kick, tear, bite, smash, jab, gouge, bruise, claw, destroy. A face to detest. Did it really happen like that? Big bouncer, small bouncer. Sirens approaching, something's kicked off. Tip of geezer's nose hanging from cotton-thin sinews; a baby dribbling snot onto its bib. Yes, something like that.

This time you know where you're going. You know where the van is. Instinct. You know where it is. It's along here somewhere. It's along here. Looks different in the dark but it's along here. Dawn must be approaching. Birds are singing. Sing your hearts out, you cunts, if you've got something worth singing for. You would have sung for her if she'd asked you to. No. No you fucking wouldn't. The girl's a fucking skank. Cuckolded you. Naïve you. Fuck you. Fuck her. Fuck everyone. She made you sing inside. No she didn't. This is the drink talking. No one has ever made you sing inside. You met her, fucked her, moved in with her. She left you. Get it? She. Left. You. Nothing you could have done to stop her. Her choice. Nothing. Nothing on your mind but revenge. Bite stray skin from your knuckle and chew. Nothing. Nothing but loneliness. Incandescent loneliness. No one. Legion of one, legion of one. Finish this. You and you alone. Finish it. Finish it how? Kill her? No, don't kill her. Death is too good for that cunt. No. No it isn't. You love her. You hate her. You do, you love her. Beg her to come back. Beg her. No, don't beg her. Beggars can't be choosers. You choose, your choice. Choose right.

At the van, banging on the door. Light still on. You can see Dunc and Ade through a gap in the curtains. They've got a game of poker on the go. Fag ends and roaches litter the tarmac. The catarrh-ridden hacking of your grandfather's tracheotomy resonates in your ears. The way he had to wipe the mucus from the hole. The way it oozed viscous fluid like tired yellow spunk squeezed from an octogenarian prick. The way he covered it to bark orders at you. The way you wanted to shove something sharp and serrated into its dark orifice.

Bang the door. Let me in then, you cunts. Bang bang bang.

Ade's face. Just a face. A shattered face. No. Forget that face. Ade's face.

'Matt, what…?'

'Someone attacked me,' you hear yourself say. 'Someone fucking jumped me. They fucking jumped me.'

It's raining now. Fuck this. It splashes onto your face and rolls down your cheek.

'Matt?'

Fuck, it's not raining. It's not raining. Are you crying?

'Matt, come inside, okay. Just come inside, man.'

And it happened like this. It happened just like this. It happened nothing like this.

FORTY-ONE

SHAUN

They did it. They discharged me. Back at home, the TV for company, nothing to do but wait around and get flabby and stupid. Whoever did this to me doesn't have to suffer any more. It's over for him. He did what he did and then he removed himself from the equation.

It's been two days. Two days of home life. Two days of sofa-sitting. Two days of TV meals. Two days of fussing. Two days of, 'Is there anything we can get for you, love?' Two days of visits from family and friends who gawp at me like I'm an exhibit in a museum of atrocities. Two days of embarrassment. Two days of David. Two days of being too weak to do anything about it. Two days. I'm sick of it already.

Now that I have so much time to think things over, I find myself questioning my morals. After all, when I first got with Steph, she had a boyfriend. I didn't know it at the time, and we'd only been together a few weeks. She didn't tell me until the day after she split up with him. At first, I didn't really care. I thought he deserved it. The way she described him made him sound like an egotistical maniac, a sociopath, a pig-ignorant and self-righteous arsehole with an increasingly violent temper. I didn't feel guilty about it at all. But as time went on, I understood that although she hated him in their final weeks together, there must've been something there at the start – some spark or other – to bring them together in the first place. I began contemplating the fact that, just because Steph and I were getting on okay, it didn't mean that she wouldn't two-time me with someone else if she ever fancied it. It doesn't really make sense, but as soon as that seed was sown, I started to treat her as though it had already happened. I gave her so much shit about it. I didn't trust her, and she didn't trust me either. I don't blame her. I was always trying to cover up the stuff me and Tone got up to when she wasn't around.

When you cheat on someone, the first time must be the hardest. It's the one time that either makes or breaks you. Afterwards, you have two options. You might think that what you've done is unforgivable, that you can't believe you sank this low, that you have no option but to come clean and tell your partner that you've been playing away. Guilt gnaws at you like fungus on a tree trunk. It rots you from the core. Everything you see, hear, smell, taste, touch, feel, breathe, think, reminds you of your trust-betrayal. Or, on the other hand, you might realise just how easy it was. As soon as you've made the decision to stick your dick in some other girl, or to even kiss another girl, you know that you're doing no harm. As long as the cheated one never finds out, then everything's fine. You're happy, she's happy. The second time is easier. The third is easier still. Soon, there's no emotion attached. It doesn't feel like you're doing anything wrong any more, because you've convinced yourself that you aren't. But once a cheat, always a cheat? That can't be true. Some people, surely, make genuine one-off mistakes?

How do all these pieces fit together? Do I deserve all this because I'm the guy she was cheating on her previous boyfriend with? Even now, I'm not sure. I tell myself that it isn't my fault, that I didn't know she was with someone else; but then I think, well, why the fuck didn't I step away once I found out? Because she was, technically at least, cheating on both of us; she was seeing both of us at the same time, making up stories to me about where she lived and who with, and no doubt making up even more elaborate stories to him to cover her tracks after she'd spent the night with me. I must have been happy to accept it at the time, and that makes me a hypocrite, because even though I said I was fine with it, I'd constantly bring it up. Especially when I was drunk. I just couldn't leave it alone. I did it more and more as time went on.

I don't like cheats. I don't like infidelity and I don't like liars, even though I'm a liar myself. It comes from my mam's affair with David, and from what I saw it do, not just to my dad, but to me and my grandparents and all the friends of the family. No one wanted to take sides. Or, more accurately, people wanted to take sides because they felt inclined to defend whoever they thought was in the right, but they didn't want to be seen to do so, because it hinted at some betrayal of the other party. Mam blamed Dad's work for it, but that's bollocks. He worked a lot of hours, sometimes doing seven-day weeks and going on long business trips, but that doesn't mean she automatically had the right to go and find someone else. It makes me sick.

Dave with his smarmy smile and grey highlights, with his capped teeth and designer shirts. The thought of the pair of them meeting up and fucking – her just into her fifties, him four years younger – curdles the acid in my stomach. She wasn't thinking of anyone but herself when she acted like that. She wasn't thinking about me or Jodie or about anyone else in the family who might be hurt by her actions. She was thinking of herself. Pure hedonism. And then, after Dad left, Dave had the gall to move into the family home, and to pretend like he was my mate or something. He bought me a new game for the PlayStation. The stupid cunt should've realised that you can bribe a kid with gifts but not a grown man. I told the wanker to shove his fucking presents up his arse, and left the house to see my dad. We were never particularly close because of his work hours but I thought it was my duty, as the eldest child, to make sure that the poor fucker was all right. Needless to say, he wasn't. It was 3 p.m. when I got to his new place. It was a flat that belonged to a friend who's into property development. He was living in it at a discounted price until he found somewhere else. It was a nice gaff. Well, nicer than the flat I eventually got, anyway. This was before he lost his job and had to go down the bedsit route. Anyway, it was three in the afternoon, as I said, and he was pissed. Not tipsy, or even just drunk, but completely fucking paralytic. I had to let myself in through the unlocked door. He couldn't walk, or sit up straight, and he could barely talk. When he did manage to address me, he referred to me as Leonard. Leonard's his dad – my grandfather – who I've never met. He died of a heart attack before I was born. I still don't know to this day whether he was having some sort of bizarre hallucination in which he saw my face as that of his dead father – in which case I have no idea why he'd address me by my first name and not as 'Dad' – or whether he simply couldn't remember what the fuck my name was. He cried as well, and it was only the second time I'd seen him do that. The first time was when I was twelve, when he was clearing out the garage and dropped a sledgehammer on his socked foot. To me, but not to him, that episode was absolutely fucking hilarious. But to see him whimper like that now – this strong, self-assured, high-flying business type – was one of the hardest things I'd ever had to witness. This is it, I thought. He's going to drink himself to death, for sure. He didn't, or at least hasn't yet. But he's as cut off from reality as it's possible to be without being sectioned. He hasn't been to visit me since the injury. I wonder if he even knows it happened.

I've seen what infidelity does to a relationship. What happened between Steph and her ex is on a much smaller scale, obviously, but everything has to start somewhere, and I feel as though I'm fully complicit in it because – even though I was unaware of the situation when we first got together – I still stayed with her afterwards. Despite the lies I told myself and her, I really was not okay with it, and I made her suffer because of it, which is totally out of order. And, ultimately, it was an argument over precisely this matter that set it all off in the club that night.

Was it ever really love? I think I loved her. I think I still do. Whenever we argue she makes me out to be the bad one: the one who can't control his impulses, the one who's off the rails and who doesn't listen to anybody and who doesn't care if he hurts other people's feelings. I'm starting to realise now that she's right. But I can't help thinking these things.

You don't choose your thoughts, your thoughts choose you. And she did it before. She did it before and I just couldn't shake off the fact that she might do it again – and even if she didn't, the mere thought of it was just as debilitating.

It really is the not knowing that kills you.

FORTY-TWO

TAG

She must be in the toilets, Tone says. She must be in there. We've looked everywhere else. I'll go find someone to have a look inside.

When I'm pissed, it comes in waves. I feel pissed for five minutes, then I'm sober, then back to pissed. Now, though, I'm sober. My anger has turned to terror. Sheer, ice-cold, glass-jagged terror. If I see that scrawny little cunt in the red New York hoodie then I'll beat the fuck out of him, but what I want most is to find Steph, and to put my arms around her, and just hold her like that for a while and stroke her hair and let her cry tenderly into my cheek and then, after all the screams inside have faded to silence, I want to stand back from her, just at arm's-length, my hands on her shoulders, facing her, and to look down into those eyes and finally apologise for the things I've said and done. I was out of order. I can admit that. It takes a man to admit he's wrong in front of a girl, but most blokes I know don't see it that way. They think that to see the error of your ways – and, to a greater extent, to be so brave as to admit it – is to show some kind of weakness. Fuck that. It takes a man to admit he's wrong.

If something's happened to her then all that's going to be on my conscience is that last argument. When I said something to her. I don't know what I said because I can't remember the conversation; I just know that it was cruel and unnecessary. I've got a sick feeling in my stomach, as if the fallout is still inside me somewhere, still affecting my nervous system, despite the fact that I can't call to mind anything that was said. I have an image of her face though, welling up, and an image of myself, leering towards her, stumbling over my own feet, unable to speak properly. Either or both of these mental images could be incorrect. I always do this to myself. Always invent scenarios that haven't really happened. The problem is that I think about them for so long that the line between nonsense and reality becomes blurred. Before long, I know nothing. I am genuinely unaware of the truth or falsity of some event which I had a concrete opinion about only minutes before.

The fear builds. Logic flees. Where the fuck is she? If I did speak to her, then what did I say? Or have I ignored her? Is that why she's gone off somewhere? To prove a point? I don't even know how long I've been inside this place. Ando and Brian look nervous. Nick's gone off to fuck Sorel. Tone's still on the lookout. None of them really wants to be around me; they're all giving me these funny looks and I'm not surprised. I get my phone out, text her saying, *Hi babe, Where R U?* There's no signal where I'm sitting. My mind's sober but my body's weak. I pass the phone to Ando, ask him to hold it up until I get bars. He does it and hands it back when the message sends. Please reply to this, I'm silently begging.

Please. I'm hoping that this is one of those dramas that kicks off when you're pissed and then seems trivial the next day. It fucking happens all the time. The silence after the storm. Please be okay.

Five minutes and still no reply. A report flashes on my phone saying *Message Sent*. I run my hands through my hair and try to think of something else. Her face won't leave me. The broken images of tonight's antics swirl and swell in my brain and my gut. Tone's not back yet, either. He's still looking for her. Wants to put my mind at rest. Should I leave her? What's she doing right now? Who's she with? Has she already decided to leave me? I've made a dick out of myself tonight. In front of her and in front of my friends. It isn't the first time. I've got to stop doing this to myself. If I don't then I won't have any mates left. Tone gets into fights, he throws his weight around sometimes, but he doesn't do it every time we go out. I need to get a grip. I've thought this before. But then I always revert back when it's time to go out on the town again. Still no sign of Tony. Where the fuck is he? And still no reply from her. She might be deliberately ignoring me, to piss me off, or to worry me, or to make it clear she doesn't care any more. To show me I've pushed her too far this time. To prove that she's gone for good.

I've got to stop doing this.

FORTY-THREE

COLBECK

Ade smokes a cigarette as he drives. He's wearing his sunglasses even though it's overcast, and you don't know whether it's to disguise his bloodshot eyes or because he thinks it looks cool. His skin is pallid, almost blanched, and you wonder if he slept last night. His clothes are creased and ill-fitting, as if he's borrowed them from someone bigger than him. There's a sleeping bag spread out in the back, and Dunc is sleeping under it. You came back in a state and they had to put you to bed. You don't remember much. The beer paranoia. The 'what did I do last night' feeling. What you do know is that you lied, and you have to stick to the story. The key to telling a good lie is to not actually *lie* but to tell less truth than there really is. It's an art you mastered long ago.

'So what happened?' Ade asks. He's facing forwards, but for all you know he might be glancing sideways at you through his shades. The fact that you don't know for sure what he's looking at unnerves you.

'I stayed in the club,' you say, 'and some fucking lairy cunt shoved past me. I let it go cos it could've been an accident. Then he did it again, like he was deliberately goading me. Fucking trendy prick. I told him he was rude. He shoved me into the bar and went to hit me. So I fucking bottled him. I would've just walked away if he hadn't gone for me. Anyway, the bouncers got me before I could escape. I was on my own; all his mates were after me; I had no one.'

'Why a bottle?' he asks. 'Why not your fists?'

'I panicked, I suppose.'

'Good job I wasn't there. I would've kicked the cunt to death.'

Nice one. That means he's on your side. He obviously hasn't gone soft like you thought.

'It's unbelievable,' he carries on. 'I mean, what's the point? What's the point in him doing that?'

'I think he took exception to the fact that I told him he was rude,' you say. 'I told him he needed to learn some manners.'

'Fucking right he needed to learn some manners,' Ade says. 'You can't just shove someone out of the way and expect them not to say anything. At least you tried to talk to him in a civilised manner.'

He puts out his cigarette in the ashtray.

'What was he like anyway?' he continues. 'Was he a proper geezer?'

'Yeh,' you say. 'Usual type. Fucking stupid haircut, shirt, showing off in front of the skanks, acting cheeky. Right fat cunt as well.'

'Fuck,' says Ade. 'I wish I hadn't left early.'

'It doesn't matter,' you say. 'It's for the best, really. It'd look less like self-defence if there were two of us.'

'True,' Ade says. Then he lights up another cigarette – which involves taking both hands off the wheel – and he asks, 'So, did the bouncers get hold of him or what?'

'I don't think so.'

'Fucking what?' He turns to face you, his mouth straight and tight like a cut from a fresh razor.

'I think they saw me as the guilty one and him as the victim,' you say, trying to hold back a smile.

'What do you mean?' He looks forward again. For this, at least, you're grateful.

'They think that I assaulted him, unprovoked.'

'Oh, fucking come on!' he shouts, smashing his fist on the dashboard. Dunc stirs in the back. 'Did they actually say that? Did they actually have the fucking gall to tell you that you were in the wrong?'

'Yep.'

'How the fuck did you get away?'

'They had me in this yard out the back of the club. Once they got me out there, where no one could see, they fucking jumped me. They really fucking laid into me. I saw an opportunity, and I ran. I waited until they were distracted and then I went for it. There was a fence, but I got over it. They chased me but I was too far ahead.'

That's what happened. That's just what happened. Isn't it?

'What the fuck's going on?' says Dunc, emerging from under the sleeping bag.

'Nothing,' you say. 'Just a minor setback.'

'Well,' says Ade, 'where's the best place to go tonight to get some fucking lairies? I tell you what, Matt, I'm gonna fucking kill someone today, I can sense it.' He turns to face you again, but you can't tell exactly how angry he is cos you can't see his eyes. His jaw is clenched shut though, like he's anticipating a punch: like something inside him is about to explode and he's bracing himself for the aftershock.

'I'm sorry,' you tell him. 'If I'd left with you and Dunc last night then this would never have happened.'

'Fuck that,' Ade says. 'Anyone who would give up freedom for security deserves neither freedom nor security.'

You stare through the windscreen, not saying anything, wondering who he's quoting now.

'I tell you what, Matt,' he continues, 'someone has to sort this fucking situation out. This fucking country.'

The boys are back in town.

Fucking Bingo.

FORTY-FOUR

DUNCAN

Ade's expression suddenly turned sour like he'd remembered he'd left the gas on back home or someshit. He was flicking his eyes towards the rear-view more often and saying shit like, What's the deal with these cunts behind? I twisted round in the back seat to have a butcher's out the rear windscreen: there were some boy racers up the arse of the van, a coupla feet from the bumper like, pressing us to gun it more. Ade put his foot down on the pedal and black smoke poured out the exhaust, but the van didn't accelerate – it just made a painful grinding noise like shifting gears without the clutch down. Doing fifty with the weight of us three and a load of beer was obvo pushing it beyond its limit. I goes to Ade, Fuckin pull over or someshit so they can get past, but he was having none of it.

Fuck that, he went, shaking his head. If they think I'm letting them intimidate me they can fuck right off.

Don't try and speed up, goes Colbeck. Slow down instead. Show them who's boss.

Guys, I said. There's no need to be fuckin immature about it. I turned round and looked at the two geezers in the car. The driver was banging his hands aggressively on the steering wheel and mouthing shit at me. I turned back round.

They aren't happy, I said.

I don't give two fucks whether they're happy or not, Ade goes. They can fucking wait. Christ, I wish some fucker'd teach these cunts some manners.

Colbeck laughed. Then he goes to Ade, Slow down a bit more. Let's really get them wound up.

Fucksake, I said. You two never learn.

What the fuck's that meant to mean? Ade spat. I've told you, Dunc, passivity is more dangerous than aggression. You need to stand up to these types. And he eased off the accelerator a little more.

I turned to the geezers again. They were proper up behind us, revving the engine, flashing the headlights and switching them to full beam and off again, presumably trying to dazzle Ade into submission.

The fact that I was facing the wrong way in my seat made it all the more shocking when it happened. The hideous screech and the loud crunching sound that followed put my heart in my mouth. I jerked out of my seat – backwards – and ended up between the two front seats, facing the back windscreen with the handbrake wedged between my arse cheeks. I tried to get myself up with my elbows, but I was proper stuck. Ade and Colbeck were already out of the van and I could hear them shouting: What the fuck are you playing at, you fucking daft cunt? You fucking want some? That was Colbeck. It was only now that I began to make sense of what'd happened. Ade had slammed the brakes on, it seemed, just to make these fuckers crash into the back of us. I was getting myself out from between the seats when I heard that fuckin noise I've told you about before – the sound that turns my blood cold, the sound of fists on faces. More shouting. Indistinguishable screams. I got myself up onto the passenger seat and dragged myself over it, falling out hands-first onto the road. The white Nova was partially embedded into the back of the camper. Considering where I was sitting and the force of the impact, it's a fuckin wonder I wasn't seriously hurt. I could hear Colbeck shouting and I could hear a sound that reminded me of when I used to throw rocks onto the metal slide at the park when I was younger. My heart was beating to fuck. I got up and ran round the front of the van so I was standing by the driver's door, still open from Ade's departure. I could see Colbeck. He had this fuckin geezer by the back of the head and he was smashing the guy's face repeatedly onto the roof of the Nova. The white paintwork was smeared with blood and he – Colbeck like – was screaming something I couldn't make out. The geezer was silent, surely unconscious, his eyes open, his face frozen still in the contorted agony of the first few hits that'd knocked him out but with the profile becoming more concave with each impact. It was and still is the most horrific act of violence I've ever witnessed, way worse, even, than what happened in the club only a few days later. Up till this point I hadn't noticed Ade, and it was only then that I saw he was behind the Nova and from the way his body was jerking I could tell he was kicking someone to death. Now I was shouting. I was crying too, I think. Stop it! I was screaming. Fuckin stop it!

Colbeck smashed the geezer's face into the roof a final time then let him go. He fell to the floor, limp; his jaw caught the edge of the door on the way down. Ade ceased his assault too and came to stand by Colbeck. His jeans and shoes were splattered with blood. He looked like he'd been wading in it. The three of us stood in silence, me shaking my head in horror, them leaning on the Nova as they got their breath back. Colbeck's nose was bleeding – from the adrenaline, I think, cuz I didn't see him take any punches like. He snorted and spat blood on the geezer on the floor then wiped his mouth, saying, That's for you, cunt. I hope I've got fucking AIDS just so you can have it too. I don't know how long we stood there after he said it, but it was headlights approaching from the distance that sobered Ade up. Get back in the fucking van, Dunc, he said.

I didn't. I went over to the geezer Colbeck had mashed. He was lying on his back, eyes glazed, face like a fuckin tumour. He looked like a shotgun suicide. I'll never forget it. It still haunts me when I can't sleep.

Dunc, don't be a cunt, Ade said. Get in the fucking van.

The headlights were getting closer, but I couldn't hear the engine. We were on a narrow country lane and it was impossible to tell how far away they were. I turned round just as Ade was getting into the driver's seat.

Dunc, he said, leaning out the window and looking back at me. You know damn fucking well that I won't drive off and leave you here. But if you don't get into this fucking van right now, then I'm going to come out there and fucking put you in it. Now get in!

Still in shock, I walked backwards towards the van. Without a word I opened the sliding door, got in, shut it behind me and buried myself under Colbeck's blanket. I cried and shivered under it until Ade stopped the van again.

◎

Colbeck was sitting next to me when I poked my head out.

It's okay, he said.

No it isn't, I sobbed. You killed them!

Shut the fuck up, Dunc, went Ade. Of course we didn't fucking kill them. And who cares if we did? They fucking deserved it. He got out the van, slammed the door and went round the back. I could see the cherry of his cigarette as he inspected the damage from various angles.

They didn't deserve it, I said to Colbeck. Don't tell me you agree with him?

He opened the sliding door and got out without saying anything. He didn't close it behind him, and I could hear Ade going, Look at the fucking state of it. It's a cunting write-off. My parents are gonna go mental.

Now, as I'm writing all this shit down, the idea of Ade going on about the wrath of his parents seems almost funny, but at the time it wasn't. Nothing was funny any more.

Colbeck was saying, Nah, it's okay. It still drives, doesn't it? So it's not a write-off.

A write-off just means it's beyond economical repair, Ade said. It's got fuck all to do with whether or not it's technically mendable.

I got my phone out. I opened a new text and typed *this is my last bit of cred. plz call me wen u get chance. v.urgent xx* and found Sorel's number. I had my thumb on the Send button when I realised how futile it would be. I had no idea where we were other than that we were somewhere on the south-east coast of England, which placed us a good four hours from home. It was getting late. At this time, and at that distance, what the fuck could I expect her to do? What was I asking her to call me for? What could she possibly say that might help me? And what kind of person would ask her for help in this type of situation anyway? All it would do is mess her head up and cause a shitload of panic. I exited the message template without sending.

I could still hear them two. Colbeck was saying, I think you need to talk to Dunc. He's really panicking. He might go to the cops.

Why don't you talk to him?

You know him better than I do.

All the more reason for you to talk to him, Ade went. He won't go to the cops. And I don't care if he does. It has to happen sooner or later.

Fuck that, Colbeck went.

We need to go back, said Ade, after a slight pause.

Back where? Back to those fucking geezers?

No! Ade goes. Back home. We need to go home.

Colbeck argued, but Ade had made his mind up. We were heading back to the flat first thing in the morning cuz there was no point sticking around any longer. And just like that, the road trip was over. That's all I have to say on the matter, cuz to this day it still shakes me. I've learned that sometimes it's better to just admit defeat and say nothing.

A TELEOLOGICAL SUSPENSION OF THE ETHICAL, LIKE

Deny yourself the luxury of passivity.

— Patrick Jones

FORTY-FIVE

SHAUN

She stands in front of me, her eyes wet and mine filling up.

'I'll leave you two alone,' my mam says awkwardly, and she walks out of the kitchen and closes the door behind her.

Steph sits down at the kitchen table. I'm already sitting down, on one of the hard-backed wooden chairs, because I fucking hate the wheelchair and I don't want her to see me in it. As soon as Steph texted to say she was five minutes away, I shouted upstairs and asked for help as I hopped and staggered across the room. This whole meeting was arranged yesterday. Steph's dad rang and asked how I was. I spoke to him. He said that Steph was sorry she hadn't been to visit while I was in hospital. He said that she was too upset about what had happened to us both, and that seeing me would have been difficult. I told him I understood.

'Oh my God,' Steph says, breaking the silence. She stands up and puts her arms around me, crouching down. We hold each other for a long time, neither of us saying anything, just comforting one another. Her scent's different, she's not wearing the perfume I got her for our three-month anniversary. No one celebrates three-month anniversaries, I said, but there you go. It was a peace offering for something we'd fallen out about; I can't remember what now.

She's lost weight. Her cheekbones are more defined, the skin tighter and less supple, her clothes hanging loosely on her body. She seems taller too. I need to get used to seeing people from this perspective. We release each other and she looks down at me. She shakes her head.

'I'm so sorry.' Her voice is weak; the words sound tiny and frail.

'There's no need to be sorry,' I say. 'What are you sorry for?'

'It's my fault,' she says. 'It's all my fault.'

She sits down, ashen faced, staring at the cupboards on the wall directly behind me. 'It's all my fault,' she repeats.

'It isn't your fault,' I assure her. I want to stand up, go over and put my head on her shoulder, to comfort her somehow.

'It is. It's my fault.'

'I don't understand. Why do you keep saying that?'

'Because of what I did,' she says.

She bursts into tears. There's nothing I can do about it: she's on the opposite side of the table. I try not to watch, the lump in my throat swelling and my eyes stinging. I want to push her to continue, but I can't bring myself to. Instead, I say, 'I hear that someone confessed.' My voice is trembling. 'I hear he did himself in.'

'Yes.'

'So,' I say, pausing to swallow, 'who was he?'

She wipes tears from her eyes. 'I can't... I don't want to talk about it. I never would've suspected him. I never thought he was capable of something like this.'

I watch as she sniffs back the tears. Still, I want to comfort her. 'I'm sorry,' I say. 'I'm sorry, but I have to ask you these things. It's killing me, just like it's killing you.'

'I know.'

I wait for her while she rubs her eyes.

'I don't understand,' she says. 'He said that he drugged me, but he didn't rape me.'

'He's fucking lying,' I say.

'It's all my fault,' she says again.

'Steph,' I say. 'Come on, babe. Come on. It's okay.' I realise that I've spent the last few weeks being told the same thing. 'Actually,' I say, 'it's not okay. I know it's not okay. But we can work through it. Or around it. We'll make sure things get better.'

She stops sobbing for a few seconds and looks me in the eye. Then she starts again, the tears flowing quicker now, the spasms more hysterical.

'Shhh,' I plead. 'Come on, we'll sort it out.'

She shuts her eyes, as if she's begging to be transported somewhere else. When she opens them, and realises that she's still here, still in this fucking kitchen, she hangs her head, staring at the kitchen table. After a while she says, 'I can't understand why this happened to us. What did we do wrong?'

'Nothing,' I say. 'We didn't do anything wrong. Neither of us has done anything wrong. Okay? Always remember that.'

She pauses.

'I have,' she says.

'No you haven't.'

'Yes I have!' she says, firmly, staring me straight in the face.

I blink at her. There's not much else I can do. 'What?' I ask. 'What have you done?'

'The night that it happened—' she begins.

Then I understand. 'You mean the argument,' I interrupt. 'Tony told me about that. You don't have to worry about it. I can't even remember it. It was probably just me being drunk and stupid as usual. There's no need to even mention it.'

'Yes there is,' she says. And she starts crying again.

'Please,' I say, trying to reassure her but with knots writhing in my stomach like baby snakes. 'Please.'

But I'm thinking: What did we argue about? What the fuck have I done to her this time? What did I say to her? What did I accuse her of?

'Look at you,' she says. 'I'm so sorry.'

The nausea. The confusion. 'What for?' I ask.

'It wasn't him that raped me. But I know who it was. You see… you see, the night you had your accident, I was… I was…'

She sniffs back the tears then exhales, and, with her voice weak and quavering, she says, 'I was with someone else.'

◎

And the world falls away. Everything besides this kitchen table and four chairs, two occupied and two not. Sheer nothingness. My head drops; saliva slavers up the back of my throat as I choke back the vomit. I look up at her. This is it. The final thing to lose.

'What happened?' I ask, too weak and too full up with self-disgust to be angry. 'Just tell me what happened.'

She watches me for a few seconds before she starts.

'We were in Zanzibar. We fell out because you were… well, you were being a bit aggressive and accusing me of looking at other lads.'

I nod. I was always too jealous. I should've known that it would come back to bite me.

She continues: 'I told you that you were being stupid, that you'd had too much to drink, and then you…'

She wipes her eyes.

'Then you called me a slag. You said, "No doubt I'll bump into you later, acting like the slag you are." And you walked off and went to find Tony.'

I shake my head. I should learn to fucking control myself. I want to apologise, but I know it means nothing any more. My apologies aren't even worth the air the words float on. I bite my lip.

'Carry on,' I say.

'So I thought to myself, if that's what he wants, fine. Fuck him. So I went off on my own. And there was this guy, and we got on really well, and we… well… we…'

'Well what?' I say.

She stares at me, face blank.

'I'm sorry,' I say. 'I'm sorry.'

'I don't know what happened,' she says. 'I danced with him. I kissed him. He bought me a drink. I can't remember anything else. I can't remember going home. When I woke up the next day I just felt really weird. I knew something was wrong but I didn't know what. He fucking raped me, Shaun. He fucking raped me… and the only reason I know all this is because Tony called me to check I was okay.'

'Who the fuck was he?' The words come out slow and measured. 'I'll fucking get him, Steph. I'll fucking get him.'

'I'd never seen him before,' she says. 'I'd never seen him in my life.'

'What did he look like? Would you recognise him if you saw him? Did any of your friends see him?'

'They weren't there. I'd gone off on my own. He was skinny, maybe. Sort of scruffy. I think he had a hoodie on. It was dark in there so I couldn't even tell what colour it was. I told the police all this. It's not much for them to go on.'

'You must have got his name?' I say.

'Yeah,' she says, shaking her head as the tears start again. 'Probably. But I can't remember, Shaun. I can't fucking remember.'

I believe her. I really, totally believe her. 'Babe,' I say, 'the person who spiked you, have the police said he's the same person who did this to me?'

She thinks about this for a while. Finally, she nods.

'I need his name, Steph. I need to know who it is.'

She looks up at the ceiling. Then, slowly, she dips her head and meets my gaze. 'I think you know, don't you?' she says.

We stare into each other's souls across the kitchen table. Seconds pass as she chokes back the tears. We inhale, we exhale. And then we both say his name at the same time.

FORTY-SIX

DUNCAN

Colbeck and Ade were both in fuckin shit moods all the way home. Ade had barely slept at all, so he said he'd drive for a coupla hours then pull over at a service area and sleep off his hangover. Colbeck was in the front, not saying anything, just glaring through the windscreen at his own reflection and the passing cars. I sat in the back, writing in my notebook and thinking shit over.

When Colbeck turned up, when Ade and I were playing poker, I saw a different side to him. It was like the rage had expired and turned to despair. Now, of course, I realise that the rage was most definitely still there, concealed beneath the surface. He looked like he'd been crying too, but it was difficult to tell cuz Colbeck sometimes gets red eye from drinking, same as I get it from smoking weed. He was bleeding a bit from his head, and when he said he was attacked I believed him, but you could tell that most of the blood on his clothes had come from him wiping his hands. It was fairly obvo that whoever attacked him had come second.

I didn't mention the guys in the white Nova. Colbeck and Ade didn't want to hear it. As far as they were concerned it was acceptable behaviour. If someone's giving you shit, having a bit of road rage or whatever, then they should be prepared to deal with the consequences, however extreme. It was rattling me. I kept thinking, What if they're dead? What if I've just witnessed a fuckin double murder? What will happen to me if I don't say anything and the cops find out later that I was there all along? They assured me that the geezers were defo not dead, but how the fuck could they tell? How many people die from one punch? Sometimes it's not the punch that kills them, it's the way they fall. And those guys took a lot more than one punch each. I kept telling myself I'd done nothing wrong, which I suppose I hadn't. And if them two ever got caught and charged for battery or assault or wounding or grievous bodily harm or manslaughter or fuckin murder or leaving the scene of an accident then I was certain they wouldn't dob me in. Cuz they'd have no need to. In fact, it would be to their benefit if they didn't say anything. They knew I was the only witness and they knew I'd tell the truth (cuz I'm fuckin scared of the police) which would, realistically, make them appear even worse. It was them who instigated the violence. Most people would have either pulled over and let the other car pass or, at most, given a fuckin V-sign in the rear-view or someshit.

This, for me, is when it changed. June 7th, 2003. They'd stepped up the violence and at the same time relaxed the rules that governed how they inflicted it. I still thought of them – Ade in particular – as my best mates, though I don't know why I didn't suddenly say, Fuck this, I can't deal with this shit any more, and walk away. Maybe I was scared. One thing for sure is that I felt safe with them. Because the pair of them were fuckin hard as nails, and I'm certain neither of them would ever have laid a finger on me no matter what I did. I know I say shit about Ade ripping my bollocks off for the whole Sorel thing, but I don't mean it. He'd probably have got mad, but I'm as sure as I've ever been about anything that he never, ever would've hit me. I can't explain it any more than that. I've tried to explain it to myself since, but I've never got any closer to what it was that somehow set me apart from everyone else. Cuz every other fucker like me (lazy, lacking direction, uncultured) they despised. I don't suppose I'll ever figure it out.

I'd filled half the notebook in five days. That was pretty good going, I thought. I hoped Sorel wouldn't ask to read the shit I'd written. A lot of it was about her. I'd come to the decision that I was going to ask her out. I figured I still hadn't repaid her for all those drinks she bought me at The George, and I also wanted to tell her how I felt. Maybe she'd been dropping hints all along like – and they seemed to be pretty big hints that I should've fuckin picked up on. It was like she was encouraging me to make a move if I wanted to, but I'm just so fuckin shy. Course, I could've got it all wrong, and if I actually came out with it, proper asked her out like, and she said no, then what the fuck would I do? I couldn't stay in the flat. The embarrassment alone would kill me, never mind the awkwardness. And I couldn't leave the flat cuz there'd be nowhere else to go. But thinking about it and looking at both sides like Ade always says you should, I had to figure out what I'd regret more – saying something, and it backfiring, or not saying something, and then realising when it was too late that she liked me after all.

Oi, Dunc, what the fuck're you writing about now? Ade said, breaking my concentration.

Same as always, I goes, just thoughts like.

Well how's about you stop writing, yeh? You press the pen too hard on the page. The scratching fucking irritates me.

Fucksake, I said. I snapped the elastic shut on the notebook and put it in my leg pocket.

◎

It was about ten-thirty in the morning when Ade took a slip road and parked up in a service station, saying, as he jerked the handbrake up, Sorry lads, it's only an hour back home from here but I'm fucked. Gonna have to get some kip.

Colbeck had been asleep against the window. He came round slowly and nodded to Ade, then adjusted himself in his seat slightly, scratched his balls and pulled his boxers out of his arse, and rested his head against the window again.

You gonna come get some food, Colbeck? I goes. I leaned forward and nudged him.

Fuck that, he went, without opening his eyes. I'm shagged, man.

Okay, I said. I didn't wanna irritate him when he was so fatigued. I decided to go and look for a restaurant or something cuz I had a coupla quid in my pocket from somewhere, and I might be able to get a brew or someshit for that much. I wanted to ask him about what happened the other night, but he obvo wasn't in the mood. I'd heard the majority of his convo with Ade, anyhow; they thought I was asleep.

I got out the van and headed towards the building. Ade'd climbed into the back and was trying to set up the bed so he could sleep in as much comfort as possible. Might as well just leave them two to it, I thought, cuz it'd only annoy them if I hung around, if I didn't die of boredom first like.

I walked through the automatic doors and immediately smelled bleach. The place was full of families on their ways to and from places, and kids running round screaming, and people chatting over coffee, and one or two blokes sitting with laptops. There was a food court ahead of me so I strolled inside and found a vacant table in the smoking section.

I unbuttoned the leg pocket of my combats and took out my notebook and put it on the table. I was trying to decide whether or not I wanted a coffee. It was a self-service place, so there was no risk of being bothered by anyone if I decided to just sit and write. There were cans of beer for sale in a chill cabinet for £1.80 each, but there was no point buying one cuz the van was full of booze.

I took a cigarette from the packet and inspected it. I tapped it on the top of the box a few times, like Ade does, even though I still don't know why people do that. Ade says it packs down the tobacco. After a minute or so I put it in my mouth and lit it, inhaled and bathed.

I stared at the blank page in my notebook. This shit's not gonna write itself, I thought, knowing that for some reason I wanted to write something down even though I didn't know what that something was. I looked around me, searching for some kind of inspiration. All I could think of was Sorel, back at home, and about the fact that if I didn't say something to her soon then it might all slip away.

FORTY-SEVEN

COLBECK

You are losing your mind. Shaking, unsettled, sentences failing, sentenced to suffer. You've heard it said that the true definition of insanity is a failure to understand that your own thoughts and behaviours are irrational. You, on the other hand, are one hundred per cent aware that your reactions to recent events have not been proportional to the gravity of the events themselves. Fucking ergo: the fact that you realise you're so unhinged makes you the sanest cunt of them all.

That odd twitching and tugging feeling, that new kind of compulsion, is back again, budding like a maggot and burrowing its way outwards, through your core, from deep inside you. It's the sort of anxious, excited, thrilling feeling that tells people to stick their fingers into electric sockets or shine TV remote control units into their eyes or poke sharpened pencils into their ear canals – just to see what will happen. Will it hurt? Will you die? Who fucking knows? And now, it's telling you to get in touch with her, arrange to meet up, see if she agrees, see how it makes you feel. See what it makes you fucking *do*. You're on the way home now, and maybe it's that metaphor of cyclicality again, the gimmick of things having physically come full circle and of wanting to reconcile the symbolic with the real. Or fucking something along those lines, anyway. And so, just like that, you decide it's time to convene with her. The decision appears in your head like someone else put it there. When you text her, she agrees immediately. From a purely practical perspective, which is the way she tends to think about life, there are things to sort out. Money things, for example. There are things of yours that she has, and you want them back. There are things you need to say to each other that could and should only be said face to face.

You have a brief text conversation with her and sort out a meeting, and she still has the fucking audacity to put a fucking kiss at the end of her message.

◎

The venue for this impromptu rendezvous is a cafe around the corner from the post office. That means you can knob two skanks with one johnny. You have to go to the post office anyway, to collect your social welfare allowance from the cunts who pay you to sit on your arse all day, so you might as well meet her somewhere nearby. You've already had to get one bus and don't want to have to get a second just to meet her. Sitting on public transport with batty old cunts and the stench of piss and tweed is not your idea of fun.

You get there and order a coffee, and the waiter tells you he'll bring it over.

'I asked for it black,' you say, when he places it on the table in front of you.

'The cream is complimentary,' he says. 'No extra charge.'

◎

Ten minutes later you notice her over the road. You study her through the dirty glass, feeling very much the Baudelairean flâneur, as she looks left and right, her hair blowing in her face, checking that it's safe to cross. She scurries across the road and onto the pavement, pushes the heavy door, struggles with it a bit, before she notices that it says PULL. You smile despite yourself, memories tugging at your sleeve. She surveys her surroundings once inside, unsure as to whether or not you've kept the appointment. Your eyes snag on hers as her gaze sweeps the room, seeking a face she recognises. You don't wave and neither does she. She goes to the counter and orders something. Probably a chai latte unless her tastes have changed since you parted company. She pays and then she's walking towards you.

'Matt,' she says. 'How are you? Thank you for meeting me.'

'Like I said,' you tell her, 'there are things we need to sort out.'

'Yes, there are.'

You take a sip of bitter coffee, and she sits down opposite you.

'You've lost weight,' she says. 'You look good.'

This pleases you, because you happened to notice immediately that she's put weight on. You're shit at guessing things like this, but you'd say it's at least half a stone, maybe more. And it's all gone to her jowls, the poor cow: her delicate jawline is hidden beneath a quilt of quivering flab.

You want to point this out, to confirm the decline that she's surely privy to already, but you don't. It's nothing to do with wanting to be polite – it's all to do with wanting to appear less spiteful towards her than you are. Your silence is worth a thousand crippling insults, and she knows it. Under the table your leg is jittering, and the vibrations rattle the spoon in the saucer on the table.

Her drink arrives. A chai latte. The saucer chinks as the waiter puts it down on the table. You stare at the liquid as it settles, and you think of revenge. Fucking cyanide, maybe, or Rohypnol.

No. You push the thought from your mind. That's not right.

'So,' she says, with a condescending demeanour that would better suit a financial advisor, 'we're in arrears on the flat. I didn't realise at first, because I was still paying my half. Then I got a letter from a debt collection agency. So I was thinking, if you'd just write a cheque now for the money you owe, then we might get our deposits back, which I'm sure we—'

'You cunt.' The epithet cuts off her tongue.

'What do you mean?' she asks, after a confused silence that makes your cock twitch.

'Fuck you. I'm not paying a penny.' Your mouth is a punctured sewage vessel and your words are the raw filth that spews out of it. There's no resistance and no filter. Your response to her is purely reflexive.

'You can't just come out with things like that, Matt,' she says. 'This is supposed to be a civil conversation.'

'And that's exactly what it is. I'm telling you civilly, face to face, that I'm not prepared to pay.'

'You can't do that.'

'Yes, I can.'

She shakes her head, her gob half open, her gums pink and wet like slabs of raw steak.

'And how can you justify that?' she asks.

'Because it was your decision to leave. You entered into a contract and you are the one that dishonoured it. As far as I'm concerned, all of the outstanding payments are your responsibility.'

She looks at you disgustedly. She still hasn't touched her drink. You pick up your cup but notice your hand is shaking. You take a quick sip, which burns the roof of your mouth, and place the cup in its saucer.

'I can't believe it,' she says. 'I wanted to be mature about this; I wanted to get everything sorted. If I have to take you to court then I'll do it, Matt.'

'Will you really?' you say, grinning. 'Take me to court. See if I care. It's just a day out as far as I'm concerned. A walk in the park. You'd never win, they'd tell you to fuck off. No one likes a cheat, do they?'

'What?' She's losing her armour.

'They'd ask why we split up. And then I'd tell them that, one day, you announced that you were leaving and left me to deal with everything myself. And the reason that you decided to leave? Because you were seeing someone else.' You take another sip. You're immune to the hot coffee now.

'Getting involved with you was the biggest mistake I've ever made,' she says. 'You know what? I'm glad I cheated on you. Because you deserved it. You never treated me with any respect. He's more of a man than you ever were. He doesn't have to put other people down just to make himself look big. He doesn't have to bully people and manipulate them to get them on his side. You should be ashamed of yourself. You're absolutely pathetic.'

You laugh. She might be telling the truth, but she doesn't look like she believes it. Inside, though, you don't feel like laughing. You feel like smashing something. But you smirk instead, like a stupid schoolboy being told off in front of his friends.

'So I take it you're still with him,' you say. 'I hope you're very happy together. I'm sure that soon enough he'll learn the error of his ways, the poor cunt.'

'Everyone is laughing at you, Matt,' she says. Her face is flushed now, and her eyes are manic: she's really getting into it. 'Just look at the state of you. Yeah, you've lost weight, but you're still fat. You have a degree that you can't afford to pay off, and where's it got you? A job in a call centre! Jesus Christ – talk about the modern success story. And it gets better, doesn't it? Apparently, you're unemployed now. Word gets around, Matt. People have seen you. Pathetic!'

'You're repeating yourself now, Steph,' you say. 'I mean, I know you have a limited vocabulary and all that but—'

'Just fucking look at you!' she screams. Everyone is staring now. 'You're a complete loser! How many friends do you have left? Like, real friends? One, maybe? Two at most. Even your own parents can't stand you. You're a fat, bitter, unemployed, *unemployable* piece of shit. You're a failure.'

You blink. What can you say to her? Think. Fucking think.

She goes on. 'I hate you, Matt. But guess what? I left you for someone else and we're all having a great time without you. Him and his mates all think you're just as pathetic as

I do. We're all laughing at you! All of us. You're a complete fucking joke. I'm not scared of you, and neither is he. What are you going to do, you fucking loser? What the fuck are you going to do?'

A beat. No words come.

'Just as I thought,' she says. 'You're not going to do anything, because you know what I'm saying is true.'

Still, you have nothing to say.

'I've had enough of this,' she says. 'I'm going. Have a nice life.' She stands up and storms out, her untouched drink still shimmering in its mug.

FORTY-EIGHT

TAG

Tone's making no sense. She's in the toilets, he's saying. Man, she's in the fucking toilets. He's downstairs, with her, and I'm on the balcony. He's talking to me on my mobile and I'm pacing around with my finger jammed in my free ear.

So that's good, then, I'm thinking. He's found her.

She's in here, Tag, he says. She's unconscious.

She's passed out?

Yeah.

She pissed?

I don't know, man, it doesn't look good.

What the fuck?

She's...

He pauses.

She's what?

Something's not right, he says, eventually.

I lean over the balcony, listening to half of Tone's conversation with someone else.

Where the fuck are you? I interrupt.

Still in the bogs.

I'm on my way now.

I take the stairs two at a time.

Tag. Fucking don't, he says.

I'm coming. Just tell me what the fuck's going on.

Something's not right, okay? he says again.

I reach the bottom of the stairs. I've got this feeling. I think it's dread. Push my way past people. I'm lost. Where the fuck are the toilets? I see neon lights on the far side of the room – ladies and gents – and push my way through, keeping to the perimeter where possible so I don't get caught up in the dance floor tangle.

Tone, I say. Where the fuck are you?

Toilets, he says. I told you already.

Yeah, but which ones?

Downstairs. By the bar. The girls'.

I'm coming in, I say.

Tag, wait—

I cancel the call and push open the doors to the corridor. I'm just outside the gents' – the place I last spoke to Steph, if the argument actually happened – but I keep going towards the other door, the ladies', at the far end. I put my phone in my jacket pocket and my hand brushes against something: feels like a baggy. A bit of Nick's stash is still in there and I'd better get it back to him before he fucking thinks I've done it on purpose. But it has to wait. For once Steph is more important than drugs, and if that'd been the case all along then none of this shit would've happened. I'll see Nick later. I zip up my pocket and shove open the door to the bogs. You're going in the wrong one, mate, someone shouts. Friendly advice that I ignore. The door hits the wall and bounces back. I walk into the sterile stench of disinfectant and perfume, the chemical headache of flickering strip lights.

At first, the place looks empty. There's no one at the sinks or the mirrors, and all the cubicles are open-doored and vacant. I head round the corner. More cubicles. My footsteps echo and I hear Tone's inimitable drawl.

He's kneeling down inside the far one. There's a girl in there with him, also crouching down, someone I've never seen before.

Tone, I say. He turns suddenly. What the fuck's going on?

I don't know, he says.

I step towards the girl and she stands and moves aside for me.

Steph.

She's sprawled on the floor, comatose. Her top is ripped, exposing her bra. Her underwear is half on and half off, hanging loosely on one leg. There's a small crust of dried spittle in the left-hand corner of her mouth.

I found her like this, says the girl.

What the fuck's happened to her? I'm shouting, and the acoustics of the empty bathroom make my voice sound even louder.

We don't know, says Tone.

I get my arms under hers, try and sit her up a bit.

Don't move her, Tone says. You're not meant to move people when they're unconscious.

We could put her in the recovery position, the girl suggests.

I ask the girl if she knows Steph. No, she says.

What the fuck's happened to her? I ask again, to no one in particular. It's that fucking guy she was with! I fucking told you, Tone. I'm gonna fucking kill the cunt!

Tag! Tone shouts.

It makes me jump.

You're not helping, he says. Let's get her awake first, okay? Then we can get whoever's responsible.

Tone and the girl roll Steph over onto her side. I crouch down again to help them. None of us has more than a vague idea of what the recovery position is. We bend one leg and cross it over the other, move her right arm and slide it under her face.

Fuck, I say.

What?

You're meant to check the airways first.

So we roll her the other way, onto her back. Her chest's moving – she's breathing quietly and regularly, so calmly that it's difficult to notice without watching and listening intently. Tone's taken his jacket off and put it over her. I open her mouth and stick my fingers inside, not sure what I'm meant to be feeling for. It feels clear. We roll her onto her side again.

I'll go and get someone, says the girl.

◎

A couple of minutes later she's back with a middle-aged woman who's wearing a security uniform.

I'm Lucy, the woman says. As soon as she sees Steph, she asks, Has anyone called an ambulance?

Tone and me look at each other, and both take our mobiles out.

Can I just ask you lads to move out of the cubicle? she says.

We go and stand with the girl a few metres away. Tone's on the phone making a 999 call.

What's her name? the woman asks.

Steph, I tell her.

She crouches down.

Steph? she says. Steph? Can you hear me?

She turns to the three of us.

Has she taken anything tonight? she asks.

No, I say.

Are you sure? It's very important that you tell the truth. There's no point trying to protect her.

She hasn't taken anything, I say. She hates drugs. She doesn't even smoke.

Do you know how much she's had to drink?

No.

She turns back to Steph, still vacant.

Ambulance is on its way, mate, says Tone.

Is she going to be okay? I ask.

Lucy looks up. She'll be fine, she says.

Me, Tone and the girl stand in silence, watching.

Please wake up, Steph, I think. Please wake up.

Tone lights up a cigarette.

Could one of you go to the bar and get a couple of pints of water? Lucy asks.

I'll go, says the girl.

Take some money, I say, handing her a tenner. They charge for water in here.

She's gonna be all right, isn't she? I ask Tone.

She'll be fine, mate.

I'm going to fucking kill him, I say. I'm going to fucking kill him when I find him.

Lucy turns back to us. Kill who? she says.

The bloke she came in here with, I say. Some fucker brought her in here.

You don't know that, Tone says.

It's fucking obvious! I shout. He's got her pissed, brought her in here, and fucked her!

Lucy's chatting on her radio. Two-seven to five-zero, she says.

The radio crackles. Go ahead two-seven.

I've got a girl in the toilets on the bottom floor, looks like she might've been spiked, over.

Spiked? I say. Someone's fucking spiked her drink?

Lucy doesn't reply. She's saying something into the radio again.

About thirty seconds pass before the door opens. Two more security guards – men – come in.

Who're you? they ask, pointing at me and Tone.

I'm her boyfriend, I say.

How long has she been like this?

I don't know, I say.

I found her about ten minutes ago, says Tone. We were looking for her and we didn't know where she'd gone, so I asked someone to come in here and check.

Who did you ask?

This random girl. She's gone to get some water. She'll be back in a sec.

There's an ambulance on its way, Lucy tells the other two security guys just as the girl returns clutching two bottles, minus caps.

I know who did it, I say. I fucking know who did this to her.

Shut up, says Tone. You don't know who did it.

I fucking do!

We'll talk about that once we've revived her, says Lucy.

It happens before I realise what I'm doing. Before I have time to consider not doing it. Just like throwing a punch at someone. I make a dash for it. Out through the doors and into the corridor.

Tony's behind me in a second.

What the fuck are you doing? he shouts after me.

Going to get him.

He gets me by the neck and holds me against the wall. Tag, no! Just leave it. It's not what Steph wants.

I shake him off. Storm back into the club with him chasing after me.

FORTY-NINE

DUNCAN

I was sat with Sorel in the living room in front of the new TV, which was turned to mute. Colbeck'd gone out to meet someone – fuck knows who, he was being proper secretive – and Ade was at the bookies cuz he reckoned there was a dead cert on one of the horses today like.

So, Sorel went, turning to me. What went wrong? Back a bit sooner than I expected.

Someone crashed into the back of the van and fucked it, I said. And then those two went mental and Ade said we were coming home. Just like that.

She sat up and pushed a strand of hair behind her ear. Of course, it wasn't exactly 'just like that' but I didn't want to say any more. If I told her the full extent of what happened, then she might tell someone else and as soon as someone else knew there was no denying that I was there too. As it stood, only five people knew: them two, the perpetrators; me, the witness; and the two guys in the Nova, who I guess you could call the victims, although there's no way Colbeck and Ade'd see it like that. Anyway, that was enough for me.

Was anyone hurt?

Well, we weren't, I said. We weren't going that fast when it happened. I'm not sure about the guys in the other car though. It wasn't a serious crash.

Was that a lie? I thought. No, it wasn't a lie. None of us were hurt and I had no idea how the other two guys were. All the truth. You can say anything you want and it will be true providing you say it the right way. Maybe that's what Ade means about a good vocabulary being the best weapon there is.

Well, just as long as you're okay, she goes. She bit her lip and I remembered why I'm so into her. I thought about the diary entry I'd made the day before. I couldn't lose another opportunity. I had to take her out and just make it plain obvo to her that I liked her. I was even considering saving up my next dole payment and spending it all on her. Giros are the way to a woman's heart like.

Sorel, I said.

Duncan, she goes, mimicking my voice and making me feel almost sick with fuckin adulation. I summoned my courage.

I was wondering if you fancy going out somewhere, I said. I know you said it didn't matter, but I really want to pay you back for all those drinks that you got me that time. I had a really good night and I want to repay the favour.

Sure, she goes, casually like. When?

Later this week sometime.

She laughed. You're so specific, Dunc, she said.

Okay then, I said. Friday.

Friday it is.

Fuck me, I thought. That was easier than I expected.

So, where we going, then? she asked.

I don't know, I said. And I don't want to plan either. Cuz it's good to be spontaneous. As long as it's somewhere where we can have a decent convo then I don't mind. And it'll be good to get out of the flat for a bit; good to get away from them two when they're acting up and shit.

And how shall I dress for this occasion? she asked, smiling and widening her eyes.

Just dress normally, I went. Be yourself. Fuck me, you're gonna make me nervous.

Well, she said.

Well what?

I like it when you're nervous. It's kinda cute, you know.

I didn't know what to say to that, so I just said fuck all.

I'm really glad I met you, Dunc, she said.

Thanks, I went. Then I added, And I'm really glad I met you too. It's nice to have someone sane to talk to for a change.

Ha, she laughed. I wouldn't go that far.

FIFTY

COLBECK

Steph's words are still ringing in your ears as you stride into the flat and slam the front door: *What are you going to do, you fucking loser? What the fuck are you going to do?* Dunc and Sorel are sitting on the sofa, too far apart to be lovers but too close to be friends. You wonder if Dunc got his end away while you were out. You couldn't care less whether he did or not, but you store the mental image of Sorel doing the old reverse-cowgirl to slap your granny to later. You go straight into the bathroom and run the cold tap and hold your hands under the stream to ease the swelling. You had to stop on the way here and give a brick wall a good fucking beating, much to the bewilderment of the small flash mob of elderly pedestrians who gathered to watch.

'Where've you been?' Dunc shouts from the next room.

You dry your hands and go into the living room and sit down on the other sofa. 'Why are you so inquisitive?' you ask.

'I suppose it's in my nature.'

Sorel obviously likes this. She prods him in the ribs playfully and he yelps with delight, like a puppy that knows exactly what it has to do to get a treat from its owner. It makes you fucking sick.

'What are you glaring at?' he asks.

'Nothing. It doesn't matter.'

He lets it drop. 'So where were you?' he says.

You put your throbbing hands in your jacket pockets so they can't see the torn skin and mangled flesh on your knuckles. 'If you must know, I went to meet up with Steph.'

'Who's Steph?' Sorel asks, as if she's suddenly interested in listening to you instead of her beloved.

'Steph's his ex,' says Dunc.

'Ooooh,' she says, in a completely over the top and annoying way.

Dunc sees your disgust and jumps to her rescue. 'But I thought you hated her?' he says.

In your head, you're thinking, Yeh, I do hate her. I despise her. I fucking detest the bitch. I fucking hope she gets cancer. Luckily, you manage to bring it under control in time to say, in a calm fashion, 'Fucking hell, Dunc. I don't hate her. I know I said that before, but that was because the wounds were still raw. There's no point hating her. I'm not angry any more. It doesn't achieve anything. Buddha says that being angry is like holding a hot coal with the intention of throwing it at someone else. You are the one who ends up getting burned.'

Dunc wrinkles his brow. Fucking hell, you think, you should get an Academy Award for that load of bollocks. Probably shouldn't have put the bit in about Buddha at the end though.

'So how did the meeting go?' he asks, eventually.

'Good,' you lie. 'Very good, in fact. I don't think we'll

ever be friends, but it was civil.' You're rather enjoying this little missive on life, love and loss. You continue: 'What's important is that we sort everything out properly and get the comfort of real closure, so that we can both go our separate ways contentedly.'

'I think that's really good, Matt,' says Sorel. 'I think it takes a real man to forgive in the way that you have.'

Dunc's visibly hurt by Sorel's sudden interest in your various manly qualities. If only you actually believed any of the things you're saying. Still, if it educates them both and gets her to flutter her eyelashes at you then at least some good's come of it.

'So,' you say, eager to change the subject before the rage surfaces, 'who's up for a night out on the town this Friday?'

They exchange glances.

'We've got plans Friday,' says Dunc.

'What plans?'

'We don't know yet, just… plans, y'know.'

'Since when?'

'Since a few minutes ago,' he says. Then the cheeky little fucker adds, 'What's with all the questions anyway? You get all shitty with me when I ask you about things.'

'I'm just interested, that's all,' you tell him. 'I mean, no offence, Dunc, but you aren't exactly a social butterfly, are you? Not exactly turning down invitations every day, you know?'

Sorel laughs.

'Fucksake,' says Dunc. He taps his leg pocket like he always does when he's agitated and looking for a fag.

'Calm down,' you say. 'I'm only having a laugh with you.'

'I owe Sorel some drinks,' says Dunc, 'so I've asked her if she'd like to come out with me, and she's said yes. What's the problem?'

'There is no problem.'

'Well then.'

'Well then what?'

'Well then, it's sorted. We can't come out with you. End of debate. Thanks for the offer though. I'm sure you'll have plenty of fun without us.'

The sarcastic little fucker. He finds his cigarettes and lights one up and relief shines across his face.

'The offer's still open if either of you changes your mind,' you say, looking from her to him and then back to her again.

'I really appreciate that,' says Sorel, 'but I don't think I fancy it, to be honest. I'd prefer a few quiet drinks somewhere.'

'Suit yourselves,' you tell them.

She makes some remark and goes into the kitchen. Dunc turns the TV volume up cos a chat show's just starting and there's not much else to do in the daytime around here. Not much at all.

You stare at the TV, your eyes boring holes through to the back of the screen.

What are you going to do, you fucking loser? What the fuck are you going to do?

FIFTY-ONE

DUNCAN

It was my big night.

I spent most of the day sitting in the flat gearing myself up for the big show like, choosing what to wear and all that shite. I wanted to go for the type of look where it appeared that I'd not really made any effort, but where I still looked cool as fuck. But with the type of shit that I had in my clothes pile, that was going to be pretty fuckin difficult. I went for the fuckin 'old faithful' combo that had never let me down – Converse, jeans, a plain white T-shirt and the red New York hoodie.

I still wasn't sure where to take her either. I had the week's dole money, so that wasn't really an issue, but I wanted to make sure that it didn't feel like a date or anything. Cuz if it started to feel like a date then that's when I'd start getting even more proper nervous than usual, and when I get nervous I'm liable to say shit without putting my brain in gear first like, as you already know by now obvo. Also, there was the fact that if it felt like a date, she might be expecting something at the end of it that she wasn't going to get, like some kinda big romantic gesture that I'd surely balls up anyway.

So, I decided that a good place to start would be The George, cuz that's where we went last time and cuz familiar settings are good for this kinda thing. I'd given myself a rule, and that rule was that I'd only allow myself to drink as much as she did. Cuz I drink proper fast when I'm nervous and if I wasn't careful I'd end up unconscious within an hour. If I didn't get any more drunk than she was then I was also less likely to make myself look like a dick by tripping over or falling off my chair or puking. After The George, I'd ask her where she wanted to go. That was the plan anyway. We might just end up sitting in there all night. But if she wanted to move on somewhere else then we would – even if it was to one of them bars up town that I despised. I'd still go there for her like. Or maybe she'd wanna go see a film, and if that was the case then I reckoned we should opt for a horror. If she got scared easily by stuff like that then she'd be more likely to get up close to me, and then I could put my arm round her and comfort her like the big strong man I most certainly am not.

But these were just minor details, really, and in fact it all came down to one thing: if it all went to plan, then by the end of the night I would have done the one thing that all this boiled down to, which was to let her know in no uncertain terms exactly how into her I was. I wouldn't let the chance slip like I did with countless others throughout my life. Even if she took it really badly, I could console myself in the knowledge that at least I did it, grasped the nettle with both hands or whatever that fuckin saying is; at least I learned from all my previous mistakes and finally had the balls to admit my feelings. Cuz if I never told her then I might spend the rest of my life wondering what would've happened. Little decisions like this can affect a person's life forever. Small and seemingly trivial matters can trigger a chain of events with just the same gravity as momentous ones. And, for all these reasons and for many more, I knew that I had to get everything right that night. I felt as if my whole fuckin life depended on it like.

FIFTY-TWO

SHAUN

The physio continues. I'm starting to get headaches. Apparently, that's normal. There are particles of memory in my brain like dregs in a coffee cup. My arm strengthens. I can move my fingers. I can grip objects. My leg doesn't seem any better, but they assure me it's on the mend. They say these things take time and I don't know whether to believe them.

The day after I spoke to Steph, the police came to see me. They basically confirmed what I already knew, with a few details missed and a few extra ones put in. An inquest is ongoing, but they have a confession, and it all seems to make sense. The only question they can't answer is who attacked Steph. They're still making inquiries. They're taking it very seriously, they assured me. But it seems they're not holding out much hope of catching anyone. The subtext is that they probably think he did it, even though he said he didn't. That would make a lot more sense.

There's more stuff to be dragged up, of course. More to be gone over. In light of these developments, they want to speak to everyone who was there, most of whom they've spoken to at least once already. So that's all Steph's mates, all my mates, anyone else who comes forward. Tony saw the whole thing and he says it definitely wasn't just one person who attacked me. The police say they are keeping an open mind, but that suggests to me that they aren't actively looking for anyone else. And there's one thing that everyone seems clear on, even my own mates: it was me that started the fight.

I don't know what to believe any more. I don't know whether to believe Tony's version of events, my mam's, the police's, or Steph's; or whether to reject the whole lot; or whether to take bits and pieces from each story and assemble my own narrative. I don't even know whether to believe myself when I run all these thoughts round and round my head. And this other guy, the skinny, scruffy guy in the hoodie, well who was he? How did she get talking to him, and when did it all turn sour? Perhaps he got pissed off that she wouldn't put out and then he forced himself on her. Perhaps. It's all maybes and what ifs and whys and hows: especially hows. How did this happen? How could it have been *allowed to happen* in such a big club as Zanzibar with so much security and with me and Tone and a load of others there with her?

And as for *him*: how could he have been allowed to kill himself? How could he have been allowed to escape the punishment he deserves? Why won't the papers print his name? Out of respect for his family? What about their respect for me? Everyone in this town, everyone in the country, should know what he's done. And what about Steph? Does she hate him as much as I do? I've seen her once since the accident. Once. That's all. The time we sat at my kitchen table, when she told me that her memory of that night is just as fucked up as mine.

The conversation with the porter at Samantha Farnworth's clinic is still fresh in my mind. The decision comes quickly. There's only one reason behind it – my unfounded but unshakeable belief that the answers to all of these questions are still locked somewhere inside my head, like a sleeping monster waiting to be awakened.

Dr Farnworth's number is stored in my mobile. I call her, but she doesn't answer. Instead, it rings for a minute or so and then redirects me to an answerphone.

'Hello,' I say. 'It's Tag. I mean Shaun. Shaun Taggart. I met with you a couple of weeks ago. I'm the guy who was attacked in the nightclub. Could you ring me back as soon as you're free, please? It's quite urgent.' I run through my mobile phone number, twice so she's sure to get it, and then I hang up.

An hour later she calls. I recognise her voice.

'Shaun?'

'Yes. Thanks for ringing back.'

'What can I do for you?'

'Do you think that regression hypnosis might help me remember what happened to me?'

'Where's all this come from?'

It came from the guy who escorted me from her office, of course. He didn't say it explicitly, but his words resonated with me and got me thinking – specifically when he said that the best person to ask for answers is myself. I don't want to get him in trouble though, and I'm not sure whether he was supposed to even speak to me. They have some funny fucking rules, hospitals, when it comes to patient care and due diligence. So, I just tell her: 'I can't stand it any more – I can't stand everyone else having their own opinion of what happened to me and me having to make my mind up based entirely on what they tell me.'

'Regression hypnosis can be very dangerous. It can reveal things deep inside the subconscious – things that are kept in the subconscious for a reason.'

'I understand that. But might it help me?'

She sighs. A long, heavy sigh. 'I doubt it, Shaun. Part of your brain has been damaged. It's not as if you've simply forgotten something. There's no memory left to be recovered.'

'But it might work, mightn't it?' I say.

A long pause.

'It might work, yes. Although it's very – no, not just very, but extremely – unlikely. You could be opening a whole can of worms.'

And despite everything, I nearly fucking laugh. *Rorms*. 'Why?' I ask.

'Because it might leave you even more confused. The mind blocks out certain things for a reason. You might end up with more questions than answers.'

'Do you know someone who could do it for me?' I ask.

'Shaun,' she pleads, 'you're ignoring my advice. This could be extremely dangerous. I strongly advise against it.'

'But do you know someone?'

'No, I don't. I don't know anyone personally.' She hesitates. 'But I know *of* someone. If you insist on going ahead then I want to be sure you're at least employing someone who knows what she's doing. I can give you a phone number. This lady has a reputation as being very good. But I can't stress enough how much I advise against this.'

'What's the number?' I say.

'She isn't local. You'd have to travel.'

'I don't care. Just give me the number, please.'

'Shaun, you must promise me that you'll consider this very carefully before you decide to go ahead with it. It could be extremely detrimental to your mental recovery. It could gravely affect your depression.'

'I've already told you,' I snap, 'I'm not depressed.'

She goes quiet.

'I'm sorry,' I say. 'This is very difficult.'

'I know. And you might be about to make things a lot harder for yourself.'

'I understand what you're saying,' I tell her, 'but will you please just let me make my own decision?'

She gives me the number.

FIFTY-THREE

COLBECK

You should be used to this by now, but you're not.

A group of lads queuing a few metres in front are shouting to a group of girls across the street, and the girls are fucking loving it. There isn't much worse than a rabble of flabby skanks wandering around town, wearing clothes fucking three sizes too small, pissed up and thinking they look great. One of them – fat, ginger, stupid – turns around and flashes her arse at them. She's wearing a thong. She'll probably need a pair of pliers to get the fucking thing off. The lads are laughing and egging each other on. The girls move on and the lads continue to laugh among themselves. Then they start chanting. Christ almighty. Please, someone, send a disease to wipe all these cunts out. You'd happily sacrifice yourself for the cause. What else can save this generation? When the piss and shit and blood and vomit is washed away, what will remain?

'What you thinking about?'

For a moment, you forgot Ade's with you.

'Bunch of fucking pricks,' you say, hoping one of the

lairies in front will hear it and turn around and confront you, so that you have an excuse to mash his fucking face up.

'Matt,' he says, nudging you, 'what you thinking about?'

'About committing a mass murder,' you say, pointing at the idiots all around.

Ade laughs. 'Now, now,' he says, 'they might be all right once you get to know them.' He grins and takes out a cigarette. 'But then again,' he adds, 'I wouldn't want to get to know them. I'd rather take them at face value and fuck them up. That's why it's so important to make a good first impression.'

'Indeed,' you say.

He lights his cigarette.

'You're not worried about getting charged cos of that shit that kicked off while we were away?' he asks.

What the fuck? Why's he asking that? And what does he mean? Does he mean when you bottled that cunt, because you could have been caught on CCTV, or when you both got to work on the two geezers in the white Nova? There's the shit with the bouncers too, but he doesn't mean that cos he knows fuck all about it. And it might not have even happened. Either way, you don't want to let your guard down. And you couldn't care less whether you get charged anyway. You couldn't care less whether you get sent down. If they brought back the death penalty just for you then your sole chagrin would be the fact that they could kill you only once. 'Course I'm not fucking worried,' you say. 'Are you?'

'Nah,' he says. 'Bring it on. Live by the sword, die by the sword, and all that shit.'

There are about ten people in the queue between you two and the door. One thing that's worked out well for you is the fact that this time neither of you has any visible bruises, and your beanie is covering up the scab on the side of your head. It attracts unnecessary attention when you try to get into a club covered in bruises. The bouncers automatically think you've started a scrap with someone. They never assume you're just an innocent bystander, or someone who's trying to put things right.

'What the fuck's Dunc doing with Sorel?' Ade says suddenly.

'How the fuck should I know?'

'Has he said anything?'

'Fuck all.'

'Has she?'

'Nope. Not to me. Why would she?'

'Something weird's going on. It's making me para. He's not her type. She goes for bad boys usually. Why's she so interested in Dunc?'

'Maybe he's got a huge cock.'

He glares at you. 'Maybe he does. But if he goes anywhere near her with it, then I'll fucking cut it off and shove it up his arse,' he says.

He throws his cigarette end on the pavement, steps on it, and emits a throaty cough.

'Here we go,' you say. There are only a couple more people to be let into the club before it's your turn.

'Hey, Matt!' someone shouts from further back in the queue. You turn around.

Fucking Dodgy Nick. You haven't seen him in ages. You don't like socialising with the fucker. You don't even like the idea that the cunt's gonna be in the same club as you. But fuck it. You aren't scared. He's not hard, really. He's just a bit of a Del Boy who's also dodgy as fuck. You turn, exchange a bit of small talk, ask him how shit's going. 'Come here a min,' he says. 'Got something for you.'

You tell Ade to wait a sec and to hold your place in the queue, and nip back to see what the fuck Nick's up to. Turns out he's got a shitload of ket on him that he wants shot of fucking pronto. 'Someone owed me money, and they couldn't pay, so they gave me this instead,' he explains. 'I want rid of it so I'm selling at half price.'

You politely decline and tell him to have a good night and that you might catch up with him later. When the pleasantries expire, you head back over to Ade.

He takes out another cigarette and puts it in his mouth. He changes his mind before he lights it though, and sticks it behind his ear instead.

'Who was that?' he asks.

'Nick.'

'Nick who?'

'Don't ask. Just a guy I used to know. Hardly spoken to him for years.'

You step up to the doors.

'Just hang on a sec, lads,' says one of the doormen.

'Sorry, mate,' Ade says, and he takes a step back. You want to glance at him, but you don't, because you know that if you do then it might look like you're on edge. Which you are, but there's no need to advertise the fact.

The bouncer is looking over his shoulder into the club, waiting for the punters to move out of the reception area and into the building proper.

'Go on, lads,' he says, ushering you through.

Fucking result. Now it's showtime.

FIFTY-FOUR

DUNCAN

I watched Sorel's hips sway confidently from side to side as I followed her to The George. I kept trying to catch up with her, but her legs were too long and besides, I was enjoying the view like. We necked a few gin and tonics before we came out which made me feel a little tipsy already cuz I hadn't eaten. I just seemed to forget, which I often do, what with all the worrying about getting tonight right and all that.

We walked the same way through the estate as we did when we first came here a few months ago. We took the shortcut behind the shops; no little scallies there this time. Same dilapidated fences all daubed with graffiti and discoloured by moss and weathering though. I picked up the pace so's I was walking at her side again and listened to the sound of her heels on the tarmac, distinctly at odds with the soft padding of my Converse.

So, she said. How's life? I don't feel like we've had a proper conversation lately.

Okay thanks, I went. What about you?

Feeling a bit weird, to be honest.

We got to the top of the alley and turned left; the pub was just ahead of us.

How come? I asked.

Complicated, she said. I'll explain when we're inside.

We reached the doors and I held them open, let her through first. It was fuller than it was last time we came here. The table we sat at before was vacant though, so I took off my hoodie and hung it over the back of one of the chairs.

What you having? I asked.

She sat down and played with her necklace. A gin and tonic please, she said. Thanks, Duncan.

No worries.

I went to the bar. The same middle-aged woman stood behind it, the one that served us last time we came here. I noticed that she'd had her hair dyed though. Fuck knows how I could remember so much about her appearance.

All right, love, she went.

I got a gin and tonic for Sorel and a beer for myself and brassed up the lady. I told her to keep the change cuz I hoped that Sorel would hear and put a gold star next to my name in whatever list existed inside that head of hers. When I got back to the table she was sending a text on her phone, but she put it back in her bag just as I sat down.

Cheers, she goes, and we clinked.

So, I said, taking a sip. What's up?

Oh, she said. Just stuff.

What stuff?

If I tell you, then you can't mention it to Aidan, she said.

Like I would, I goes. I put my glass down on the table.

It's my ex, she said. The guy I told you about.

She had my full attention now. I goes, What about him?

He's been texting and ringing me lately, asking me to get back with him. I don't know what to do. I went to see him while you guys were away and, you know, stuff happened.

It was like a fuckin boot to the stomach. I was winded by it. I just said: Oh...

That's why I was so glad I was going to get to chat to you tonight, because you always give me honest advice. I can't really talk to anyone else about this kind of thing.

I took a big swig of my drink. What about your mates? I said.

Most of them don't like him.

Well, there's your answer then.

I reached over the back of the chair to get my cigarettes from the pocket of my hoodie.

What's that supposed to mean? she went.

Well, they must dislike him for a reason.

I've told you all about that, she said. About how he hit me once.

Fucksake! I went. A middle-aged couple a few tables away turned and flashed me the evils. I shrugged an apology and turned back to Sorel.

What do you mean? she asked.

I mean, I said, lowering my voice, if he's hit you, and you split up with him, then why the fuck would you get back with him? I lit the cigarette and turned to the side, so I wasn't blowing smoke in her face.

He's said he's sorry, she explained. He's said it was a mistake, he can't believe that he did it and he's a mess without me.

Well, that makes it all right then, I said bitchily. I took a drag of my cigarette and thought about burning my arm with it.

Don't be like that, she said. I don't want to fall out with you. But you've never met him and you shouldn't just dismiss him when you know nothing about him.

I know enough about him, I said.

What do you know about him?

I know that he hit you. And it's not just because I care about you that I don't like him. It's because you're a girl, and any man who hits a girl is a fuckin coward.

I took another big gulp of my drink, draining the glass.

I explained to you that he has problems, she pleaded.

Well, he'll have a few more problems if Ade ever finds out about any of this.

Dunc, she said sternly. Don't you dare mention this to Aidan. It isn't fair.

I'm not going to mention it to Ade, I said. But that's not to protect your ex. It's because you asked me not to and I'm true to my word.

She touched my hand. I shivered.

She carried on talking but I wasn't really listening. She was doing that thing people do when they make it sound like they're justifying their actions to someone else, but what they're really doing is trying to convince themselves. I took long, deep drags of my cigarette. Her revelation had scalded me. I couldn't believe how stupid I'd been. Obviously she never liked me in that way. Obviously we were just mates. Obviously, when she held my hand that time as we walked home from the pub, it was just a friendly thing. I guess I didn't make it clear enough that when I asked her to come for a drink, I was asking her out. Like, y'know, fucking *asking her out*. I wanted to just fuck off home and get into bed and hide.

She stopped talking and looked at me like she was waiting for me to approve whatever it was she'd said.

Right, I goes. You really want to know what I think?

Okay, she said.

You're an adult. No one can stop you doing what you want to do. People say that everyone deserves a second chance, but I think that's bollocks. Some things, like cheating on someone, or hitting your girlfriend, are so inexcusable that anyone who does it shouldn't be given the opportunity to do it again.

I understand, she said. But he won't do it again.

You can make sure he doesn't do it again by not getting back with him. If you do get back with him then you're not the person I thought you were.

She looked at the table, sneeped. I'd hurt her by saying that, and I instantly regretted it. But it was the truth – and I figured that I owed her my honesty. It's what friends are for.

Sorry, I went. But you know what I mean. How can you possibly know that he won't do it again?

Because I trust him.

And did you trust him before?

Of course I did. I wouldn't have been with him otherwise.

Well, he's broken your trust before, hasn't he? Why wouldn't he do it again?

I just really believe him. He sounds so different. He's even been to anger management.

I think you've already convinced yourself, I went. I think you're just trying to get other people to reassure you that you've made the right decision. But no one's going to agree with you, because it just sounds so… stupid. You just have to do what you want to, I suppose. It won't change the way

I feel about you as a friend or anything. I just think you're making a mistake, that's all.

She nodded slowly, her eyes still locked downwards.

Anyway, I said. You want another drink?

Thanks. Same, please.

I got up and went to the bar, seriously pissed off by this whole new spin on events. There was no way I'd get with her tonight obvo, and, even though I'd never met this fucker she used to go out with, he sounded like a right twat to me. I found myself thinking: if I was wired-up differently, and I thought I could get away with it, then would I go after this cunt and give him a good beating for what he did to Sorel? And the conclusion I came to, standing there at the bar, was that yes, I probably would.

I ordered a beer and a gin and tonic, paid the woman, said cheers and headed back to the table with the drinks. Sorel was on her phone again.

You wanna move on after this one? she asked.

Where to? We've only just got here.

Some of my mates are up town. We could go and meet them if you like.

Well, I said. I don't really…

Fuck it, I thought. I might as well. There's no point just sitting here with her while she rabbits on about her ex. At least if we go to a club then I can get fucked up and have a bit of a dance and it might take my mind off this shit until tomorrow. But only until tomorrow. All this shit'd still be waiting for me when I woke up. And the next day. And the day after that.

Fair enough, I said. And just like that, my fate was sealed.

FIFTY-FIVE

COLBECK

Ade gets the drinks because he wants change for the gamblers. You can't be fucked to get crushed in the struggle for the bar, so you lurk at the side of the room, next to the DJ box. You watch a group of girls gyrating to the music, pouting at the boys, all clutching Smirnoff Ice bottles with straws poking out the top. A couple of lads dance over to them, shout into their ears, get behind them and grab handfuls of arse. The skanks seem to be having a competition to see who can dance the most raunchily. You shake your head and look away, the first tentative throb of a headache attacking your temples.

Then you see her.

Oh fuck.

She sees you too, because she instantly turns away and moves through the crowd so that you no longer have to look at each other. This is weird. How can you go so long without seeing her and then, as soon as you've actually agreed to meet up with the bitch, end up seeing her in a club less than a week later? If this is something to do with fate, then he's a cunt.

You notice Ade heading over to you with drinks.

'Fuck this,' you say to him. The music's loud and you have to shout. 'Let's drink these then go.'

'Why? What the fuck you on about?'

'I've just seen her.'

'Who?'

'Fucking *her*,' you shout back, taking the rum and Coke from him. 'You know, Steph.'

His eyes widen. 'Who gives a fuck?' he shouts back, after a few seconds. 'You can't leave just cos you've seen her. If anything, it's a reason to stay.' He lights a cigarette.

'How do you work that one out?'

'Cos if she notices that you've left as soon as you've seen her then that gives her the upper hand. Makes you look like you're scared of her. Like you're a pussy or something. Just fucking stick around and prove to her that you aren't bothered.'

You shake your head. 'One meeting a week is enough. I just want to have a good night and not have to think about her. She brings out the rage in me. And if I end up bumping into her new bloke then I don't know what the fuck I'll do. I'll end up losing it.'

'So lose it then,' Ade says. 'It might help clear the air. Like when it's really muggy and then there's a thunderstorm.'

'It most certainly wouldn't.'

'Well, be pleasant to your enemies, then,' he says, with a toothy smile. 'Nothing annoys them more.'

You watch his grin widen. 'Who says that?' you ask.

'I don't know.'

'Well it's bollocks. Never heard so much fucking shit in all my life. Fuck your enemies up, mate, that's what it should be. Because nothing annoys them more than a broken jaw.'

He laughs.

'And what the fuck are you on about anyway?' you continue. 'You're not pleasant to your enemies. Fucking anything but.'

He nods. 'Correct,' he says, 'but you're forgetting the fact that I reserve the right to contradict myself at any time.'

You roll your eyes. Fuck this shit. 'Okay,' you say. 'I take your point. I'd better go and say hello to her. Back in a sec.'

Of course, you aren't going to say hello. You're going to find somewhere you can watch her without Ade sticking his fucking oar in. There's a place near the fag machine, just next to the doors. You tuck yourself away and burn holes in her with your eyes. As far as you're concerned, each and every cunt she talks to (and she's getting attention from a load of different lads who she may or may not know already) is potentially the one she cheated on you with. You have no idea what he looks like. None of these pricks looks anything like you. He could be anyone. Something's wrong, you can feel it inside you, because your first instinct would normally be to stride over there and stick a jagged glass in each of the lads' throats. But now, you're thinking something else. You don't want to hurt them. Not really. Not as much as you want to hurt her.

What are you going to do, you fucking loser? What the fuck are you going to do?

You're picturing a big cat stalking its prey, getting in all the different angles as it plans its best method of attack, all twitching tail and salivating jaws. You're going to fucking get her this time. You're going to fuck her up. You're going to fuck her up so bad she fucking stays fucked up. You're picturing those three girls you met that night, the night that seems so long ago now, the ones you tried to help because they were underage and one of them had been spiked. Chloe, one of them was called, you think. And Nathan, the guy you gave five quid and change to. Did he spend it on booze as you feared, or did he put it towards a bed for the night? It doesn't matter. He'd have been back in the same place the following night regardless. Your money would change nothing. Kindness changes nothing. Steph, this girl here, this one you spent two and a half years of your life with, has fucked you. She has fucked you both literally and metaphorically. Now, you are going to fuck her.

You duck into the bogs to make a phone call. You've had an idea that's so beautifully messed up that you can scarcely believe you've conjured it. What's more, it popped into your head so neatly and fully formed that you're inclined to believe it was delivered by a higher power.

Once you're safely inside the shitters, you get your phone out and see whether you've still got Dodgy Nick's number saved. Turns out you have, so you hit the button and call the fucker. He doesn't answer. It's fairly obvious that the cunt's unable to hear his phone in this place, so you text him instead. As you're doing so, your phone buzzes: incoming call, number withheld. It's got to be him.

'Yeh?' you say.

'Matt?'

'Hey, Nick, how's it going?'

'All right. What's up?' He's shouting and you can hear the music from the club, the same fucking shithole club that you're in right now.

'What we spoke about earlier, yeah? I've changed my mind. Can you sort me out?'

‘Meet me outside.’

‘I’d rather not, mate, can’t we sort it in the bogs or something? I don’t wanna get caught bringing it back in. They do searches here.’

‘No. Not inside. That’s kind of a rule.’ He’s still shouting. Fucking conspicuous fucker. You’re in no position to argue.

‘Okay,’ you say.

‘Now?’

‘Yeh.’

‘Safe.’

He cancels the call without saying bye.

◎

Twenty minutes later you’re a vulture scavenging for carrion. That bitch has ruined you. Your eyes dart from left to right as you edge across the dance floor towards the bar. You’re not avoiding her any more. You’re not trying *not* to bump into her. You’re actively seeking her. You’re geared up for the fucking showdown. By the time you get to the other side of the club, you still haven’t seen her. You wonder if she’s fucked off somewhere else. You keep looking for her. You’re not done with her yet. Fucking skank. Fucking leaving you for some other cunt. Fucking making you the cuckold. Fuck this shit. Your chest tightens. Keep it in the can, you think. Keep it in the fucking can. You walk the length and width of the dance floor, circling the rabble of gyrating spastics. Try to remember what Steph was wearing. Doesn’t matter anyway cos the only colour that stands out in this place is white, and even that looks purple in the ultraviolet light. The ultraviolet. The ultrafuckingviolent.

Every cunt in here dresses the same. Striped tops, designer labels, hair highlighted. You continue to circle the dance floor, clockwise, anticlockwise, like a lion taunting its prey. Eventually, you see her a few metres away in the centre of the throng of writhing bodies. You make your way over.

As soon as she sees you, she edges away. After a few seconds she turns and elbows her way through the crowd, towards the bar. You follow, shoving the cunts out the way and attracting stares that bounce off your beer armour. You corner her at the stairwell.

'Steph,' you say.

'What do you want, Matt?' she shouts back. 'Can't you just leave me alone?'

'I'm sorry,' you say. 'I wanted to apologise for the other day. I was, well, an idiot.'

She shakes her head. 'I'm not interested in your apologies,' she says. 'I've got nothing to say to you.'

'Will you at least let me buy you a drink?' you ask. 'A peace offering. You never have to see me again if you don't want to. It'd just help lay things to rest, in my mind at least.'

You watch her consider it.

'I don't think—'

'Please,' you say, cutting her off mid-sentence. 'I'd really like to.'

'And then you'll just let me get on with my night?'

'Of course.'

'One drink,' she says.

You head to the bar and she follows. There are a few of them in this place, on opposing sides of the room and up on the balcony, so you go for the one on your right, the one with the smallest queue. You wait your turn patiently. She stands a few metres away, watching you, and you think of your encounter with the girl on your road trip.

There's a baggie in the coin pocket of your jeans, half full of white powder. Three grams of ketamine, the same stuff they use to tranquilise fucking horses in larger doses, liberated from Dodgy Nick's stash for forty notes. *An absolute fucking steal,* he assured you. Even now, you're not entirely sure why you're doing this. You're not entirely sure what the endgame is going to be. But this is going to fuck her up. And when – fucking *if* – she finally comes round, she might have vague suspicions that it was you, but she'll never know for sure, and her memory's bound to be fucking fucked anyway. She'll feel stupid and vulnerable and scared and she won't know what to think any more. She'll no longer feel safe anywhere she goes. She'll remember the night she let her guard down and she'll carry the fear with her forever, just the way you'll carry this hatred with you forever. She'll have that nagging thought tugging at her nerve endings: *anything could have happened. I could have died.* There will be a forever gap in her memory where she won't know what she's done, or with whom, or where she's been. You know her well. You probably know her better than anyone, and she likes to be in control. She doesn't take drugs. She doesn't really drink much. She rarely gets drunk. She hates the idea of not being in command of her own actions, of exposing herself to danger. This is going to fuck her up. Just as she has fucked you up. This is something that she will not be able to come to terms with. She'll no longer be able to trust anyone, and her faith in those around her will be destroyed. She will feel how you feel. She will feel how *she has made you* feel. Everything that she thinks she knows about herself will be questioned. You're going to dose this bitch. There are endless possibilities – you could even be the superhero who comes to save her afterwards. Who'd have fucking thought it? After all she's said, you're still her fucking knight in shining armour. Nah, fuck that. You want her out of the fucking way. Just throw her to the fucking lions and leave them to decide whether they lick her face or eat her alive.

You get her drink, and a pint and double JD with ice for your own courage. It's sensible to get your drinks in twos in shitholes like this to minimise time waiting at the bar.

Using the pads of two fingers you pop open the baggie, still in your pocket, and scoop most of the powder into the palm of your hand. You hold it there.

You neck the JD and pick up your pint. Can you really do this? The swinging brick in your chest seems to miss a beat.

You reach forward and grab Steph's drink from the bar. In a quick movement you draw back your fingers and let the powder fall into the glass. There's a light fizzing of liquid against your palm. A few metres away Steph smiles a vacant smile that does little to hide her social awkwardness, and you love her and you hate her so much all in a single blink of the earth's eye, and you smile back at her.

FIFTY-SIX

DUNCAN

What a fuckin mess it was turning out to be.

As soon as we got into the club, Sorel grabbed my sleeve and pulled me up the stairs, saying that her friends were on the first floor. I fuckin hate clubs cuz they make me nervous. I sparked a cig, trying to take in the surroundings as casually as poss as we squeezed past punters and headed over to the DJ box.

Hey! she shouted, waving her hands in the air to get the attention of a group of girls dancing in a half-circle a few metres away. We pushed our way over, she tapped one of them on the back, and when they turned around it was all smiles and hugs and kisses and *Oh my God long time no see!* and me just left standing there trying not to look stupid even though they all had their backs to me.

Oh! goes Sorel. This is Dunc.

The girls said hey and I awkwardly said hi back, already regretting my decision to come here. To make it worse, there were some guys with them. The sort of guys that Colbeck and Ade would have a prob with. You know: proper lecherous creepy metrosexual fuckers. Lairies, basically. I wondered if they knew Sorel's friends or if they'd simply tagged on, eager for some action. Fuck this: I was in a shit mood already. I put my arm round Sorel's shoulders and asked if she wanted a drink. She nodded.

They didn't do gin and tonic at the bar, so I got her a vodka and lemonade. The whole process of getting served and getting back to her took about fifteen minutes and when I found her again, in more or less the same spot as I left her, she was chatting to one of the geezers. I handed her the drink and sort of stood there, wondering whether I should fuck off or wait to be introduced or someshit. He looked like a fuckin meathead and I didn't want to give him any excuse to take a dislike to me.

She ushered me in. This is my friend Dunc, she said to the guy.

All right, he went.

All right, I went back.

This is Nick, she said. There were a couple of seconds where my eyes were locked with hers, like she knew what I was thinking. And what I was thinking was, Nick who? Am I supposed to give a fuck?

My ex, she mouthed, subtly, but I sensed that he picked up on it.

Just when I thought this shit couldn't get any fuckin worse.

Oh, I said. And the two of them carried on talking like I wasn't even there, and after thirty seconds or so, I necked my drink and fucked off back to the bar to get another one. Might as well get pissed to try and salvage something from this pile of shit.

◎

I was waiting in line at the bar, getting proper pissed off at all the people shunting into me and giggling and shouting and acting with general disregard for every fucker out of their own social bubble, when someone hit me on the shoulder. I tried to ignore it, cuz I knew that if I turned round then some cunt was prob gonna deck me. But then it came again, harder. Then a vicious poke in the centre of the spine. I turned round.

What the fuck are you doing here? went Ade.

Fuckin hell! I shouted back. I'm pleased to see you, man.

Why? What's happened?

I'll tell you in a min, I shouted. Let me get another drink.

So Ade moved to the back of the mob and I waited till I got served by the guy behind the bar then made my way back over to where he was standing smoking a fag.

What's up? he asked.

Came with Sorel, didn't I.

He frowned.

Don't fuckin worry, I went. She bumped into her fuckin ex and abandoned me.

Sounds like Sorel to me, he laughed.

What's that meant to mean? I went.

She's not very good at cutting strings. Always running back to ex-boyfriends and shit. And always leading people on until she finds someone she likes more.

That's bollocks, I argued. She's not like that.

How would you know?

Cuz I've been hanging around with her, haven't I?

Fuck this, he said. You seen Colbeck?

No.

Well, he saw his ex as well. Looks like there's a fucking pattern emerging here.

He's not gonna get back with her, surely?

God knows.

I'm going to the bog, I told him. Just wait here for me. Don't move else I'll never fuckin find you again, and I can't be arsed with that shit.

Be quick, he said. I wanna find Colbeck. His face changed a bit, exposing something that might even have been fear. I'm a bit worried about him, he said.

I walked past the stairs towards the DJ box. I wasn't going to the bog really. I was going to see if there'd been any developments with Sorel and her ex like. When I got there, they'd gone. I scouted around a bit, hoping to see them, but I couldn't, and so I headed back towards the bar, necking my drink on the way. Then suddenly they were right in front of me on the dance floor. Her and him, fuckin all over each other. They were so caught up in it that they didn't even notice me standing there.

I pushed my way back to the stairs, feeling sick and pissed off and in the mood to kick the shit out of someone, and I didn't like that feeling and I wasn't used to it and I waved to Ade and gestured towards the bar and got in line and ordered myself a big fat fuckin drink.

◎

An hour later and I'm far too pissed. I can barely even see straight. I've got with this girl somehow: I don't remember exactly how I ended up talking to her, but she's holding my hand now and pulling me through the club and I'm trying not to throw up and trying to think of something other than the nausea. I imagine Sorel smiling at me and for a moment I forget what's happened and why I'm here with someone else and what a total fuckin let-down this night has turned out to be.

Where the fuck are we going? The music's being played through water now. Corridor is looming. Pass through double doors, white, with circular glass windows, and into the light. Fuckers leer at me as we pass them. One gawps at me and gobs off saying he's had better days or someshit like that and I scowl at him. Yeah, mate, I have had better fuckin days, and I'm trying to take my mind off it if you wouldn't mind leaving me to it.

Fuckin sterile as fuck, man. Lit like an operating theatre or someshit. Notice we're in the toilets. White tiled walls and some fucker's left the tap on, I should prob turn it off in case the place floods. No urinals in here though. Confused. Must've come through the wrong door. Then I remember. Remember her. Remember I'm with someone. Where's she gone? Here she is.

No time to stop the impending flood. She shoves me into a cubicle and kicks the door shut. Turns round to lock it, smiles seductively with painted lips. My face on her neck and my hand on her thigh under her skirt. But where the fuck am I? I'm in the toilets with this girl. In a club somewhere.

She hitches her skirt up, unbuttons me. One leg up and she supports herself on the opposite wall. What the fuck am I doing? She pulls my face into her chest, think I've ripped her fuckin top. Wonder if she knows. Wonder if she cares. Scent of perfume overwhelming and I can hear giggling outside and I know it's directed at me and I don't care.

She's fuckin breathing heavy and so am I through the sweat and alcohol. But it isn't happening. It isn't going up.

She grabs it and rubs it against her, trying to guide me in but I'm too fucked to do anything. I can't even tell if I'm hard. What the fuck's this? She's on her knees and she's sucking it, pushing her hands up and her fingers into my mouth. I'm moving her hair out of her face and she's looking up at me, eyes like blue ice.

But it isn't happening. It isn't happening.

This isn't happening.

◎

Both of us are too drunk to talk. I don't know if what just happened can be classed as sex. I'm too numb to feel anything. I collapse onto her. She sits down on the bog and says something I don't understand. One leg in her underwear and one leg out, she rests her head on the side of the cubicle and says she needs to sleep. Says she'll find me later.

I stagger to the sinks and it's not until I notice my reflection in the mirror that I realise my trousers are unbuttoned and my dick's still out. I try to make myself look presentable. She breathes heavily in the cubicle and I pull the door shut before I leave.

FIFTY-SEVEN

TAG

There's the cunt!

Tag! Fucking leave it!

Tone grabs me again. He won't let me go. The fucker grips me with those fucking tree-arms of his round my waist like a bear hug.

Get the fuck off me!

I struggle free.

Tag!

His voice is hoarse.

I steam over to the scrawny cunt, who has his back to me. Grab him by the hood. Spin the twat around and smash him a good one on the jaw. He's not expecting it at all: it's a proper fucking sucker-punch and he goes down like a sack of shit. Tone pulls me out of the way before I can stamp on the cunt's cranium. I give him the elbow and he grabs my face.

Tag! Fucking stop it!

Shut the fuck up, Tone!

I elbow him again, shoulder him, bite him.

The cunt's on the floor shielding his head and cowering like a scared animal. I stamp on him, but I can't get to his face because his arms are in the way. Someone grabs at me, throws me to the floor, and I stumble and land face down.

Fucking calm it, son, he says, spitting the words out round the cigarette that hangs from the corner of his mouth.

Who the fuck's this prick? I stand up and go for him in a frenzy. He tries to hit me but misses. People jump out of the way. The cunt's still on the floor, blinking, bleeding. He rolls to the side as I aim for his face again. He's shouting. What the fuck? he's saying. What the fuck?

The other guy grabs me once more. Fucking calm down! he shouts. Tone gets between us, tries to calm me down as well. He's shouting, the guy's shouting, the cunt on the floor is shouting, every fucker's shouting and still I can't hear anything. Fucking pandemonium. A cattle market. An angry mob swelling up, unsure of who's siding with who.

Now someone else is going for me. I spin in attack mode. Where there was one guy there are now two. A hard skull smashes against me and my nose explodes. I realise I'm on the floor. I see stars. I see fragments of glass and cigarette ends. I try to get up, disorientated. Punch-drunk. I can't move. I don't have the strength. A boot smashes against my chin. Blood gushes from my nose into my mouth. I see girls' legs, smooth, skirted, fake-tanned, and I see chivalrous guys pushing them out of the way.

The scrawny cunt's on his feet again now, wiping nose blood onto the sleeve of his hoodie. I see him leer over me with the other two. Freeze-frame as he weighs up what he's about to do. I don't know who this person is, but I know he's hurt Steph and now he's about to hurt me. I'm sprawled out like a starfish, completely vulnerable, but I can't seem to move or defend myself. Where's Tone? I can hear him, but I can't see him. If this was a film, they'd be playing it in slo-mo now, a spiralling close-up shot of my face with soft focus. I need to get up. I need to get out of the way. My limbs flail hopelessly as I try to pull myself to my feet. Then a sudden rush of noise, back to twenty-four frames per second, into hyperspeed, and pan out wide. And then the stamping starts.

Screams.

Are they coming from me?

My eyes roll back.

Stillness everywhere.

Still.

Still.

◎

I'm conscious of being moved. Conscious of the music turned off. Hours could've passed.

◎

What's your name? Can you hear me?

◎

Hello?

◎

Stay with me, okay? Stay with me.

◎

Something soft under my head. Unthinkable pain in my face and chest.

◎

Shit, is he dead? Is he fucking dead?

He's not dead. Do you know his name?

◎

Shaun? Can you hear me, Shaun? Do you know where you are? Do you know what's happened to you?

◎

His girlfriend's in the toilets. We think she was spiked. Security were looking after her... She wasn't responding. I think she's still in there, on her own... can you send someone to check on her?

◎

There's no one there...

What do you mean there's no one fucking there?

◎

The stillness.
Still.
Still, and silent.

◎

There was the silence, and it blanketed me, and then there was nothing.

◎

Nothing for days, and then the wall clock tick-tocking.

◎

And here it comes.

◎

The Surfacing.

FIFTY-EIGHT
DUNCAN

I was standing at the bar, hoping that the girl might make an appearance and wondering whether I'd fucked her or not and trying to remember what she looked like. For the first time that night I noticed Colbeck across the room. His eyes scoured the club nervously. He was chewing on his lip, making his way over to me. I was so pissed that I could barely think. What happened next is a blur of photographs on a slide show.

There was a huge surge in the crowd, I remember that. A few people fell over, but I wasn't one of them cuz I was supporting myself on the bar, being by this point too pissed to stand without assistance. I didn't realise I'd been punched until I was on the floor. I didn't feel it, but I felt the warm blood soak my face and neck. A sick tingling in my jaw. From the floor, I could see someone going for me, screaming all kinds of shit that I didn't understand. I was screaming too, screaming for Ade to help me. But I didn't even know where he was.

Fuckin help me! Fuckin help me!

No cunt wants to know. I'm trying to shield my face but it's absolute bedlam now that it's kicking off. A trainered foot narrowly misses me.

Then Ade's here. Colbeck too. Thank fuck. As they're laying into the fucker that's just hit me, I manage to get to my feet. There's blood all over my hands from protecting myself. Everything seems quiet. The noise in the room is as trivial as a fridge buzzing. The guy is on the floor now. I don't recognise him. Maybe Colbeck and Ade were right. Maybe these people who lay into someone for no reason other than their own satisfaction deserve a stern reprimand and I'm fuckin done with it. My actions are like a knee-jerk. I stagger over to where he's lying, not thrashing about as you might expect, but flat on his back, staring at the lights above him. Who is this person? I don't care. I'm fuckin fired up and he fuckin started it. I stand with Colbeck and Ade, my friends, the fuckin three musketeers, peering down at the guy on the floor like we're staring at a hole we've just dug in the garden. Suddenly the guy springs to life like he's trying to get up. And so do we. It's like someone's fired a starting pistol and we're seeing who can deliver the most kicks within five seconds. Together we stomp the guy on the floor until he stops struggling and lies limp.

◎

He's lying on the floor, mouth open like he's sleeping, but with wide unresponsive eyes fixed on someshit above him. Inside my head I'm not in this club with the lairies and skanks, caught up in this brawl with someone I've never met. Inside my head I'm alone and in silence. Fuck me, I'm thinking, all mute panic. I've fuckin killed the cunt.

Then bedlam returns. Pumping beats. Throbbing bass. Guys and girls gobbing off, some of them unaware of what's gone on. Where are Colbeck and Ade?

Before I realise it, I'm in the corridor next to the bogs, then I'm forcing open the fire doors and I'm climbing onto the recycling bins and pulling myself over the wall with people shouting after me, and I'm away.

This is both the beginning and the end.

It is June 13th, 2003.

FIFTY-NINE
SHAUN

'Are you sure you really want to do this?' she asks. Me and my mam are sitting in the car parked outside the offices of the hypnotherapist I was referred to after my conversation with Samantha Farnworth.

I tell her that I'm sure and she opens the driver's door and climbs out. She walks round to my side of the car and helps me to my feet. I support myself by resting my left arm against the top edge of the car door while she gets the wheelchair out of the car boot and unfolds it and smooths the seat out ready for me.

'Ready?' she asks.

'Yep,' I say. She helps me into it and wheels me towards the entrance of the building.

◎

The lady tells me that she's going to hypnotise me using a standard script. When I'm under, she will deepen the trance by asking me to picture myself in a room, with a chair, a table and a shelf full of books. I will be encouraged to take a book from the shelf and open it at a random page. This page represents today. After focusing on my life as it is now, I can turn the pages backwards to see how it used to be.

'Do you understand?' she asks.

'Yes.'

'Okay. Can I just ask you to lean back on the couch? Make yourself as comfortable as possible.'

She helps me into position.

'Would you mind waiting outside?' she asks my mam.

'Of course not.'

She leaves the room.

◎

I'm standing in a large wood-panelled room in what seems to be a stately home or manor house. Mahogany bookshelves line the walls, there's a battered old leather chair by the window, maroon curtains drawn, stepladders propped up in the corner, the scent of damp paper, dust, time. I step forward, study the spines: hardback books, decades old, sun-faded and weathered, and I can't make out the titles of any of them, or the names of their authors.

All except one.

SIXTY
DUNCAN

The taxi cost me six quid. I stomped up the stairs and burst into the flat. Ade was sat on the settee, smoking solemnly. His eyebrow was bleeding.

You fuckin prick, I said, slamming the door. I strode into the living room, noticing as I walked past that Sorel's bedroom door was wide open; she'd probably shacked up with her cunt of an ex-boyfriend somewhere. Fuck her. I didn't need her any more. I didn't need any of this any more. Colbeck, Ade, they didn't care about me. Fuck them.

Dunc, Ade said, face grave. Get over here now.

Fuck you.

What?

You heard. Leaving the club without me. Neither of you gives a shit about anyone but yourselves. You don't care what happens to me.

Dunc, said Ade, you don't understand.

Oh yes I fuckin do.

No, he shouted, making me jump. You fucking don't understand. He stood up, grabbed me by the arm and pulled me into the kitchen.

What are you talking about? I went. And where's Colbeck?

Shh, he said. Colbeck's gone to bed. Listen. That girl you were with tonight, yeh?

Fuck. I'd forgotten all about that. And how the fuck did Ade know anyway? Guess I wasn't being as discreet as I thought like. What about her? I asked.

Do you know her name?

No.

Did you tell her yours?

How the fuck am I meant to remember that? I was fuckin leathered.

Well, she's called Steph.

Is that supposed to mean something? I goes.

He shut his eyes for a few seconds, then opened them again. She's Colbeck's fucking ex-girlfriend, he said. If he finds out, he'll fucking kill you. And if the new guy finds out who Colbeck is, then he'll fucking kill you as well. That's why they were after you. Some fucker spiked her drink before you got with her. That doesn't look good, Dunc. So, don't you fucking ever say that I don't give a shit about you, all right?

My heart was in my throat. Oh fuck.

If Colbeck finds out about this, then you're in a fucking lot of trouble, he said.

Yeh.

He opened the secret cupboard and took out a half-bottle of Jack Daniel's and took a swig. I ran my hands through my hair. I was shaking. What the fuck had I done?

What the fuck have I done?

SIXTY-ONE

COLBECK

Life goes on.

It goes on until Monday – June 16th, 2003 – when you see the headline in the local paper as you walk past the newsagents on your way to the offy. You pick the paper up and you scan the article. A girl, Stephanie Harrison, 20, found drugged and raped in the toilets of a nightclub. Her boyfriend, Shaun Taggart, also 20, assaulted, in hospital, critical. Is this what you wanted? You wanted to get your own back on them. You knew what you were doing when you drugged her. You knew the dangers. It was sheer spite, but you couldn't have predicted this would happen to her. This is not how her life was supposed to turn out. You would never wish it on anyone.

You put the paper back on the rack. You head for the offy in a daze, buy 70cl of cheap vodka, trudge back to the flat, trying to think of some way to justify your actions. Try to think of some way to excuse yourself, to divert the blame.

There's no way.

◎

Days pass and melt into weeks. You continue to sign on every Monday. You sit in the flat all day, drinking. Ade and Dunc go to all lengths to avoid you. Steph was right when she said you only had one or two real friends left. But one or two real friends – like *real* friends – that's all anyone needs, isn't it?

That was then though, and this is now. The fact is that you're bringing them down. Their absence speaks volumes. They are cutting you out because you're sucking the life out of them. Even the way you walk has changed. You don't stride any more, you shuffle. You keep your eyes down, scanning the pavement. You are flabby and stupid. The hatred has cauterised all your nerve endings and you can no longer feel anything at all. Hate may be a negative emotion, but at least negative emotions are capable of producing a call to action. You're now so numb that you are incapable of even hating. You have nothing to look forward to but a lifetime of pandemic inaction. Never before have you felt so close to suicide. But, if you do it, then how? You need to get it right first time. You can't wake up and go through all the explanations and apologies for your actions. Pills seem like a good idea. A few packs of aspirin and some vodka, clichéd but effective. But you've heard stories about this. People assume that you just take the pills and drink the booze and fall asleep and it's all nice and fluffy and you don't feel a thing. But in actual fact, it's agony. Aspirin is one of the messiest and most complicated overdoses around. It affects every system in the body unpredictably, meaning that different people react in completely different ways. On top of that, aspirin is an acid. It burns the gastrointestinal tract from the inside. It changes the blood's pH level and can even make the blood acidic. But it also accelerates breathing control, making the lungs churn out carbon dioxide at twice their normal rate. It destroys your kidneys and lungs and produces a fever which burns out your nervous system.

Maybe different pills are less painful but equally deadly. You still have a bit of the ket left. You could empty the medicine cabinet and take the whole fucking lot in one go, but it's unlikely it'd even make you high – let alone kill you. You've broken everything and everyone around you, but you just cannot seem to break yourself.

Blades. That might work. A lot of blood though, and very traumatic for whoever has to find you. You need to override the guilt and do what you want to do and ignore the feelings of everyone else, just like you've always done.

Ade once told you there's a way to extract pure nicotine from pipe tobacco. A few drops of that in a cup of coffee are enough to kill a man, apparently. And you get a huge buzz before you go. Maybe that's the one. Go out on one last chemical high.

Alprazolam. That's the one. Some people call it Xanax. Fatal in high enough doses. You can get hold of it, illegally but easily.

Oh fuck. Why are you thinking this? How close are you to actually doing it? Your thoughts are scaring you. But it's for the best. It has to be. The guilt will always be there, like a wraith in your peripheral vision.

◎

You sit alone in the kitchen. Ade's house-sitting for two nights at his parents' place. Dunc's in bed. He goes to bed as early as he can to avoid having to spend time around you. He gets up late and goes straight out. Sometimes, in the evenings, you walk into the living room and he's in there, not really doing anything, just sitting. But the second you're through the door, he grabs the remote control and switches the TV on, or he snatches a book and pretends he's reading it, or he picks up the crossword from the arm of the sofa and studies it. Anything to avoid a conversation, to avoid eye contact.

You open the bottle of vodka. Its vapour burns you. You don't enjoy it like you used to. It is a symbol of joy turned into despair.

This is just something you have to do.

You take the pills ten at a time. Swallow them with water then drink as much of the vodka as you can until you retch. You think of Steph. You wonder if she will recover from her ordeal. This is the final chapter in yours. The weight of guilt has crushed the life out of you.

Twenty pills. Thirty. How many do you need to take to be sure that this works? You'll swallow them until your eyelids fall, like the lid of a grand piano slamming shut after one final performance.

Here it is. Here it is. Sleep greets you warm.

EPILOGUE

It isn't dying that's sad; it's living when you're not happy.

— Octave Mirbeau

SIXTY-TWO

SHAUN

'And... awake'.

My eyes open. Am I in hospital? No. I'm still here. On the hypnotist's couch. What have I just experienced? I saw them. I saw them all, but I can't remember them. It was the most vivid dream, but I can't remember. My eyes fill with tears and I wipe them away.

'There was a lot of emotion in what you just told me,' she says.

'What did I just tell you?'

'About the night of the attack.'

'What did I say?'

'You were angry and hurt and aggressive. You felt regret and remorse. You felt that Steph was wrong for always trying to keep a leash on you. You were afraid when you were attacked. You wished you'd have been able to see their faces.'

'I did see their faces.'

'That's not what you just told me.'

'I saw them. I knew who they were.'

'You're confused, Shaun,' she says, standing up and giving me the all-too-familiar smile of fake empathy. 'The things that you told me when you were under don't correspond to the things that you're saying now.'

My eyes fill up and my face burns. I've done everything I can.

◎

I will never know. I'll never know for sure who did this to me. I'll never know why they did it. I'll never know how much of this is my fault. I'll never know who to blame, who to hate, who to hurt. Right now, the only person I can hate is myself.

Will I ever recover physically? Maybe. Will the memories ever return? No. Never. They're gone. Maybe they never even existed.

For my part in this mess can I not, at least, be forgiven?

SIXTY-THREE

COLBECK

You know the scene, at the end of *Othello*, where Iago's manipulation has been exposed, and still he refuses to divulge his motives? That used to be me: no compromise and no justification and every action an end in itself. I say it 'used to be' me, because it isn't any more. It's come full circle. I set out to do something, and I carried it to its logical conclusion, and now, as I sit here, pen shaking in my hand and a packet of pills in front of me, there is only one thing left to do: try and explain. But I can't, at least not in any meaningful way. Not in a way that will bring comfort or closure to anyone. So, make what you will of this note. I'll try and keep it short.

Dunc - okay. Listen up. I know how worried you are about everything that's happened. I can see the way it's chewing you up. You've witnessed some brutal things and I'm sorry you had to see them. But you have to get over this, Dunc, and just put it behind you, because I know the type of person that you are. You'll torture yourself over it for the rest of your life, even though you've done nothing wrong. You'll obsess over it until it completely ruins you and that's exactly what happened to me. Don't make the same mistake.

Please forget everything that you think you know about that night - June 13th, 2003. I'm not claiming to know exactly what happened, but I know more than anyone else, and I think it goes something like this:

I was trying to get my own back on Steph. It wasn't planned. I didn't really think it through. I just wanted to scare her. I wanted to make her feel vulnerable. I didn't want her to come to any physical harm. So I slipped some ket into her drink. Later, I guess someone must have seen she was out of it. She must have staggered into the toilets and someone must have followed her in there and attacked her. It's all my fault. It means nothing to you now, and it's unrepairable, but I am so sorry for my actions. That's it. It was me. I drugged her, and someone raped her. I never wanted this to happen. I just wanted to show her my pain.

When the fight happened, I had no idea who

Shaun was. I was just trying to defend Dunc. I guess Shaun was trying to get to me, and Dunc somehow got in the way. I'll take all responsibility for it: the kicks, the stamps, the punches. Whatever anyone asks you, tell them you weren't involved. Tell them you were trying to stop me. There can be no forgiveness for what I've done.

I can't expect you to forget, either. Instead, remember me as a weakling - someone who was bitter to the end, hateful, irrational, full of spite, worthless. Remember me as a shadow. Remember me as a boy, not a man: a scared child, pathetic, and now full of remorse. Remember me as nothing. But please also remember me as someone who made a terrible mistake, and whose actions had consequences far worse than he ever intended.

Ade. If you look under your mattress you'll find an envelope with a few grand in it. That's all my savings - I drew it out so that you and Dunc can live the dream for a bit longer. Take whatever Dunc owes you out of it, and consider his debt cleared. Keep the rest of it, and spend it on whatever. Don't get a fucking job.

Thanks for your wisdom. Thanks for the good times. This ride we've been on, it has to end here. I'll write to the police and give them my final confession that I acted on my own.

This is it then. The final indignity. I'm not worth your time. People like me have to die alone.

Will someone please tell Steph and Shaun for me: I'm so sorry.

Maybe I'll see you around.

Matt.

SIXTY-FOUR
DUNCAN

As soon as I've finished reading the letter, I allow the tears to flow. I must've read it a hundred times over the months that have passed since he wrote it, but I still don't know who I'm crying for. Am I crying for Colbeck or for myself? For Ade losing his best mate? For Steph? For her boyfriend and what we did to him? For Sorel? For everything else that's been lost?

It didn't arrive until four days after I found him. He posted it second class on the day he did himself in. He duplicated it, copied it out in that tiny, precise handwriting of his, and sent it to me and Ade (both at the same address). He sent a letter to his parents too, and according to the local paper he also sent one to the police. I've no idea what it said because I've never seen it, but it's obvious he took all the blame for what happened, not just to Steph but to Shaun as well.

Someone must know though. Everyone knows everyone around here and someone must have seen me. Even now, the investigation is still ongoing. It's only a matter of time before the police come looking for me again. They've interviewed me a coupla times already, and Ade too, as part of the inquest. I told them exactly what Colbeck told me to tell them, and I felt fuckin guilty about dropping him in it, even though that's what he wanted. I'm sure they have reason to believe that Ade and me were involved in the fight, but they just can't prove it. It all happened so fast.

Of course, Colbeck had no idea what went on between Steph and me in those brief moments of drunken stupidity: both she and I were completely pissed-up but neither one of us was forced into anything. It wasn't even proper sex, for fuck's sake. We barely fuckin did anything. But look what it's fuckin led to: this has ruined her life, and it's something she'll never recover from. The worst thing of all is that so many different lives have been destroyed and it can all be traced back to something that never even fuckin happened.

She thinks she was raped. But that's what everyone thinks: as far as everyone, including Steph, is concerned, Colbeck spiked her as the result of some stupid fuckin vendetta and then someone else got hold of her and attacked her because they thought she was out of it. That's what set this delicate house of cards tumbling and Colbeck died because of it, yet I'm the only person who knows the full truth. Ade just keeps telling me to leave it. But it's an impossible situation. Can I really let her go the rest of her life thinking that she was raped when in actual fact she wasn't? Would anyone believe me even if I confessed? Or would they charge me? It'd be my word against hers. No proof either way. But it doesn't look good. Fuck, it doesn't look good.

Sometimes, horrendous situations can be traced back to one thought, to one instant, to one wrong decision or action made when you didn't have time to consider the consequences. I always knew that, and yet I still did it. I still stood over him and delivered kick after kick after kick. Another life fucked beyond repair.

Ade's been in a real state. He moved the furniture around in the living room, put the sofa at the opposite end, fucked the kitchen table off and got another one from a charity shop. His way of making a fresh start, I guess. He spent ages one week putting his books in alphabetical order. Then he did the same with his videotapes, and then his CDs.

Finally – and you're not gonna fuckin believe this – he decided to quit smoking. This was five weeks ago, and he's not had a cig since. He told me: Matt always went on about how much he hated smoking. He told me that I'd die *way* before him, because I smoked and he didn't. I told him it was bollocks, and that I was bound to outlive him. I didn't fuckin mean it, mind you – I was just arguing for the sake of it. Anyway, we made a bet while we were at uni – if I outlived him, I had to quit. And of course I agreed to it because I never thought I actually would outlive him! We shook on it and everything. Now, every single time I'm pissed off and gagging for a cig, it's going to make me think of him, and I know he'd take great pleasure in that, the cunt.

Sorel's back at her parents. She came back to the flat for a while, but then moved out again. Last time I heard from her, a coupla months ago, her and Nick were making another go of things. And then there was Colbeck's funeral. It got delayed cuz of police procedure. Testing him, the inquest, an autopsy, that kinda shit. Official cause of death: suicide by ingestion of alcohol and Alprazolam.

I flicked through my notebook today. It was under my bed. I haven't written in it for a while, and I decided to leave it that way: an unfinished testament to who I was and how

I felt in that chapter of my life. I still think of Sorel a lot, but she's just a name now – one of those words from the past, rooted in history. I have to let her go. They say you should never visit the places where your happiest memories took place because, if you do, then they – the memories like – will surely be destroyed. And that's how I feel about the time I spent with the three of them, up until the night where it all went so wrong. The problem is that I'm still here. I'm still here and it just isn't the same. You see, the people who tell you that your schooldays are the best days of your life are lying. They say it to shut you up and to make you grin lugubriously and bear something which you would otherwise bitch and moan about. The best days of your life are the days when education is no longer compulsory and when you're taking your first tentative footsteps into the big wide world. You're invincible – for a few months at least – to all that's thrown at you, and you're at this magic point in your life where you can do pretty much anything if you sit up and put your mind to it. I used to be invincible. I didn't realise it at the time, but Sorel was right. I could've got out of this shit town. I could've lived a happy life. But that window of opportunity was open for such a very short space of time, and now it's slammed shut again. I can't blame anyone else. After the decisions I made, and after the impact they had on me and on others, I'm not sure it'll ever open again.

Something makes me want to take a walk. I put my coat on, grab my notebook, head out the front door. Down the stairs and out into the street. Ade's at the bookies – he says it's his escape. With Colbeck gone and Sorel away it's back to how it was originally, just me and Ade and our late-night drinking sessions and his rants about the ways of the world. The joy has gone now though. It's kinda like he's doing it for the sake of it; like he's parodying his life as it was six months ago.

I head down the street. It's five in the evening and bitterly cold; starting to get dark like. I pull my coat around me, my breath making clouds in the air in front of me as I move along, head down. I walk briskly. Cut through behind the shops, walk down the alley. For some reason I'm not as scared now that I'm alone. I arrive at my destination before I even realise where I'm headed: The George and Dragon. I haven't been here since that night.

It's warm inside and pretty empty. The smoke chokes my throat. I get a pint, sit at a table, mine and Sorel's table, and light a cigarette. I reach into my pocket, flip open the notebook, and start reading. I remember the day I made these notes: in the camper van, heading south, music blaring on the stereo and Colbeck with a beer in hand sitting shotgun. And, as I read, I can almost hear him and Ade going, Fuck me, Dunc, what's that shit you're writing? and I can almost sense Sorel at my side telling me, Ignore them, Duncan, it's important to write these things down. But I pay no attention to any of them, cuz I know they're just ghosts.

ACKNOWLEDGEMENTS

Thank you to everyone at the Manchester Writing School who oversaw the earliest drafts of this novel – Andrew Biswell, James Draper, Paul Magrs, Livi Michael, Nicholas Royle – and of course, the MA Massive – Alex, Dan, Jonny, Katy, Kayte, Lily and Red. Also Stephen May and all at Lumb Bank in May 2007.

Thanks to Anne Barber, Jo Cole, Frank Coyle, Myriam Frey, Stephen Galbraith, Kerry Hadley-Pryce, Sarah Jasmon, Danielle Jawando, Fionnuala Kearney, Dimmi Khan, Kate Lord Brown, Stephen McGeagh, Romola Parish, Geeta Roopnarine, Catherine Rose, Graeme Shimmin, Anstey Spraggan, Louise Swingler, Megan Taylor, Daniel Touré, Sally Wag, Anne Worthington, Emma Yates-Badley and all at Moniack Mhor.

Thanks also to Ivan Mulcahy, Tilly Vercoutre and all at MMB Creative; Gary Budden, Kit Caless, Sanya Semakula and Jordan Taylor-Jones at Influx Press; Max Edwards, Helen Francis and John Mills.

Cheers to the Clifton Street Crew, Stone Scribblers, and CreepJoint; Gary Steer and Caoibh for info; Silvia at Moleskine Italy for donating the notebooks I sketched ideas in; everyone I wrote to who took the time to write back and offer encouragement and advice; Toe-laaa for believing in this book from the beginning; and the New Smithy Inn where I wrote it.

Love to Jade, Toby, family, friends, and all the interesting and inspirational people I met along the way first in Stoke-on-Trent, Birmingham, and Manchester, and then in North Wales, London, Dublin and New York.

Finally, thanks to anyone I should have included, but forgot (in which case it's nothing personal!)

Please visit www.joegilligantrust.co.uk.

ABOUT THE AUTHOR

Steve Hollyman was born in Stoke-on-Trent and currently works as a Senior Lecturer in Creative Writing. He is a graduate of the Manchester Writing School, where he completed an MA and PhD. He is the vocalist and guitarist in the three-piece alternative rock band CreepJoint, whose most recent album *A Generation of the Dark Heart* was released in 2018. Find him on Facebook at @stevehollymanofficial

Influx Press is an independent publisher based in London, committed to publishing innovative and challenging literature from across the UK and beyond.

Lifetime supporters: Bob West and Barbara Richards

www.influxpress.com
@Influxpress